A Mighty Collision of Two Worlds

By

Safi Abdi

ISBN: 1-4033-2266-X (ebook)
ISBN: 1-4033-2267-8 (Paperback)
ISBN: 1-4033-2268-6 (Rocket Book)
ISBN: 1-4033-3226-6 (Dustjacket)

Library of Congress Control Number: 2002091472

This book is printed on acid free paper.

Printed in the United States of America
Bloomington, IN

1stBooks - rev. 10/14/02

Dedicated to:

Kinsi

Amina

Yaseen

Zahra

&

Mother

*Time spent on this work was
time spent away from them.*

Acknowledgements

Special thanks go to our friend Claus E. Feyling for his tireless support. He was a Godsend, for without his enthusiasm, the draft of this book would still be yellowing in the closet, today.

I am eternally grateful to Professor Hassan Al Naggar for his time, patience and valuable comments, which helped sharpen my own thoughts and allayed my fears.

Special thanks go to my friend Imola for her balanced review of the book and to Suhair and Salaah for their support, and to Mariam Combes for her feedback.

I am also grateful to Literary Consultant, Mr. Harald Horjen, for his professional evaluation of the draft, and all those others that contributed, directly or indirectly, to this work. Thank you all.

Foreword

It gives me great pleasure to introduce this marvelous work by Safi Abdi, a budding artist with whom I recently became acquainted.

Quite frankly, I found it hard to believe, as I read through the manuscript, that this is indeed her first work. What impresses me the most about Safi's craft is her outstanding ability to handle the clash of cultures – which the book focuses on – with fairness and objectivity. Her subject-matter is only matched by her fine technique which superbly highlights the difference of two distinct world-views of which even the two central characters seemed to be unaware of at the beginning.

Safi gives great attention to character, and this, together with her eventful plot and suspenseful dialogue, makes the book a pleasurable read. A Mighty Collision of Two Worlds plays a major role in bridging the gap of cultural misunderstanding which is, unfortunately, so rampant in our world today.

Prof. Dr. Hassan A. El-Nagar
Lecturer at ISTAC, Kuala Lumpur

Chapter One

Rako Island

May God steal from you all that steals you from Him
[(Doorkeeper of the heart –Versions of Rabi'a)]

The front door stood ajar. Anisa pushed through the narrow opening. As the gray metal door clicked shut behind her, her mother's voice grounded her to the hot asphalt.

"Are you saying what I'm thinking you're saying?" Her mother was saying to someone. "Not that I've any regrets about being a homemaker, but I'd rather Anisa went on with her studies."

Eventually, when she found enough strength to move on, Anisa tottered to the farthest corner of the open courtyard and flopped onto a cement bench underneath the cool shade of a cluster of palm trees garlanding the kitchen entrance. This was the family's favorite spot – a leafy corner in an otherwise austere patio. Anisa's fingers caressed the batches of orchids, oleander and periwinkle blossoming freshly beneath the smooth trunks. These were her late father's pride before death claimed him last summer. She had just turned fifteen then, and her brothers, the twins, Hassan and Hussein, were not yet three.

Anisa's eyes moistened with apprehension, dreading an unknown adversary. She was transported to a time, not long ago, when all she did was patter around the patio, *the-right-hand-lady* of her father, helping him with this or that, doing small jobs here and there. She was, in fact, there when her father single-handedly painted the wall around their house all white, and she remembered chiding him for not waiting for her to hold the ladder for him. She'd scolded him in the same way for coating his new white shirt green while painting the kitchen.

"Did you hear me say that Anisa must quit her studies at once?" said a new voice, stifling Anisa's reverie. *This must be Aunt Huda,* Anisa flinched.

"I merely reiterated Rahma's wishes. Jibreel's not any other young man. He's the state secretary's son, and a humble, intelligent young man at that."

The speaker paused. Anisa's dark hazel eyes squinted at the blinding brilliance of the turquoise sky as she waited for the speaker's next words.

"Moreover," Aunt Huda continued, "Rako Island's no longer Rako Island. Fatima, take a good look around you—girls much younger than Anisa are being spotted everyday in the company of young men, sometimes even in the arms of the *kafir*. Here's a good chance for you to steer her away from such foolishness."

"I hate to say this to you, Aunt Huda, and I know you mean well," Anisa's mother replied, "but I know my daughter."

"What mother doesn't know her daughter?" threw in Aunt Huda.

"Well, I know my daughter and the last thing on my mind is to put into her head any ideas that might conflict with her schooling. Her uncle and I'd rather she went on to further studies. And I do have high hopes of her spiritual growth. I put my trust in Allah and hope that she won't betray that trust."

"But, dear Fatima," butted in another voice, this time Aunt Rahma's, "we're not here to curtail a young girl's life...nor are we prophets of doom."

Aunt Rahma was Aunt Huda's constant companion, and, if one was parked somewhere, the other was sure to be there too. These two weren't exactly Anisa's blood relations, but tradition made an older person either an aunt or an uncle, and the very old were either a grandpa or a grandma.

"However," continued the Aunt, "Jibreel's my own nephew and my late sister's eldest son. On his return from one of those frequent jaunts of his, I was, in fact, the one who insisted that he cease his vagabonding and settle down for once and all..."

"More tea, Aunt Rahma, Aunt Huda?" interrupted Anisa's mother. "Tea's very good at this time of day, or so it's said."

"They say it even cures colds," coughed Aunt Rahma before she continued with her story.

Observing Anisa here the other night, seeing what a beautiful young lady she'd become, how could she possibly resist mentioning Anisa's name to her nephew? Her nephew had laughed, dismissing the whole idea with a light shrug of the shoulders.

"His reluctance," said the Aunt, "only helped fuel my own plan of affiancing these two."

Cold indignation blanketing her very bones, Anisa tore herself away from the women's stuffy drivel and sought refuge at the kitchen sink. How could they do this to her? She cried into the running tap, dabbing her tears away with wet hands. What kind of aunts were they? she moaned. *Meddlers! Observers! Simple match-makers!* She wept in hushed resistance, crest-fallen. They were parading her for sale, as though she were a product for grabs – *their* product. Even her own mother wasn't allowed to have a say in the marketing of this *common* commodity. She swallowed her hurt, dispirited.

"You crying, Anis." The twins stood in the doorway, and they had never looked been more dusty.

"Sssh," she said, raising her head from the sink. "I'm only washing my hands."

"You pulling your head off!" said Hassan, the speaker of the two.

"I still have my head on, big mouth!" she whispered, forgetting her heavy heart as she pulled them into the kitchen and put her hands on their mouths, making them squeal with delight.

The women's voices could be heard from the terrace. And then they were bidding salaam to her mother.

"This heat, this heat," sang Aunt Huda, "time we rushed home. Fatima, *Ma 'assalaama.*"

"*Ma'assalaama!*...Aunt Huda...Aunt Rahma."

The minute the door closed behind them and her mother returned to the living room, Anisa and the boys emerged from the kitchen.

"You met Aunt Huda and Aunt Rahma outside, dear?" wondered her mother. "And how was the exam?"

Ignoring the first question and mustering up a smile that didn't quite touch the heart, Anisa beamed at her mother.

"*Alhamdulillah!* Not bad; glad it's all over, though."

"But that's wonderful, *Alhamdulillah!*" said her mother. "Your uncle's coming here right after the *Jum'a* prayers. You'd better go get changed."

"*InshaAllah,*" Anisa replied, nodding.

In the kitchen, Fatima's thoughts slipped back to the two women. Perhaps she'd been too harsh on them, she wondered. There was nothing wrong with what they said and absolutely nothing wrong with the young man; it was the way they put it that rubbed Fatima up the wrong way.

And she, too, was aware of the pitfalls of being young and susceptible today. Since the opening up of the island to the outside world, more and more scantily clad foreigners were pouring in. At first, these so-called tourists, who the government said were good for the island's economy, were mainly concentrated at the beach resorts. There the skimpy clothing in which they came was skinned away, and the flesh fully exposed to the sweltering rays of the sun – the unblushing bodies a common feast for all. No longer confined to the outlying strands, these sentinels of bad taste were now swarming the neighborhoods.

In the evenings, it was said, these freshly baked potatoes would make a bee-line for bars and dancing places, where they whirled crazily, drank themselves silly and mingled until dawn. They returned to the hot shores later in the day for another dose of sunrays before they again hit the town bars for another mad restless night. This cycle repeated itself until the time came for them to depart to wherever it was they came from.

While some of the island's non-Muslim population were said to have voiced some mild reservations about this primitive trend, the small Muslim community's raised alarms were falling on mute ears and were being dismissed by the non-Muslim ruling elite as the blind assertions of an archaic folk who refuse to change with the times.

"Ah, there you are," Anisa's reappearance interrupted her mother's thoughts. "Come, give me a hand with these," she said, pushing a plate of carrots towards Anisa. "Now that exam's over, you girls must be delighted."

Fatima stole a sideways glance at her daughter. Gone were the plump cheeks of a year ago. In fact, she now looked more developed than her sixteen years, with a face that was beautifully oval and a pair of eyes glossy bright and almond-shaped. Her velvety complexion glowed amber-brown, as if lighted from within. Anisa's grown into a dainty replica of her father, she thought. The only thing she got from me is her tiny observant nose.

Oblivious of her daughter's awareness of the day's conversation, Fatima smiled, "You know, looking at you today, I suddenly felt time pass by."

"Yes, Mother, I know," said Anisa, trying to be game. "I'm also aware of the fact that I'm a head taller than my own mother." In spite of herself, Anisa couldn't help teasing her mother. "I can easily pass for your elder sister. Look!"

"My little pumpkin!" said her mother. "So you've been secretly measuring yourself against your poor mother. That's unfair."

"You remind me of how I used to do the same to your grandmother," Anisa's mother chuckled. "Can you believe it? Even after I got married, I still entertained ideas of outgrowing her somehow. No luck, though. Ultimately, I had to reconcile myself to my fate—your grandmother remained taller."

"Mother," said Anisa tentatively, "how old were you when you and father...you know?" Anisa could hardly bring herself to say the word "married," but her mother got wind of it.

"Well, I was fifteen when we got engaged," replied her mother.

"We wedded a year later, immediately after your grandfather died. By then, your father was already working."

"*Ya Allah!* How awful! I can't believe it!" Anisa rolled her eyes in a show of utmost shock. "First your own father dies and then you're dashed...off, as though nothing had happened!"

"You know," her mother said, unruffled, "at the time it was perfectly normal for girls to get married early, sometimes even as young as fourteen. At any rate, you wouldn't have been a head taller than me today had a terrible delay occurred."

Curious at her daughter's sudden interest, she ventured lightly, "Maybe we shouldn't delay yours either?"

"Over my dead body!" pronounced Anisa, with a vehemence that almost shattered the tiny kitchen window.

"Whoever said there was a market for dead brides," returned her mother. *Did Anisa know more than she was letting on?* her mother pondered.

"By the way," she went on, as she began to grate the carrots for salad, "I do have higher aspirations for my girl than I had for myself."

Anisa's mother relished the crunchy taste of carrots. They were good for the eyes and teeth, she also believed, and made sure everyone had a hearty portion of her favorite salad. Anisa winced at the thought of having carrot & raisins salad, yet again.

"And I know the importance of education," Anisa's mother went on. "I assure you, if a prince knocked on my door today, he'd be sent away empty-handed."

"Now we're talking sense," Anisa said, relieved.

"I also need," her mother said on a serious note, "your promise to stay away from that girl...Now put fire to the stove."

"You mean Rebecca?" asked Anisa as she dried her hands and reached for a matchstick. "But, she's just like the rest of us. I don't understand why you're so concerned about her. Is it her not being a Muslim?"

"That, too," said her mother. "And why not stick with Faiza, your cousins, and other Muslim girls your age? Must you mix with her as well? You know, she's no good. Her father's a drunkard, and her mother's never home."

"But that's not her fault."

"When I was your age," said Anisa's mother wistfully, as she took out a handful of raisins to wash for the salad, "we never did have the need to mix with the *kafir* population."

11

"Well, this is 1978. The world has changed, Mother, and for the better, I think."

"It sure has changed, and now it has become as the prophet had forewarned, but if I were you I wouldn't be too keen on certain changes," her mother said. She paused, and then added. "The right way will never change, Anisa. Never."

"Mother, I know that, and I'd never imitate others in anything. I'm a big girl. I can look after myself."

"Well, Anisa, that's what they all say."

"Mother, I'm very much aware of the differences."

"Then does that mean we understand each other, Anisa?"

"Exactly."

"Which brings me to the question of your *Salat*." Fatima turned from the sink.

"*Ya Rabb*! So you noticed?" she blurted out, meeting her mother's gaze. "Mother, I'm really sorry. Starting today, I'll be more than careful—you've my word."

Chapter Two

St. Joseph

Sister Anne, Anisa's school principal, could hardly contain her amazement at finding Anisa's name on the short list. Not that she doubted Anisa's abilities, but it had never been a school policy to include Muslim girls in the school exchange program. To get to the bottom of the matter, she called out for her secretary, "Cynthia, please call Sister Margaret to my office."

Sister Margaret was Anisa's class teacher. Her arrival in Rako Island coincided with Anisa's bereavement, and she had developed a soft spot for her student. A few minutes later Sister Margaret was ushered into the principals' office. Motioning the younger nun to be seated and pushing the list towards her, Sister Anne pointed an over-sized finger that had seen better days at Anisa's name and asked, "Whose idea was it to put this girl on the list?"

"Mine, Sister Anne," Sister Margaret returned, as she began to balance her body on the bantam chair she was offered to perch on. It was hardly enough for a child. The principal looked down at her from her sturdy armchair, "I suppose you're ignorant of the school policy?" The principal intoned from her throne of power.

"I don't understand," groaned the younger nun.

"Sister Margaret," the principal said, pulling down at her head habit with both hands the way one would clutch at a runaway scarf on a windy day, "education's a waste on these people, and I'm amazed at your ignorance of that basic reality."

"I see."

"The more you teach them, the more impudent they become. There's no place for our teachings in their hearts."

"I see."

The principal compressed her mouth into a virtual nonentity. "Sister Margaret, you're being evasive," she said.

"Maybe so, but aren't we dealing with school children?"

The principal's mouth reappeared, "A line must be drawn somewhere, though," she said.

"I don't understand."

"I take it you're allowing your own personal perceptions to come in the way of your missionary work?"

"It's just that…"

"Sister Margaret, I'm afraid, such wishy-washy sentiments are best left unsaid," said the principal as her glance brushed against a large portrait of a handsome young man.

"But unless the heat's gone to your head," she released a wicked breath, willing the young nun to follow her gaze, "I'd say you know why we are here."

"But converting Muslim kids?" whispered Sister Margaret, taking her cue and fixing her eyes on the portrait of their lord Jesus. "I'd no idea that figured in our work. Or perhaps it does?"

"Sister Margaret!" the principal hissed. "You know very well what it really means to be a missionary! Please don't force me to spell it out for you."

"I beg your pardon?"

"While it's pertinent to keep up appearances," Sister Anne fumed, "it'd be ludicrous not to expect handsome returns for our humble endeavors. God forbid we are not without purpose, and nowhere have we ever shied away from stating our holy agenda."

"Our holy agenda?"

"That being, if I must say, the Christianizing of everywhere we set foot," replied the principal, without mincing words, "and by all means. If that can't be achieved, we may as well pack and leave."

A dull thud was heard as Sister Anne's hands landed on the pile of sheets atop her desk.

"I'm afraid," she continued, her voice filling every nook of the room, rising with every syllable, "these people have always been, and still remain the greatest impediment to our total success in this island. The only weapon we have is to see to it that they remain at the bottom of the social hierarchy until they come to their senses. We didn't come here for mosquito bites; we've work to do."

"Sister Anne," Sister Margaret said, "if all we want is to convert the locals, why are we wasting our time teaching school children?"

"Teaching's a weapon," the principal breathed, "one of the many hooks we put out for the sake of the lord Jesus. To ensure a sphere of influence during the tender years of a child's development, we give to all. But, if the child grows and is not affected, we drop that child for a more adaptable one. Of course, there're loopholes here and there. We can't be too obvious."

"I see," swallowed Sister Margaret.

"The rule is: no fish, no success."

The principal paused to reveal a side portion of her false teeth, which the younger nun was supposed to take for a natural smile.

"What about people of other creeds?" Sister Margaret reminded her, still clutching at the sides of the Lilliputian seat. "Those who still find themselves out of the fold—shouldn't they be kept at the bottom too?"

"Sister Margaret," cried Sister Anne. "I'm afraid, you've chosen the wrong calling, but let me tell you this: No. No. It's not our policy to keep anyone else at the bottom. These people are easily persuaded. Their conversion's the century's success story. They're not a threat to us, and we're not a threat to them. We know how to get them, and our success is proof of that. Even those who don't make it into the fold know and acknowledge our superiority. They look up to us."

The younger nun swallowed. *So this was Sister Anne's version of Christian charity?* It was a depressing thought. "Is it that important that people look up to us?" she asked finally.

"Absolutely."

"And the Muslims…they don't bow to us?"

"Absolutely not!"

"You must excuse my confusion, Sister Anne," said the younger nun, steering the older sister back to Anisa. "I'm perhaps too sentimental, but considering her recent tragedy…not only that…but I do find Anisa ambitious and focused and reckoned that good enough reason."

"How forgetful of me!" exclaimed Sister Anne, suddenly all giving and majestic. "So this was the poor kid who lost her father?" The principal closed her fox-like eyes, but only for a split second.

"You may have a point there, Sister," she said, scrutinizing the younger nun's candid face for any shadow of irony. Finding none, she continued. "Very kind, very thoughtful, indeed a very Christian thing to do."

She must find a replacement, and very soon, the principal decided there and then. Like a cat, she then bounced off her chair and literally shooed the pitiful amateur out of the door, leaving the younger nun to ponder over the diabolical turn-about.

It was the final day of school. Everyone had gathered at the school compound for the day's ceremony. Sister Anne gave her usual speech and was full of praise of the year's school performance. She also informed the assembly of her joy to announce the lucky beneficiaries of the year's exchange program. A dead silence permeated the crowd, and the senior girls held their breath. The principal donned her reading glasses, and, snapping up two envelopes from under her arm, she went on to announce the year's lucky girls. Peering at the two envelopes, she called out, "The lucky recipients are: Jane Philip Jandawani of 4A and Anisa Ali Haaji of 4B. Girls, come forward and take these envelopes home to your parents. Everyone clap your hands for the lucky girls."

Amid the sound of cheers and hip-hip hoorays a thunder struck Anisa pushed forward to claim her letter.

"Thank you, Sister Anne, thank you," she murmured as she sleepwalked back to her row, where the girls were already abuzz with youthful excitement.

The principal went on with her speech, citing the two girls' responsibility in their new environment. She went on about how they were a window through which the host school would be observing this very school, and so on and so forth, leaving Anisa's mind in a spin.

The contents of the letter were rather brief: The host school was a boarding school. Only lucky girls attended such grand schools, and one had to be terribly lucky to obtain such a fortuitous chance as Anisa now received. The principal made sure that important fact was not left out in her message to Anisa's mother and uncle. Of course, she phrased it differently, but the meaning was clear. The period of study would be one year, starting in the fall. Words of congratulations came from everyone. Anisa wished them a pleasant holiday and was in a hurry to break the news to her mother.

On their way home, as Anisa and Faiza, Anisa's classmate and childhood friend, went over the pros and cons of going abroad, Faiza's sudden remark almost twisted Anisa's heart.

"What if Aunt Fatima says no?" Faiza asked. The conversation overheard the other day was now a beating village drum, the furious echo pulsating in Anisa's very head. *Jibreel's not like any other young man*, her head drummed. *He's the State Secretary's son.*

"You think she would refuse?" Anisa replied. "Honestly, would you refuse to go if you were in my place?"

"Search me," Faiza replied. "I'm not really as brave as I'd like to be. Going to the other side of the globe's kind of scary, when you think about it. But then again, going there could open doors."

"What'd you do," Anisa said slowly, "if, for instance, something very personal made you want to go?"

"Like what?"

"Just answer the question."

"Then I'd use every trick in the book," Faiza said.

"No details, please," Anisa said, as they reached Faiza's door.

"Good luck, I miss you already."

21

Chapter Three

Farewell

Still in a daze, Anisa buckled her seat belt. The Captain was now welcoming the passengers on board. Yet again, she glanced through the tiny almond-shaped window and peered down at the white and blue colored building of the airport, where she knew her folks would still be pressing their faces against the glass pane, for a last glimpse of the jumbo jet as it sped down the runway and took off into the skies.

As the plane gathered pace, jerking here and there as it negotiated its way through the mass of clouds and gained upward mobility, the batch of land gave way to a tiny blotch in the vast ocean.

So that's how small we look to the birds? she thought, at the sight of the receding spot, her home of sixteen years. *A slight flurry of the sea wings*, she reflected, *that was all it'd take to drown her folks.*

Her neck was beginning to hurt from looking down. Reluctantly, she tore her eyes from the receding speck.

"We're not going to a funeral, you know," Jane whispered into her ear. "We should be glad, not sullen."

"Well, I'm happy, but I can't help being sad too."

"So am I," Jane said.

"Bone tired," Anisa yawned.

"Me too." Jane unclasped the seat belt.

"Is this your first trip abroad?" Anisa asked following Jane's cue and unfastening her seat belt.

"Yeah. I take it this is your first ever?"

"Yes," Anisa replied, then added, "So now, what's going to happen next? Any clue?"

"According to Sister Anne's instructions to the crew, I understand we should be served a meal, but that's only if we exhibit good conduct and don't call out for food."

"Is that so?"

And, if nature calls, there's a loo on board!"

"What if everyone wants to go, all at the same time?" Anisa asked.

"It's a case of first come, first served. See, that stewardess over there? She's the loo-usherette. You just go over there and register with her, as soon as you see people lining up."

"Very informative, indeed. Now I understand why Sister Anne wanted to get rid of you! But one more thing, how do I know what I'm being served, I mean, food-wise?"

"Like I'm planning to do, eat whatever you can grab from those girls."

She'd been too excited to eat properly the last couple of days, and the smell of food wafting from the kitchen made her hungry, "Well, I can't eat everything, you know," she said.

"Bad luck, Muslim girl," sang Jane.

The food trolley had now moved towards them. A flashy stewardess suddenly curved over them and two plastic plates dropped onto the girls' laps. Anisa peered into her plate. Aha...she could recognize some of the stuff, but, "What's this?" she nudged Jane.

"Give me a break! Haven't you seen chicken salami before?"

"Looks too pinkish to me," Anisa said, as she began to eat the rice and vegetables. Finding that she was still hungry, she picked at the lifeless flesh. Yes, it did taste like chicken.

"If you don't want it, just pass it over to me," said Jane as she cleaned the plate and started on the pudding.

A little later, Jane dozed off to sleep. It was now something like 7.00 PM. Too exhausted to sleep, Anisa pulled up the window screen and gazed down at the now darkening clouds.

Somewhere below, her mother would be getting ready for *Maghrib*. Anisa's cheeks dimpled with amusement at the thought of her little brothers' whereabouts and the state of their clothing at this time of day. If they were lucky, at least one of them knew where he last left his sandals. Soon after Maghrib, her mother would set out on her search, which would most certainly end up at anyone of the three street lampposts on the narrow lane. For as long as she could remember, she had always felt some sort of a mystical pull toward these posts, once the lights came on. Ending up under anyone of these lampposts, between *Maghrib* and *Isha*, was a kind of a ritual the neighborhood kids experienced during their growing years.

Her uncle would be there for the night. Fathiya, one of Anisa's cousins was also coming home to Anisa's mother's house to stay until the reopening of school.

Thinking back to that fateful day when she first handed the envelope to her mother, vivid images of the scenes leading to her journey passed through Anisa's mind.

"Could you explain what this is all about?" her mother gasped.

"It's an offer for me to take part in the exchange program."

"And what does that mean?"

"That means I'll have to study in the USA for a year as an exchange student."

"There's no one else to go?" her mother asked, as though Anisa was doing the school a favor.

"Mother, plenty of girls would change places with me. Going to America is every kid's dream. This is a chance to see, study and get first hand knowledge of other people and cultures." As she said this, Aunt Rahma's voice was already a hammer in Anisa's head: *But dear Fatima...we're not here to curtail a young girl's life...nor are we prophets of doom.*

"Mother, please!" Anisa pleaded.

"No...no...this is out of the question," said her mother. "You're not going out of my sight, Anisa. You finish your schooling here. You have all the people and all the cultures you need here. The school must find another candidate."

What if, after this, they managed to convince her mother? No, she couldn't allow that to happen. Here was her chance of escape. And on she went, "Mother, please! At least, think it over. It isn't as bad as you think. I'm going for education. You've always wanted me to study. You never did have the chance to study properly. You've a problem writing your own letters. Mother, you know you couldn't even read your own letters until you started going for those evening classes, and then even after that you still have problem reading everything by yourself. Mother, you're constantly in need of others, and this is a chance in a million. Sweet Mother," she pleaded as her mother grappled with herself. "At least let's discuss this with my uncle, please?"

"I'll bring it up with your uncle, *inshaAllah*," said her mother in a softer note, "but I can't see him disagreeing with me."

27

Next day, right after Maghrib, Omar, Anisa's uncle, and step-father since her father's death, pulled up to a stop at the gate, making Anisa half jump from the terrace bench where she'd been helping her mother with some needle work. Having exchanged the formalities of greetings, Anisa's uncle made himself comfortable on the bench Anisa had just vacated after she blew into the kitchen on the pretext of brewing some tea for supper.

At her reappearance, her mother nodded for her to fetch the letter. Anisa's heartbeat could be heard as her uncle concentrated on the letter. After what seemed like an eternity he looked up, "Well?"

"Well?" Anisa's mother echoed.

"Well?"

"Well?" Anisa's mother replied.

"And what's my girl's opinion?" he glanced at Anisa.

"My opinion?"

"Your opinion."

"Uncle wants my opinion," she threw at her mother.

Her mother cleared her throat.

"Omar, I already said no, and I don't have to repeat myself. You have to remember we are on the same side, and we are speaking with one mouth."

"It's a very big leap," he said, then turned to Anisa, "Since your old grandfather's trip to the holy land, many, many years ago when I was a naked lad of two, no one in this family had ever ventured outside the walls of these waters. For all we know the sky could be green on the other side."

Anisa and her mother exchanged glances, but neither interrupted Anisa's uncle, for Omar had not yet said what he was going to say: "Having said that," he said, "I think Anisa's too young to go anywhere on her own."

"Young?" she cried. "There's another sixteen-year-old going. If her parents can trust her, why can't you? Is something the matter with me?"

"For all we know the sky could even be blue on the other side too, so, wouldn't it be just as well if Anisa completed her schooling here?" he asked.

"Uncle! You, of all people?" She switched on him a pair of woeful eyes. This had the desired effect.

"Well, if you really feel this will help you, and it's only a year, and you'll be looked after by the school," said her uncle with a scratch of his head. He was having second thoughts, and Anisa grabbed the moment.

"Yeah, it's only a year. By next year I'm back," she babbled. "Perhaps this might even give me the chance to continue with my further studies here. You know how difficult it is for Muslims to go on to tertiary education even here? We all know that, don't we?"

"Well?"

"Is that all you can say, Omar?" It was her mother's turn to push her case. "Are you tongue tied all of a sudden? And is it normal to send a sixteen year old girl to the other side of the globe?"

"It'd be an enriching experience," said Omar, still deliberating, and wondering what her father would've done under the circumstances. Granted, he loved Anisa with all his heart. He was her uncle, her late father's only brother, and since her father's death, he'd filled her father's shoes, and married her mother, so now he was also her stepfather. But, if he refused her now point-blank and things didn't go right for her here, he might never forgive himself. Education was life and had never been more important.

"If the sixteen year old knows what she's doing," he said slowly, "and is aware of who she is and what she stands for, then I see no reason why she shouldn't be allowed the benefit of seeing how the other half lives. What does my girl say?"

"Yeah, and it's only one year," she said, closing the deal.

"Omar, you're too trusting," her mother said, looking from the one to the other.

"Shouldn't I be? What cause do I have to be otherwise?"

"I really don't know. Maybe we should sleep on it."

Her mother's tone was also giving in and within no time she was also surrendering.

And so it was. And in the days and weeks that followed, Anisa became the sole focus of her mother's worries and attention. The way her mother carried on and on about everything from hygiene to eating and praying and reading the Qur'an, you would think Anisa was never coming back.

The scores of aunts and uncles that came with special advice and free counseling had further fueled her mother's worries. There were tales of youngsters who, even after ten or so years' absence, were still to return. An old aunt who didn't know her son's whereabouts since he went for further studies to the United States some nine years ago had with her a letter and some homemade sweets for the son whom Anisa was to locate when she set foot in America.

Adding to the general excitement around her, were two aunts whose frequent presence on the premises touched a special core in Anisa's sensitive mind. It seemed these two were making more trips than were good for Anisa's peace of mind. She watched out for these two with the alertness of a good alarm clock ready to go off any second. The other aunts' and uncles' concern she bore with patience.

As the departure date neared, her mother took pains to cover all areas of concern. Nothing was to be left to chance.

"You know what you have to say before you go to bed?"

"Yes, Mother."

"Say it aloud."

"Please, Mother, I know. I'm a big girl."

"You see, Anisa, no one knows you as much as I do."

"Yes, Mother."

"*Alhamdulillah*, you've always been a good child, but still, it's a long way off."

"What can possibly happen to me, Mother? It's a boarding school, and it's only a matter of one year."

"My dear, plenty can happen in such an environment, and I'm particularly worried about your laxity. Young lady, I'd be lying if I said I was impressed with your daily prayers. Anisa, you're missing your *Salat* almost all the time. Now, I wonder, how you'd fare without me."

"*Salat* is the connection between the created and his Creator. Right, Mother?" Anisa responded, dispelling her mother's worries. "And without *Salat* man is lost, lost to the wiles of the accursed *Shaitan*."

"Right Anisa," said her mother. "If you keep your Lord in your heart, He'll provide protection, so keep your link with Him and you'll be all right. *Salat* is what keeps a Muslim from going stray."

"Yes Mother."

"*Salat* protects from evil. It purifies the body, cleanses the spirit and keeps one from bad deeds."

"*Salat* also keeps you alert and punctual, right Mother?"

"That's right, dear, it's also your only link to your Lord, and you'd be severing that bond at your peril."

"Who in their right mind would do such a thing?" Anisa said. "I'll bet only a booby would do such a thing!"

"You have another problem, Anisa."

"Mother?"

"You're easily overwhelmed by others. You have a very thin skin when it comes to that. And you do like being in the swim, don't you?"

"Mother!"

"No one knows you as much as I do, Anisa, not even your uncle. He trusts you more than he trusts his own daughters. He thinks you've got a mind of your own."

"Mother!"

"Your uncle thinks the world of you because he doesn't know you as much as I do."

"Mother, please!"

"Now promise to write."

"I'll write every day, *inshaAllah*."

Still gazing into the now darkened space, and murmuring, in all honesty, "I'll write everyday...and may I be a booby if I ever neglect my duties," Anisa dozed off to sleep.

Chapter Four

Life Changes

After the excitement of landing at the gigantic airport, the long drive to the school that took ages to reach, and the weeks the girls spent in the principal's quarters where they got acquainted with the staff and their surroundings, the first day of school came as an anticlimax. Jane and Anisa ended up not only in two different classes but also in different places.

By the time Anisa's roommate crashed on the scene with her belongings, Anisa had already settled in her part of the room. Her clothes were all hung in the cupboard. Her prayer mat and head scarf neatly folded by her side, and the few books and stationery that she and Jane received from the principal were already on the shelves, with the copy of the Qur'an duly placed on the side table. The new girl's "Hi!" as she rolled into the room, luggage and all, somewhat intruded on Anisa's peaceful disposition.

"Hi!" returned Anisa, half jumping from the bed where she'd been reclining with a book.

Relieving herself of her weight, the new girl, yellow curls and all, tossed her jeans-clad bones onto the empty bed.

After a minute or two of stretching her twiggy arms and legs, she propped up her massive curls in her hands and fixed a pair of brooding eyes on Anisa. Her eyes were so blue that Anisa wondered if the girl's eyesight was okay.

"Got any name?" she squinted at Anisa.

"Anisa...And yours?" Anisa flashed her own brown fire.

"Wait a minute," she waved a rather bony hand, "do you mind saying that again?"

"ANISA," she spelled out.

"You're a complete stranger, aren't you?" the new girl frowned.

"Yes."

"I'm Florence. My friends call me Floor. You may call me Floor, but there's no walking over me, is that understood, girl?" Anisa had no intention of walking on anyone. But before Anisa could respond Floor added, "Tell me, what do your friends call you?"

"Anisa's just fine," she wrote it on a piece of paper and handed it over to Floor.

"And so it shall be." Floor shoved the paper into her shirt pocket, dug her fingers into her jeans and resurfaced with a packet of cigarettes. She fished one out and lit up.

"This stuff's forbidden, you know," she said as two columns of smoke wafted out of her nostrils and mingled together in mid air.

"Care for one?" she offered.

"No, thanks."

"Never?"

"No," replied Anisa, at which Floor frowned.

Changing the subject, Anisa asked, "Is this your first year at Fairwood?"

"No."

"Do you like it here?"

"Somewhat."

After putting out the cigarette, Floor went down on both knees to unpack. And out came layers upon layers of shirts, T-shirts and jeans, pants, underclothes, and shoes. Albums, loose photos, a year's ration of sweets, chewing gum, cookies, potato chips and chocolates followed a dozen or so novels. Next came the toiletry and makeup, the likes of which Anisa had never beheld. Moving over to Floor, Anisa offered her help.

"Sure," replied Floor, making it look like she was doing Anisa a favor, "make yourself at home."

Working swiftly, they crammed stuff into every empty nook and crook of the tiny room. Still, there were things that didn't find a place and had to be returned to one of the suitcases.

"Good," Floor grinned. "You've so little yourself...not like my ex-roommate...am I glad the needle-wit's out of my hair!"

"Where is she now?"

"The hell with her!"

Zipping the suitcase shut, Floor looked at her watch, and then made a rush for the door.

A couple of weeks later, Anisa was to learn the reason behind Floor's rage against her former roommate. Lisa, otherwise known as *needle-wit* by Floor and her friends, was in fact the brightest pupil in Floor's class. Lisa's mother, Floor told her, had committed suicide.

"But why?" Anisa asked.

"Search me," Floor replied curtly.

"But how could she do such a thing?" Anisa insisted.

"Had a cheat for a husband," Floor conceded. "The *Needle-wit*'s father was a cheat…like daughter like father…Can't blame the poor woman for wasting her life so."

What irked Floor the most was Lisa's stealing of her boyfriend.

"The most handsome guy you ever saw," Floor said in unconcealed nostalgia, "and the cheat stole him in broad daylight."

"I haven't seen any boys around here," Anisa said.

"You're dumb!" Floor shook her head.

"And what does your man say about your coming here?" The question caught Anisa off guard.

"I…well…nothing. I don't have one," she admitted.

"Never?"

"Never."

"Is this a normal thing in your part of the world?" Floor doubled with laughter.

"Yes."

"Of all the bizarre things I've heard the last couple of weeks," she said, "I must admit this is the weirdest of all."

At times like this, Anisa found Floor's behavior downright rude. On the other hand, she knew her roommate did not really mean harm. She was just having some fun, at Anisa's expense. Floor wasn't a bad sort, though, quite the opposite. She was extremely helpful to Anisa, and a good friend once Anisa passed the initial test.

It was only those few things…like her not eating everything, which the others saw as picky, her prayers and so forth…that made Anisa into some sort of a freak. But apart from those minor things, the others considered Anisa normal, even likable.

A far cry from the authoritarian sisters back home, Anisa found the staff at Fairwood quite friendly and less distant. Although a milder version of Sister Anne, Ms. Hope, the school principal, was also a disciplinarian in her own right. Many were the girls who ran afoul of the school's strict rule against smoking, and so on.

During their evening chats, the two girls were also learning quite a bit about each other.

Safi Abdi

"Let me get this straight," asked a rather amazed Floor one night, "you mean, after your old man's death, your own uncle, your father's brother, had married your mother? And that on top of all that he'd already a wife and children of his own?"

"That's right," Anisa said. "My father's only brother had three daughters and a wife of his own when he married my widowed mother."

"But that's bigamy!" Floor exclaimed, and reaching for the bed lamp switch, she gave a long hard stare at Anisa's dark silhouette against the off-white wall. Anisa's long wavy curls glistened darkly in the lamplight.

"In Islam," Anisa replied, unruffled by the incredulity in Floor's voice, "a man can have more than one wife, it's not forbidden. On the contrary, it's preferable to mistresses, family break-ups, child-neglect, surplus women, you name it." Anisa paused a little, but, finding that Floor was still too stunned to respond, she went on. "Look here, Floor," she said, Floor's open mouth a welcome scene, "a Muslim man can marry more than one wife, if all parties agree to it and he can provide for them. But there must be a good reason. There's also a

42

condition that the wives be treated equally, and the transaction done honestly. Everything's above board."

Until that night Anisa had never given much thought to the reason behind polygamy. But, having heard it mentioned so often, she knew some of the reasons by heart. And since her father's death, she was able to see the wisdom behind it.

"In Islam," she went on, warming to the subject, "a child's happiness and security is also very important. You see, Floor, relatives are bound by Allah to help the helpless, the old and the orphans."

"Really?"

"It's a God-given right, and it's the duty of relatives to fulfill those rights." Anisa said. "Anyway, the important thing is my family's very happy. My two brothers and I have a father who loves and cares for us. Life was so empty until Uncle came into our lives. I love my uncle with all my heart. You see, Floor, we love each other, my aunt, my cousins, we're family," Anisa concluded, meeting Floor's troubled gaze.

Floor winced, as she knocked the light out.

Her voice came from the darkness. "So, everyone's happy down there?"

"Muslims are duty-bound to help the weak and the unprotected," Anisa said, savoring every second of her roommate's fluctuating mood. "My brothers were barely three when my father died and my mother wasn't about to marry anyone. And the boys and I needed a father, and that was a good reason for my poor mother and dear uncle. And my uncle's wife understood that point. She knew her husband better than anyone else. And she knew he had good reason for what he was doing. It's an island we live on, and we're a very small minority. So we like to stick together."

"I just can't endorse such a social network," Floor said.

"Well, that's your problem. Our community's, however, duty-bound to help the widows and the orphans."

"Duty-bound," breathed Floor, "kind of archaic, don't you think? Somehow, I can't see it working in real life."

"It does work in my family," Anisa said, then added. "It wasn't easy, though. The idea of my mother and uncle's marriage was just as difficult for all of us, my cousins, my mother, my aunt, and, worst of

44

all, for my uncle, who was torn between loyalty to his own family and his duty towards his brother's family. But after the initial fears, and with the community's help, everything began to work. Got it?"

"I'm not deaf," conceded Floor, "but it isn't as though I were buying it."

"Well, this one's not for sale," snapped Anisa.

"Well, I wouldn't buy it, even if it were the last option," Floor said.

"But it does work for us and that suits us just fine. My father may not be here to see my brothers grow, but they sure have a happy home."

"Talk about happiness!" Floor snapped. "But hey, I was happy too, at one time, but that was until one fine day," she whispered, "Mom split with a man, a complete stranger, a vain moron."

"What?" It was now Anisa's turn to sit up in bed and switch on the lamp.

"I was thirteen then," Floor's voice was almost inaudible. "You can't imagine how many times I cried for Mom."

Anisa's mouth flipped open in horror. "What kind of a mother abandons a child and bolts off with some stranger? *Ya Rabb!*"

"Then one day, I got this damn letter explaining away Mom's actions, and her rights, and a lot of other crap I didn't quite catch. I still don't. All I ever wanted was for Mom to come back."

"And what did she say for herself?"

"Said she was happy and in love for the first time in her life. And that if I loved her, I'd be supportive and be happy for her."

"Back home, it's different, you know."

"Heaven on earth!" Floor hissed.

"I'm sorry, I didn't mean to boast. And then, what happened?"

"Then the most natural thing happened," Floor said, twirling the yellow curls between her fingers, "Dad took to the bottle, and an old flame came to the rescue. They're now living together, and I've to put up with her two brats from some previous partnership."

"You mean your father married his old flame?"

"What a thick head!" Floor sat up in her bed to explain. "My dad and this woman are living together." Floor entwined her two forefingers as if trying to communicate in sign language. "But these two adults aren't married. She's his live-in, if you know what I mean. In this country, the only official paper that makes sense is the driver's license. Who in their right mind would waste their time on a piece of paper when it's business as usual with or without it?"

"Get real!"

"The damn paper didn't prevent Mom from kissing me goodbye, now did it?"

"Living under the same roof? And not married? Floor, please! I've had more than I can take for one night!"

"And you haven't heard anything yet!"

"I do understand your point," Anisa said, "but then I get the feeling that you're not very fond of your father's live-in old flame or whatever. If she was legally his wife things wouldn't have been that bad."

"Legally his?" Floor spat.

"See, if she was his wedded wife, then you perhaps wouldn't feel so cheated, and there would be a sense of permanence in the home, a commitment. Now this affair must be one hell of an *arrangement*.

And God knows how many more brats this woman will be taking back with her when she decides to leave."

Floor lit a cigarette.

"This mother of yours, where's she now?" Anisa asked.

"The last I heard from her," Floor blew columns of smoke onto the wall," the moron left her high and dry. Poor woman, she's still putting the pieces of her life together, whatever that means." Floor wept.

Still moaning softly, the cigarette butt dangling between her fore and middle finger, Floor lulled herself to sleep. Anisa rose from her bed and extricating the butt from Floor's fingers, she put it out by putting it under the faucet and returned to her bed.

The two girls were now inseparable.

Anisa was also fast learning more and more about the host country. Slowly but surely she was also beginning to understand and sometimes even adopt, albeit, unconsciously, some of the mannerisms and habits of her girlfriends. Except for some minor escapades during weekends and holiday breaks, however, the last semester had come almost to a close without a major change in Anisa's outlook.

Salat was suffering, though. She wasn't purposely neglecting her prayers, but there was so much else to do during the day. And when she finally retired to her room, she had time only for *Isha*, the night prayer, which she performed like a thief, for fear of being seen by the others.

The problem was no longer her roommate. Floor had come to accept what she termed her friend's bizarre habits. Still, Anisa felt *inhibited.*

She kept in touch with her folks back home. In her letters to her mother, she'd write something or other happened just before "I adjourned for *Asar"* or, having overslept, "I just had to rush through *Wudu*, ablution, and perform *Fajr* in full speed." And so on.

Anisa hated herself for resorting to this kind of speech. She knew the Almighty God was watching her every word and move, but she was so afraid of hurting her folks that she'd just write whatever came to her mind, though this also left her in cold sweat afterwards.

On the other hand, there was absolutely nothing shameful about her academic performance. With the Foreign Students Aid Scheme, Anisa could even start college the coming fall, if she so wished. It was a chance she couldn't pass up, so she painted a saintly picture of herself. She was at times a bit honest with Faiza, but, even with her, she took care not to divulge too much.

Graduation day was almost around the corner. Jane and Anisa, who had kept an odd kind of relationship throughout, each having found a circle of friends, were both excited about the future.

Like Anisa, Jane was also adamant on staying on. They'd already received the go ahead from home and applied for admission to three different colleges.

Anisa's uncle and mother greeted the new developments with misgivings, but after being deluged with their daughter's correspondence, they had begun to reconcile themselves with the idea of Anisa's further absence; her mother's fears being assuaged by her daughter's detailed description of her host country.

The picture Anisa conjured up in her letters was that of a simple, hardworking, generous folk whose only fault was their complete ignorance of the One True God.

What appalled Anisa even more was how many of her friends, including Floor, had gloried in this ignorance of theirs, as if it were *something praiseworthy*. Proud was how they felt about this ignorance of theirs, and flaunt it they did, without so much as a speck of embarrassment clouding their empty lives.

"Mother," Anis would write in total disbelief, "fancy going to bed every night without remembering Allah, and waking up to daylight every day without so much as a word of thanks to Allah? The one Who willed them to be, the one Who has their souls in *His* Hands, Mother, how could they forget so?"

"And I've yet to meet anyone who truly cared, *really* cared about *Isa* the Messenger of Allah. The way I see it, this *Jesus Christ* business is for many only a put-on, and an excuse for celebrations. Mother, these friends of mine are not Christians. I repeat—I haven't met a single Christian in this country. I'll bet Sister Anne, faulty though her belief, would have a heart attack if she came here! Poor thing, she's so innocent, cut off as she is from everything! She just doesn't know what's going on in the real world!"

While Anisa honestly believed to be true what she wrote about her hosts, she knew she wasn't exactly honest about her own deeds, which were becoming more and more questionable.

She wrote minutely about the kind of food she was eating daily. She gave a graphic description of the school, the girls and the teachers, but thought it best to keep mum about certain things.

About her daily religious duties, she exaggerated to a maximum, and sparing her mother some of the thorny details from Floor's life, she rightly lauded her roommate's many virtues.

"Floor's all heart," Anisa would write, "In my next holiday, I'll make sure she comes along. She's such a kindly soul, a pity her silly mother ran off with a man, a *tattooed* moron!"

Back home, Anisa's letters became the subject of admiration and debate within her family's intimate circle. The hitherto pessimistic attitude of some of the aunts turned to one of sanguinity and envy. Even Aunt Huda, who had never admitted defeat even when she knew she was wrong, had to admit to her miscalculated prophecy of doom.

And as the clove-spiced whiff of the steaming tea caught their nostrils, her mother would relate to the spellbound aunts, "The rules governing morality are so strict that even those suspected of things like smoking, would immediately be taken to task. And Allah help those caught in the act."

And, "Venturing out of the school premises on their own is simply out of the question. And if and when it's done it happens under the strict supervision of the teachers."

Anisa's letters continued well into her sophomore year, although she was now, with time, growing a thicker skin and inadvertently becoming less and less detailed about her non-existent spiritual life.

Her uncle's pleas for Anisa to return for the holidays also fell on deaf ears, and the summer holidays kept passing by them, a point that worried Anisa's uncle, since nothing prevented his niece from coming home, at least for the summer breaks. Although he was moved a few times to bring up the matter with Anisa's mother, he decided against it, hoping that he was perhaps over-reacting. And who knows, he reasoned, Anisa was perhaps taking into consideration the family's economy, as she pointed out so many times? And since her mother had already taken in everything, he thought it best not to burden her with his misgivings.

Even though she pushed it to the farthest corner of her sub-conscience Anisa did not always feel at ease with herself. And the times she spent with herself alone were not always the best of times.

The minute her head hit the pillow, thoughts of life and death would converge on her brain, but these would just as soon get dispelled in the morning, and the good times with friends and the weekend disco continued unabated. In recent times, the *Isha* prayers of her high school days had also become a thing of the past.

No longer was she dwelling on them in her letters to her family. She was now too grown-up for that sort of thing. She still respected her folks, but she had come to believe that her prayers and social life were now things that concerned only her.

In college she was also meeting more and more other Muslims from different parts of the world. And she was consoled by the fact that they were also no different from her. Like her, they went to the nightspots and disco joints. So brazen were they in their ways and mode of speech that you couldn't set them apart from their hosts. This was the late Seventies and the early Eighties, and it was hip for many to flow with the tide.

The crux of the matter was that she wasn't alone in her fascination with the *exciting*, individualistic life style. Everyone enjoyed life on the fast track, and the loud riotous music had an *appeal* of it's own.

The whole thing was so fleeting, so very much a *now-thing*, that they made the most of it while it lasted. None of them, it seemed, including Anisa, had for one moment taken that way of life for real, nor did they see it as lasting. It was a dream world with disco lights instead of real stars; a dream from which they hoped to awaken one day soon.

However, these Muslim friends and acquaintances provided much needed material for her correspondence with her folks. She conveniently dwelled on their origins and backgrounds, which, although diverse, were not so different from her own. That pleased her mother, and she would be encouraged letter after letter to keep her friendship with the Muslims. That, her gullible mother assured her, would further boost her remembrance of God.

At the end of her sophomore year, Anisa pledged to save enough money from her stipend and part time job and promised to see the family the following summer. And as the time neared for her departure, Anisa's excitement knew no bounds.

She was now nearing twenty and, among the crowd of friends both on and off campus, there was a young man who was becoming dearer and dearer to her. He was already working and a few years her senior. They met on a Saturday night at one of the dancing places she and her girlfriends frequented on the weekends. He'd noticed her a few times, but, until that night, he'd not summoned up the courage to speak to her.

That night he came alone, hoping to see her again. Coming over to their table, he smiled at her and asked for a dance. Without a second thought, she breezed like a dry leaf in a blustery autumn morn onto the dance floor with him. He introduced himself as Mike. Asking her for a date became the most natural thing in the world.

On their fifth date on their own, to Anisa's throbbing heart, he whispered, "You have a most beautiful name, befitting a most perfect person."

"Perfect?" she almost choked on her Coke, as thoughts of her foibles whizzed through her mind.

"Yes, perfect," he said, leaning on the table, "and blessed with the most perfect set of teeth."

"We don't eat everything, bad food is bad for you," she stammered foolishly. "I mean messing with swine is certainly not the best way to healthy living. You see, you become what you eat. That's probably why we have good teeth."

"And we don't," he suppressed a smile. "I guess that explains it somewhat. As you said, you are what you eat."

He'd been to the library and skimmed through some literature on Islam, just to get some idea of the girl's thinking.

"Why aren't you married? What're you waiting for?" The question charmed him.

"Had few girls here and there," he said airily, indulging her further, "but they all seemed so shallow, irresponsibly flighty, if you know what I mean. One day they are with you, the next with your best friend; perhaps this flip flop has something to do with the swine syndrome?" he said, puckering his smart nose at her. He was enjoying himself, uttering whatever came to his head.

He was already filled in on Floor's silly mother, and knew about Sister Anne's complete unawareness of what went on in the real world, *cut off as she was from everything.*

Leaning forward, he added, "You know, I've just noticed something funny."

"Yes?" She took a nervous drag of the cigarette.

"For how long have you been smoking?"

"I don't know…two years, two and half. What is it to you?"

"Two years and you still don't know how to hold the cigarette, and you can't even inhale!" he mused.

"Are you a religious person?" she asked off the cuff, not knowing why she was bothering the cute fellow with that.

"What kind of religion are we talking about?" he asked and swung around in a rather funny way, as if chasing after a lost object, looking rather *cute*. They were in the same disco where they first met. His *boldness* intrigued her. But she didn't think him half as smart as he would have her believe.

"How silly of me," she laughed away her foolishness. "Of course, you don't have to answer that. You're simply too cute for that sort of thing!"

A couple of days before her departure, Anisa and Floor sat at their favorite corner of the campus coffee shop where they both worked as part-time helpers. As the girls relaxed at the end of their shift over Coke, Anisa asked, "What do you think of him?"

"Cute. Kind of exotic," Floor said, adopting Anisa's mode of description and gazing up at the ceiling, as she had seen Anisa do often. "Very persevering. Not pushy. Not so bulky, if only he were a Muslim."

"But what do you think of him, I mean, as a person?" insisted Anisa. They'd been over that line before.

"I'd say," Floor said pressing her lips together so as not to giggle. "I'd say there was something terribly wrong with this person. And I'm sure his mother would agree with me."

"What're you wearing that stupid smile for?"

"You're naïve, you know, what I'd call *dumb-naïve*."

"Even so. That's probably why he prefers me to the wise girls like your highness here."

"We'll wait and see."

For a minute Floor was tempted to confide in Anisa. Her boyfriend of one year and she were in fact planning an abortion that very evening. Notwithstanding Anisa's outgoing nature, her liking for music and dance, to her Anisa was still the *square board* she had met at Fairwood. Despite the cigarette puffs, the discarded prayer mat, the disappearance of the Holy Book, and the general worldly-wise airs she assumed, Floor knew that certain things would never find favor with Anisa. Things like pregnancies and their causes were the kind of stuff Anisa had *yet* to deal with.

Floor gazed through the haze of smoke, stared into the heavily mascara-ed eyes and had to admit with a healthy dose of gloom, "My friend, I can see you've changed a lot the last couple of years, but you still have a long way to go. Your kind of change is what I'd call, *a scratch on the surface.* Deep down you still believe in the *love after marriage* theory, right?"

"But, of course."

"Then why are you wasting the poor man's time? This man believes in *the love before marriage* practice, love before marriage, Anisa, *before*, not after. The way I see it, you guys are traveling in two separate boats, sailing in opposite directions. So why are you wasting your time, if I may ask?"

"The trouble with you girls is you are programmed to think only of one thing, and, before you know it, you're crawling in the mud with a total stranger. How *disgusting!*"

Floor took a sip from her Coke, "Tell me if I'm wrong, but isn't it like this with you guys: Old aunts meeting. Conversation in subdued tones, then, before we know it: Engagement. Wedding. Children...And Love? A *maybe*."

"Superior to your hop into bed first. Children second. Marriage third—with the illegitimate progeny serving as best men and best women—isn't the aftermath what we used to thrash out at Fairwood? Hop into bed. No commitment. Children. Stray about like cats and dogs. Sail. Then cast anchor at another port. Children sacrificed."

"You don't forget things, do you? From the look of it, I think you're wasting the poor man's time. And I won't be surprised if your mother hasn't already singled out a very nice boy from the community for her dear daughter. And by the way, aren't those devious aunties of yours still on active duty, scouring the neighborhoods for brides?"

"But, honestly," said Anisa, steering Floor back to Mike, "what do you think of him?"

"I think he's crazy in the head. And if America wasn't such a free soil, I'd sound my warnings to him." Floor broke into laughter as images of a prostrating Anisa hit her brain.

"You little bugger! Talking to you is like talking to the wall! Good bye!" Anisa got up. She'd a date with Mike. They hadn't seen each other for over a week, and now, he told her on the phone, he was anxious to see her that very afternoon...talk to her about something very important.

"See you later," Floor threw after her, "and don't do anything I wouldn't do."

Anisa was a few minutes early. Searching her mind for things she forgot to buy for her trip home, she entered a supermarket by the sidewalk.

When she returned to the parking lot, his car was already parked and Mike was deep in concentration staring into the open space. He didn't even look at her when she entered the car.

Instead he put the car into gear and drove in silence. Soon he was pulling the car to a stop by a small lake, not very far from the campus, but secluded all the same.

"Why are we here?" she asked, getting slightly edgy, and wondering what the fuss was all about. "And why are we acting so strangely?"

"Anisa?" he said, gawking through the windscreen.

"Yes?"

"I'm suddenly overwhelmed by a sudden urge—something I never knew was in me—and I feel like getting married, you know, committing myself for life. What do you say to this new me?"*So that was it?* she grinned, relaxing…*Mike was back, and* yes, yes…*the man was still playing smart pranks on her!*

And it was *he* who wanted to get married, that was it. *He.* And he must be out of his mind, her mind raced, to call on a port that was hardly known to him. He couldn't even pronounce her father's name, nor did he ever bother to get it right. And now *he* wanted to get married. *Pronto!*

"Good for you," she said, bolting out of the car and rushing over to the edge of the lake. The water was still and crystal clear, and she could gaze at herself standing over the giant mirror, looking rather comely in a purple ankle-length skirt and a white cottony top. Before

Mike's ancestors raided their lives, Anisa thought, how many of the natives must have washed their hair right there where she stood and utilized this giant mirror while they plaited their hair? And she'd wondered now, as she did so many times before, if Mike ever got any guilt trips from the way his ancestors uprooted the real owners of the land?

"Your parents, how are they?" she asked, craning her neck, and viewing herself, as the native women of the stolen land must have done hundreds of years ago.

"Good, good, busy as usual," he threw from the car. "Hobbies have a way of stealing people's hearts."

"And time," she added. "If I were a senior citizen in this country, I'd most probably want to have a hobby, too. Takes your mind off things."

"I think I'm falling in love," he whispered, still gawking through the windscreen. "Let's get married and get it all over with."

"You know, that's just not the done thing."

"And why the hell not? What's preventing us from doing something we are both dying to do?"

"Your condition, Mike, your condition."

"My condition? Had no idea I was ill!" He flew out of the car and joined her by the water.

"You're a *kafir*, Mike, that's what's wrong—nothing that we can see in the water."

"For God's sake, what's come over you?"

"A *kafir*'s a *kafir*, that's it, Mike. That's your problem, you're the sort of man I could never take to my folks."

This wasn't the first time she was babbling in a foreign tongue, but what she said just now told him something funny was afoot.

"What's wrong with me?" he asked again, peering down at his own reflection, not a single hair out of place.

"You're a non-believer in Islam, happy?"

"So?"

"My dear Mike, let's quit the pretending. You're an unbeliever, and you're very much aware of your condition. It isn't as though you didn't know of your *kufr*. You know you're an unbeliever, and there's nothing you relish more than the state you're in. And so does everyone else I know."

"I was born into unbelief, Anisa. I live and drink it everyday. This air is thick with unbelief. This condition's part and parcel of life in my home turf. I can't help it. But what's this little handicap got to do with us?"

"You see, a believing woman should know better than to get involved with such as you. Unless and until that condition of yours is changed for the better, Mike, marriage is out of reach for you, it's *haram*."

"What?"

"Forbidden. No good. Bad. Very bad."

"How do you know it's no good? We're not married, are we?" he asked, completely puzzled. "And how come you never spoke in this fashion before? Did I miss something?"

"You mean you couldn't guess at any of this?"

"Taken me for a clairvoyant, haven't you?"

"Did you tell your parents about getting married to someone you don't even know?"

"Yes, I sure did," he chuckled.

"And what did they say?"

"My old man wasn't exactly bowled over, but the old man's a man of few words and I respect him for that," he grinned. "If you were a golf club, maybe then he'd spare a word or two. Who knows."

"Just as well I'm no golf-club," she laughed. Mike was so cute, she reflected.

"Mother," he went on, "was more obliging, though. She's a firm believer in the division of people along race lines. A very sensible sort, if you ask me, what I'd call a good race-organizer, like with like."

"I just hope she's not a member of the *Klu Klux Klan*?" she laughed.

"This lady's in a class of her own," he grinned. "Confounded her with your picture yesterday. *'Pretty dark, pretty girl'*, Mother shivered."

"Apparently," he added, "I'm out of touch with the world scene, messing around with people given to terrorism, and only God knows what else. Mother diagnosed lack of information on my part and prescribed more television."

"You know your mother's right," she beamed at him. She needed time herself. In the meantime, let his mother shiver, she reflected. While his mother's worries were *only* skin deep, Anisa reflected, it was *his* condition that was most worrying.

Direct. Not pushy. Perfect size. If only she were able to change his condition.

"People must be doing *Maghrib* now," she said, thinking aloud.

"What?"

"You know Muslims are supposed to pray five times a day?"

"Oh, yeah?" he grinned. "Never caught you in the act."

"But we're supposed to, you know that."

"So? It's a free world," he said. "My best friend's just returned from vacation. He's busy now erecting this shrine in his own kitchen for this hideous statue he brought with him from God knows where. He burns foul smelling stuff in front of this unsightly thing, and he speaks to it. He even offers California oranges to it. It's a free world, Anisa. This is America."

"You don't understand," she glared at his reflection.

"What am I supposed to understand?"

"We Muslims," she said, "we're supposed to pray to the Almighty God five times a day. This prayer of ours has nothing to do with your friend's ugly, foul-smelling, orange-eating statue. We're supposed to offer our prayers to the Almighty God, the all powerful God, the Creator and Sustainer of this universe we're in, the Owner of this very air you're breathing right now. Not some ugly lifeless object that can't even beautify itself out of its hideousness! Now you understand why we're Muslims and why we're supposed to pray and seek His help five times a day?" she glared at him.

"Wow, that was some shot!" he said. "Incidentally, what am I supposed to understand, your doing it or your not doing it? Frankly speaking, I doubt if I'll ever understand either way."

Then without warning, she was crying.

"I'm sorry. Did I say something I shouldn't have?" he asked gently.

"It's nothing," she said, wiping away the tears with the back of her hand. "It is not like me to be so mushy, could be I'm coming down with the flu?"

"I'm starving," he said, returning to the car. "Let's go find something to eat." He put the car in motion and sped towards a fast food restaurant. A few minutes later they were back in the car.

"I hate the stuff," he said, as he unwrapped his burger and bit into the juicy beef. "These burgers, they're all garbage. I miss my mother's cooking."

"I think I'll miss my burgers," Anisa said.

"What else will you miss besides the bloody burger?" he asked.

"The car."

"And?"

"The burger buyer and the car driver."

For a while they ate in silence. Swallowing the last bit and washing it down with coke, he turned to her and said, "You know something?"

"Aha?"

"I think you're becoming more and more materialistic, with every passing day."

"Shouldn't that make us very happy? Man, you ought to celebrate!"

"Perhaps I should thank my lucky stars that everyone's becoming like me, eh?"

"Isn't that what the *Media*'s all about? To make everyone into a carbon copy of Mike Peterson?"

For a moment he was tempted to move towards her, but he kept his hands to himself. He knew she would recoil. He couldn't explain his condition to anyone. It was weird and very unlike him to exercise so much control over himself. He would've split there and then, but something or other kept him going all these months. He was glad no one guessed at his predicament. To anyone who saw them together, their relationship seemed as normal as anyone else's.

"A whole month without you," she said, breaking into his thoughts. "However, if you find a nice girl who is ever ready to hop into you know where with you, please marry her while I'm gone and save me the troubles that I see ahead."

"What troubles?"

"I'm not sure yet. But, we'll manage, won't we?"

"I foresee nothing but bliss," he said, staring out of the window. He was confident of the future. His mind was made up. As far as he was concerned, religion was a personal matter. If she managed to keep hers to herself, and it didn't spill over to him, he was sure everything would be just fine.

"We sure will manage," he said. He put the car into gear and headed towards the campus-housing complex. Three days later he returned to drive her to the airport.

Chapter Five

The Visit

The jumbo jet made a landing sweep over Rako Island. The engine roared for the final touchdown on the tarmac. Anisa's tired eyes blinked in the piercing sunshine. Soon, very soon, she'd be meeting her family.

Hardly waiting for the *Fasten Seat Belt* sign to disappear, she unbuckled the seat belt. And no sooner did she enter the tiny terminal than her eyes fell on the waving crowd on the other side of the glass partition. Retrieving her luggage from the baggage lounge, she made a dash for the exit as she had nothing to declare to the customs.

A whole crowd surged forward to meet her. *Kisses. Cries. Laughter. Shouts.* Her brothers had grown so much. Which was Hassan and which was Hussein? She was at a loss for a moment. They were almost identical and too tall for their age. She hugged them both. Her mother, her uncle, Aunt Rukhiya, Aunt Aisha – she

73

embraced them all. Tenderly, she brushed against her cousin's protruding tummy and recognized the young man at her side from the pictures she received two years earlier. She squeezed Faiza's nervous hand, and the two girls jumped up and down as they hugged one another.

Then they were all piling into the pick up, except for Aunt Rukhiya, Fathiya and her husband. As the car picked it's way through the heavy downtown traffic and into the long narrow road to their shabby neighborhood, to Anisa's surprise, everything looked smaller than she had remembered—the streets, the buildings, the sidewalk, the traffic lights – it was as though everything shrunk into a miniature of the original.

By the time her uncle had swung into the narrow dusty street of the neighborhood, it was already *Dhuhur*, the midday prayer. And the beautiful voice of the *muezzin* touched a cord in Anisa's heart; uplifting her heart in a swelling gladness. Her eyes moistened, and it was as though she had never left. There was something about that voice that had reminded her of her father, for as long as she could remember, his goings and comings had been timed and accompanied by this celestial call.

Her uncle had at last pulled the pick-up to a stop in front of her home. Lugging the baggage into the house and planting a kiss on Anisa's forehead, he called for the still wonder-struck boys, and hand in hand the three hastened towards the little mosque.

Upon seeing the car, excited neighbors crossed the street. Salaams, hugs and showers of kisses flew everywhere. "She must be very tired," Faiza's mother said, her voice rising above the din. "Let's all disperse now. *InshaAllah*, there'll be time enough later." She gestured for everyone to leave and tore the reluctant Faiza away. Anisa and her mother made the few steps to their house in silence.

In the privacy of their home Anisa's mother examined her daughter closely, "Anisa, you're so skinny, actually much thinner than you looked in the photos." On recollection she cried, "But then, what did I expect? Away for so long, without kith and kin to care for her. All skin and bones, poor baby!" Her mother's eyes dampened as she bid her daughter to turn round and round for further inspection.

Anisa was at last in the bathroom for a much needed shower. Meanwhile, her mother waited on her at the door, as if afraid someone would snatch her daughter away.

Minutes later, her mother was still shaking her head. "Bare bones, poor child. One more year and it'll all be over. White bones."

The minute she reemerged from the bathroom Anisa was greeted with, "Have you already had your *wudu* dear?"

How could she forget? She couldn't remember when she'd last done *Wudu* and stood up for *Salat*, but now it was as though she had never missed a single prayer. "Yes, Mother."

Already rejuvenated by the *Dhuhur* prayers, Anisa made her way into the newly painted kitchen; it was still green, her favorite color.

"Home sweet home. I'm so tired I could sleep all day," she said and flopped onto the old mahogany kitchen bench. It was as old as she was, but, surprisingly, just as sturdy and shiny as the day she left. Her uncle must have given it a new polish.

"You'll sleep all you want, *inshaAllah*," Anisa's mother said as she handed her a large bowl of her famous lamb soup. "But first, let's put some nourishment in those bones of yours. Drink it all up. It'll give you strength. I've also prepared your favorite lunch," she added as she briskly turned the chicken on the stove.

A knock on the door and the boys, their uncle, together with two brothers from the mosque, entered. At this time of day, when it was too hot to sit out on the terrace, especially when guests came along, the male members would take their meal in the sitting room. As usual, her mother had enough food to feed a whole village.

Before she knew it, Anisa was fast asleep on the bench, prompting her mother and uncle to half carry her to the bedroom.

It was already past 8.00 PM when she woke up the next day. The boys had already gone to *Madrasah*. School was closed for the summer. She could hear her mother and others in the kitchen. Anisa stretched her legs before she got up to get ready.

Her mother, Faiza and her mother, and Aunt Huda were all present in the kitchen. At Anisa's appearance, all conversation stopped. They had been waiting for her. All eyes fell on her as she made a handshaking round, hugging a breathless Aunt Huda. "*Assalamu 'alaikum*, auntie."

"*Wa'alaikuma salaam!*"

"There you are," Faiza said, motioning Anisa to sit beside her. "We thought you'd never get up. I've got some leftovers for you here," she teased as she handed Anisa a plateful of warm pancakes and a glass of milk.

"You're heartless. You don't expect me to eat all this?" Anisa gasped at the sight of the piled up plate, and the story invariably turned to Anisa's physical state.

"Aunt Fatima's right," said Faiza feigning shock. "If I saw her on the street today, I wouldn't have recognized her, but for the smile. Yes a walking skeleton, a bundle of white bones."

Later in the room when the girls finally extricated themselves from the women, Anisa stumbled onto her bed.

"I must thank you for your concern," she said. "I'm so full I could burst at the seams. By the end of the month, I think I'm going to need a crane to help me about." Propping herself up with her hands and scrutinizing Faiza who was now busy rummaging through her suitcase, Anisa narrowed her eyes.

"You know, Faiza, except for some minor sprouts, here and there, you're not only the same old bully, you're also the same old twiggy, and no one seems to notice. Talk about white bones! Now, now, before you mess up my stuff, just tell me what it is you're looking for, and I'll direct you in all sincerity."

A bar of chocolate in the mouth and a colorful photo album in her hand, Faiza finally rose from the floor and climbed onto the bed alongside Anisa. "Since your letters haven't been exactly newsworthy," she said opening the album, "I'm looking for some juicy first-hand knowledge from here."

Pointing to a bespectacled young man, whose presence seemed to dominate the pages, Faiza turned to Anisa.

"Wow, Mr. Lucky?"

"You could say that."

Faiza peered at the white form, and then returned her gaze to the long lost form of her friend.

"Chalk-white!" she breathed. "He could use some sunshine!"

"Pinky-cream, silly; there's blood in those veins," stated Anisa.

"Whatever. I wouldn't mind casting him in some dye, any dye. Poor thing, hasn't he heard of suntan lotion? Does he think yours will rub off on him, eh?" she snorted.

"He wears glasses, I'm sure you know what that means."

"What does he believe in?"

"Only in himself."

That made Faiza giggle, "Not even in his dog?"

"He's allergic to dogs. His grandmother's puppy once nipped the skin off his ear. There's this permanent mark; a fine scar supporting his phobia."

Faiza gave another glance at the snap, "No dog, chalk-white, and he likes my friend," she said, thinking out loud. "Something must be very wrong here. It's dead serious, isn't it?"

"Ah! If my heart had speech, it'd tell you all about it."

"My dear Anisa, you're disrupting nature...does he have a name?"

"Mike Peterson!"

"Mike Peterson & Anisa Ali Haaji, what the world's coming to!" Faiza shook her head, then sighed, "You know the plans we've got for you up here?"

"No."

"You mean, you can't even guess? Not even after bumping into Aunt Huda?"

"No." An uncomfortable throb made her heart ache.

"The State Secretary's eldest son's finally ready for a serious undertaking...no more vagabonding for Aunt Rahma's nephew." Faiza grinned.

"What's that got to do with me? I'm on vacation here. Everyone knows that."

"I don't know who put the idea into his arrogant head, but it does seem the gentleman's eyes are set on the world-wise Anisa, or *so* thinks Aunt Huda." Faiza suppressed a smile. "Why else is he procrastinating? And he's not getting any younger."

"I thought they'd forget all about me and find some other dummy for their precious hobo – but, no, no, it has to be me. But let me tell you this Faiza, I'm not the frightened Anisa they shipped off to America. I've learned quite a bit since, and one of the skills that I've picked up is how to say a simple no."

"Don't tell me the silly women had anything to do with your absence?"

"So, so. I thought it'd all pass, but apparently, I was wrong."

"Cool it, Anisa. You know, no one can force you into anything. It's probably only something the women are cooking up on their own. The man's never home anyway. Moreover, you still have a whole year in college. Take heart."

"Well, thanks for the warning," said Anisa. "Incidentally, how's your teaching career going?"

"Beautiful. Once we get our bits of papers, the Ministry of Education's sending some of us trainees abroad for seminar, before we finally embark on our careers. Don't you think I'll make a good teacher?"

"Of course, you'll, with that mouth of yours, I wouldn't worry a second," Anisa grinned.

"By the way, our engagement date's already set."

"Sa'id, isn't it?"

"Yep."

Anisa hadn't seen him since his high school years. "How old is he now and what does he look like?"

"Just turned twenty six. But, I'm afraid, he's not as exotic as our Chalky here. Too earthly-normal, if you know what I mean." Faiza paused for a second. "What I'd give for a little uncertainty – a dab of the extraordinary would surely spice things up a little bit. Now, with Mr. Chalk, we don't know a thing…it's like being in this vast place, exploring a whole new world; and with a daub of *suntan lotion*, things can change before your eyes."

"The same old clown," Anisa grinned.

"With this Sa'id, it's the same old tale. Nothing to pique the senses, nothing worth exploring, and certainly not a *river* of lotion will do away with that dusty look. His hair's already taking leave of his scalp, and I've for sometime suspected something of a kangaroo pouch forming on his tummy. It's a no win situation here."

"You see," she carried on in the same vein. "When my father brought him to our doorstep, I said to myself, *cheer up girl. This better be a bad dream.* All Dad said was: talk to him, look past the specter, and talk to the man."

"And what kind of language does the man talk?"

"All I can say is words like disco dance, music, etc, these just don't figure in his language. The poor fellow hasn't even heard of Michael Jackson's latest Album!"

"Get real!"

"Apparently," Faiza said, "he's never set foot in a disco joint—all those years in Europe – what a waste! Never did he set his sensible feet in *Shaitanic* premises, says he, and he wasn't about to start it in Rako Island, not even for my sake."

"Explains his lack of style, doesn't it?" said Anisa who could hardly hide her own chagrin. "Did he say where he used to *walk* his *sensible feet* in his spare time?"

"Yes, he used to do voluntary work in an Islamic organization, says he, whenever his studies allowed." Faiza rolled her saucy eyes. "I was about to tell him to shove his impressive record," she continued, "but you know my father; he can be pushy. Keep talking, he said. And I really don't know what it was that did it, but for the past months, we've done nothing but talk!"

"You see," continued Faiza, "he and a couple of other guys are into this liberation movement, the *Islamization* of not only the non-

Muslims, but also people like you and me, or what he calls *Muslim hypocrites*!"

"You sure landed yourself in a mess!" Anisa gasped.

"You could say that again! But wait until you hear this. Come the faithful day, he said, and he wants a real woman, properly attired when in public, and not this *plastic copy* of a female! But he's in for a big surprise!"

"I'll bet you can't wait for him to finish the talking, and come down to real business, eh?"

On seeing her brothers at the door, Anisa jumped from the bed. They hadn't seen each other since her arrival. She embraced them both, and setting them on the bed like porcelain she dived into the suitcase. While the boys scrambled for their stuff, she gave Faiza some chocolates and a small beauty case.

"Hey, what's all this?"

"Now you understand why I'm so thin, saving for a whole year. Now get out. I've things to do."

Turning to the boys, Anisa wanted to know all about her brothers.

"We're going on to grade two after the holidays," Hassan said. "I got the highest marks in class. The teacher said he made some silly mistakes this year," he added, referring to Hussein.

"But I did better than him last year," Hussein retorted.

"Now boys, what do you want to be when you grow up?" she asked.

"I want to become a pilot, so I can travel like you," said Hassan.

"How about you, Hussein?"

"I don't know. I'm not ready for anything yet."

"Now tell me about your Qur'anic studies." Anisa knew everything. Her mother briefed her on everything, even when one of then sneezed in his sleep.

"I think we are both good, *inshaAllah*," Hassan owned up.

"We don't miss *Salat*, we pray at the *masjid* whenever we can," Hussein's eyes twinkled with pride.

"And before we go to bed," Hussein said, "Uncle insists we read the Qur'an to him. We've such beautiful voices; it makes Uncle so happy to listen to us. It must make Allah even happier."

"And we know all about the prophets, peace be upon them, these were real brave men," he added as another bar disappeared into this mouth.

And then she was hugging them again. "You know, the last four years, you've really made great strides."

In the kitchen, Anisa's mother was already putting the finishing touches to the lunch, her daughter's favorite.

"Smells good, Mother," Anisa said as she entered the kitchen. "By the way, do we have any tea in the thermos?"

"I keep forgetting you're a big girl now," her mother said as she handed Anisa a cup. "There you go."

"Isn't uncle coming tonight?" Anisa asked after settling on the bench with her tea. "I'm dying to meet everyone."

"He's bringing the whole gang this evening."

"*MashaAllah*! I hope pregnant Fathiya's tagging along," Anisa snorted. "She looks so funny, I bet she's carrying many heads!"

"Wait for your turn, then it won't be so funny."

Oblivious of the call to prayer, Mother and Daughter chatted on and on about everything under the sun. They filled in on each other the latest tidbits and on the happenings of the last four years. It was as though time stood still for Anisa and she had never left Rako Island.

Two weeks later Anisa was still the latest news in Rako Island. It was a Friday night, and Anisa was all alone in the house, for the first time since her arrival. Her mother and siblings were away attending a social gathering on the other side of town, and were not expected until much later.

Although half expecting Faiza, or the odd neighbor to drop by, she still looked forward to a relatively quiet evening. Reclining on the terrace bench and browsing over a book under the fluorescent light, and contemplating on whether to write Mike a letter or whether she should let him miss her, the abrupt halt of a car broke her reverie. Her uncle wasn't expected that night. Wondering whom it could be she sat up on the bench. Two doors opened and closed simultaneously and then a light knock followed by a push for this door was never closed unless everyone was in for the night.

It was her uncle and he had a man she'd never seen before with him.

"*Assalaamu 'alaikum!*" Her uncle clasped her hand in both hands and clung to it, shaking it vigorously every now and then, until all the formalities of greetings and inquiries were made; much to the discomfort of the man hovering behind him. Still holding her, he now turned to the younger man.

"This is the much publicized, Anisa. I think you'll do a better job introducing yourself. I'll be around the corner if you need me." With this he took leave of the stunned Anisa and the equally puzzled man.

"*Ma'assalaama!*"

"*Ma'assalaama!*" they echoed after him in unison and then broke into a nervous laughter.

Shaking her head, she said, "That's my uncle, in a nutshell."

"I like his style. By the way, I'm Jibreel," he said.

"Jibreel? Have we met before?" she breathed, an invisible whiff of arid atmosphere blocking her airways.

"The last time I met you," he said pointing to a small chair beside him, "you were this size."

"I don't remember ever meeting you," her throat cracked.

"I'm a very scarce breed," he said, putting a stamp of approval on his vagrancy. "I'm never home. So there was no way you could've met me, even if you wanted to."

"Let me get you a cup of tea," she managed finally before blowing into the kitchen. *So this was the spook that haunted her all these years?* She had to *thank* him for sending her to America and keeping her there as well.

"I suppose you're the famous son of the famous Secretary," she called out from the kitchen.

"I don't know about the famous bit, but I'm who you think I'm. No need to rub it in," he said curtly. *Was the man ashamed of being the State Secretary's son?* Anisa reflected. That was nice to know. Praying under her breath for Faiza or anyone else to show up and disturb them, she told him to, "please be seated while I make a nice cup of tea for you."

After a few minutes or so she handed him a cup, took more time in the kitchen, making herself another cup and returned to her bench.

"Now, what can I do for you?"

He smiled at the question. Like uncle like niece. A sip of the tea and he almost choked.

"I came to see with my own eyes the much *publicized* Anisa," he couched, trying to swallow the bitter tea.

"Now that you've seen her, what's your next step?" she snarled at him, silently wishing him to choke some more.

"My next step is to force myself to drink up this lukewarm brew before it turns cold," he said. "By the way, I thought you'd been gone long enough for the water to boil at least! Fancy calling this a nice cup of tea!"

"Got the message, haven't we?" she hissed at him. *Oh, how she despised the rolling stone!* she thought in disgust. *Sending women on marriage errands! Doesn't even have time off from his vagrant career to look up things for himself!*

"A very *un-lady* like thing to do."

"If it's a lady cook you're looking for, Sayid Jibreel, you won't find her here! So, how about taking your troubles to some other door?"

"Absolutely no! This is my kind of door, and we're just beginning to say salaam. And I can see very little fault with my aunt's choice, I'll bet the lady's never been offered a nice cup of tea!"

"Should I get you something cold, then?"

"No, thanks. I was fine when I walked in that door; I want to walk out in the same form. But just for the record, what have I done to deserve this lovely evening?"

"I'm particularly averse to famous people, especially those who're never home," she said. She wasn't about giving him the satisfaction of knowing all about her fears and heartaches.

"We're like-minded."

"I'm on vacation here," she said, packaging her whole face in a threatening mode. "I came back to see my folks, nothing else. I think I can also safely tell you that I can do very well without the *match-making* of your aunts."

He let that pass.

"And," she continued in the same fashion, "the next time you hire them to run nuptial errands for you, teach them some manners, show them the ropes of their chosen profession, impart some niceties to them. That's the least you could do when hiring old aunts who don't know their job. As it is, the people you've recruited aren't doing you any good. Or perhaps they're doing the job for free and needn't be out-and-out?"

"What are you majoring in?" he asked, politeness itself.

"English Literature," she said simply.

"Very hot stuff. What a waste of talent!"

"I like acquainting myself with different cultures, and literature is a window…"

"To what?"

"I don't know what your talking about, and I'm not in the least bit interested in learning anything right now."

"Enamored with all things western, aren't we?" He crossed one long nomadic leg over the other. *What a wacky irritant!* She let out a breath.

"Well, my career's none of your concern. Perhaps you should go home, if you're stumped for ideas," she clenched her teeth.

"When you compare notes, wouldn't you say that life's that tiny bit boring on this mound of sand we call home?"

"Yes, very much, especially, when one finds oneself in the company of someone as distinguished as your nomad islander."

He laughed at the outburst.

"What's so funny?"

"I think I'm beginning to like you and hope this will become the beginning of a new chapter for both of us."

She was at a loss but just for a moment, then she said, "I hope you'll take into consideration our mutual disagreements on all the issues raised thus far. And hope that you'll henceforth abstain from the publication and promulgation of everything that's been said here tonight."

A contrite smile on his lips, he raised himself from the chair.

"Anisa, I think you're confusing me with someone else. However, if you ever happen to change your mind, I'll be more than happy to pursue the subject of my coming here tonight. Give my salaams to the family. *Ma'assalaama.*"

"*Ma'assalaama* and farewell, too!" she hissed after him as the door swung shut behind him.

"Not really the stuffy creature that haunted me all these years," she later told Faiza who had already seen him from her window. "But I'm not sorry to see him go."

"You sure you won't change your mind?" Faiza asked.

"Can't wait to get back."

"What if Mr. Peterson refuses faith? What then?" Faiza demanded.

"Mike will embrace Islam and might even become a better Muslim than you are, Faiza. When he puts his mind to it, Mike does things well."

"It's not that easy, you know. One can't just switch from non-faith to faith, just like that. There's something called motivation."

"He'll be motivated," she said slowly.

"Mr. Chalky? Motivated? Isn't the material world enough for him?"

"Whoever said Darkies had a monopoly on the truth? On the other hand, I'd be careful about sweeping remarks."

"So you think he'll become a good Muslim, eh?"

"Well, that remains to be seen."

"Let's not forget that faith had never entered his heart—isn't that what you were saying the other day? If I were you, I'd ponder that glaring fact – unless you're dying for regrets."

"You're free to make your own judgments, Faiza."

"If you're so serious, why not put your cards on the table? Hearing your family's opinion won't hurt, you know."

"You must be crazier than I thought!"

"They trust you, you know, and you'd be shattering their picture, if they found out…"

"That I was just as corruptible as everybody else?"

"I couldn't have said it better!"

"You're grinding my nerves. What a lovely evening! First him, then Faiza. How many times do I've to tell you that I could trade him for the likes of his royal nomad…any day!"

"His royal nomad will wake you up for your dawn prayers, Anisa, somehow I can't see Mr. Peterson forsaking his bed for the sake of his spirit! Isn't that why you're keeping the material boy under wraps? You need to come clean, Anisa."

"So I could be helped before things get out of hand?"

"It's the least we could do."

"Give me a break. I can perfectly take care of myself. And it so happens that I love my family too much to cause them misery."

"If I were you I'd rather sadden them a little bit now and get some First Aid than wait for a major operation!"

"*Ya Rabb! Ya Rahman*! Faiza, I'm developing an acute migraine!"

Anisa shifted her gaze to the sky. Not a single cloud hovered above. The stars shimmered like so many live diamonds, pure and vivid.

"Have you ever wondered," breathed Faiza, "why Allah made the sky so beautiful?"

"Faiza, a thing of beauty's a joy forever," said Anisa, quoting a well-known poem.

"Not really," replied Faiza, "even beautiful things fade, you know, people fade, too. Anisa, nothing abides forever, except for the face of Allah. Countless stars have already phased out. Everyone's moving on, everything's wearing out—and if the interior's never been lit by faith won't one be left with a slacking unlit shell? Are you prepared for that my friend?"

The question caught Anisa off guard.

"So you think I don't know that?"

"If you know that, then why aren't you straight with yourself?" Faiza asked.

"I just can't picture Mike as a fading star. Faiza, Mike's flesh and blood. He's not a faceless star. All he needs is a little knowledge of Islam to get him started. And once he's sufficiently motivated, he'll kindle his own spark. Trust me."

"You don't know that, Anisa, all I can see at this point is that you're running after a mirage, and dying to make yourself *miserable*."

"He's so gentle. It started all too *easy*, and I didn't think it'd come to this…and now, I don't know what to think, Faiza. It's so peaceful around him. In fact, I'm more peaceful around him than around me."

"Peaceful around the happy kafir?" Faiza arched her eyebrows.

"I very much doubt Mike's really that happy in that condition," said Anisa thoughtfully. "Complacent, yes, but happy? No, Faiza, I don't think Mike's happy with his lot, at all, there's always been something missing, he told me once. I think he's looking for something and he doesn't know it."

"Then why not let him come here?" said Faiza seriously.

Until now, Anisa hadn't thought of that angle, and she had immediately fallen for the idea.

"Let him embrace the faith first and once that's done, we'll come here right away. Faiza, thanks!"

Chapter Six

Back to America

Anisa's departure was finally closing in on the family. Two more days, and it'll once again be Ma'assalaama. That evening her uncle was to have a heart to heart talk with her. She was no longer the little bundle he was afraid of dropping onto the floor, some twenty years ago. Anisa had grown into a strong willed young lady, very much like her father. She knew what she wanted. He was proud of her and marveled at her educational brilliance and hoped that, with her qualifications, she'd have a decent future in the country. Degrees opened doors, especially when obtained from overseas universities.

He'd also derided himself for having doubted his niece's sincerity. He still did have misgivings about the regularity of her *Salat*, though, and that was, exactly what he wanted to bring up with her. He took her out and as they sat by the window of a busy restaurant facing the creek, he said, "My dear, we're going to miss you. This has been the shortest month of our lives."

"Me too."

"What do you intend to do after graduation?"

"Write. I still don't know what, but write I shall, *inshaAllah*."

"You don't have to tell me that," he smiled, thinking of the flow of her letters.

"But I don't know if I'd be qualified enough with my bachelor's degree."

"You could attend a course in journalism here. I don't know if you've noticed, but it seems as though things have been picking up here in Rako, as well."

"Anisa," her uncle added, "do you know how much you resemble your father?"

"But only on the outside," she grinned nervously.

"Did you know that he's never intentionally missed a single prayer in his life?"

"But, he was different. It's hard to measure up to him."

Safi Abdi

"You also know that *Salat* is one of the five pillars of Islam, second only to the *Shahada*, and that it is a special favor conferred on the Muslims by the merciful Allah." He paused for a moment, then added, "Let's put it this way, if you, for example, needed a personal favor, let's say from the highest authority of this island, and that if the said authority, which is already aware of your needs, graciously allowed you to petition for yourself at certain given times, wouldn't you, the petitioner, grab that chance?"

"But, of course."

"Need I say more? Anisa, it's the servant who's in need, and not the other way round. And that was never lost on your father."

"Yeah, I know. He was different."

"If you willfully refuse to petition for yourself, Anisa, who'll do it for you?"

"I know, Uncle, I know it, but…"

"No buts, Anisa. Even if you'd been thousands of miles away and you thought you could get away with things, maybe, I was wrong, but I thought you were smart enough to know that there existed a Being who saw and watched your every move."

Did her uncle know of her hidden treasures? The thought hit her like a splash of scalding water in the face. She glanced away from his keen perception, and her thoughts vaulted over the window.

Outside on the corniche, there mingled people of every kind and hue. The tourists were no longer content with the *two-week-seaside-sunshine* of earlier times. They were now setting up home in Rako Island. And the place had never looked more cosmic – in fact, the corniche and the people it hosted showed signs of being more world-wise than Mike's own hometown.

"All I'm trying to say is that one should never take one's faith for granted." His measured tone whisked her back to her seat. "Islam's a way of life. It's not a label that one puts on or off whenever it suits him."

The next remark made her jump in her seat. "You also know the rules of modesty, don't you?"

"Yes."

"So, when are you going to look on the outside what you are on the inside?"

"Wearing *hijab* is tough these days," she released yet another sigh, making it look like she tried and failed.

"Islam's *a way of life* and you've *to live that life,* or *you've nothing,*" he said softly.

"I know."

"That's the spirit," he said, "now here's a little something for my girl." He put his hand into his trousers and handed her a tiny red jewelry box.

"*MashaAllah!*" she beheld a most exquisite set of gold. "Thanks, Uncle. This is so lovely!"

"What do you make of him?" her uncle asked shortly, making Anisa's mouth flop.

"Jibreel? Him?"

"Yes, him."

"Well, I don't know…is this something I should think about while I'm still studying?" she stammered.

"Your studies come, first, of course," he said. "But you know how women are, your mother, Aunt Rukhiya, they all think very highly of him. Frankly speaking, so do I." He paused for a minute, and then added, "Of course, you're not expected to like the chap, since you don't even know him. He's also aware of your being tied up in your studies. He doesn't seem hurried, either. But then, again, like I said, he's a nice man, indeed very much unlike the father. And a year's not that long...wouldn't hurt if you kept in touch, would it? Not that the man has any permanent address. Still there must be a way."

"I don't know what to say, Uncle." The words rattled off her tongue. "The problem is, I really don't want to make any commitments I can't keep...and like you just said, the man doesn't even have a steady life-pattern, if I understand you correctly? Of course, where there is a will there is a way, but then again..."

"That's my girl," her uncle glanced out the window. *Was he seeing what she'd just seen*? Anisa wondered.

He saved her day. "If that's the way you feel, then we should let the matter rest, at least for now. In the meantime, let the man find a place of rest."

On the way home, her uncle said something, which completely shattered her composure. She learned for the first time that her Aunt Rukhiya, her uncle's first wife, was seriously ill.

Safi Abdi

Staring into the dark her uncle said, "She's diagnosed with cancer and may soon have to go for a major operation."

"But no one said anything!"

"You know Rukhiya."

"Yeah, she's a carbon copy of Mother. Always more concerned about others. But this is dreadful!" She could hardly control the tears.

"I wasn't supposed to tell. Now, wipe away those tears."

Chapter Seven

Pacing up and down the arrival hall, Mike's mind was in a spin. The plane was delayed. Something Floor said about *arranged marriages* had created a tiny spark of suspicion in his mind, and the spark was now a ball game for his doubt-loving emotions. If such a possibility existed, his emotions pondered, what then? Granted, Floor was given to exaggerations, but then again, the doubts returned – one never knew where one stood with those people.

Immediately the thought hit his discerning conscience, he realized he was thinking like his mother, doubting people without actual evidence, hanging markers on a clan he'd never even met.

A reshuffling of the arrival board rescued him from his conflicting self, and before long the plane was landing. And then, he was able to catch a glimpse of her as she queued up at the passport control. He waved from behind the glass partition. She waved back, a dimpled

grin on her face.

Chapter Eight

The Merger

The year was 1982. Even though Mike changed job location and had to travel a great deal, their relationship came to a head. Anisa's graduation day came and went. Mike made arrangements to meet her that night.

He was already seated when she arrived at the Latin food joint, INDOORS. Mike was in mid conversation, trying to impress Charles, their friendly Mexican waiter, with his meager Spanish. As usual Charles was gesturing with both hands and Mike's hands kept flying about, that being, as he told her so often, a good way of dislodging the foreign words from his throat; a scene so familiar to her that Anisa suppressed a grin.

The place was as yet empty of customers and as she walked towards him she knew her heart wasn't lying to her. Mike was a nice man and once his heart *embraced* faith, she was convinced, he'd make a good *faithful* husband.

"Hi! Sorry, I'm late," she said nervously as she took her place in front of him. Charles had already performed one of his disappearing acts, only to resurface with a large glass of fruit punch for Anisa.

"Especially for Miss," he chortled as he placed it in front of her. "No foolishness added, a healthy drink, as usual."

"You see," he continued, "I'm still pinching myself for adding foolishness to your drink last year, without your knowledge and full permission. Miss, you'd every right to blame me for taking you for granted. And I'll never forgive myself even if I lived to be hundred."

"Thanks, Charles. You're very considerate, but that was a long time ago," she grinned. Charles was still his funny self, she thought, and that, in spite of being rounded up a few times for overstaying. But as he so often joked, re-crossing the border was a piece of cake for him. "When you're from Mexico," he told her and Floor the other day, "crossing borders ran in your blood. And it was no big deal crossing over to big brother America. My own brother was caught so many times that nowadays the customs just look the other way.

They're simply weary of catching him. With all the deadly drugs coming from South America, who in their right mind would want to net empty-handed neighbors?"

Once they extricated themselves from Charles, Mike was then able to sound his congratulations to Anisa.

"Pity, I couldn't make it. So, how did it go?"

"Perfect. Everyone's celebrating. Floor's throwing this big party at her new apartment. Care to join?"Neither of them had eyes or ears for anyone else. They didn't even know what Charles served them for dinner that night, and as the evening coursed on, and she hung on each and every word he said, without the usual disputes cropping up, she knew some portentous forces were at work...goading her *further and further away...*

Once or twice she tried to unlock her gaze from his, but to no avail. At long last, the question she dreaded and waited for all night grated the air.

"You know why we're here?" He reclined back in the fragile bamboo seat but was far from reposed. *The food was good in the joint,* he thought as he waited for Anisa's response, *but the owner didn't* know a bit about anything else. And if it weren't for Charles, he'd never show his face at the place.

"I think I do," the words splashed out of her mouth, her mind a whirlwind of confusion, and she felt like a piece of someone else's *handiwork*, crocheted by clever fingers, hemmed in with a metal thread—*leave a man and a woman alone and Shaitan becomes the third*—it was an echo from the past. *Leave a man and a woman alone and Shaitan becomes the third.*

Mike was talking again, and he was saying what she'd been dying to hear, "What would you say if I said I wanted to marry the woman of my life?" The chair creaked under the impact of his weight. *He must remind Charles' boss to do something about the furniture*, he thought, *before a well-meaning customer informed on the poor immigrant and the authorities came down on the place and rounded up Charles and his friends.*

"When?" The tempo overwhelmed her, rendering her disabled. The *effect* he was having on her these days was no news to the man; her obstructed mind demurred weakly.

"Very soon."

He was leading her to an altar, she knew, and worse, she was running before him, holding the slight ribbon that held her neck to him, for him.

"But how?" she trembled, terribly enthused against her own better judgment, her head spinning, spread-eagled on the altar of submission.

"There must be a decent place where lovesick birds can tie the knot," he laughed a sure laughter.

"And where's that?" she quivered, light as a feather.

"We begin the search tomorrow at my parents' place. They do have a right to meet their future daughter-in-law, don't they?"

"But what am I supposed to do?"

"Just act being in love, that's all," he grinned graciously. She didn't have to act at all. He was just being cordial. She was already in it. *Leave a man and a woman together alone and Shaitan becomes the third,* she heard it whispered again.

"I'm frightened," she shivered, the hair on her hands stilling to a standing position, spike-stuff.

"It's going to be just fine." He gave off an aura of graciousness, exuding perfect authority. "Leave everything to me," he commanded, like a disciplined soldier in a well-practiced drill.

Seemed like he knew what he was doing, she reckoned, helpless without an effective body-guard, "But you don't know the first thing about *Islam*," she voiced weakly, totally incapacitated, incapable of detaining herself.

"I promised I'd embrace faith, didn't I?" They'd been discussing it and he was all for it just to make her happy. He already knew the rule: No *Islam* no Anisa.

"You mean it with all your heart?"

"I thought you knew me by now," he said. "When I say something I mean it, Anisa, but I need time, before I commit myself. I think that's more than fair?"

Here was a most pragmatic man. How on earth did she expect him to jump into something he didn't know?

"Of course, I know you," she said, acquiescent, caught in the moment. Her earlier resolve of first *faith and then wedding* forgotten in the meekness of utter pliancy. "And I love you too."

Chapter Nine

On Retrospection

Several weeks later, Mike and Anisa were pronounced man and wife. A quiet reception at his parent's home followed. For their honeymoon, they flew to an isolated spot in the West Indies, followed by a rowdy celebration at Floor's apartment, before the newly weds finally made the long drive to the next county.

Like a mirage, the first three months of their civil marriage whizzed by. So absorbed were they in each other that time simply stood still. And except for the hours he had to spend at work, they lived their lives in each other's company.

One evening, after a stressful day at work, when Mike was looking forward to a relatively quiet time with his wife the dreary question of his awaited conversion shattered the peace.

"Well, I'm still working on it," he threw at her. "What's the hurry? Why not do it after the baby?" He made what he thought was a sensible suggestion.

"Now that there's this," she said, aggrieved, kneading her stomach, willing her insides to perish, "there's every reason to hurry things up. You promised." She was in tears. For how long had she been crying? He gaped, strangely unmoved by her rueful emotions.

"All right, all right, so I promised," he said, dryly. "But, the point is, do I know what I'm getting into? Could someone please explain?"

"It's quite simple," she swallowed. "We make arrangements through the nearest Islamic organization. Or we get in touch with that Muslim man I told you about. He may be able to help us. Once you embrace the faith, we get married in the Islamic way. Quite simple."

"Excuse me?" he panted like a beaten long distance runner. She never did explain this part of the deal or did she? He wondered, flabbergasted. She did talk about weddings and stuff, but somehow he never did take them seriously, never saw them as affecting his life, their life. "So now you're telling me we aren't married, after three months of married life?" he cried.

The next few sentences made an unkind wedge in his panting heart. "I thought I was married, too. Please, don't ask me why I thought so. But now, I'm beginning to get the uncomfortable feeling of…"

"The uncomfortable feeling?" he cut her off in mid sentence.

"The uncomfortable feeling of," she repeated, looking towards him for support, "yes, the uncomfortable feeling of living in sin."

"Living in sin?" he shrieked, stupefied. "Living in sin? Of all the words in the world, why did you've to pick out that silly phrase? Living in sin?"

"I don't know what came over me. We shouldn't have rushed things," she moaned. "Oh! My emotions where have you led me? These three months of my life where was I?"

His lightweight eyes brooded, flickering blue, dejected, "So you aren't happy with me no more?" he croaked like an old tired frog.

"I know, we're happy, we've been happy, yes, too happy," she admitted, contrite, panic stricken, "but since I came to know of the baby, I haven't been myself. I just didn't want to dishearten you.

After all, you didn't force me into anything. Oh! My emotions, to what they have led me!" She lamented, coated in misery.

"Well, I really don't know," he said with a sagging spirit.

"I don't know how to describe it, but I can't deny it anymore. I know it as I must've always known that some things are just not right. That's how they're. Not right. Totally wrong, and there's no way around them than to avoid them. I can't even bring myself to tell my family. I haven't written to them since graduation. *Ya Allah*! Where am I going from here?"

"You mean you haven't told them at all?" He had never been so injured.

"They don't know you exist," she had to admit, with a heart weighing heavily upon her like a massive boulder. But seeing the hurt in his eyes, she added. "But we'll write and tell them as soon as you've embraced the faith."

"So, after all, the faith's more important to you?" He was despondency itself.

"But of course. I love Allah, and I love my faith. I just can't understand why I chose you over my faith. *Ya Allah,* what have I done? All these years of my life, where have I been? *Ya Allah! Rescue me just this once!"*

"And you would put Him before me?" he gaped at her, conspicuous disbelief mounting his heart.

"But of course. I love Allah," she stated with such ease, as if that was the most natural thing to say. He felt pounded.

"And what's next, if I may ask?" he queried, sounding like a schoolboy. "What else comes before me?"

The man can't be right in his head, her ton-weighing heart cried. "Mike, you must be crazy to think that the feelings I have for you is in anyway comparable to the love I have for my Maker, for my faith, or for my beloved prophet."

"And as far as your precious family's concerned," he said, bitterness incarnate, "I don't exist at all, if I'm not mistaken?"

She was mystified. The man must be off his rocker, she thought. Simple mound of clay comparing itself with the Lord of Heaven and Earth? She wondered, Faiza's remarks flashing at the back of her mind: *And if the interior's never been lit by faith won't one be left with a slacking unlit shell? Are you prepared for that my friend?*

"Mike, you're weird," she said at length, chiding him for his childishness. "Small wonder that faith had never set foot in that dusky heart of yours. And the problem isn't Christianity at all, now is it?"

"I have my reasons for not believing," he bellowed, "and they're bigger than the opinions of a third-world citizen. But the simple truth is, the simple undeniable fact is, the woman I married has taken me for a ride. Not only that, I'm just beginning to understand exactly where I stand with her. And of all the things that are important to her in life, I, her very dear husband, the man who wedded her just three months ago with glee and cheer in his heart, find myself tossed down right to the bottom of her who-is-who list, right at the bottom."

"Oh, really!" she cried, "so now, my husband's not only a proud non-believer without a single creed to call his own, he's also in full competition with his Creator?"

"Mike," she went on, censuring him for his childish haughtiness, "you're nothing but a simple morsel of flesh, queuing for termination, next in line for a sure end. You get that into that God-given brain of yours, you're nothing, but simple clay. And if it weren't for Allah, you'd remain just that anonymous clay, like any other type of earth, without class, description or spirit. Now tell me what's so *first-worldish* about a faceless mound of earth lying sprinkled flat, somewhere on the face of Mother earth?"

"Here I was thinking myself the happiest man on the planet, and my wife can't even bring herself to acknowledge my existence."

He had never felt so beaten. He sprang out of his seat, dashed off to the kitchen and raiding his own refrigerator, he pulled out a bottle of beer, and hurling himself on his cream leather seat in the same speed, he twisted the cap off, and as he did so, his gaze fell on his living room.

For three whole months he had been living there and until that moment he hadn't realized just how vacuously un-American the whole setup looked. They did have the usual bric-a-brac. But wait a minute; he was beginning to miss something.

"Hey, what have you done to my paintings?" he asked, "And to my lovely sculptures?"

"Lovely sculptures," she groaned. "If you must know, these lovely things of yours give me the creeps. I can't stand them, hard as I tried.

Safi Abdi

But don't you worry, I've decided to give them to my mother-in-law," she added, hoping this might lessen the bereavement.

"You're going to hand over my paintings and my lovely sculptures to my mother?" He banged his fists across his chest. "You take me for dead, woman? My dear wife, I'm right here, ticking away like a brand new clock!"

She chortled at his outburst.

"I may even pretend I'm being thick with your lovely sister and present her with a fine piece of art, or two, if you don't want your mother to have them. You relax and leave the house stuff to your wife. Now about the real issue, the spirit, Mike, the spirit."

"Crude! My paintings? My sculptures? You know how much these pieces of art cost me?"

"They'll cost you even more in the Hereafter, if you don't stop nagging about them," she said. Mike was such a peculiar man, lavishing such great value on such earthly trash.

"Now, now, Mike, let's talk sense and come down to the burning issue of your state, you promised." She was again in tears.

122

"I promised to embrace faith," he said, nursing the cold bottle between his fingers, "and at this stage of my life, any faith's welcome to my heart, and if it's my wife's why the hell not?"

"And marry you again, I shall, if I have to," he seethed further, collecting himself. "You just say where, when and how, and I'll do your bidding. In the meantime, I'm going to write to your family. I may as well show some probity, give myself the liberty of introducing myself, and break to my wife's highly distinguished family the happy news of their daughter's blissful marriage." He took another swing from the bottle.

"Can't we wait until we're done?" she pleaded.

"Or perhaps you mean to say until Mike Peterson's done? Properly done? I'll bet that's how you want to present me to your folks?"

She had never seen him that way and was taken aback by the new attitude.

Fixing her eyes on the bottle in his hands, she blurted out what she'd been dying to say but dared not voice until now. Before their marriage, she had already convinced him about the ill effects of pork, and he took her word for it, after all she was doing the cooking. But the beer was altogether a different matter. Mike's attachment to beer had been a casual love affair, and Anisa thought it best to wait before she ultimately quickened the break up of that happy liaison.

Mike was by nature a contented fellow, but there were moments the drinks seemed to fill a vacuum, every bottle filling the void where faith should have been, Anisa suspected. Only true faith in God, she reasoned privately, would cure Mike of that need.

"Once you've embraced faith," she said, fully determined, "you'll expect no more folly from that fridge."

He ignored the statement, half-flew up the stairs and blew into the bedroom. Rummaging through the pile of papers she kept on her side of the bed, he found not only her home address, but pieces of other papers as well. Unfinished letters that got discarded in mid pages, halfway through mid sentences. For a moment he was tempted to take a peek and see for himself what sort of pain she was trying to compose to her sensitive family, but decided against it. He still had some decency left, he reasoned.

Next morning, seeing her lying there on the immense sofa, all alone, looking every inch a foreigner, her knees crouched up to her foreign chin, breathing softly like a foreign child; he grimaced at his rashness. He rushed back up the steps and returning with a sheet, he covered her up. He didn't wake her up, for he was still mad with the woman. This reminded him he had to do something about the alien's green card; thanks to him she was no longer a foreign student.

Two hours later he called from work. "Darling, I'm sorry."

"Me too. My fault."

"You're not made at me, are you?"

"No, I've no right to be mad with anyone. *Ya Allah!* What have I done? My purblind feelings, where have they landed me!" She began to weep into his ear.

"I reckon, we're in this together," he said gently. "I've been thinking, high time we got it out of the way. Why not call this man you met in town? See what he can do?"

"You mean it?"

"Of course," he laughed into the receiver. "If I were to marry my wife a thousand times, I'd do it. You're a foreigner and we do have certain rules for foreigners here."

"I'll call him straight away," she laughed, cheering up.

"Good. I'll see you later, bye darling. And do forgive me, will you?"

"My oh my!" It was Bill, Mike's colleague. "I couldn't help overhearing what you just said." Bill was a great guy. He was a confirmed bachelor. Since the day he turned fifteen and he came upon his first love making it with another fellow, a scrawny pimpled no-good, he promised himself not to ever take any woman seriously.

"Man, what was this about marrying the same wife a thousand times?" Bill pulled a chair and supported his bulging arms on the mahogany table.

"That was my alien wife," Mike grinned at the confounded Bill. "This is what happens when a country boy becomes a member of the Muslim nation."

Before putting down the receiver, Anisa hurriedly made another call. That done she grabbed her handbag and hastened to catch the bus to town.

Catching her breath at the entrance of the Islamic community's branch office, she hesitated at the door for a few seconds to adjust her disheveled hair before pulling the door towards her to enter.

"*Assalaamu'alaikum*, Sister," a young woman clad in loose trousers and a blue scarf walked towards her. "I am Khadija, Yusuf's wife. You must be Anisa?" The woman said as she led Anisa into another room.

On seeing her, Yusuf rose from his chair and after the exchange of salaams he motioned for her to sit.

"May I get you something?" he asked.

"A glass of water will do, thanks."

"Plain water for an honorable guest?" he grinned. "What take you us for? You hold it there, lady. I'm getting us some fruit juice—you look after yourself, I'll be back in a jiffy." With this he dashed out of the room.

Safi Abdi

This gave Anisa a chance to wind down and look around her. Except for a large Qur'anic calligraphy on the wall behind Yusuf's chair, a large round table and a few houseplants, the room was bare. Anisa leaned forward to read the Qur'anic message. It was chapter two, verse 221.

"I see you're busy reading," Yusuf said as he placed the juice on the table. "You must be proficient in Arabic."

"No, I'm very bad," she admitted. "Where I come from only the very old know Arabic, and most of them are perhaps extinct by now. I understand some Arabic words, though. I can also read the whole Qur'an and know some of the chapters by heart."

"*MashaAllah!*" he said, grinning. "A friend of mine's offering Arabic classes. So once you're more settled you could attend these classes, and also bring your husband along, and your hometown's welcome too."

"Thanks," she smiled. "You're very generous."

"Now," said Yusuf, as he handed her the juice, "I understand your husband's finally ready to make an honest woman of you. I take it that's why you're here?"

128

She wasn't his first case. He had met several Muslim women like her who got themselves into things in haste, and then lived to regret it.

The lucky ones got help early. But these were few and far apart. There were also those who didn't know they had a problem at all, and these made the bulk of Muslim girls marrying outside the faith, and without the knowledge or the blessings of their parents.

He met her a week ago, at a fast food restaurant. The place was fully packed and seeing an empty seat at her table, he asked for her permission to sit there, and was pleasantly surprised when she greeted him with a salaam. He introduced himself and once he realized that she was new to the town he gave her his business card. Before long, she was telling him all about herself, and all the while he listened to her narration, he kept thinking: *What a tragedy! What a tragedy!"*

"Right now," she confided in him, as if she'd known him all her life, "the worst part's my family. Being away from them all these years, my return was taken for granted. And now all these months of dead silence! They must be worried sick! I didn't leave a forwarding address. So there's no way they can get in touch with me. Strange how I forgot about them all these months!" she sighed, despondency flowing in her veins; the whole affair just as amazing to her as it was to him.

"I really don't know where I've been all these months!" she concluded, baffled.

Before they parted, he urged her to take a closer look at her life and to get in touch with him.

"Anytime," he said, pained on her account, commiserating with her weakness, "don't forget, I'm your brother, and I'm only a click away, and don't forget it's not too late for you to remedy the situation. You've only one life. Think hard." He wasn't of course aware of the new life germinating in her belly.

Now facing her, he hoped he could be of some help, before the situation got out of hand.

"It took a week to convince him – not bad," he said, as his right hand pulled out a slim file from the desk drawer.

"Since your husband's not here," he went on, as he spread the file in front of him, "I need your help and if you catch me asking boring personal questions, don't get mad at me. I don't mean harm. I'm only trying to help."

"No problem," she pressed her lips together.

"First of all," he said, "besides your being in love with the man, what do you know about him?"

"He's a nice person, that much I know," she conceded. "Perhaps too nice. My husband's kindness itself."

"Islam's a practical religion and a couple can only live together in peace if there's total harmony," said Yusuf. "No matter how emotionally involved two people get, if there's no other force backing that emotion there's bound to be a gap. At the end of the day, it'll all end up in pain. In a real marriage emotion is not enough. There must be some form of inner compatibility as well. You follow me, my sister?" He paused to gauge her reaction.

"I think I do," she whispered.

"First of all, don't misunderstand me. I'm not a *love-hater*. On the contrary, I'm all for love so long as it's *within* the boundary of Allah's limits. And as we all know, a marriage without *love* and *mercy* is a defunct union. But, I assure you, that alone won't be enough in a permanent relationship."

"Right," she nodded in affirmation.

131

"Eventually," he continued, "you'd want a family, you know, children and the responsibilities that come along with them; are we still together, my sister?"

"Yes," she swallowed; her eyes fixed on the verse behind his head. She could read, *but what did it mean?* she wondered.

"And when one grows older, and hopefully wiser, things do get to change—things that didn't matter previously suddenly get to matter – and as you very well know, Islam's a way of life, meant to be lived, and practiced here on earth; am I still doing fine, my sister?"

"Sure." She stole another glance at the Qur'anic message. *Would that she knew what it was all about?* she thought.

"And children have a way of getting in the way!"

She grimaced at this, but he didn't notice.

"And spiritual matters have a way of knotting things. Sister, I really don't want to scare you but these are hard facts. Shall we go on?"

"By all means," she said.

"Now, I don't want to pry, but I'd like to determine whether you guys can at all be helped. Shall I go on?"

"By all means."

"If Mike has certain liabilities, his kindly heart notwithstanding, say: gambling, alcohol, drugs, foolish ideas about God, makes fun of the prophets of God, etc, then we'd have to think harder about things, you do get what I'm trying to say?"

"I think I do." Sigh. The juice was by now a sour crust on her tongue, but she wasn't at all irritated with the man.

"Moreover, we've got to give due considerations to the type of *jahiliya* society we're living in right now. If we lived in a society that forbade those things, I wouldn't be asking these absurd questions, and you wouldn't be here answering them." She winced at this, but if he was going to help then he might as well go all the way, he thought.

The last case he had a year ago had ended up in a fiasco. The smooth handsome fellow he helped convert to Islam and then arranged for marriage to the beautiful Muslim girl turned out to be a hard-core gambler. He almost killed the girl and the newborn baby in a drunk driving accident. Shortly after, the fellow took off and left the Muslim wife and the baby to fend for themselves.

There was also the tragic demise of the Muslim woman who lost her mind, after being married for ten whole years to a confirmed atheist who still refused to believe in God, even after embracing the faith.

This Atheist maintained that, since before Islam he was an Atheist under the guise of Protestanism, as a Muslim, he saw no disharmony in what he was before and what he was now.

He only changed shirts, he confided in the courteous Muslim marriage counselor whose home he and his wife frequented at the weekends – before one fine day the wife quieted down, politely declining to attend non-beneficial counseling sessions; only to flip out utterly a month later.

None of her friends knew where the woman resided after that. But the merciful angel of death knew exactly where to go for the unhappy corpse, in a mental hospital.

This hapless woman, Yusuf swallowed, left behind four children, and the only version of Islam these children ever got to know was the constant warring of their father and mother over the existence of God.

Yusuf knew that people who converted and got married the same day were only using the center to get a marriage certificate, and more often than not, ownership of the said paper provided comfort only to the sensitivity of whichever party was religiously inclined.

And it wasn't always Muslim girls who converted their non-Muslim husbands. Some Muslim men were also fooling themselves, wishfully thinking that they were persuading self-satisfied agnostics, and warding the marriage certificates in *their strife-ridden* homes – as a way of cheering themselves up. Still, the jam was no less jammed than the *born-Muslim-woman-new-convert-man-muddle*.

Not all such relationships were maddeningly faked, Yusuf knew. There were a good number of couples that really made it, *ultimately*. But there was no way of determining the genuine from the phony. They were of course there to render help but these hasty marriages between Muslims and new converts were no good. Character assessment was inevitable. These girls' parents were thousands of miles away.

"Tell me about his spiritual inclinations?" he asked shortly, hoping against hope. "Would you say Mike was religious at all?"

"Not really," she affirmed Mike's own admission, nipping Yusuf's hope in the bud. "But then again, he wouldn't really mind visiting the church. There must be good enough reason, though."

"Like the birth of someone or the death of an old uncle, right?" Yusuf's head popped up from the file, already disheartened.

"Exactly. And of course the odd church weddings of his friends," she went on. "Fortunately though, since we met, the need never did arise."

"Good," teethed Yusuf, before adding, "it wouldn't hurt anyone, though, if he were more spiritual..."

"But there's not much we can do about that now," she said in a small voice. "It's not my fault, you know. He was like that when I met him."

"Sister, I'm not blaming you for his lacking," Yusuf returned, his fingers warming the pen in his hand. "Rest assured, if he wasn't a real Christian before you met him, he wasn't going to be one after he met you...now, you might want to tell me about his drinking habits..."

"Mike drinks to socialize."

Drinks to socialize? Yusuf marveled at the popular expression while another part of his mind screamed: *Why can't he socialize without benumbing himself? What's he afraid of? Is he frightened of himself and is that why he's unable to hold normal conversation with people without a glass in his hand?*

The cold juice tickled her throat and she began to cough. He waited for the cough to subside, feeling the heated pen. The beautiful Muslim girl of a year ago also said the same thing, his mind raced. Anyway, you couldn't paint everyone with the same brush. After all, this was America. The one who truly stuck only to the occasional social drink deserved a medal; when the time came to quit, such a person found it easier to shake off the yoke.

"You're certain, my sister?"

"Yes, very certain."

"Also no drugs?"

"Also no drugs."

"No gambling record?"

"No gambling record."

"No criminality of any sort?"

"No criminality of any sort."

"No sympathy for nudists?"

"No sympathy for nudists."

"No history of incest?"

"No history of incest."

"No parental hate?"

"No parental hate."

"No abortion advocating?"

"No abortion advocating."

"No friend of Israel?"

"Not unless he's hiding things from me."

"No other hanky panky you can think of?"

"No other hanky panky I can think of."

"No animal friends?"

"You mean this Western doggy business?" she paused to ask.

"That's the idea."

"A dog once literally chewed his right ear off," she said. "So Mike may salute a poor dog from a distance, but his phobia would never allow him any close intimacy, no way brother, I know Mike."

"Good phobia." Yusuf nodded.

"Perhaps in your case, this is not so important," he added looking rather grim, "but there's something I would like to mention."

"Brother?"

"What do you think of your husband's standing with the so called gay community?" he asked, the words bursting out of his mouth, beetle-fashion. "Does he humor this sad fraternity, you know, like they do on TV? I mean, is he in the habit of making these imbeciles look good?"

"Aha!" She broke into laughter, thinking of Mike's relentless aversion towards the sad group. "Brother, you should meet Mike. His phobia against this lost humanity far exceeds even the one he has against dogs. Mike, he just can't be bothered to feel chummy with perverts. It's not his style."

"*Alhamdulillah!*" Yusuf said, brightening up. "Half the battle's won. And by the way, have you had such questioning before?"

"No."

"Then you're simply perfect," he let out a breath. He gave her a napkin to wipe off the sweat from her face.

"Now," he said, "having taken your word for it that the man of your choice is nothing of the above. You may now tell me a little bit about his knowledge of Islam."

"He'd been reading stuff, on and off, going to the library…but I really don't know how much of it has sunk in." She twitched in the old comfortless chair. The chair didn't seem like it belonged in the America she was getting acquainted with since she wedded Mike. It reminded her of the restaurant INDOORS of her student days.

As she began to wonder about Charles, hoping against hope that he was still his true self, and wondering why she didn't remember him at all, until that moment, Yusuf's words cut into her thoughts.

"The library, you say?" he asked. "Well, many of these library books are jotted down by biased pens. When reading about Islam, about any religion, it's best to stick to authentic scholars, in this case real Muslim scholars." Yusuf paused, before adding. "Of course, there're those written by open minded scholars be they Christians or people of other faiths, though even these may not be flawless, but at least, they don't disturb the basic facts. However, books pushed by deceitful pens, are more often than not either misleading or at best confusing."

"I didn't know that," she said, shaking her head. *So that was how devious pen pushers operated behind the scenes?* She thought in disgust. *Deceive and confuse unsuspecting folk about Islam?* She'd have to take that up with Floor.

"As you can very well see, this joint can't afford to keep many books, good or bad. Books cost money, however, I'll give you a copy of a book called *Islam in Focus*. This should give him an overview of what good Muslims are always saying. Let him read it for a month or so. In the meantime, be a good Muslim and help him with whatever questions he might have and come back to me when he's ready for submission and can say the *shahada* on his own free will. The more questions the better. Questions mean interest. If he asks questions you're unable to answer, he's welcome here. On the other hand, if he doesn't ask questions, ready yourself for more questioning," he grinned, then asked.

"I take it you have a copy of the Holy Qur'an?" he asked.

"Yes," she mouthed.

"How about a translation of the Qur'an?"

"No, never seen one."

"Then I'll give you that, as well. It'll help you understand what you're reading."

"That'd be nice. Thanks."

The next question struck her numb.

"What do you think of your present marriage?"

"Present marriage?" she choked.

"Sister, do you feel married?" He turned in seat to look at the calligraphy behind him.

She followed his gaze, "Not really, not anymore, anyway," she said in a small voice.

"Do you understand the meaning of this verse?"

"No, but I can read it no problem," she said. "What does it mean?"

"It means," he began: "And do not marry the idolatresses until they believe, and certainly a believing maid is better than an idolatress woman, even though she should please you; and do not give (believing women) in marriage to idolaters until they believe, and certainly a believing servant is better than an idolater, and Allah invites to the garden and to forgiveness by His will and makes clear His communications to men, that they may be mindful." Yusuf stopped at the end of the verse.

"I wasn't aware of the meaning of this verse," she said candidly, pulling at her left ear, "but I knew I wasn't allowed to get involved with an unbeliever. So, I don't know why I did what I did. I really don't know what came over me. I can't explain anything. It was as though someone else has overtaken me." She paused to look at the verse again.

"But what's preventing you from doing the right thing now?" he asked.

Her hand darted to her belly, and she was about to blurt out, "But it will be okay, after he has believed, won't it?" she quickly put in instead.

"But it must come from him," said Yusuf. "He mustn't force himself to rush into things, just to marry you. It won't work. Sister, I hope you understand what you've got yourself into."

"You know, he's not even a real Christian," she sighed.

"Let's just hope then he's not an atheist," Yusuf sighed.

"He doesn't have the looks of an atheist, it's just that he just doesn't know. He's like a blank sheet of paper."

A lump came to Yusuf's throat, "Let's just hope you have the right pen to write on this blank sheet of paper," he said.

"He thinks he's married, you know," she sighed again.

"Well, he has no reason to believe otherwise, or has he?" Yusuf sighed. "But now that you know," he coughed the words, "you'll have to explain things, meaning, you'll have to suspend the relationship until things are sorted out..."

He had to say this, and wondered if he should offer her a place to stay, but decided against it. If he now forced her to take herself out of the mess, and she didn't learn anything from the first mess, before long he'd find her in another mess. He had to let her sense the burning sensation of her first mess, Yusuf thought. Even children were wont to play with fire until the flames teased their little fingers. And it was normal with people to appreciate their own little efforts best. She was already getting a whiff of the pain; he had to let her have it all.

He was tempted to ask if she was herself a true Muslim, but decided against it. If she were a practicing believer, would she put herself in this mess? He doubted that very much. But she needed his help, and it wasn't in Yusuf's nature to turn away a fellow Muslim that needed help. He go up, disappeared into another room and then reappeared with a blue covered book titled *Islam in Focus* by Hammuda Abdalati and a translation of the Holy Qur'an by Abdullah Yusuf Ali.

Once out of the Center, a breathless Anisa called Mike from a phone box.

"A very nice man," she rattled into the phone. "It all went ever so smoothly."

"Great. What're you doing now?" He was still embarrassed at his conduct of the previous night. It wasn't like him to be so mindless.

"I was thinking of having lunch in town, would you care to join me?" She'd already forgotten all about the night before, and now she had to break the news of their being not married.

"How could I possibly say no?" he said in that husky voice she loved. "I'll be with you in half an hour."

Chapter Ten

Breaking News

On a bright Thursday morning and amid fermenting speculations as to what could have happened to Anisa, at a time when she was expected back any moment, Mike's letter was delivered to her uncle's shop.

Her uncle was contemplating a search effort. How he was going to go about it, he still didn't know.

Noting the American stamps on the envelope he quickly opened the letter. Expecting to see his niece's sprawled handwriting, Anisa's uncle was taken aback by the neat script. His eyes darted to the undersigned: Neatly written in capital letters was the name MIKE PETERSON. He quickly began to read the content.

The writer introduced himself as Anisa's wedded husband. He, Mike, had known their daughter for exactly two years, three months and seven days. He fell in love with her the minute he set eyes on her, and that instant affection known as*: love at first sight* later developed into a serious commitment.

A product of a normal white American society, he wrote, he never had the NEED to belong to any religious category. The closest he ever came to the supposed faith of his land was his nametag; a label with which he became so comfy that the thought of losing the tag altogether had never really pressured his complacent mind.

He had to admit, he wrote, he knew very little about Christianity and next to nothing about other faiths. The little he knew of Christianity, not that he really knew enough to nail the faith, had put him off all religions—not that he really cared. In fact, he wrote, he prided himself on his ability to disassociate himself with much of what he was taught in Sunday school—a scenario that wasn't exactly uncommon in his part of the world.

Prior to their marriage, he wrote, once he realized the importance Islam played in Anisa's upbringing, and the NEED she had to belong to that faith, he did promise to convert to Islam. After all, he didn't think he had anything to lose. However, he had to admit: Rome was not built in a day, but as of that day he was more than willing to do the right thing, and would be glad for any help or advice that might make things easier for him and his wife.

The writer touched a little bit about his background. Both his parents were active and working. The writer concluded his letter by saying that Anisa was now carrying his child. He sincerely hoped to meet them one day and looked forward to hear from them both.

Dumbfounded and at the same time touched by the letter, Anisa's uncle was glad there was no one else in the shop at that moment. He had read the letter several times before it downed on him that what he was reading was in fact a letter from a man who claimed to be his niece's husband.

If there was anything Anisa's uncle valued in people, it was frankness, and the writer of this letter, Omar thought, had plenty of it. That was some consolation. He folded the letter as nicely as he could and put it in his shirt pocket.

When Omar left the shop, Abdullah, his assistant was already crossing the road. He greeted him outside the shop and still nursing the piece of paper in his pocket, he headed home to Rukhiya, his first wife.

"The whole thing's entirely my fault," he began a heartfelt lament, "and to think that she was different from the others! And to trust her so much! Would this happen if I didn't let her go?"

"Omar," said Rukhiya, "whatever you did, you did out of love and respect for your niece. In any case, we've no reason to believe things would've been any different even if she were here. Right now, there isn't much we can do. First of all, she's thousands of miles away. She's also carrying a baby. The only option open to us at this very moment is prayer. So please send him a letter immediately, and if he agrees to embrace the faith, and is willing to learn, let him marry her."

"*Ya Rabb*!" There was anguish in his eyes. "Why did I marry her mother if I wasn't going to be a father to her? Would she have done this if her father were here today?"

"Omar!" Rukhiya shook him, "Get a grip on yourself, Omar, and what didn't you do that her father could've done better? You know what kind of children we are raising these days. Omar, look around you."

"And how on earth am I going to break this distressing news to her mother?"

149

"I'm coming with you, *inshaAllah*," said his wife, fighting her own distress.

"He does say he's working on it," he said consoling himself. Yet again he unfolded the letter. "There's some room for hope yet," he comforted himself, "and the poor man's working from scratch…and as he said, Rome was not built in a day."

Having sufficiently consoled himself, and having clothed the situation in his best inferences, he later concluded his own rendering of the story to Anisa's mother.

"To be honest," he said to Anisa's mother, hoping for a lightening of her pain, "this man's straight to the point, a very truthful man, if there ever was one."

"I wish that were enough," Anisa's mother mourned, "but it isn't."

"Mike Peterson doesn't beat around the bush," voiced Anisa's uncle, and strangely gaining some conviction in his heart that the situation was perhaps not beyond repair, he went on. "Fatima, we've here no less than a very honest man. For all we would know he could have said anything to save face, but he chose to speak the truth, instead. Now, tell me, how many worthy Muslims there're in the world, today, and how many of them are truly honest with themselves? Count, how many?"

"Omar," the mother's heart wept, aggrieved out of her wits. "Are you now telling me that my daughter, my only daughter has married an honest man? And a non-believing man at that? I ask you, where's the honesty? Where's the belief? Stripped of godliness, and devoid of truth, how stands honesty?"

"Now, I ask you," he said, still nursing the letter in his pocket, and mysteriously siding with a man thousands of miles away, "of the two absentees, who's more believable? Who's more plausible? Fatima, of the two absentees, who's more sensible? Our hiding taciturn Muslim daughter or our honest forthright non-believing son-in-law, the very father of our forthcoming grandchild, the honest writer who took the trouble to pen down this innocent letter I have right here in my pocket? Of the two, let's be fair, who is more accessible?"

Chapter Eleven

The Conversion

In spite of his busy schedule, Mike made sure he read the blue book from cover to cover. The contents eluded his intellect altogether. His only concern being the salvaging of his marriage, however, this did not ruffle him one jot. He did ask general questions, though.

"If Islam's the true path, and the only path to God is Islam," he asked, "why are the Muslims split into so many sects? Why isn't there one Islam? And where does Khomeini fit in all these?"

"Mike, I don't know anything other than what the media tells me about Khomeini, and right now, this man is the least of my worries," she told him, "but as far as God is concerned, there's just one right way, and there's not much we can do about it other than to live with the truth. But before you make any promises you can't keep, please read the book again."

"How come Khomein's not mentioned here?"

"Mike, get a life! Islam's not about *Khomeini*," she spoke slowly, as though talking to an impaired child. "Islam means obedience to the *Will of the Lord*. Not obedience to the *whims of man*, and that includes all the Khomeinises of this world. I hope you're now getting *the picture?*"

"If the man doesn't figure anywhere in this book, why are the papers full of him?"

"Perhaps we should reserve that question for the *Herald Tribune?* Today, it's Khomeini, tomorrow, it will be someone else. So why are we bothered at all?"

"If Islam means submission to the *Will of God*, then why do Muslims submit to Muhammad?"

"I just hope you're not confusing Islam with some *other* faith?"

"What if I did?"

"For your information, Muslims don't worship Muhammad, they follow only what he brought to them from God. Mohammad was a *servant of God*, the last of God's prophets. Why is that so difficult to grasp, Mike?"

"Well?"

"On the other hand, there are people on this planet of God who worship a servant of God," she would explain, "They call him lord Jesus, and it is them that we should be concerned about..."

He waved away her comments. "Now, let's not waste time on Christianity. I'm simply not interested."

"And why not? You were baptized in Church, weren't you? And given a Christian name..."

"Wife, these problems of mine are bigger than you. They're bigger than this book, too. Don't get yourself involved. This is a private matter. Don't jump into it."

"Well, you asked for it."

"But only in passing, now let's forget it, shall we?"

"Suit yourself."

"Now, this book, what does it say about Islam?" He would wave the book at her. "And what does it say about your belief in Jesus?"

Anisa was pricked. *Was something the matter with the man?*

"You've just read the book, Mike. It's in English, in your mother tongue! You want me to translate it for you?"

"Just answer this: Do you really believe in Jesus, I mean the real Jesus?"

"Now, the belief in *Isa* son of Mary," she would say, again and again, "is compulsory on Muslims. Compulsory. Compulsory…"

"So it's compulsory for you guys to believe in Jesus, is that what you're saying?"

"Yes!" she would breathe out, scratching her head for all the synonyms she could think of. "Obligatory. Mandatory. Required. Inescapable. Necessary…Now, give me a hand…"

"Stop! Enough! I got it! Now what were you saying about Jesus son of Mary?"

"Mike, please, if you ever fancy becoming a Muslim, you've no choice but to believe in *Isa* son of Mary. In Islam there is no pick and choose. It's not Mike who sends the prophets; it's God the Almighty. So you either take all or you leave all. Simple as that."

"No one said I'd to believe in Jesus, too."

"Then if you've a problem with *Isa* son of Mary, then we might as well call off the whole thing."

"Well, well…that what I call news."

"The belief in *Isa* is an *article* of faith in Islam, because *Isa* or *Jesus* as you like to call him, happens to be a Messenger of God, submitting to the Will of his Lord and Creator. He was a good man and a prophet of God. Now what reasons do you have for not believing in a prophet of God? And who are you to give orders to God as to who to send and who not to send?"

"Oh yeah? Now, how do you explain the Christian point of view? Say, I'm just plain curious, not that I believe in it."

"That problem should be addressed to those who worship *Isa*, not me. I'm innocent, Mike. Thanks for raising the question, though, but I'm afraid you're talking to the wrong person. Thank you. Thank you."

She was exhausted to the marrow, and was beginning to get morning sickness now, and he was nowhere near accepting faith. And strange as it seemed, she was now getting the stinging feeling that Mike had more problem with Jesus than he had with Muhammad.

"What do you say about man being made in the *image* of God?" he shot into her predicament.

"The arrogance of S*haitan*!" she was vexed at him for voicing such an absurd claim. "Man of clay, if I were you I'd think twice before putting my little feet beside the Creator of heaven and earth. Man of clay, look at you! Now go over to that mirror, and take a peek. I assure you, you won't find the image of God there. Please Mike, be serious, for once. Come to think of it, you were never serious about faith. It's not Islam, now is it?"

"Boy, this is weird," he thrust the book away. She knew he was beat, too, but nearly not as desperate as she, she thought glumly. He wasn't carrying someone's child. She was. *Would that she were buried with this child still deep within her, while only God knew her shame.*

"Dear, Mike," she bounced back to life, pondering her condition, "now, look here, this book's supposed to open your eyes and make you understand things. All I know is I'm a believer. I may not be the best of believers but I honestly believe in the Almighty God. And I'm frightened out of my skin. I don't know if I will see the light of day tomorrow. I'm so confused Mike. I pray to God to guide me, and wish that you too would come with me, and that together and with this child I have in my belly we may seek his Grace. Islam is peace. Let's not fight. This baby I'm carrying, it doesn't need fights. Peace, Mike, peace."

"If Islam means peace, why the absence of peace in the Muslim world? Why the absence of peace in this half Muslim home?"

"Islam means peace and only those who truly follow it are peaceful, got it?" She'd been skimming through the book herself, behind his back. "And while we are on the subject of this half Muslim home," she continued, a huge knob mounting her throat, "how do you think this home will ever attain total Islamic peace if the other half refuses to rally for this Muslim peace? How then?"

"Around the world and especially in the Muslim world," he said picking up the book again, and waving it at her, as though she were the writer, "a lot of people are suffering. So much warring. So much bickering. So much tragedy. What's Islam doing about all this?"

"A lot of people are suffering here in America, too," she would retort, "and they're not Muslims."

"There're far too many poor people in the Muslim world. Why aren't the loaded Arabs spreading the God-given riches?"

"Money isn't all, Mike. Our poor people happen to have things that are way above the reach of any loaded American...*contentment*. As for our rich brothers, well, all I can say is some of them do share, but perhaps just because they don't make it a point to *advertise* their compassion on TV, their generosity is known only to God?"

"The only freedom Muslim women have in Islam is found only in books."

"How do you know that?" she asked, piqued. This was the only book that he'd truly pondered on the subject and now he was acting as though he had read every single book on the face of the earth, "Even after reading, you still don't have a clue. Yet, you've already made up your mind, what kind of reasoning is that, Mike?"

"The oppression of women in Islam's scary, when you think about it." He nodded his head with all the vigor in him, in complete agreement with what he had just said.

"I come from an Islamic community and I've as yet to meet these so called oppressed women," she quipped. "On the other hand, there's no dearth of subjugated, battered women who're in dire need of your attention here, in this very country. If your concern for women's indeed for real, shouldn't charity begin at home?"

"Look, there's no freedom in the Muslim world."

"But the question is are these governments using Islamic Law to govern their lives?"

"Then why do Muslims terrorize the world?"

"All this talk about Islamic terrorism is a mighty diversion, if you want to meet true terror, you're living in the right place. Why, you people are not even allowed to see Islam for what it really is, the true path to Allah? We Muslims, we're very much aware of this fact. And it's time you knew it, too. You're oppressed, Mike, for there's nothing like spiritual dictatorship. And please let's not talk until you've attained your freedom from the media."

"Why can't I be who I am? After all, no one's perfect."

"No, we can't abandon you when we know there's hope. Now, go back to your reading and don't talk until you've had time to think, and don't forget to read the translation of the Qur'an as well."

"Aha, wasn't the translation for you?"

"You know I'm a born Muslim, I know things that are simply Greek to you, and it's this knowledge that's now killing me, now get on with it, there's no time left, you'll need to declare the *shahada,* soon."

"I know God is one, had always known, long before I started reading this book. Why broadcast it?" he persisted.

"Because, unless you declare your belief openly and state what you know of the truth with that mouth of yours, how would we know of your state? We're Muslims, we're not psychic."

Two months later and he was still unable to make head or tail of what the religion of Islam was all about – not that he had any doubts about the existence of God as such. But he just didn't get it, and his wife wasn't exactly the best of teachers. Not only that, hard as he tried, he just couldn't shake this image of Islam that was already a part of him. It wasn't really the belief itself that had his brain busted, it was all the other things that he over the years associated with Islam, which perhaps, didn't even have much to do with Islam the religion.

While yet in this wavering state, Mike Peterson was to report himself at the gates of the Islamic Center where he became the recipient of a Muslim name, and said, on his own admission, the profession of faith: The declaration of: *Ashahadu ana Laa Ilaha Ila Allah, Wa' Ashhadu anna Muhammadan RasulaAllah* (I bear witness that there is no god worthy of worship but Allah, and I bear witness that Muhammad is the Messenger of Allah).

Having uttered the Arabic declaration, which strangely glided off his tongue with the least of effort as though it were the most natural thing to say, and whose non-offending meaning was nicely typed out for him, Mike Peterson was then issued a certificate attesting to his new identity as a Muslim. For better or worse, within the span of fifteen minutes, the American now named Ali Ahmed Peterson took Anisa Ali Haaji as his wedded wife.

The happy couple invited those present at the mosque for a well-earned meal in town. And if the bride didn't chastise the happy groom, Ali Ahmed Peterson might have entertained his guests with a few bottles of champagne, to celebrate the happy occasion. As it was, his wife whispered in his ear that these honorable guests would rather have chilled coke and orange juice. They were not the kind of

Muslims he was accustomed to during Anisa's college days. These were real Muslims, she murmured in his ear.

Chapter Twelve

A Trial Run

The first three years of their marriage, their relationship went as smoothly as the clash of cultures allowed. Although, most of the time they couldn't see eye-to-eye and even small things like personal hygiene became a bone of contention, the situation remained manageable to a degree. Mike was a peace-loving person and the pressures were mainly coming from her direction. She was after him all the time, following him around as though he were a mere child, and she his mother, with orders like: "I hope you've brushed your teeth before breakfast, dear?" or "Hope you haven't forgotten to wash after toilet, Mike?" or "how come you haven't washed your hands before eating, Ali?" or "Man, you're taking food with your left hand! Ali!"

Breakfast in bed was out of the question, as Anisa had already read too many novels, and seen too many movies where the hero or the heroine just bolstered up in bed from a night's sleep, propped up the pillow behind his back and just began to relish the breakfast without so much as a mouth wash!

Of course, Mike was no filthy cowboy, yet his total ignorance of basic Islamic *adab* (etiquettes) would drive Anisa against the wall, but then as always Mike would give in and things would get back to normal. The hygienic part did not worry him at all, but that these had to be followed so religiously—that was what piqued him often. So this was what it meant to be Muslim? He pondered. If he wasn't living with one, he'd never have guessed the amount of water used daily by an average Muslim—one who wasn't even practicing her faith.

After the birth of their daughter, Nasra, approximately a year after their marriage, they also took the much-awaited trip to her home country, where Mike became a very hot topic in Rako Island. During the one month and half they stayed there he was the sole charge of Anisa' uncle, while Anisa and the baby Nasra immediately fell under the care of his mother-in-law.

Anisa's uncle treated him like royalty, escorting him personally everywhere – every now and then, giving Mike the opportunity to do something with his sometimes-bored princely hands – by letting his son-in-law help him fix his hoary pick-up. And every time Anisa's uncle felt that his guest was perhaps in need of a change of scene from all the kind attention he was getting in the neighborhood, the two would go from place to place, looking for spare-parts for the ancient pick-up. And from the inner city, the open markets, to the outskirts of the island and to the few mosques, the two men went, where men crowded over them – awed by the American believer, for many viewed Mike's conversion to Islam as something short of a miracle; his *conversion* somewhat breaking the long held assumption that the white race was inherently *kafir*.

On their return to the United States, Mike knew by heart all the formalities that were necessary for the ritual prayers. Although it never failed to make him wince every time Anisa introduced him by his Muslim name (which she clung to with an obsession that bordered madness), and never pretended to like being called by these names, his empathy with the folk of Rako Island was such that he could even endure being called by these names, while there.

Indulging them further by greeting them with *Assalamu 'alaikum,* also became the norm. It wasn't as though he were pretending. He really liked the simple community life of the people so much so that their next vacations were also spent there with them. And as far as the family was concerned, Anisa's choice of husband wasn't such a bad deal, after all. Their son-in-law proved to be more than they bargained for, given the circumstances.

If the long distance between them and their daughter and grandchild proved painful, the family did not hold it against him. They bore the longing with fortitude and they looked forward to the vacations.

Excepting some uncouth remarks hurled from over the wall— before the family raised up the wall to shelter their son-in-law from public curiosity, while he sun-bathed, on his wife's insistence – no one of real importance had in reality reacted negatively to his color, or the lack of it.

He was pleasantly surprised that to his wife's community, race wasn't really a burning issue, and had never been so. People's worth were drawn along spiritual lines. If you were a believer you were a brother. Period. For the belief in Islam meant that God only looked at the *heart* of men, and that it was piety alone that could put man above another man, and that neither race nor wealth could bring man closer to God if true piety did not exist in the heart.

A new member to the *Ummah,* was indeed a welcome addition, and this created in Mike a fellowship feeling that he had never felt anywhere before. And once Mike's terribly undernourished skin received a much-needed dose of healthy sunshine, after a week or so of reaching the island, Anisa's mother would heave a sigh of relief.

On the home front, during those first three years things also remained under steady control, except for minor squabbles over basic issues such as the naming of their child and Anisa's blanket refusal to partake in Christmas merriment, Easter and Halloween witchery, as she believed these to be archaic pagan traditions that had absolutely nothing to do with the son of Mary.

The only major crisis so far had been when Mike's mother brought to their home a four-legged friend, as a surprise gift to her two-year-old grandchild. Anisa's hysterical response to the little beast's licking of Nasra's face after the grandmother handed her the puppy was such that the well-meaning grandmother was naturally scandalized, and she made a speedy exit from her son's home, with the equally stunned fluffy paws clinging to her protective arms.

For weeks his old mother refused to speak to him. And when she finally found her tongue, to Mike's horror, a Pandora's box of the things that were hitherto kept under wraps became unleashed.

"Mother," he said in defense, "Anisa is my wife, she doesn't hate you, she loves you, but we've to respect her way of life."

There was no denying Mike was a good son. Had always been so. But the black alien had practically taken over their life, vexing the family further by calling Mike by some barbaric names, and shooting her mouth off about how the alien heart constricted before Mike embraced faith – making it seem as though Mike had no faith at all until his forced conversion to Islam.

No one knew how she got the idea, but the alien never did take them seriously, Mike's mother reflected, recalling the many discourses she had had with the alien, before the message finally hit her head that the alien was in fact serious about what she was saying. That was the joke of the century, the family balked. But, it was a joke they suffered for three whole years.

Even his sister, Charlotte, who had earlier gone along, albeit reluctantly, with the idea of an alien sister-in-law, just for the heck of it, and who in all honesty expected some sort of a door mat and a baby-sitter rolled into one, couldn't hide her dismay. The appalled sister confided in her equally stupefied friend.

"You know," Charlotte told her friend, "I expected some submissive creature, you know the sort, and if I know my brother, that's exactly what he had in mid. Frankly speaking, though, this woman's out of her league! Doesn't fit anywhere!"

"What a misfit!" breathed the friend.

"If all he wanted was a black woman," Charlotte continued, "plenty of pretty homegrown blacks these days. Beats me why he had to import some alien creature from some island down the lower hemisphere? An alien who's put into her silly head that she's something? What a joke! Won't even celebrate her daughter's birthday! A waste of time, says she!"

"A waste of time? Her own daughter?"

Somehow, they all thought he'd soon tire of her and hoped privately she'd flee in haste when events got a tad too much for the primitive soul. What they didn't bargain for, however, was that it was they, and not the alien, who ultimately did all the compromising, and made all the adjustments...all in the name of family. Having lived through the absurdity of all three years, Charlotte had of late opted for the severing of all familial cords with her own brother and his alien family. Her two boys would rather go to Grandma's when their little cousin Nasra was sure to be there as well, but their mother Charlotte had at last decided that the boys rather become chummy with the colored children down the road, to make up for the loss.

It was wacky, sending your children off, to play and become chummy with some colored folks down the road, but if it helped mitigate the loss of the alien's child, then what the hell? It was worth a try. Even after they played with the colored kids, Charlotte's boys still kept up the bugging and pestering about their ticklish baby cousin. They both agreed that it was more fun playing with their cousin than with the neighborhood kids. But their mother wouldn't budge.

Though Charlotte was now succeeding in totally avoiding her brother, the mother could hardly be expected to cut the umbilical cord with her boy.

Although the puppy pandemonium made her say to his face some of the things she'd been saying behind his back all along, she was still his mother. But to her son's further bewilderment she proceeded to say her mind.

"To be circumcised by a woman!" his mother sizzled in a fit of anger. "Son, the bottom line is, you're circumcised, ritually!"

Did the doctor flap his mouth behind his back? Mike wondered, but did not say it. Instead he stated with all the patience in the world. "And so was Jesus, your Lord!"

Disregarding the last remark, his mother demanded, "Tell me now, what's your name? Aren't you the same baby I baptized in church?"

172

"And little good it did me, Mother!" Mike broke into chortles.

"I used to take you to Sunday school, well, didn't I?"

"I'm not complaining, Mother, but why are we kidding ourselves? We know the truth about my Sunday school teacher," Mike snorted.

"So what if he turned out gay?" his mother shot at him. "There're thousands like him around. Why are you singling him out?"

Mike gasped at his mother, "Mother, I happen to have principles. I just don't like perverts. A disgusting lot, that's what they're. And believe you me, my Sunday school teacher was one weird priest. How this abnormal being ever came into the fold of the clergy is beyond my imagination."

"Son, this woman doesn't believe in the *lord Jesus*," said his mother, changing the subject.

"Mother, please, let's not forget, as far as this woman's concerned, Jesus is a messenger of God, a human being, like you and me."

"Nothing more than a human being?" she shot at him.

"So what if she says Jesus is a man? It's her mouth that's saying it, not yours."

"Our Savior Lord's nothing more than a human being?"

"My Sunday school teacher believed in this Savior, and little good it did him, too!" he balked.

"But this woman, she believes in Allah. Son, you're being blindfolded."

"Is that an offence," he cried, in spite of himself. "Since when did believing become an offense? Mother, you may not be religious yourself, but come to think of it, you've always been on my back for not believing. Why are you now taking offense at her beliefs? What is it to *you* if she believes in Allah?"

"But she doesn't believe in the *lord Jesus.*"

"As far as she's concerned Allah is *the God.* And she's free to her beliefs. Everyone's free to his or her beliefs. Why are we denying her, her rights to her beliefs?"

"But to say Jesus is man, you call that belief?"

"The last time Jesus was seen he was every inch a human; a fact known even to the Jews. Why are we bashing her for things we already know?"

"Son, this woman's not a Jew."

"See, what's wrong with *our* perception, Mother? We'd accept anything from a Jew, but when it comes to Muslims, it's a no, no...and to think that it's the Jews that don't give a damn about Jesus...while Muslims accept him as a good prophet of God. See what I mean?"

"What has she been feeding him?"

"No disrespect meant, Mother, but I think I'm developing a softer spot for Jesus now that I'm getting acquainted with the man. And it's Islam I should thank."

"Son, this woman's no good. She's different. She'll never be like us. And to think of Jesus as nothing more than human...who the heck does she think she is? This woman's not a Jew. She's an alien, with a green card, and that's all there is to it."

"Let's face it, Mother, Jesus was a man, the son of a woman. Christian scholars are falling all over themselves to bring that point home to us. Mother, please, Jesus was a man, let's not deny facts."

"But that's all in the past. He's God now."

"And were you there when he became God, Mother? Was anyone there when this unnatural incident came to pass? Mother, no one becomes God, it's a rational impossibility. You can't prove it and you can't make the impossible possible."

"And were you there when Muhammad became God?"

"Muhammad never did become God anymore than Moses became one. According to Muslims, Muhammad's the last Messenger of God. And there's no way we can *disprove* that...that's if we're truly honest with ourselves. *We weren't there.* I maybe Muslim only on paper, but I guarantee you I'd have less problem agreeing to this version."

"Good!"

"Now, now, since when did Muslims ever claim divinity for any prophet? Since the answer is a never, then why are we putting words into their mouth? Why do their sayings rub us up the wrong way? Why are they having this effect on us? Who are they by the way? Third world citizens, why are we taking them so seriously?"

"Then why are we taking a third world citizen with a *green* card seriously...you tell me?"

Mike was truly depressed. "Mother, please, you aren't exactly spiritual. Why can't you let her be? So what if she doesn't want to be licked by a dog?"

But once uncorked, his mother could hardly stop.

"But I'm white and Jesus is *my* Savior Lord. Now who is *she* to ruffle my feather?"

"Is that it?"

"Everything's forbidden, everything," she said, pacing up and down her cushy living room. "We can't even have a decent family get-together without consultations as what to put on the dinner table! The whole thing stinks. You may keep that woman, but as far as we're concerned it's over."

Steering her back to the subject, he said, "Mother, let's not build a mountain out of a mole hill. You know, I've nothing against dogs. They're good animals, but why force them on her? Isn't this America? Whatever happened to the freedom we love so much? The freedom to choose, the liberty to differ, why aren't we suddenly so concerned with that? Is it because of the shade of her color? Or perhaps the green card has something to do with it?"

"Force it on her? I've every right to celebrate my grandchild's birthday, and with whatever takes *my* fancy! She's no right to take that away from *me!*"

Now that she spilled the beans, she was beginning to have second thoughts. Religion wasn't exactly her cup of tea. Mike was right. Her dislike of all things spiritual fringed on agnosticism. She never bothered to find out why she was being touchy on the question of her daughter-in-law's like or dislikes. But she was white, and never did take orders from anyone. And Christianity was a *badge* of honor and a truly *white* tradition; and she wasn't about bowing to the blabbers of some *black* alien daughter-in-law. However, Mike was the perfect son. She knew she could count on him more than she did on her daughter. Never would she dare to say to her half the things she had heaped on him. Her daughter was no angel, but then, she didn't bring a total stranger into their midst.

"Naturally, you developed this phobia, after what happened at Grandma's...but after all these years, I thought, you somehow outgrew the angst..." With this, his mother set about the task of setting the table for coffee.

"I still don't get it, this thing between Muslims and dogs," voiced Mike's father who'd been watching his favorite match on TV, while half listening to the old lady and her son's rumpus.

Mike who had been on his feet all this while now flung himself on to a settee. He'd already consulted the puppy issue with Yusuf and now he tried to relay what he had gleaned out of Yusuf's remarks to his father.

"Islam considers a dog's saliva impure. So naturally, cuddling is out and so is licking. If one becomes in contact with a dog's saliva, one must wash seven times: once with earth and six times with water."

"Once with earth, and six times with water?" yelled his mother from the kitchen, almost dropping the saucer she had in her hand on the marble floor. "Son, I'm very sorry for *you!*"

As an exhausted Mike took leave of his somewhat pacified parents, the long drive home gave him time to reflect on his plight. Even though Anisa was not really involved in her faith, there were still rules and regulations that never let him off the hook. Right from day one, he found himself walking on a tight rope, balancing himself between his wife's taxing rules and his society's unrelenting scoffs at those rules. True, he was Muslim only on paper, but that too was enough to give everyone the opportunity to *badmouth* the faith, though Anisa was for the most part spared the snide remarks. In spite of everything, however, he never ceased doting on his wife and daughter, and now looked forward to the unborn child with exactly the same passion he awaited the birth of his first child.

Chapter Thirteen

Private Agony

When trouble toucheth a man, he cried unto Us (in all postures) – lying on his side, or sitting, or standing. But when We have solved his trouble, he passeth on his way as if he had never cried unto Us for a trouble that touchet him!
(Qur'an:10:12))

Some six months later, after they all thought they had put the puppy mess behind their backs, an unwarranted crisis was now plunging the very pregnant Anisa into the thick of an unexplainable dilemma. A battlement that so sapped her energies – a predicament so personal, that no one could either share or relieve the pain. Neither the doctor she consulted for her ailment nor the loving husband by her side could help her with her burden.

"Cheer up," said her doctor, "you're in perfect condition. The baby is growing beautifully. Pamper yourself and drop by in two weeks, if you haven't delivered by then."

"I keep hearing this heavy metallic pounding in my head," she complained, frantic for a cure. "Doctor, I can't sleep. Can't you do something?" she pleaded with him.

"Get plenty of fresh air. Eat plenty of fruits, and take an hour's walk before sleep. Take care." The doctor buzzed for the next patient.

To any casual onlooker her life seemed normal and happy enough—a nice house, a car, a few good friends, a caring husband, a healthy beautiful child, a second child on the way—what more could she possibly want? Why was *she* so ripped up *inside*? Tossing and turning on her side of the bed, she was once tempted to wake him up, as she had done many times before, but decided against. He had work in the morning. And what could he possibly do to lighten her pain? Easing her heavy body off the bed, she ambled into the room next door.

Lying in bed so peacefully was their daughter Nasra of two and half. She moved the child to one side and made a place for herself alongside her. Lying thus, so close to the warmth of her child, fanned by the gently breath of her daughter's innocence, some of the heaviness of the heart uplifted and a benign drowsiness sent the pregnant woman into the pool of the unknown.

A couple of nights later, propped up in bed, flipping nervously through the pages of some *Woman* magazine, and dreading yet another sleepless night, a sudden sensation of horror darted shafts of terror down her spine and submerged her in stifling angst. Attempts to ease her panic with the *shahada* also came to naught. Dry and stiff, her tongue returned to her. She found she could no longer affirm her faith in God. The *shahada* of *La Ilaha Ila Allah* (no god but Allah), the same phrase she used to utter in reflex movement, even in sleep, she found, she could no longer *verbalize*. The new find disquieted her.

For the first time in her married life, the utter degradation of her condition became clear to her. She did sense emptiness before, but never that bottomless abyss.

She flung the magazine on to the floor and cupping her face in her hands, a frantic shriek escaped her, "Ali! Ali! What have *I* done?"

"Now, what is it?" he leapt off the bed as if suddenly bitten by a python.

"It's *awful*," she trembled.

"What's awful?" He flopped back onto the edge of the bed.

"*Our* marriage."

"Here we go again!" He glared at her. "Now, say it, what the hell's wrong with *our* marriage?"

"In the eyes of God it's null and void," she sobbed.

He was appalled, "I can't help you there, Anisa. And as far as I'm concerned I am a married man. I married you not just once but twice. All your Muslim brothers and sisters were there to witness the whole process. We've two nicely signed certificates to show for it. And now you're telling me *our* marriage is null and void?"

"*Ya Rabb! Ya Rahman*! I'm doomed, *Ya Allah*, don't leave me! *Ya Allah*, don't let go of me! You're all I have! *Ya Allah*, don't take up issue with me! *Ya Rabb*, I need You! Help me! Help this poor being, and she'll serve you for life. *Ya Rabb!* Don't let go of me!"

"There're people out there, Anisa," he said with a patience that went beyond perseverance, "who can't even boast of a single piece of paper and they live together, happy and without a care in the world. I don't know what I'm doing wrong."

Warm tears flushed down her cheeks. Channels by the corners of the mouth, the torrents rained onto the belly and trickled further down her thighs.

"It's not your fault," she choked on the saline waters.

"Okay, okay, then let's keep it that way. Good night!"

He turned his back on her. She turned hers on him.

She was now nine months pregnant. Any day now, she'd be bringing into the world another child. Whether that child was to be the product of a divinely ordained bond was hard to tell. They did have an official marriage certificate. After witnessing his conversion, the people at the Islamic Center were kind enough to follow it up with the marriage ceremony. That was not the issue. The thought that was gnawing at her now was not whether they had an official paper to prove the legality of their marriage to themselves. Rather it was whether *he*, Mike Peterson, was ever going to be capable of carrying out the responsibility that came along with being a Muslim.

Believing was never a known orbit with Mike. She knew that on the fifth day of her date with him. If he was a non-believer in the faith of his ancestors then, he was a non-believer in Islam, today. She now realized that all the allegations he so loved to hurl at Christianity was nothing more than a dying wish to stay a non-believer for life. *How blind she must've been to fall for his anti-priesthood tactics*!

And now that she'd done what she'd done, she had let herself into the trap of his disbelief, and became one with his doubting heart.

As he said so often, he did convert to Islam for *her* sake, didn't he? Didn't he fulfill his part of the deal, by going over to *her* camp? Wasn't that in itself a favor? She did want him, at least as much as he wanted her, didn't she? Then on what grounds was she complaining? What did she want him to do? What could she possibly do now in her condition? Wrench his doubting heart from him and plant therein a believing one? It was an impossible task, and she cried the impasse away on the pillow.

For God knows how many nights in a row, she tore herself away from her miserable thoughts and turned to the safety of the room next door.Next morning, Anisa awoke to her daughter's screams. Nasra was already up, playing with her toys under the bed where her mother slumbered, fitfully.

Nasra was not only the most beautiful baby, she was also a most good-natured child. She was in every respect what you would call an angel. There was an unspoken understanding between Mother and Daughter. It was as though the child understood her mother's pain. If it wasn't for the insistent ringing of the phone, Nasra might've kept on amusing herself with her toys and let her mother slumber on some more.

"Mommy! Mommy!" Nasra rushed to pick up the phone.

"Coming, dear." Anisa yawned a "hello" into the mouthpiece.

"*Assalamu 'alaikum!* Anisa, it's me, Khadija."

"*Wa'alaikuma salaam*! What time is it now?" Anisa peered at the clock on the wall.

"Anisa?"

"Yes, Khadija?"

"Don't go any where, okay? I'm on my way."

"Welcome, welcome." Anisa yawned.

An hour or so later, Khadija and her son of four were already at the door.

Since Anisa and Mike's marriage at the Islamic Center, the two had become good friends. Khadija was a very reticent person, though, and since she took for granted that Anisa was happy and contented, Anisa could never bring herself to talk to her about the inner agitation that'd been building up during this pregnancy.

Khadija on her part could never have guessed at her friend's inner turmoil. Anisa was always so laid back and cheerful. In fact, Khadija and Yusuf thought very highly of both Ali and Anisa. And since Ali was already an accepted member of Anisa's family, their initial fears were soon forgotten. Of what they had seen of him, they also believed that Ali was a very nice man, though they long suspected he was a slow learner. Still, they somehow believed in him. And Yusuf hoped that one day in the near future Ali would join him in the Friday prayers.

Yusuf did not want to push him. He did try to explain a few things, conversely, not only about Islam, but also about all the different aspects and similarities of existing beliefs, so as to give Ali the benefit of putting Islam into perspective, and to bring home to him the *unity* of God's message to mankind, lending him a book every now and then.

Yusuf was also aware of Ali's *personal* antagonism towards his ancestor's faith, though Ali had never given any learned opinion to support his anti-Christian feelings.

But, he didn't want to push him, or take Ali's blind aversion of his former faith as an opportunity to spring Islam on him. Ali was otherwise a very thoughtful person, and Yusuf felt it best to let him be guided by his own reasoning powers.

Moreover, when one converted to get married, one was bound to be slow. In his case, patience was perhaps the best medicine, so reasoned Yusuf. So far, Ali and Anisa's partnership was his best case, and he wished this marriage success.

Pouring a cup of tea for her friend now, Anisa was startled by Khadija's remarks.

"Ali called you? What about?"

"I'm not sure," Khadija said, reclining back in the cream-colored leather sofa and taking in her surroundings. Anisa's home was charmingly uncluttered. A selection of flowery abundance craned their heads against a wide balcony. Underneath, a light blue rug gave out a sea view ambience to a row of balmy plants on the floor. And on the opposite wall, a stack of books filled the shelves, while pieces of wooden artifacts and brightly colored ceramics and seashells further heightened the room's foreign character...as though, Khadija surmised, Anisa longed to capture something of her hometown.

"I really don't know, Anisa," Khadija shook her head, as she took the cup from Anisa's extended hand. "But what's the matter, Anisa? What's going on? It's very unlike Ali to call us so early in the morning. I must tell you that he sounded rather upset, and worried, saying that he couldn't get through to you. And thought you might not be feeling well."

"I'm in perfect condition, Khadija," she forced a crack of laughter, but it didn't quite sound like one. "The doctor said so." Her hands lolled in the cool air of her living room, limply, like two mildewed branches in a gusty parching atmosphere.

"Ali doesn't think so, said you're driving yourself crazy with worry and that's no good for you in your condition. Honestly, what's the matter? It's not Ali, is it? Forgive me for saying so, but I always thought everything was so perfect between the two of you."

Anisa's teeth jittered, "Nothing was ever perfect." Her jaws shook. "It was all a make-believe world, an experiment, and it isn't working, Khadija."

"Now, start from the beginning. You know you can confide in me," said Khadija getting down from the sofa and sitting down on the ruddy fluffy carpet under the sofa with Anisa.

"I really don't know where to begin. All I can say is that the whole thing's a lie, and you'll never know the pain until you've lived it." Anisa sighed, stretching her cramped legs on the carpet.

"I don't understand." Khadija frowned.

"I'd known it all along, deep down. I'd only kidded myself, Khadija."

"Go on."

"He never lied to me; always saying he accepted the faith because of *me*. *Me*, Khadija, not Allah."

"And you went along with it?"

"Never given it much thought...until now...not until these past few months." Anisa's eyes were intense red, laden with sorrow, the lashes damp, matted with tears.

Khadija swallowed, "I don't know what to say, but are you saying that Ali has renounced Islam?" she asked.

"No, no, he doesn't deny anything, nor does he admit to anything. He's so vague about the whole thing, and he could go on forever like this...but I can't, not anymore. Khadija, I'm frightened."

"He knows Allah is one, doesn't he? He knows the world didn't just come by itself, and that there's only one God responsible for all this?"

"Of course he knows that," said Anisa. "But how do I know he's Muslim in the strict sense of the word? Almost four years since he said the *shahada,* and he still believes he's Muslim only on paper. And proud of it too, I'm sure."

"He's Muslim only on paper?" Khadija's generous eyes widened. "But he did declare his belief openly, we were all there. And unless he went back on his word, wouldn't that be enough to qualify him as one?" Khadija's thoughts were all muddled up. Ali had never ever hinted at anything, and they all took his Islam for granted, thinking that though he did not exhibit any of the religious fervor that new Muslims always brought with them, he did seem to carry out his obligatory duties such as fasting during Ramadan, and prayed the daily prayers whenever in the company of Muslims.

"It's his heart that worries me," Anisa said, "and I don't know if you guys have noticed it, but the only time he seems to pray is when he is at the Center or with Yusuf, a habit he must have picked up from me."

"What?"

"And he can't stand his Muslim name."

"We always call him Ali and he doesn't seem to mind," smiled Khadija, relaxing a bit, and taking a sip at her tea.

"Call him that in front of his people, and you'll see the redness in his eyes!"She wept.

"Maybe that's because he's not used to it and feels embarrassed," voiced Khadija helpfully. "He's human after all. He's got some adjusting to do, Anisa. Family pressures to come to terms with. I mean he's not an island unto himself. These things take time. But are there other things, besides the name, that's worrying you? The name's not that important, really."

"Never has a good word about Muslims," she sniffed.

"He does like us, though, and we happen to be Muslims," Khadija grinned.

"He despises the Muslim world. He makes fun of the Arabs. How can someone who calls himself a Muslim hate the Muslim world and make fun of the Arabs: I find that hard to believe."

"Well, we shouldn't take this personally," Khadija said softly. "You know, first of all he's a Westerner and the average Westerner whether he's in Europe or in America, has this intrinsic misconception about Islam, believing without thinking whatever they're told, so it's the media we should blame, not Ali."

"Shouldn't people think for themselves?"

"These people just aren't given enough time to think beyond the food on the table, Anisa. They're like programmed mules doing drudgery for a paycheck, and they just can't be bothered about things for which they aren't paid. So this vague, general dislike for Muslims is simply a healthy reaction, considering all the stuff they're being fed. You've to realize thinking costs time, and time is money. We've

to forgive them. They simply don't have the time to think."

"But shouldn't he be different, after all, he's supposed to be one

of us?"

"I don't think you're doing Ali justice, Anisa. Of what I've seen, I

think he's a very nice person. We all like him. Everyone likes him.

Yes, I do think Ali's a kind person."

"Sure, to animals and flowers, and to the trees in the forest, he's

very kind! But when it comes to Muslims and Arabs, I don't think

he's kind at all," she lamented, resigned to that deplorable condition.

"In any case," Khadija said, "Muslims and Islam the religion are

two separate issues."

"He doesn't like real Christians, either," she sobbed. "Nor does he

hold any tender feelings for the Jews!"

"Anisa?"

"Of course he would side with the Jews, that *he* would, but that's

only because *he* happens to love the Muslims less!"

"Anisa!"

"And he scoffs at the Jeffersons our neighbors, just because they happen to be devoted Mormons!"

"Are you sure?" Khadija's nose wrinkled. She'd no idea Ali was that bad!

"Oh, Khadija, I wedded a man for whom faith is one big zero! Believe me, he was already into faith ridiculing when I met him. Whether they're Jews, Mormons, Coptic, it really doesn't matter. He just can't stand people of faith, and he makes no bones about it. Mention the name of the Pope, and you'll be inviting trouble. That's the man of my choice."

"Now let's forget about all these other people of faith," breathed Khadija. She had no idea Ali was like that. "And please let's not bring the Pope into this. This is a family matter. Let's now, in all honesty, get back to you, Ali and Islam. What's it that doesn't click there? I must confess I'm still confused."

"Khadija, this person Ali is fake, that name isn't worth the paper it's written on," she said, her heart constricted with agony. "This man's a faith-abuser. I'll bet if he was wedding a believing Christian or a staunch Hindu, for that matter, he would've done the same thing: Convert without scruples!"

Khadija's mouth became a wide cleft.

"Are you now saying Ali's conversion to Islam was done without a nickel of conscience? Is that the message I'm getting, Anisa?"

"Yes, he just happened to be at the wrong place at the wrong time. And so was I. And now I've ruined my life and the life of my child. And now, look at this." She threw a morbid glance at the protruding stomach. "Khadija, this baby's father has never bought faith."

"Allah is the Almighty Lord, Anisa, and no sin, however great, is above his mercy or forgiveness. It's never too late, for you, Anisa. Despair not of the mercy of Allah."

"The first day I came to the Center," Anisa wept, her heart dilating out of her chest. "I remember Yusuf telling me that passion alone wouldn't be enough in a marriage. He was warning me, but I just didn't get it, at all. Even when he read it out off the wall, I didn't get it. At the time nothing seemed to make a dent in me. I just didn't care. Nothing seemed to move me."

"But we still thought the two of you were somehow different, not like the others," Khadija said, pondering her own density.

"Even after he gave me the books and followed me out, he told me to think. 'It's never too late', he said. But I didn't listen. I heard everything he said, and yet I didn't hear a thing. Khadija, why didn't you stop me?"

"Come on, Anisa," Khadija said, her gaze falling on Anisa's stomach. "We knew you were already...you know? I knew it the minute I saw you. You were in such a hurry. And we thought it best to let him embrace the faith and hoped things would work out."

"Yusuf knew it, too?"

"Yes, but not immediately. In fact, he was on the verge of dissuading you from the whole thing, but once I told him...he agreed it was perhaps best that way. And so did your uncle after he received Mike's letter. Mike had done some homework on his own by approaching Yusuf without telling you about it, since he said he wanted to do everything correctly this time. That's also why your uncle wrote back to Mike to give his permission, empowering Yusuf to stand in his stead should Mike embrace the faith. And that's why we were all in such a hurry to get you married, and once we got to know Mike better…"

"So my uncle knew of the baby too?"

"Mike didn't tell you?"

"No," she said in a small voice. She was crying again, ashamed of what she'd put her family through. *So everyone had tidied up after her?*

"I'm living in sin, aren't I?" she sobbed.

"Stop it, Anisa. This man married you in a proper manner, we don't know what was in his heart, but from what we had witnessed he did everything correctly. But as far as his heart is concerned I'd leave it to Allah to be the judge. I've come to know a few things about Ali and I think he's an honest person, and meant everything he said. But I believe he still needs time. In the meantime, why not set a good example yourself and show him personally what it means to be a true believer?"

"*Ya Rabb!*" Anisa's mouth jerked open only to snap shut again.

Khadija shook with fright and the words began to rattle off her tongue, "He now has this version of Islam," she said, like one possessed, "the affluent Muslims who won't help their own and squander their money on nonsense; the easily corrupted Muslims; the so-called Muslim governments; the desperate, violent Muslims. Anisa, here's a chance for you to change that concrete picture he has and show him personally the other side of the coin."

"What would I know of the other side of the coin?" Anisa wept.

"This Islam is within you, Anisa, bring it to the open and let him see for himself the true spirit of Islam; an Islam that's shorn of all pretensions. Let's face it, Anisa, we so called Muslims, we're standing in the way of honest people. And let's not for a moment pretend we're representing God. Everyone's representing their selfish selves."

"I severed the bond with my own hands, and now I'm at a loss as to how such as me could ever approach God? How can I possibly face Him in this condition?"

Khadija took her hand in hers. It was ice cold, "You still can."

"I was frightened last night and tried to say the *shahada*," she said with her eyes glued to the ceiling, "but couldn't, it was then that I'd realized how far I'd traveled…"

"No sin is beyond the forgiveness of Allah. His mercy transcends His wrath. His door is never closed. Open yours, Anisa, and let yourself in. Take a step in and He'll come running to you. That's Allah."

"Is His door always open, even to one such as *me*?"

"His door is never closed, it's you who needs to enter," Khadija lowered her gaze, ashamed of herself. *How did she miss all this anguish?* she swallowed.

"Since the day I came to this country," said Anisa, "I'd been leading a double life, except for the few times I'd been home, even then it was just for the sake of my family. Can you believe it?"

"Allah has said," Khadija replied, "if my servant walks to Me, I go to him at speed."

Still holding the trembling hand in hers, Khadija began to relate the story of the man who took a hundred lives, "Yet the door of Mercy never closed on him," she told her. "Learn from that story, Anisa."

"He also said," Khadija went on, quoting another part of a *hadith,* "O sons of Adam, were your sins to reach the clouds of the sky and were you then to ask forgiveness of Me, I would forgive you."

"He also said," Khadija added, quoting a Qur'anic verse, "if my servants ask you concerning Me, I am indeed close (to them), I listen to the prayer of every suppliant when he calls on Me."

It was at this point that she felt her stomach heave. She was at first not sure and as they went on the subject of forgiveness and mercy, with Khadija doing all the talking, and Anisa all the weeping, that the latter let out a cry of pain, "Khadija! I think the baby's coming!"

Chapter Fourteen

Mohammed

"If I hate my sins, will God love me?"
"No – But if He remembers you,
Then you will remember Him – so stand in wait."
[Doorkeeper of the Heart (Versions of Rabi'a)]

Early next morning, a beautiful boy came into the world via a Caesarian birth, just like his sister.

Back home, the proud father of the newborn baby made a long distance call to his wife's family.

"They're both fine, Omar. It was a quick operation like the one she had before," he yelled into the phone.

"What's his name?" Omar yelled back.

"We don't know yet."

"It's important that he gets a good name," Omar persisted, "I wouldn't mind helping you out…"

"We'll keep that in mind," Mike thanked him, then placed another call, this time to his parents. Since the puppy issue they'd been avoiding each other.

"It's a boy!" he told his mother.

"A boy! It's a boy!" His mother relayed the message to the grandfather. "But that's wonderful. And every things' okay with you?"

"Very good."

"I've just the name for him," said his mother, forgetting her own promise not to ever get involved in her son's alien affairs. "We'll name him after your grandpa."

Mike chuckled, "don't you worry about the name, Mother, we'll cross that bridge when we come to it. The boy's just come into the world, give him a break."

"No strange name, Mike, is that a deal?"

"I've got to go now, I'll see you later. Bye."

"And where's Nasra? Isn't she there with you?" she asked. "I hope she's not still coughing from that bad cold she had when I gave her the puppy?"

"She's doing great."

"Good. I'll see you later."

He made another call to Yusuf and Khadija and was told Nasra was already asleep. Khadija told him not to worry about her, and would be more than happy to have Nasra until Anisa and the baby were released from hospital.

No sooner did he put down the receiver, and then a call came through to him. It was from the intensive care unit.

"Mr. Peterson, come to the ward, immediately, please," a male voiced urged him.

"What is it?" he asked, but the line had already gone dead.

"It's your wife." The surgeon who had delivered the boy took his elbow and walked him towards the intensive care unit. "It's probably a false alarm."

"She was fine when I left," Mike began as his eyes darted to the still body of his wife. "What happened?"

"She has problem breathing, very high blood pressure. She's in heavy sedation."

"But what're you going to do? Is she going to lie there?"

"I'm going for consultation," the doctor said patting his shoulder. "You keep an eye on her. I'll be right back."

An hour or so later, the surgeon reemerged followed by several nurses who immediately got to work on the still body.

"We're reading her for another operation...we need to open the incision...just in case..." the doctor put his hand on his mouth to stifle a yawn.

"You left some thing in there, didn't you?" Mike stated accusingly, his eyes fastened on the doctor's hands. "Did you do that on purpose so you could cut her up again?"

"We need to get to work fast...now if you'd walk over to the coffee shop...we'll call you back once we're done." The doctor brushed Mike's comments aside. He'd just gulped some hot coffee himself and was sure the man could do with some too.

Before long the stomach was open again. All shiny and red in the raw reddish white flesh of the belly that yielded the beautiful baby only that morning there simmered some fresh blood. Everything was nice and clean when last sewn. How did the blood get in there? wondered the surgeon, then as he tried to sponge away the blood,

206

something foreign caught the surgeon's eye: *Infection*! It was one of those invisible hospital germs that roam around intensive care units and feed on open sores!

The surgeon moved away from the table and from the surgeon crew, slowly removed his gloves in silence and started to wash his hands in the sink. He staggered out of the hall, his eyes betraying the gloom in him.

"We need more consultation," he said to Mike.

Consultation after consultation ensued and at last the doctors decided on leaving the stomach open, so as to control the infection and let the wound heal from within while doses of drugs kept the body still, yet paving the way for a spout of pneumonia. She was lucky, though.

After fighting for breath, Anisa had a faint nightmarish memory of some of the events that had ensued after that. After a week of coma-like-posture, Anisa's eyes were at last peeling open. She could hardly focus, seeing everything in twos.

When she finally awoke to the presence of the people around her, a doctor was at hand to touch on the happenings of the past week. As his entourage of trainee medics crowded over the patient's bed, like she was some sort of a rare species in a grand zoo, the doctor said, "Such complications do occur. You've been extremely lucky. You've delivered a beautiful baby boy. His father's picked a nice name for him…"

As the doctor's soothing voice drifted on, her foggy gaze caught something in the ceiling…what *monstrous* ventilation! Fear gripped her heart and she screamed at the grisly sight of snake-line spaghetti oozing out of the vent holes…

When she once again peered through the fog the room was a-buzz with activities. These are *terrible* times, she thought, but she was being doped to the core with morphine and felt nothing but fear.

Every now and then a nurse would shoot yet another needle into her thigh, and say, "That should lessen the pain."

Having heard the good news that his wife had once again opened her eyes, Mike rushed from the coffee bar to be with her.

"Welcome back," he planted a kiss on her forehead. Shortly afterwards, a nurse wheeled a tiny cot into the room. The nurse was all smiles.

"Here comes our young man, and he's dying to say hello to his mother," she beamed at Anisa. The latter could only return a wooden stare.

Unlike Nasra, his face was long and gaunt and there was this flabbergasted look on his countenance, as if startled by the whole episode of his birth.

"The nurse scooped him from the cot and gently placed him on his mother's lap. Fed through the bottle from day one, his mother's presence was, however, of little concern to him. He wasn't alone in this unconcerned mien, though. His mother was just as indifferent to the little bundle on her lap.

She was more concerned with the grisly vent, and the terrible stench that seemed to hang about her person. The nurse and Mike exchanged glances as her eyes drifted to the ceiling.

Anisa was totally unaware of how long this state of comings and goings had lasted from the first day of her awakening. At last, when the fog began to uplift and she started to take note of her surroundings, she was now in a position to study closely the white-appareled beings who scuttled like desert ostrich all over the place, and whose bee stings she was now beginning to note.

As her eyes began to peel open some more, she was now in a position to discover the stings' whereabouts on her body and before long she knew that the bites she had been subjected to all this time, were in fact needles, and not bees, and these were coming from the hands of the appareled beings themselves.

As one of these needle-bearers now closed in on her, a sting of nothingness, as the needle thrust into the flesh of the thigh with a ruthless pinch, flooded her whole being.

And then there was the trolley pusher who'd then position herself on her right side. Anisa fought hard to focus on one of these white forms as she bent over her and began to dislodge stuff from her stomach with the help of what seemed like tweezers. Then attaching a tube onto a syringe, the white form would then shoot some liquid stuff into the tummy of the patient—repeating the same procedure twice or thrice, before stuffing in a new set of white compressors—a process that would repeat itself again and again.

After all the things she's been through, moments of highs and lows followed by deep depression were not only highly probable but also inevitable. Since her awakening she'd been wallowing in virtual torment, existing in a twilight zone, hallucinating and seeing strange things.

Unknown to others, relentless voices swarmed her ears and acquainted her with her sins. *Enormous! Unforgivable!* thundered the voices. *Who can forgive such enormous sins!*

The pathos of shame that'd been swelling in her breast during the pregnancy now matured into a full-blown explosion. All the errors of her adult life now sprouted to the fore and took on a life of their own. And the voices made sure these were dangled before her eyes.

In a moment of a fitful slumber, a vociferous voice had bellowed a warning of immense effect: *Your time is up. We'll delay it no more. Now's the time for death! You either do it! Or we do it! The sinner must go!* roared the potent voice, vengeful and unrelenting.

The physical pains, which the doctors and the cheerful nurses were so preoccupied with all these weeks, were now slowly but surely giving way to inner torment.

At one point, the pain was so acute that Anisa saw death round the corner, and made what she believed to be her last words to Mike. That afternoon, clutching at the sleeve of his shirt, she begged him to fulfill her last wishes.

"Ali, promise to take the children to my parents," she cried. "If you keep them here with you," she wept, "they'll be lost forever...we don't want them turning out like you, do we, Ali?"

His eyes swelled, yet he blinked away his tears to brush away at least some of her pain, "No, no, no...we don't," he forced a weak smile, "but don't you worry about the children, I'll look after them— trust me. And you mustn't think of dying. The worst's over, and you'll soon be coming home. Trust Allah. He'll take care of them for *you*."

"What would Ali know about Allah?" she cried.

"Now, dear, you mustn't distress yourself. You heard what the doctor said," he said.

"Ali, I betrayed my children," she whispered, framed in agony. "What was I thinking when I married you? Ali, what's wrong with me?"

"You're okay, dear, don't worry," he said, as he patted the perspiration off her face with a tissue paper.

"I failed my children," she said, gulping tangy tears. "Their spiritual need—you can't provide, Ali, but whatever you do, promise not to ever take my children anywhere near your folks...*Ya Rabb!* What a *mess* I'm leaving behind!"

Overcome by an injection the nurse had given a few minutes earlier she once again dozed off into another twilight zone.

At the end of the sixth week, she suffered a complete mental breakdown. A power beyond description seized the patient from within, and hurled her out of the room. Before she knew what was happening, the strong power had pulled the confirmation of *La Ilaha Ila Allah* (No god worthy of worship but Allah) off her tongue and the strength of the words threw the patient into a staggering delirium.

On hearing the strange cry from down the corridor, the nurses surged forward to the scene, propelled the patient onto a bed trolley, and pushed her back into her room. Someone wondered whether a Muslim clergy should be called in. The staff nurses were slowly becoming acquainted with the problems. Someone had already called for the poor husband.

A short while later, Anisa awakened to the presence of the resident psychiatrist. He was a quiet man in a tight doctor's coat, and his soothing tone had put Anisa to sleep several times before. But she was wide-awake now and his soft tone did nothing to ease her burden.

"You're looking at a sinner," she said firmly. "Look at this Muslim woman. She is a mother of two children and she's doubts about her marriage. How does that grab you?" She giggled.

"After what you've been through," the doctor said, "your situation's quite normal."

"Doctor, is being married to an unbeliever normal? Perhaps it's so in your world, but certainly not in mine. My situation's the opposite of normal. That's why it's so normal for me to feel so abnormal. But what amazes me is how did this abnormal situation ever come to pass? *Who* actually got married to Mike? Was it Anisa Ali Haaji or the real *me*? *Who* do you think got married to this man?"

"As far as I know, your marriage's no secret," he said softly, "your husband's at this very moment on his way here. But you've a wound on your stomach and we're trying to help you heal well. You've to help us too and not make things more difficult." He had to be firm with her. She wasn't insane.

"He's a liar this husband of mine, a big liar," she whimpered. "Four years and still no sign of change. And I'm a very dishonest Muslim. That's it. The sinner is married to the big liar."

"Why do you say that?"

"Anisa Ali Haaji, she's the trouble-maker," she said. "Her poor parents trusted her, and she'd violated their trust. Yes, she had faith, but what good?"

"Well?" asked the doctor, making himself comfortable and leading the patient on to diagnose the root of her own afflictions, and if possible, prescribe her own remedy. In fact, his life's drudgery ended at *Medical School.* Once he secured his bits of paper from the said establishment, he was a free man. The doctor chuckled to himself, thinking of his old grandfather's remarks before the old battle-ax vacated the world for good.

"Let the cerumen wax, if you dare," gibed the toil-worn battle-ax, aiming a swipe at what he called his grandson's mad idle profession, "and I guarantee you, you'll soon be on social welfare, just like *your* father…"

"I was created free," the patient's sorrowful words speared through the psychiatrist's pleasant reminiscence. "The day I was born, I was born *free* of sin, and so is every child."

"Is that so?" There's always something new to be learned, sniggered the doctor to himself.

"Has the doctor any doubt about my being born without sin?" She glared at him.

"I wouldn't know about that," said the doctor, "indeed we're in *opposite* worlds where what's normal in one place might be abnormal in the other, but as a medical doctor who's been raised as a Christian, I wouldn't say I was born without sin…"

"*Shalom!* So you're a Christian?" She caught herself in the middle of her faux pas. "So sorry, I used the wrong salute. For a moment I thought you were a good *Jewish* neighbor! So you're a Christian? But that's great! Peace!"

"Peace?"

"But isn't that how Jesus used to greet people?"

"But, of course, I'm a Christian and that's how I'd greet people if I were following Jesus. Thanks for reminding me. Peace!"

"Peace!"

After a moment's reflection, the psychiatrist's smooth forehead pleated a little, "For a brief moment you thought I was a Jew, why is that?" he asked, looking bothered, for while being taken for a friend of Israel was politically correct...but to be mistaken for a Jew even for a split second...that was altogether a different ball game...

"Honestly, what made you think that I was Jewish? Do I look like one?"

"My dear brother, what's wrong with being a Jew? Isn't it enough that you're not anything like my poor husband? You've admitted to faith and that's all that counts with me. My husband would blow my head off if I for *once* mistaken him for a Christian."

The doctor relaxed.

"I went to a religious school, you know," she said, lowering her voice, like one confiding a secret in a friend. "And I'm very much aware of the quandary."

"The quandary?" the doctor's eyes flipped.

"Doctor, your lord started out as a prophet of God, and before he knew it, he was promoted to the position of a son of God, and then before he knew what was happening, *boom*! He melted into the Father in heaven and became one with Him! And now that everything's so jumbled up, you guys can't figure out who is who. Honesty, who's your Lord, the Father or the Son?"

"What're you talking about?"

"You believe in the divinity of Jesus, don't you?"

"What about it?"

"Back home, in my old school," she said, "we had a nice portrait of Jesus, or so believed Sister Anne. But brother, the truth is whoever it was that painted that picture had never set eyes on Jesus. The kids somehow knew, but not Sister Anne. After all, the portrait was in her office. We could take a peek if we felt like it, but that was it. The portrait belonged in Sister Anne's office."

"What!"

"Brother, you've faith, and in this part of the world you're my brother-in-faith. We can help each other out, you and I."

"Right now," the doctor said, steering her away from the topic, "you're the patient, not I." He too had his own reservations about the dogma, but he wasn't about discussing it with this alien patient.

"You're evading the issue, aren't you?" she demanded.

"Don't you think it's time we got back to the real issue?" he asked, not even pretending to be polite.

"Brother, I was born free and I put myself in fetters," she frowned, and then giggled at the absurd thought of putting fetters on oneself. "This woman has manacled her soul. You can't help her there, but she sure can help realign that head of yours."

"Oh yeah?"

"Brother, the good news is the day you were born you were a stainless infant. It's only after you developed grand ideas about yourself that you became mired in things."

"Get real!"

She waved him aside.

"Brother, you're not honest with yourself. Blaming others for you doings won't make your misdeeds blow away, just like that. Puff!"

"Puff?"

"Yes, puff, blow away!" she said. "Doctor, learn from your own patient, own up your sins, they aren't hidden from God, so why kid yourself?"

"For your own sake," said the doctor, eyeing the strange patient, "and for the sake of your two children, wouldn't it be best if you scraped the religious bit and started concentrating on getting well?"

The doctor was at a loss. He was no expert on the spirit. He thought he was dealing with someone with a momentary loss of sanity. But what he had now was a sphere far beyond the ken of his professional expertise. If she told him she was a product of parental neglect, or that she was a child of incest, he might have been in a position to help her, as he was familiar with such situations. This was, however, an alien sphere. But he had to keep her talking...

"Tell me about Islam," he said, exuding original willingness. He needn't buy everything the woman said, he reflected, but he didn't mind listening to his patient's side of the story, either. And his patient was more than willing to share. It wasn't everyday that he was blessed with such luck. He was a professional and he knew there was nothing like first-hand knowledge—tidings without the trappings of niceties or self-regard.

"It's the belief in the one true God," the patient said. "The God of Adam and Eve: Allah, the God. No son. No father and no partners of any sort. Just the one true God. Simple truth, without any toppings."

"And how does one attain to this simple truth without the *toppings*?" the doctor's eyes rolled.

"You simply submit to the one true God, the creator of the heavens and the earth. Acknowledge the truth, without building castles in the air. He says He is *one*. Was always *one*. That's exactly what He said to Moses. That's exactly what He said to David. That's exactly how Adam and Eve perceived Him. If He were more than one wouldn't we know it from the first man? He says He is *one*. No need to tell Him He is more than that."

"Exactly! I must concede to this," said the doctor and he really meant it this time. "God is one, now what?"

"Now, once you've rid yourself of these imaginary whims of yours, then the next step is to acknowledge your total dependence on this one God by honestly declaring your freedom from all other

221

powers and false assumptions, and that's the *shahada,* the declaration of freedom. I just said it, at the top of my voice, so as to make it known to all my enemies, to every spirit in this building, so that every *Jinn* and every *Shaitan* and every human should hear it, so that they'd think twice before messing with me again…don't tell me you didn't hear?"

"When?"

The patient rolled her eyes.

"I see," the doctor put in quickly. "But what's the purpose of this declaration?"

"You call yourself a doctor," she said with unconcealed pity, "yet, you don't even know the first thing about doctoring? How on earth did I let *myself* into this doctor's world?"

Before the stunned doctor could respond, she went on, "Doctor, sin enslaves the self. It's because of my sins that I'm now in this bed. No sin no doctor. So, now you see why I had to free myself from this bondage, with or without your help?"

"So you just freed yourself from yourself, and that if I were a proper doctor I'd know what was wrong with you?"

"You see," she breathed, "with the *shahada*, a Muslim's supposed to kiss goodbye to all self-delusions, a fact that's been dodging *me*, somehow, until this very moment," she said, then paused as a nurse administered a shot for the pain. The patient was then coaxed into taking some tablets and capsules. Having downed the pills, the patient continued, more hostile than ever, for the medicine had not yet begun to work.

"Allah has given Anisa Ali a perfect way of life. But by consorting with the baddies of this world, Anisa has belittled myself."

Cheeky patient! The doctor's mind screamed.

"In my travels," she went on, "I've bumped into quite a good number of ignorant folk, but I've as yet to meet a more uninformed person than my poor husband."

"Get real!"

"I victimized myself, imitating an ignorant folk," she said flopping back on the pillow. "And I just can't forgive myself for what I've done."

"Is that so?"

"My husband's been to fancy schools, yet he's like the day he was born. Now tell me, how does one cure spiritual ignorance? Isn't there any cure for faithlessness yet?"

"The medical profession isn't looking for one. We simply don't have the time. We've our hands full. You're a case in point."

"Then the medical profession must needs brighten up. And very soon."

At this point the door jerked open and the ignorant husband made his entrance.

The last weeks had been pure inferno and since the day she moved from the intensive care unit and she began to talk, all hell broke loose.

Mike was now a two legged paranoia, alienated, and shredded beyond mending. *Lousy* was the word that best described his being, estrangement ruling his very heart. Far from being sympathetic, his friends, his colleagues, they all thought he got what he deserved. Isn't that what happened when people *messed around* with *aliens*? And a *black* alien fanatic at that? Wow!

No one said it in so many words but that was exactly what he felt in the air. *It was a typical Western attitude,* his paranoia told him:

when you were down in the dumps, people simply gloated over your misfortune.

His mother was no less privy to her daughter-in-law's troubles; the state of her befuddled mind was not a well-guarded secret. But after visiting her and the baby at the hospital, and learning about her grandson's name for the first time, she couldn't wait to tell the blind son what she thought of the whole sad alien *affair*.

If all this public talks about Islam was enough to send her against the wall, the baby's name, Mohammed, sent arrows of fire down the grandmother's spine. And the fact that the name itself had actually come from the lips of her son didn't help mitigate the pain.

Once out of earshot of the crazy woman, she snarled at her son, "Another Muslim name, is it? My son, you're under a spell. You're being controlled, even from the deathbed."

She knew she was being mean, but there was a test of wills and she'd be damned if she was giving in without a fight. Grandson or no grandson, she was damned if she was going to cope with such a name.

"These children happen to be Muslim children," he yelled back, "and I'm damned well giving them whatever name I please," he barked at his mother. "How about Hari Krishna Hari Ram for starters?"

His saying of *Muslim children* surprised him, as he'd never seriously considered himself as a real Muslim. He'd never talked so harshly to his mother, either. But he was bone tired and was sick and fed up with their bickering.

What made it all so irksome was their selfishness, their unwillingness to help. His sister didn't even have the decency to visit his crazy wife at the hospital. And busy as they were with their lives, it was just as well they didn't have to baby-sit for him, either.

Had Khadija not taken Nasra under her wing, he might even have had to take off from work, indefinitely. As it was, he was a mad man caught between work and a mad sick woman. And the only thing that told him of his residence in his home was his ever-mounting laundry. If Khadija didn't pop in every now and then, the whole place might have caught fire.

Besides this Muslim friend, the sympathetic medical staff and his friend Bill, Floor was the only one who truly stuck by him.

He was in the middle of an important assignment at the office when the hospital call came through.

The doctor, who at seeing the miserable Mike recalled his professionalism, now tried to explain a few things to the forlorn husband.

"A mental beak-down of the sort was never ruled out," he said gently, silently chiding himself for having lost his temper with the patient. "The hormonal changes at childbirth, the amount of drugs administered for the pain, coupled with the underlying human tensions; it's been obvious from the beginning." The doctor recommended that the patient be released from hospital immediately and moved home. "Being in her own surroundings might give her the necessary stimulus for health," he told him. "But she must remain under twenty four hours surveillance, for a while, for she might get suicidal if left on her own," the doctor warned.

As predicted, a period of severe depression followed her release from the hospital. She was no longer talking now. The voices did all the talking and she moved around the house, listening to these manifold voices. A web of stench hang about her person. Everywhere she turned, dark holes gaped ravine eyes at her. Every little opening, curve and corner became a dark bottomless abyss—turning the tense hair into electric rods, rooted deep into the withering scalp of the head. The sight of food churned her stomach, and she shivered at the sight of the houseplants. Even the toothpaste tube took on a life of its own.

Authoritative voices fought for command over her, confronting her with conflicting messages, and ordering her with irrational dos and don't. She felt like a stone-age specter that had lived long ago and knew everything, but had no tongue of his own to express his woes. And she was frightened of the unspoken knowledge of this specter over which the unwise voices fought command.

Her scheduled meeting with the psychiatrist ended in a pointless swindle. If anything, the prying doctor only exasperated the patient's woes. The way he scrutinized her, studying her as if she were a rare monkey, made her writhe like an earthworm. If she was in a dire condition when taken there, she was even in a more demented form when she was at last allowed to wriggle out of the unkind couch. And she vowed there and then not to ever return to the uncouth doctor.

The tablets that were supposed to provide respite from the hellish gruesome darkness turned her into a mute, mobile, non-living matter; turning her whole being into a hollowed stolid box, and her tongue into an old leather reject.

For months on end, Anisa lived a zombie like existence. It was at this juncture of her benumbed caustic life that in a moment of grating despair, she flushed the tranquilizers and the capsules down the toilet bowl. It was at this period, in the high currents of her trauma that the grace of God turned Anisa's baffled mind to her Lord. And she learned how to cry to Him.

Sometimes, when the intensity of the depression became too severe to bag, and she could no longer hold on to herself, Anisa would bolt to the backyard and cry out for the mercy of her Creator; tracking up and down the un-kept grass in a frenzy until the tears exhausted themselves and a momentary relief came over her.

Other times she'd just flee to the woods or other deserted places where she knew she'd be alone, and really walk and walk and talk, and really cry her heart out to Him who created her, until the darkness dissipated and a flicker of hope replaced the throbbing despair of the heart, and she felt enlivened again. Her Maker became the psychiatrist and in Him she found a shoulder to cry.

The depression and the dark days persisted for a long time to come. However, as time passed and the condition of her physical state bettered, slowly but surely Anisa was now developing a mechanism, an inner mechanism to combat and control the depression bouts. But when she was reeling back from a yearlong emergency, and the family began to get ready for a vacation to Anisa's home country, another crisis took shape in the form of a car crash. Her mother's wishes to come and visit her met Anisa's blank refusals. Her family had suffered enough on her behalf, she felt, and wished to protect them from this dark period of her life.

Only Anisa and the kids were in the car when the vehicle she was driving blasted itself onto a giant rock. The kids came out unhurt. Anisa ended up with a punctured small intestine, which paved the way for another major operation. This had in turn given way to another painful year, yet again paving the way for another operation, as the doctors had to part two other intestines that somehow became glued together from all the tempering.

A voluntary reopening of the scar, which now extended almost up to the breasts, by yet more infection, necessitating yet more drugs, had once again thrown the soul into more soul-searching and more soul-baring, but this time only in the company of her Lord.

The therapeutic effects of the word of Allah, the words she discarded long ago, now helped sustain the tormented being. And as she read the meaning, she immersed herself in the caring love of His counsel, plunging the very quintessence of her being in the sea of His mercy.

Ya Rabb! She would cry, *I thank you so much for testing me.*

O sole reformer of beings, recreate me and reform me and don't leave me to the mercies of my own nature. Bless me with a new heart, Ya Rabb! You're indeed the sole designer of hearts. Ya Rabb! When You choose to return my mind, don't give me back the mindset I had before you remembered me.

For the first time in her life Anisa was really able to connect with her God. Although she cried for His help and succor, she knew too that the pain and the suffering had to take place if she ever were to look herself in the mirror. Anisa needed to be censured and she

231

welcomed it with open arms, for the suffering had lightened her burden, and helped smoothen the way for her return to the path.

If the situation was dire enough after the baby Mohammed, the once again near death scenario after Anisa became involved in the car accident which resulted in yet more operations on the fragile stomach had, if anything, only added to the pressures at home – with Anisa's religious fervor colliding headlong with Mike's fervent wish for a let up and a break. While Mike was now more or less becoming reconciled with the perpetual daily prayers, and what that entailed in terms of keeping the body pure, his body included, the whole atmosphere had gotten out of hand.

Having to live under the strict dictates of Islam was now exhausting whatever tolerance he might otherwise have had. Wherever he turned in his own home, whatever he switched on in his living room, whether it was the TV, or the video player, the religion of Islam dominated. They could no longer have a decent conversation without the intrusion of Islam into their lives. The invasion of Islamic literature into their home also meant one thing: READ.

And Anisa read, drowning herself, unreservedly, in the pages of everything that came her way, on the subject of Islam. And the more she read the more her ignorance grew. Gone was the woman who thought she knew everything, she was now like a pauper lapping up every crumb, every drop of knowledge, and the more she drank the thirstier she got.

At one time during the crazy days at the hospitals, he even threatened to tear up the copy of the translation of the Holy Qur'an apart, but the idea somehow never materialized into action.

Changing too now was the dress code. Going out with her meant suffering the Muslim scarf. People on the streets, even those who didn't know them, wouldn't pass by without first staring at her then at him, then at her and back to him. If he was colored or looked foreign, the attention wouldn't have been so negative. He'd sometimes keep a safe distance from Anisa and the children.

In one incident, as Mike hurried towards his car at the neighborhood shopping mall, with Anisa and the children trailing behind him, an old friend who already spied on the family caravan, caught up with Mike as he was about to open the car.

233

"Trying to lose the appendage, aren't we?" Tom roared with laughter as he swung the door of his car open.

"Mike's face turned purple, "What appendage?"

"The appendage, that invisible wife of yours, where's she these days?" Tom guffawed.

Anisa was now just a few meters away, but their backs were turned towards her so she couldn't have heard Tom's nasty remarks.

As she neared them, she called out, "How are you, Tom?" She hadn't seen Tom and his wife for a while. No doubt, they were avoiding them. "And how's Tina?"

He craned his neck at her direction, a conspicuous smirk on his face, he thundered, "But where are you?"

Anisa was just a few steps a way from Tom and having by now guessed what the private joke was all about, she breathed, "Here she is, right under your nonsensical nose. Understanding was never your forte, Tom, and now, it seems, you've also gone stark blind!"

"But where are you?" Tom repeated, like one groping in darkness, before he slid behind the wheel of his car and reversed in a spin of wheels and guffaws.

If there was anything Mike hated, it was the scarf. After such embarrassing moments outside, he'd unleash his frustration on her, "You! You! Why can't you be like other Muslim women and drop the peculiar cloth? What's the point of attracting attention to yourself?"

"I'm simply trying to be myself," she would say, hurt but firm. "Can't I be who I am? Haven't I run away from myself long enough? For once in my life, I'm really trying to be *who* I really am, and yet no one seems to appreciate it. For the first time in my life I'm really trying to rid myself of my duplicity, and yet..."

"How could anyone rid themselves of anything with something like that on their head?" he'd say, forgetting his own desire to let her be. "Really, when was the last time you looked at yourself in the mirror? I suggest you go and have a hard good look."

"A hard good look?" she'd say, aggrieved. "Isn't that what I'd been doing lately? Take a hard good look at *myself*? But I simply need no mirror to do that. No mirror on earth can make *me like* what I've seen of *myself*."

"Here we go again! Cut the bull, lady. I'm talking about the cloth. It doesn't become you."

"Khadija wears the same cloth and she looks just fine to everyone, including yourself, or doesn't she?"

"It's different with her," he'd say without knowing why it was so. "Khadija is so normal, not like you."

"If the hijab looks normal on her it should look normal on me too."

"If you didn't look so ridiculous people wouldn't have to shake their heads in distaste, now would they?"

"Whether you like or not, Mike, the era of showcasing is over for this woman. My hair and my body belong to me and no one else. I'm not public property, not anymore. And if people find it so arduous, then that's their problem. I want to be *me*. I've just found myself, and I'm not letting go of *me*. This is the natural *me*."

"Say, what's so natural about your life, if I may ask?" he would bellow. "All you think about is religion, more religion, and yet more religion, you call that natural?"

She was after him all the time, saturating him in Islamic literature, passing over to him every book that came her way, marking up things for him in yellow and red, as though he'd neither eyes nor intellect, but nowadays, it seemed, the odd Bible was also finding its way into his home, as though, he brooded in alarm, that were a *ladder* to Qur'an. Someone from the Center had told her jokingly one day that had Mike read the Bible and seen for himself all the mind-boggling stuff that it contained he'd make a grab for the Qur'an. And so in trickled the Bibles.

"When the time comes for me to consult a Bible," he'd tell her as nicely as he could, "I'll give my Sunday school teacher a call. How many times do I've to tell you: I don't need your Bibles!"

Although Nasra was only four and half and Mohammed barely two, he was positive, she was already working on them too, doing her bit of brainwashing. He couldn't even speak with his own children, without the word *Allah!* emitting from their little mouths. When they tripped and fell, they said: *Allah*! After feeding they were made to say: *Alhamdulillah!*

While his feelings and pride were hurt by her aloofness and her newfound certainty, he could also swear to her change of feelings towards him. He now had an ultimatum: Accept Islam, fundamentally, in it's pristine form, or face life without his wife and children.

As long as they were in the US, he knew she couldn't just split and disappear with the children and he played on her fears by threatening to take the children away from her, if she tried to leave. If she filed for divorce, he also threatened to inform the authorities of the reasons.

"I'm the perfect husband and father," he threatened her. "Just tell me, what American jury would've the heart to give away two innocent American children to a Muslim woman fanatic, who also happened to be a fundamentalist?"

Fanatic or no fanatic, he was using every trick in the book to make her stay.

"Apparently," he would taunt her, "you love your religion more since you're bent on destroying our life for some mysterious theory."

"Some mysterious theory, is that it?" she was distraught. "I really don't know what to make of you. At one moment you say you now believe in the truth of Islam, and the next moment you call it some mysterious theory? What am I supposed to believe?"

"Did you hear me deny anything? Of what I've seen, so far, all the evidence points to that same truth. I can no longer deny it, but I need time…"

He was becoming a chameleon, changing colors at will. The man who had always prided himself on his straightforwardness now played a zigzag game with her.

"If you're telling the truth," she said, "then let's see some action from your side. Prove it, act on it, then only would you become a true Muslim. You don't need Yusuf reminding you all the time, you must learn to stand on your own two feet. Do things on your own. Grow up, Ali, you know as well as I do what happens to Muslims who follow *Shaitan's* footsteps…they crack up like a nut! Go no further…just take a look at your wife!"

"You're a nut!"

"And by the way, a fanatic and one who honestly adherers to the basic fundamentals of his faith are not one and the same."

"Save the new-found knowledge for yourself, Anisa, and just because you're nowadays forced to bring out the mat, must everyone else hop on it with you?"

239

"Then embrace Christianity, there is no dearth of Bibles in this house."

"You're nuts!"

"Convert to Judaism. Tell me you're a Buddhist. Become something. Do something."

"You're nuts!"

"Own it up. Say you're a Freethinker."

"A cracking nut!"

"At least I'm something!"

"What a nut!"

"Then welcome to Atheism. I'll become your witness."

"Lady, I'm not that stupid!"

She knew he was stalling for time, and no one seemed to understand her predicament.

Floor, who was saddled with her own worries and troubles, could hardly be expected to comprehend the gravity of Anisa's situation. She was in the middle of a lawsuit, where she hoped to bring to heel her chronically unfaithful husband who not only ran off with a friend of hers, but also dropped that friend for another gullible woman.

"Give me a break," Floor said to the miserable woman. "Look around you, and that'll sure as hell cheer you up a little bit."

"Just tell me," she said in her matter of fact tone, "just tell me what you would've done if you ever got saddled with the kind of rogue that's bent on ruining my life?"

Neither Yusuf nor Khadija had also estimated the enormity of her plight, "Listen, Anisa," Khadija kept telling her. "If we knew there was no hope we would've said so. You're now forgetting all the months of suffering he went through because of your illness, shouldering the responsibility of not only two children but a sick wife as well, all by himself."

"For two whole years, Anisa," Khadija said, "two whole years of emergency, he nearly lost his job because of all the stress of coping at home. You know how he took care of you and the children all these months. It's not even a year since you had these other operations, the infections, and what not. If you had two whole years of suffering, he too had an equal number of years of pain. Don't be selfish, Anisa."

"It's disgusting living with a man for whom Islam's only some mysterious theory." Anisa felt caged. "He doesn't even know the difference between blind fanaticism and carrying out one's basic duties. If I pray on time and tell him to do the same, he says I'm 'a fundamentalist'. I say, 'come to prayer, Ali,' he says, 'here comes the fundamentalist!'"

"That's perfectly normal. He's only parroting what everyone else's saying. You can't prosecute him for that?"

"But to call me a fundamentalist when all I'm saying is come to prayer?"

"He doesn't know what he's saying, don't push him too hard."

"This home was never a hearth," she was forced to admit, "but now, it's pure hell. One moment he's Muslim, the next moment he's nothing. He's not even a Muslim on paper anymore."

"But that's a positive development. Anisa, Ali's on his way, don't put up roadblocks. Encourage him. That's what he needs, encouragement. And patience, loads of it."

"But he's no faith. I can't handle this nothingness. There's nothing in the man's heart, nothing that tells you he's something. Nothing…"

"You still need to give him time."

"I even tried to convert him to Christianity," she was perplexity itself. "Bought him a copy of the Bible, several copies, in fact, just in case that made things easier for him, but he wouldn't budge. He threw the Bibles on my face. Perhaps if he was a real Christian before and not a cynic materialist, things wouldn't have been so complicated?"

Khadija burst out in snorts, "Then, he'd have a starting point, wouldn't he? And you could take things from there?"

"At least I'd know who I was dealing with. As it is, he was neither a Jew nor a Christian. Not even a Freethinker. Never met a Taoist, he claims. He did shake hands with a Hindu, but just once. Never owned a Bible. And he wasn't about to fill his precious shelves with contradictory versions, he jeers!"

"Anisa, patience, patience."

"He scoffs at the Trinity and sneers a the priesthood. How could anyone argue with such a person and tell him where he's gone wrong? There's no platform. I may as well confess to you, Khadija: We've nothing to stand on. There's no record, no history, not even a road map. And we're at this junction and he neither comprehends from where he came from, nor does he care where he is going. Khadija, it's a crazy world we've got under this roof, and with these children caught in the middle, I really don't know what to think."

"At least, he doesn't follow blindly," Khadija was caught between laughter and sadness. "And he's definitely not anti-God. We know this."

"Even so, but he's driving me crazy, that much I know. Why did I have to have children?"

"Your health's not perfect yet, Anisa," Khadija said. "You're simply not yet ready for a full blown fight. Give yourself a breathing space. Give him time and give yourself the benefit of the doubt."

Khadija meant well, this was, however, easier said than done. Having swallowed the bitter pill of her own deviation, Anisa was now in a hurry to mend; and cementing her relationship with her Lord needed total commitment.

Patience needed time. And having already whiled away so many precious years in rebellion herself, she was afraid time wasn't exactly on her side. Waiting indefinitely around for him to see the light also meant compromising on her spiritual advancement. If he had weaknesses and problems of his own, she too had devils of her own to fight. And the battle raged on. They were now in the middle of the month of Ramadan, obviously, a further encroachment on Mike's personal freedom.

Mike was now coming home, later and later, and with the progress of her physical and mental well being, the conflict intensified to a detonation. The quarrels and the misunderstandings at home were now throwing him more and more into the arms of his old friends and colleagues who were more than glad to bring him back into the fold.

After work, instead of hurrying home to his wife and children he was now going out with his friends. His drinking habits were never above the normal Western dose, but the occasional glass of wine or beer, which became less and less and almost non-existent for sometime, now came back with a vengeance. He didn't even have to pay for them anymore, as friend after friend would pass his table and order yet another round, before Mike had chance to finish the last. It seemed as though the jinn and the human in drinking places made a secret pact between them to flood their long lost friend with months' supplies of liquor and beer. And his family saw him less and less.

This didn't escape his wife who now beyond all doubt saw for the first time the incorrigibility of the situation. The truancy gave her a respite and the right excuse for a plan of action, a drastic plan of action.

The children were already in her passport, thanks to the canceled trip to her home country after the car crash the year before. They had a joint account, she paid for the tickets with her credit card and made a long distance call from the inner city to her family.

Chapter Fifteen

Breakout

When My servant asks thee concerning Me, I am indeed near.
I answer the prayer of every suppliant when he calls on Me.
Let them also listen to My call.
(Qur'an: 2:186)

On a Sunday night, a whistling Mike pulled the car into the drive. He was out late the previous night and purposely went to his parents' place to sleep away the hangover.

His mother was more than happy to have him stay over for the family Sunday barbecue, which included his sister, her two children from her failed marriage and her latest boyfriend. All the time he was there no one mentioned either the alien or her children. His wife was bad news and the less anyone heard about the bad news and her children the better. And now that he didn't show any concern for them either, they were perfectly happy with the status quo.

Safi Abdi

Turning the key and pushing the front door open, Mike was slightly baffled by the darkness. It was slight over 9.00 PM. It was as yet too early for Anisa to go to bed. He felt a slight numbness in the stomach when he found the beds empty, but did not yet panic. He went to the bathroom to take a quick shower, and then took his time to take a coke from the refrigerator, which seemed strangely eerie and almost empty. *When was the last time they went out shopping together?* His stomach turned but he held on. Now feeling somewhat tense, he dialed Yusuf's number but gave up after several attempts. He switched on the answering machine. There were a few calls, all for Anisa. He returned to the kitchen for any tell tale signs, for any note stuck on the refrigerator. Nothing, except for a prayer time schedule. Soon it was 11:00 PM. She never stayed out this late with children.

Once again he dialed Yusuf's number, and Yusuf answered.

"Yusuf?"

"*Salaamu alaikum*, Ali."

"Any idea where Anisa could be?"

"I really don't know," returned Yusuf, "we were away for the weekend. Just a second, perhaps Khadija…"

248

Then Yusuf was back, "she doesn't know, perhaps…"

Mike didn't wait for him to finish.

A sleepy Floor took the phone. No. She hadn't spoken with her for a while.

"Another nervous breakdown, isn't it?" she snarled.

"What you mean?"

"Well, the way she carried on about the heedless non-believing hedonistic West, I just hang up on her. Who does she think I'm? Aren't I one of them spirit-swilling non-believing folk? And now you tell me she's ditched you, well, that's about the best news I've had all year!"

"She's missing…any wild guesses where she could be at this time of night?"

"There's only one place for people like her, the psychiatric sickbay," Floor hissed, "and don't you wake me up again unless you need some cheering up at her funeral!" And dead went the line. Just as he was wondering whether he should go over to the neighbors and find out when they had last seen her, the ringing of the telephone startled him.

"Is everything all right?" It was Yusuf.

"No. It isn't."

"Have you tried the neighbors?"

"That's exactly what I was about to do. I'll catch you up later." Then as he was about to leave the door the telephone was ringing again, it was Floor.

"Is she back?" she blurted out.

"No, she isn't." Mike shook his head.

"But you can tell me where the heck you'd been holed up yourself, can't you?"

"I'll call you in the morning, Floor," Mike released a breath. "Go back to sleep and don't mess with me. Am not your ex-husband!"

By the time he was done with Floor it was past midnight. It was a bit late to call on the Jeffersons, so he started with the Johnson family, sure that the Jeffersons' dog would make a scene at the slightest dingdong. No, neither the Jeffersons nor the Johnsons had seen either Anisa or the children for two whole days.

"We thought you had all gone somewhere for the weekend," Mrs. Jefferson said.

The folded newspapers on the lawn on his way from the neighbors had further confirmed his suspicion. He ran up the steps to the bedrooms only to find her passport gone. And so was his passport.

Two days later a cab driver reported to the police. He admitted to having driven to the airport a foreign looking woman and two children fitting a description of Anisa and the kids.

"When I look back now," recounted the cab driver, "I did think her quite fidgety. She did have the look of someone running away from something. She had only a pram and a backpack. She didn't have any other luggage. I remember her especially because of this thing on the head," concluded the cab driver.

After the police feedback, a distressed Mike placed a long distance call. Her uncle confirmed his worst nightmare. The kids were in good condition, he said, but couldn't say the same for his wife. And it'd be best for all concerned, her uncle told Mike, if he, Mike, kept a safe distance until the situation stabilized and the family knew what was going on.

"What's wrong with her?" he asked.

"Nothing's wrong other than what the two of you have created…"

"A nervous breakdown?"

"I wish I could give her ailment a name, Ali, all I can say at this point is that she isn't Anisa, she's someone else. And she's done nothing but weep, I hope you'll make us understand the situation."

"What about my children? And my passport?"

"Right now I'm more concerned about my niece's health. How come you never said the situation was so bad? I expected more from you, young man, why didn't you send her and the children here if she was so bad? Why were we kept in the dark?"

"She wanted to keep you in the dark. Not I," threw Mike. "Now, if you'd excuse me I'd like to have my children and my passport back. You may keep her if you want but I want the other stuff, you get me...the children...the passport, you know what I' saying...?"

"I don't think you should try such a rash action, Ali. If you don't care about your wife, there're people out her who do." Omar didn't mean to threaten the man, but that's how Mike perceived it.

"Kicking up a fuss, aren't' we?" he yelled.

"I think you should calm down," Omar said. "I don't know anything about your passport but if it is anywhere in Rako Island, I'll send it right this minute, don't you worry. Relax Ali. Relax."

"Relax? Without my children? Relax? Without my passport?"

"It isn't as though we were abducting your children. Please don't push me. I'm not the one who created this mess. I'm only trying to help. I've always been on your side, young man. Since the day you sent me that letter, I made sure I was on your side. I never blamed you for anything. And I tried to patch up things hoping for the best..." The telephone deadened in Omar's hand.

The word *abduct* struck a chord in Mike's ear drum. He headed straight for the nearest bar. After several glasses of hard liquor, he was laughing and screaming at the top of his voice.

"Hey, guys," he waved yet another brimming glass high up in the air. "Can anyone of you fools come up with the meaning of abduct?"

"Abduct...Abduct..." shouted anther tipsy fellow down the bar, "abduct...kidnap...capture...seize and carry away...how does that grab you, fool?"

"You said kidnap?" Mike charged at the fellow, "who said anything about kidnap, you…!"

The brimming glass landed on the man's shoulder, causing a cut on the skin and a free for all brawl ensued. A screaming, bleeding Mike was at last dragged off the premises. A police constable escorted him to the nearest station.

A week later a bandaged but somewhat calmed Mike reported for work. One look at him, and his boss broke into laughter.

"Been meaning to give you the sack for a while," he said. "But it won't be fun until you've had some fun. Go take a break, and don't come back until you know you can take the heat."

On his way out, Mike stopped at his colleagues' for a while and having said his good byes headed straight for the car.

Once inside the house he got to work. He had already filled three large suitcases with her personal stuff, and dumped there everything from clothes to shoes to the weird scarves. He now brought down some more cases from the attic and went ahead and dumped whatever other relics that reminded him of her. And in went everything from

Bibles to audiotapes and to the albums and what irked him the most at that moment, the Islamic literature.

Down with all Muslim scholars, he sizzled, as he dumped the vexatious literature into the cases. Down with Abdullah Yusuf Ali, he seethed and down with Dr. Al Mansour, and Mauddudi and down went Sayid Qutb and his prison life stories, and down went Yusuf Qadarawi and his rules and regulations, and down with Dr. Maurice Bucaille and his smart findings, and so went Ahmed Deedat's galling pamphlets and video tapes, for he was a huge troublemaker that man with the funny hat, Mike seethed as he unceremoniously shoved all the rabble-rousers and their smart books and videos into the bottom of the boxes. The Qur'anic *calligraphy*, these he cast in cello-tapes.

Having stored away everything in the attic, he could now relax and sit back with a steaming cup of coffee in his own living room. He was now determined to take things easy and take everyday as it came. He would be damned if he was going to throw his life away for some silly, third world citizen.

The first thing he was now going to do was to call that uncle of hers and find out about ways of remitting a monthly allowance to his children, at least for a while, until he got his bearings right and thought out ways of claiming them back.

Having done that he was determined to take his boss's advice and take a long vacation. He'd always wanted to go to the continent. What better time than now?

His mother was thrilled.

"Lovely," she said, smug. "You sure need your vacation. Thank God the nightmare's all behind us." She paused for a second as a bright idea hit her head.

"But don't you leave yet, darling. Your father and I are having a few people from the club over here for dinner this weekend, why not join us and perhaps bring along a friend?"

The said friend was a high school friend, the daughter of his parents' friends. They'd dated a few times but forgot about her when life took them apart. She married a fellow from down south, and was now in the middle of a long-winded divorce proceeding. Daisy, for that was her name, had confided her woes in him only the other night, and found in him a sympathetic ear.

He didn't mention his tribulations to her, then, but his mother saw to it that Daisy got all the tidbits.

"Deal?" his mother put on a charming smile.

Why not? He had nothing to lose. And as it turned out later at the party, Daisy too was on her way to Europe. She was now up to her ears with problems and lawyers and had to get away from it all. What a pleasant coincidence! He couldn't get a better companion and he told her so to her face.

On their return from their wild trip in the continent, the abandoned pair naturally ended up under the same roof. The diligent Daisy simply moved a few of her belongings; some at a time, into Mike's house and a cohabitation of a sort soon bloomed into a permanent partnership. This time, though, without the hassles of official stamps.

And except for the monthly bank receipts that found their way into the letterbox, for a time Mike was actually able to blank out his wife's memory from his mind.

Of all his friends, Floor was perhaps the only one who chose to differ. Bumping into him and Daisy, quite accidentally, one day shortly after their return from holiday, her disgust and horror at what she called the mans' indecent behavior had turned quite a few heads on the street.

Totally shooting past *the mouse* (for that was the name she tagged to Daisy), and charging at him like a bull, she said what she thought of him – that he was no better than the average adulterous westerner was now clear. And that, as of that day, whatever was said about the licentious western condition was a sore she'd have to live with for the rest of her life, concluded the appalled Floor who now left the embarrassed couple to quietly crouch away from the stares of the passers-by.

Much to the consternation of the two, Floor also took upon herself to pester them with persistent nuisance calls. And now Mike couldn't thank his lucky stars enough for the deranged woman was at last out of their hair.

Thanks to Daisy's presence, Yusuf and Khadija had likewise given up all hope of ever reaching him. It was just as well and he hoped their paths would never cross again. Not that he had anything against these two, but they reminded him too much of what he was trying to forget.

Chapter Sixteen

Temporary Settlement

Meanwhile, as time passed and Anisa was once again on the road to full recovery, she'd begun to hear the island's hushed whispers about the throwaway woman from America. Although her family and real friends provided some sort of a buffer zone between her and her assailants, and happy and grateful as she was for being there with her folks, the susurration didn't escape her note altogether.

She found it hard to believe, but it seemed as though, there existed within the community, some quarters, who were ready to believe the worst of her. There were also a few who took a real pleasure in her plight. While to some, the whole idea of her sickness was regarded as a ploy to perhaps cover up the girl's iniquity?

To others, the woman got no more than she deserved. All those years in America and not a single penny to call her own, they said. Not even a change of clothes. The poor mother had to rush to town to buy all the bare necessities – not only for her but for the two children as well.

Remarks of how well some of the island's people were doing, especially those of Anisa's generation, filled the air. Indeed, Anisa's rendezvous with the West was now deemed a very sad, sad story.

Even her looks changed, it was agreed. Only a ghostly version of the robust girl who took off in a whirl from the shores some eleven years ago, that was all that remained, a worn out ghost that did nothing but slouch away her time on the family couch!

Anisa's family and those who were dear to them did not budge from the cruel onslaught nor did they try to put out the flame with a counteraction from their side. They let those who chose to believe the worst come back on their own sweet time.

"Gossip is like a very slight sail boat," her uncle said. "When the current changes, the sail boat changes direction." He saw these people as that flimsy sailboat on the vast currents of the ocean. "Leave them alone," he told Anisa's mother. "We know the true story. Anisa did err, but those errors are between her and her Lord. And it's Him who should be the judge. She did not hurt anyone other than herself and the only ones who had to brave the brunt of her errors are those who loved her the most.

"So leave these people alone, they're few in number and their strength will soon dwindle with every breath," he told the tearful Fatima to let the matter rest and leave everything in the capable Hands of Allah.

And so he was proven right. The minute Anisa got on her feet and people saw how blooming and robust she again felt and looked, all around, a change of heart could be heard. What man worth his salt would let this woman and her two adorable children slip through his fingers?

And when the Lord gave something of his bounty to the throwaway in the form of a decent work in a decent place, the cries of how qualified the runaway was could now be heard. Time Anisa stood on her two feet and not depended on *kafir* handouts, they cried.

Meanwhile, Rukhiya, Omar's first wife and companion, gracefully departed from the family. Years of pain had taken their toll on Rukhiya and when the hour finally came, everyone welcomed the inevitable relief. But the sorrow was by no means less felt. Rukhiya was not only an honest upright woman within the community, she was also of a pure generous heart that gave and never expected a return. A friendship that went beyond friendship itself had always existed between her and Anisa's mother, Fatima. A lot of women shook their heads in consternation whenever the subject of Fatima and Rukhiya came up, especially since the two shared the same husband in recent years. But now that Rukhiya was no more, they were all agreeable, and in fact even admired the special traits of selflessness, which the two women demonstrated all along to everyone. We're all on our way out, said the women, sooner or later, everyone's heading that way. So, why not be charitable and kind when one had the chance to do so? *Woe to those who took the world for granted!* They moaned. The love for this flimsy world and its attractions, they moaned, was a rope with which only the stupid hung themselves. The final exist of a known and a cherished person was always an eye-opener. For how long these eyes would remain open was, however, anyone's guess. However, for the moment, said these saddened souls, woe to those who took the world for a destination and didn't see it for what it was: a *transit station.*

Almost a year had now passed since their arrival in Rako Island and the only thing Anisa saw of Mike were the signatures on the monthly allowance that came to the bank for her and the children. She was glad for the respite, worried herself sick over him, and prayed for his soul, day and night.

Chapter Seventeen

Life in Rako

The blind and the seeing are not alike;
Nor are the depths of darkness and the light;
Nor are the (chilly) shade and the (genial) heat of the sun:
Nor are alike those that are living and those that are dead...
(Qur'an: 35:19-22)

Nasra was now six and Mohammed three and a half. The whole family doted on them. Their two young uncles, Hassan and Hussein, took them everywhere their little feet could go and they simply loved all the fuss everyone made over them.

The old house where Anisa was born and bred had already been sold. The family now lived in a modern house in another part of the city. Anisa and her mother missed the old house but the family had to move while Anisa was still in America, because of the sewage problem that plagued the whole area in recent years. Too much sand had clogged the sewer pipe along the dusty lane where the house lay.

Even Faiza's family and many of their neighbors had likewise vacated their homes. And the dust-infested area was now state property and no one knew what program the state had in store for the said zone.

Now that Aunt Rukhiya had left the family, Anisa's youngest cousin, Nora, was also staying with Anisa's mother.

Anisa's other two cousins, Fathiya and Rohana were both married and had their respective families. As luck would have it, Faiza's home was a stone's throw away from the family's new house where Anisa and her two children also stayed. Faiza too was the proud mother of two lovely boys. She was a part time teacher in a government primary school. And that gave her plenty of time for her home and family. Her husband, Sa'id, had turned into a known Islamic activist and the authorities were watching him with special care.

While in the past, the bulk of the Muslim community was content with being on the defensive, and kept the *kafirs* at arms length. Sa'id and a few other like-minded people were now telling their own community to shed the *we-are-perfect-mentality*, and forget about the so-called tarnished face of Islam.

It wasn't Islam that was tarnished and needed a facelift, rather, it was the Muslims who needed a complete overhaul. For it's they, and not Islam, that was faulty. And that it was the individual Muslim who not only needed a face-lift but was also in dire need of a complete change of heart.

An offensive inroad into the hitherto ignored territory, the *kafir* territory, said these men, wasn't such a bad idea after all. But first the heart transplant.

This new tactic, as opposed to the defensive attitude of the disorganized Muslims could hardly go unnoticed by the authorities. And the new dynamism of the formerly static marginalized minority was now making some pockets quite nervous.

The Christian missionaries who for the past hundred years or so enjoyed a total monopoly over the non-Muslim natives of Rako Island were now forced to think out ways of controlling the impinging epidemic; and to this end, new youth-friendly projects kept sprouting up every now and then in Rako Island.

While on the one hand, Sa'id and his co-workers sought to break away from the isolationism of their fathers and forefathers, they didn't shy away from taking a more vigorous road to obtaining their rights as citizens of their own land. The law that previously forbade the erection of Islamic schools must go, they said.

For fear of rebellion the state was now cornered into acquiescing to the long-standing demand of allowing a standard school for its minority group. And now that the community had decided not to involve the government in the financing process as this was to be taken care of by a rich Islamic State (which didn't want to be named or praised for their kindness as they rightly saw this as their duty) the government was now eager to allocate the necessary funds, as well. But the community politely declined the offer, as they were no longer in need of the state finances.

Everyone knew what the state's financial involvement would mean: *restriction of movement*. All the community needed from their government was now the removal of the law so the community could get on with their lives with the help of their far away brothers. The community wasn't begging anyone and least of all the far away brothers. Rather it was the brothers themselves, who, having got their heart transplant proper, were now in the process of getting the face-lift.

"Better late than never," also became a good saying. These heart transplant patients were therefore more than welcome to get their face-lifts in Rako Island.

The school that would give the far away brothers the needed face-lift was to be a unique addition to the island. The syllabus was to be tailored to the specific needs of the Muslim child, offering a decent education that went hand in hand with his spiritual leanings and strengthened the inherent belief in the young heart.

Arabic was to be taught as a second language as this would make for a better understood and appreciated Qur'an. Islamic culture, history and literature were to replace the study of *kafir* literature that didn't have a direct bearing on the child's character development. *British history must go*, everyone agreed. *What was the point of lapping up the unholy ventures of unholy kings? What was the purpose of making an innocent child suffer king Henry VIII's wives? What virtues were to be learned from past European pagan traditions?*

The accumulation of unnecessary information, it was agreed, only jammed the children's memory and warped their perspective in life. This was sure to raise a few eyebrows in parliament, but the Muslims were adamant on a total Islamization of their community's education.

Why the government had all along turned a blind eye to the presence of the outmoded *madrasah*, while it at the same time objected to such a standard school, was no secret. From a very young age the average Muslim child would come to the *madrasah* nearest to his home and learn how to commit verses of the Qur'an to his heart. Since Arabic, the original language of the Qur'an was not the spoken language of the island; a child could only cram the verses without understanding. While this handicap could not be said to have in any way diminished the Muslim child's inherent belief in Allah and that stories of the prophets, the oral relaying of Islamic thought and civilization, the sayings of the prophet, coupled with the Islamic home environment, had all added to the reinforcement of the Muslim child's belief in the authenticity of his faith, lack of Arabic notwithstanding.

Still, a glaring gap remained on the bridge of knowledge, and unless one was extremely well versed in the teachings of the Qur'an, which more often than not required a super human effort on the part of the ordinary school going child, there existed a certain risk. The extra curriculum and the incessant homework also saw to it that hardly any time was left for the *madrasah* and the pursuing of spiritual knowledge.

As the bulk of the country's lawmakers were themselves a product of Christian thought, and the missionary schools could hardly be considered as local schools, this institution operated above the law of the land. The discipline was better and many Muslim parents would make a beeline for this institution.

To Muslim children, the *madrasah* was some sort of a pre-school institution. Many of the children never returned to the madrasah once their ordinary schooling began. Only those whose parents were particularly headstrong stayed on.

Faiza's husband, Sa'id was among the few who continued at the ill-equipped *madrasah* even into his secondary schooling. It was tough. It was tiresome. Young Sa'id hated it with all his heart, and he grumbled and grumbled about the injustice of it all. His father conceded but added that he could hardly be blamed for the injustice.

The heartless father argued that were the pursuit of higher knowledge part of the school curriculum, his son wouldn't have to suffer so. And Sa'id and the few boys like him would dream of a day when the study of higher knowledge also became part of the school curriculum so they wouldn't have to suffer so. And the fathers lobbied and lobbied for such a school, but to no avail.

The community had neither the power to change the law nor the resources to stand on their own. And the grumbling continued, but Sa'id's heartless father wouldn't budge. No sooner did he return from school and done his assignment than the young Sa'id would be shooed off to the old Sheikh until Sa'id was able not only to fully commit the whole Qur'an to memory, but his long intimacy with the *Sheikh* paid off, leaving a lasting effect on him. The intimacy had also instilled an appreciation of the Word of Allah. By the time he completed his former education, Sa'id already knew what he wanted in life. The mere attractions of the world of which the Qur'an described as *play and amusement and chattels of deception*, was not what he wanted in life.

And when the time came for him to say his salaams to the old *Sheikh*, Sa'id had also found the heart to forgive not only the antiquated *madrasah* but also the heartless father.

Notwithstanding their strong belief in the perfection of their faith, many youngsters of Anisa's age did digress from the strict path of their faith.

Now that she could reason out her own deviation more objectively, Anisa was now able to pin down, at least, some of the things that might have attributed to and even started the wheel of the tremendous errors of her life.

"Yet I can find no convincing reason for what I did," she said to Faiza and Sa'id. The night was cloudy and drizzly, a typical monsoon night. The three were sitting at the couple's balcony, as they had done so often, sipping Faiza's favorite drink – a blend of honey, lime and coconut water flavored with a pinch of cardamom. Sa'id hated the concoction but had to drink it all the same because of Faiza's insistence that it was good for his thinning hair.

Anisa suppressed a smile. Despite his outspokenness one thing Sa'id dared never do was criticize Faiza's cooking. A word of complaint and he knew he'd be exiled to the kitchen.

"My knowledge of the Qur'an might've been very little," Anisa said, sipping her drink, "but I'd the best of parents. There's absolutely no excuse, whatsoever."

While she waited for Sa'id's response, she leaned over to Faiza and then whispered, "I suggest you leave the honey bit out next time around."

"Madam, you know where the kitchen is!" Faiza retorted.

"The school environment, I think that's what did it," said Sa'id helpfully.

"You're so charitable, Sa'id," said Anisa, "I know you mean well and want me to think better of myself, so I could get rid of the guilt and get well. But, look here, Faiza went to the same school and she'd never been institutionalized. See what I mean?"

"Okay, okay, so Faiza hasn't been institutionalized? No one can say she's a better person than you are, not before and certainly not now."

"Mind you," he went on taking a sip at his wife's concoction, "she's not alone in this lukewarm situation. Although no one likes to admit, everyone has need of correction, some time or other. I'm sure you're aware of our community's many defects."

"The problem with Anisa is," Faiza said, "she refuses to forgive herself. Do tell her what Allah says to His erring servants.

"Allah has said," Anisa said, quoting a part of a Qur'anic verse: "And those who, having done something to be ashamed of, or wronged their own souls, earnestly bring God to mind, and ask for forgiveness for their sins – and who can forgive sins expect God?" She inhaled, willing the words to breath life into her chest.

"If you only knew how much comfort and solace these words gave to the troubled soul that was mine during that hellish period, if you only knew how much comfort I received from these words. I sometimes wonder what'd become of me if I, for instance, had neither the Qur'an nor the *hadith* to fall back on."

Anisa swallowed, thinking back of the horrors of that period. "I'd definitely become addicted to some tranquilizer or other if they became the only comfort I had from the nightmare of that period."

As she said this a quick film-like review of the various hospitals passed through Anisa's mind. At the ward where she stayed after the car accident, there was this scared old woman who kept weeping and yelling all night. And Anisa remembered taking the woman's shaking hands in her own weak ones, praying for a lightening of the woman's pain. "You do believe in God, don't you?" Anisa asked softly.

"You're shoving it on me too, right?" the old woman snarled, jerking her hand away from Anisa. "You're like him, this priest who's been shuffling around my bed, aren't you?"

"But, he's only trying to help," Anisa pleaded, "please listen to him and let him pray for you. That'll give you comfort...well, some comfort. I don't know if that will give you salvation, but then you need some comfort while here, so let me get you that Bible he left over there. And God is great."

"What Bible?" she pulled a pair of bleary eyes on her, and then grunted, pointing an old withered finger at the book, "It never did give me any comfort before, what makes you think it'll do any good now?" she asked, drawing muted noises from Anisa.

Further down the corridor there also echoed the persistent laments of an old man, eating his heart out in fear, yet not knowing where to turn to for help. These people had no faith nor did they have any trust in their Maker, Anisa learnt to her desolation. The painkillers and the tranquilizers were their only solace.

A year later when Anisa once gain returned to the hospital, the ward she stayed was jam-packed with elderly people, mortals in their twilight years; beaten by a life and a system that sucked the juices out of their veins and now ejected the useless corpses.

The vacant looks in their eyes told tales of humans who saw nothing beyond the limited life they now led – chronic sicknesses coupled with the specter of death and awaiting an end they mocked during their reckless years, and thought would never come.

All the good things that happened to them in life were now a past memory. All the contribution they made to society; the graceful buildings they helped build, the beautiful lawns they mowed on the weekends; the golf clubs, the continental jaunts; the Sunday barbecues; the Christmas and birthday parties, the New Year fire works; the salty television crackers and the cinema popcorn.

The tragedy of it all was, among these elderly folk she met at the hospital, there were many who had by then already forgotten about all these little pleasures for which they had worked so hard all their lives. So, what was the point of it all now that they had lived through the irony of it all?

"And I was ashamed of myself and knew instantly that God wanted me to see things with my own eyes." She pit her lip. "And the warning couldn't have been made clearer. This is the reward of those who refuse to heed their Lord. And there's no knowing what life will hold for them in the life to come."

Sa'id's eyes moistened. "There're people on this earth who call themselves Muslims and they never get to see their errors. It's a pity that we humans, despite all our God-given powers we still choose to remain beasts. We eat and drink and sleep and breathe, and eat and sleep and breathe until there's nothing left for us to eat or drink or breathe. Then what?"

She shivered as she'd done so many times, the hair on her scalp standing erect, wiry and stiff. "It isn't that I'm against the little pleasures of life, as Allah has made them *halal* for us," she said, "the ugliness of it is, however, when one remains the cow forever, but for the Grace of Allah, wouldn't the same be true of me too?"

"I think your rendezvous with the West wasn't such a sad story after all," put in Faiza. "And contrary to what others might say, I think the West's just the right place to live until people sharpened their antennas and scanned with their own eyes that all that glitters is really not gold!"

"I mean besides the theoretical part," Anisa said, "what did I know of Islam?"

There she was thinking herself a believer all this time, and albeit her own non-adherence, feeling superior and way above the rest of the world.

"But was I any better?" she said, looking from the one to the other. "Can you imagine the shame I felt: The stark hypocrisy of my life?"

"Yes, you are right, Anisa, your digression was the direct outcome of your negligence but I still believe things might not have spiraled out of hand, had you a firmer grasp of what being a true Muslim really meant."

"I did try to talk some sense into her," Faiza said, "but she wouldn't listen!"

"Faiza, time I went home," returned Anisa eyeing Faiza with apprehension.

"I don't want to pry," Sa'id said, "but can I ask you a personal question?"

Anisa nodded nervously.

"You and your husband," he said, "shouldn't things be finalized one way or the other? I mean why are you avoiding him? And why is it that we all thought so very highly of him? To be honest, we all liked him. And your uncle doted on him. What happened, Anisa?"

"I'm sorry, it had to end this way," Anisa shrugged, "but you all saw how I was when I came."

"Strange, he never did try to get in touch," Faiza said.

"And I'm thankful to Allah for that, praise be to Allah, my prayers are answered."

"I understand the children miss him, don't they?" Faiza looked at her friend with unconcealed skepticism.

"Yes, it's very painful. They think their father's coming any day. When they see a plane pass over they shout: 'Daddy! Daddy!' I didn't expect them to be like this," Anisa said. "And Nasra, she's driving me crazy. She was very attached to him."

"So what're you going to do?" Sa'id asked.

"Nasra used to be such an easy child," she continued, evading the question, "I didn't bargain for all this fuss she's making now. And Mohammed's become her parrot. Hopefully, they'll grow out of it. Time is the greatest healer."

It was a little over 9.30 PM. Sa'id got up as well to walk Anisa home. The last few years, drug related crimes were making the streets slightly unsafe. Although most of the problems were sighted in areas in and around the city center and tourist locations, still it was better to be cautious.

On his way back, just as he was about to cross the street, a car screeched to a stop in front of him and before he knew what was happening, he was blindfolded and dragged into a waiting car.

The next day, the local papers were awash with news of a busted drug ring, where the police seized two very important suspects who tried to flee from the scene of the crime. The said suspects whose names were still withheld by the police were to appear in court.

A few weeks later the said drug dealers were brought to the court of justice—the bruises they incurred in the cell now healed. The men pleaded not guilty, however. They also proved their alibi that the two weren't even together the said night they were supposed to have been together. Neither of them had any criminal record. However, the police had enough evidence to support their charges; the police report and two witnesses were all they needed to lock the two away from mainstream society.

All around, news of Sa'id and Usman's tragedy took the community by surprise. What was the state up to? Of all the people, why these two? Of all the charges why the drug ring? Why weren't they allowed a lawyer of their own choosing? Why was the case so quickly wrapped up?

Throngs of bewildered citizens crushed the gate of the state secretary's residence. The secretary was never known for his empathy with his own people. His post as personal secretary to the president was more important than the ideals and integrity of his community.

281

He knew it. His colleagues at the top knew it. And the community avoided him as best they could, as matters concerning the community were never his field.

To the state, however, he remained an indispensable representative of his community. So far the Muslim community had somehow managed to do without him. But this was no time for pride. There were a couple of other Muslim stooges in high places, but they lacked political clout and close proximity to the highest level. He was their only hope.

To the community leaders' surprises the secretary was just as mortified by the incident involving the two men. But his mortification, to their dismay, wasn't exactly like their own.

"What humiliation! What disgrace!" roared the secretary with indignation. "Who would've thought such brilliant men would act in such an abominable manner!"

The secretary was perhaps more dense than they thought? His son Jibreel was away from the island and it was just as well. Father and son were never the best of friends.

"But Mr. Secretary," said the community speaker, "we know it, and we dare say you know it too that there is more to this issue than meets the eye."

"So you're now saying the police are lying?" asked the secretary. "Why would the police do such a thing?" he stole a glance at his Rolex watch. A lavish state dinner awaited him.

"Look here Mr. Secretary," said the speaker. "We really do not want to take too much of your time, but there is more at stake here than meets the eye. We may be citizens of this island, but apparently, there are people who find it difficulty to live with that reality. But as citizens we are deeply concerned about the fate of these two men and their respective families. The people of this island are a very peace-long folk. They shouldn't be exposed to undue unrest."

The speaker paused a little to see how far the words had sunk in. He had to be scared into action.

"But how can we be so sure these men are innocent?" the secretary said, changing tactics.

"They're innocent," said the speaker. "And the people who made the arrest know it. We leave it to you to prove their innocence."

The secretary got up. He was no fool. In fact, he was an expert in self-protection. "Well, I won't promise anything but I'll see what I can do. There might be a mistake."

"And since you are a trusted friend of the president tell it from us that the deadline is tomorrow. Ma'assalaama, Mr. Secretary."

A shaky secretary later took his boss aside.

"Mr. President," he said, scared of his own voice, "these men are innocent. It's proven beyond doubt. They have the whole community's support. They're not alone. Such an action may cause undue unrest." Was the secretary drinking? The president thought.

"What men, Mr. Secretary? The drug dealers?"

"It's a frame."

"Framed by the police?"

"Mr. President, we need to do something, and promptly." Sweat dotted the secretary's face.

What have they been doing to him?

Although the secretary was in the dark, the president was fully aware of the situation.

The president was lately inundated with complaints from high-ranking people who didn't quite approve of the men's religious activities, and felt threatened, because these people were spreading ideas that were not in the best interests of the island. Revolutionary ideas that ran contrary to mainstream currents.

The president had to concede that if that was the case then the situation was indeed perilous. The impressionable youth, complained some of the fathers who lost their hitherto disco-going children to these religious sessions, were the primary targets of this new onslaught. And if this cancer wasn't nipped at the bud, and the youth not returned to the dance floor, would Rako Island be the same? A strong signal was needed to thwart these uncalled for advances, so said the few guys on top.

This was not a war. All Sa'id and his friends did was *talk*. That was all they did, *talk* in the mosques. It was a peaceful grassroots talk. But everyone agreed, this kind of *talk* was something Rako Island could very well do without. Hence, the drug ring. By framing these two, the state wanted to test the will of this minority group, and measure the level of their resistance.

But, if the secretary's sweat was anything to go by, then caution was perhaps a better weapon than a headlong confrontation?

"Mr. secretary, a mistake, you said?" The president narrowed his deep-set eyes. "I'm not personally aware of the situation. But I'll see what I can do, if only for your sake." This was made to look like a personal favor from the president to his loyal servant. The secretary was most certainly a valuable representative of his community.

"They must be released immediately, or my credibility's at stake," burped the secretary.

"If proven innocent, then I see no reason why they shouldn't be released."

The secretary sighed. He knew he could count on the President. The two always propped up each other, or so thought the obtuse secretary.

Chapter Eighteen

Mike and Daisy

It was a pleasant sunny afternoon, not too hot, not too cold. Mike and Daisy strolled, arm in arm among the tall trees of the woods, a few hundred meters away from Mike's home, where the couple resided and cohabited in the manner of a married couple. Daisy was now deeply in love with Mike and the thought of the runaway wife and children plagued her non-stop, and was now making her more and more distraught.

She long expected some sort of action from his side. However, all she got whenever she broached the subject was a shrug or two.

Almost a year and half had passed since she moved in with him, as yet, nothing, not a word about the woman, not even a mention of his own children, whose pictures he carried in his wallet. Daisy thought this kind of eerie and said so to his sister, but Charlotte was just as tightlipped about the crazy alien fanatic and her children.

A problem she'd only become aware of only an hour ago was also now an added weight on the anxious Daisy.

Although she never said it aloud, and didn't even want to admit it to herself, something else was bothering her.

In the early days of their relationship, Mike was vivacious, spontaneous and fun loving. Lately, he was becoming more and more morose. She couldn't even remember when they last went out or had fun, or even had friends over. He was always too busy, and if he wasn't drinking mineral water he was drinking orange juice—as though weaning himself away from wine. And now, she didn't know what to think any more. On his side of the bed, there was this book, this green thickset book he was being absorbed in. And when she asked him about it the other day, all he said was: "The Holy Book of Islam." Why he was reading, of all books, the Holy Book of Islam, was still a mystery to her.

When she moved in with him, she didn't sight a single religious book anywhere. But now, it seemed, there were books everywhere, strange books. Where these came from, she had no idea. All she knew was he was now being absorbed in one of these strange books.

Another strange thing she kept shrugging off was his vehement refusal to touch anything that had any pork product in it, and wondered why Mike went to great lengths to seek out kosher products. She put this to one of those things, she was herself once a vegetarian.

But it was the strange readings that had now begun to get on her nerves.

Tightening her arm around his, and leaning slightly on his shoulder, she now said, "Mike darling, don't you think it's time you filed for divorce?"

The question startled him. In all the time they had lived together, Daisy hadn't bothered him too much about his personal life, and he was thankful for the respite.

Jerking his head away from hers, he stood still for a moment as if to say something but stopped himself. Sensing his reluctance she untangled her arm from his and pulled him to a stop.

"What're you waiting for? You know she'll never come back." She made an abrupt U-turn to face him. He looked squarely at her.

"If you don't mind, Daisy, I'd rather keep that subject out of our lives."

"You can't be serious," she charged at him, treading on his shoes.

"Let's forget it, shall we?"

"Then you're still in love with the black thing!" The words escaped her mouth.

"That black thing happens to be my wife," he said, taking a step forward, but a dazed Daisy blocked his way.

"So that's it? The black thing's your wife, and that's how the black thing's to remain...your wife?"

Here she was thinking all along that everyone was happy the black fanatic was out of his hair. At least, that was the impression she got from everyone, including him. It seemed almost too good. And if it wasn't for those phone calls from the deranged woman, Floor something, she'd never know of the phantasm.

She didn't even have the slightest clue of how the woman looked. All she had was this mental picture she conjured up for herself. For all she knew the woman was pitch-black, a walking nightfall without a shadow. Not a sign of the midnight in the house, either. But one thing was sure, the nightfall was alive and breathing somewhere.

"That black thing's keeping my children from me." The almost non-audible words cut into her thoughts.

"Then why not go fetch your children from the black thing, if that's all there's to it. It's simple enough. You know where they're, and the law is on your side," she said shrewdly.

"It isn't that simple, Daisy."

"Seems simple enough to me, unless of course, there are other shadows standing in the way."

He did not comment.

Speechless and pensive they walked the rest of the way in complete silence. Later in the evening, after they'd had their dinner, she again started where she left off.

"You know you're not you anymore – you're different, you don't laugh, you hardly drink, you don't do any of the fun things you used to do. I don't know how to say it, but you aren't the same Mike."

"I'm the same person, Daisy," he smiled.

"No, you aren't," she darted another look at him. "You've this strange look in your eyes, haven't you seen it yourself? See, we don't even go out anymore."

"Oh?"

"I hope I'm wrong, but you're different. You're changing before my eyes, cloistering as we speak."

"What makes you think so?" he folded the newspaper he was reading.

There were times when he thought Daisy funny. The old girl was losing her grit, he thought, arrogance getting the better of him.

"I think you should file for divorce," she replied, staring into the half glowing tip of the cigarette she held in her hand.

"If there's anything I hate, it's lawyers, quarrels and divorce proceedings, so please let's not waste our breath."

Daisy forced a weak smile. "I'm not saying it's a wonderful process, I been through it myself, but it does help sort out one's life. And I think you should consider doing the same. This is unnatural. You need to sort things out."

"My life's been sorted out for me, Daisy, I don't have to do nothing." He tried a weak smile.

"Tell me if I'm wrong, but I think you are still entertaining some hope of the black fanatic…"

"Maybe we should stop there, Daisy," he caught her in mid sentence. "And please let's cut the coloring…It wasn't as though anyone had given us the license to color people at will."

"So you do like colored folk?" she coughed, before she realized what she said.

"To be frank with you," he took a deep breath. "The first thing the black thing used to do every time I set foot in her home country was to banish me to her mother's open backyard, until some human color crept into this terribly starved hide of mine. And if it was boring then to hear well meaning passers-by throw from over the fence: *You're turning out well, Ali! Well done! Well done*! I guess it's just as boring to hear people talk the other way round here."

"Is that so?" she arched her eyebrows.

"To answer your question, Daisy," he went on, "yes, I do have a soft spot for colored folk – I just can't help it."

293

"I think I'm beginning to understand things." She lit another cigarette with an unsteady hand.

"I'm going to bed, good night, Daisy," he said. It wasn't even 10.00 PM. They both knew why he was in such a hurry.

Once there, he picked up the book where he left it the night before. He couldn't explain it. He didn't know when or how it all began. All he was now witnessing was this urge to know. This driving anxiety to know and understand the religion that had over powered him so, and took his wife and his children away from him. Ironic but that's how it was now. The parts hadn't yet fallen into place altogether, but the mystery was slowly unfolding. The crazy wife, it seemed, was what stood between him and his God. Now that there was no crazy woman breathing down his neck he found he could reason things out, at his own pace. However, there still remained areas of darkness.

And he was angry with Islam. *Look, what it'd done to him?* And with the crazy woman, there was no describing how he felt. He had all along wondered why he didn't claim his children back. When every limb cried out for revenge, why, he wondered, did *he* humbly let it all go? He loved his children and would give anything to get them back. Yet, he held back. Even at the height of his anger and self-pity, when he could've most certainly killed her with his bare hands, something kept him from waging a war with her. Ironic, but he didn't even make a try.

Now that this urge to probe the religion that had done this to him was all over him. Yes, *investigate* that's how it all started, *investigate*, and now he was seeing her ghost in every glass he took. And now even Daisy had begun to remind him of her.

After meeting sunny Daisy, he thought, he could put the alien behind him, but sunny Daisy had now turned into a long shadow. He was afraid of hurting her feelings. She did fill a vacuum in his life, he had to admit, but as far as he was concerned, that was it. He didn't mean to use her anymore than she wanted to use him. Theirs was an open partnership. The exit doors were quite open on both sides. She wasn't obtuse and now he hoped she was getting the message.

What he didn't anticipate, however, was that Daisy was now deeply in love with him, and that she was carrying a life, his baby, and hoped for a more lasting relationship with him.

In spite of everything that was said that evening she still hoped. She was indescribably happy. Here was a man she was greatly in love with. And now she was carrying his child. If he had a dozen different living shadows frozen up in the Alps, she'd still fight for him.

Next morning, she called him from work.

"I've exciting news for you," she said. It was a Thursday and she arranged to meet him after work at one of their favorite spots. After the arrival of the drinks she raised her glass for a toast. As he began to lift his, wondering if she received that promotion, she said: "To our baby, Mike..."

"To our baby?" The glass almost fell out of his hand.

"I'm pregnant, Mike," she said, happiness radiating her face. "If you only knew how many times I tried for a baby all those years I was married to that scoundrel. And now I'm pregnant, just like that."

"I don't understand...," he mouthed, his mood clouding like an off-season wintry night. "I thought you were taking precautions."

Sporting a darkened face he now began to twitch in his seat.

"I love you, Mike, I really do," she whispered. "And I don't give a damn about that shadow of yours...what's her name?"

"Then you did it on purpose," he threw at her, hoping for the roof to fall on his head. But what did he expect? He pinched himself. Living under the same roof with a woman, what did he expect? And why was he putting the blame on her shoulders? He was shocked at himself. Putting the blame *solely* on the shoulders of the woman for something they did together was indeed first-degree hypocrisy.

How it was always the women who got hurt in this sort of situation was an irony itself. Floor was right, he thought reproaching himself with an invisible dagger. He was not only a reckless abuser, but also a hypocrite, and the disgust he felt for himself was so great that even his eyes refused to focus on the pregnant woman in front of him.

With his eyes dancing on the crystal glass before him, he fought to correct the situation, "I'm really sorry, Daisy," he fumbled. "I didn't mean to hurt you. The fool I was, I didn't exactly expect this to happen…now tell me…what did you have in mind?"

"What did *I* have in mind?" she fired at him with red-shot eyes. "What did *I* have in mind?" She pushed the seat back with the strength of an angry bear, and almost colliding with a passing waiter, stomped out of the restaurant and took off in a whirl of screeching tires.

She drove straight to his house, collected of her stuff whatever she could carry and dashed off to her girl friend's apartment. She relayed the story, verbatim, to the sympathetic ear of her girl friend.

"You were always right, Jane, they're all the same. All of them," sniffed the disheartened Daisy. "There isn't a single decent man on this continent."

"What're you going to do now? Are you going to keep the baby?" asked Jane wisely. She'd been through it herself, so many times.

"What else could I do? Kill my own baby?" said Daisy feeling like a first-degree murderess already. "As it is, I've already humiliated myself. I might as well learn to live with it."

Daisy sniffed away the remaining tears onto the steady shoulders of her friend.

Having somewhat reeled from the events of the past hour, a still shaken Mike headed home. If he weren't such a dense creature, thought the man on the rebound, if he hadn't been so stubborn and really gave ear to what his crazy wife was trying to say, none of this would've happened.

As luck would have it his entrance into the house coincided with the ringing of the phone. He picked it up with an unsteady hand. It was his mother.

"How are you, Mother?" he croaked, guilt creeping into his voice. He knew he was avoiding his mother, again.

"Your sister's on her way here," his mother said, "there's been this huge row between her and her boyfriend. Why don't you guys just hop into your car and come straight away?"

Which boyfriend? The words almost rattled off his tongue, but he caught himself by the skin go of his teeth.

"Yeah, sure and how's Dad?"

"He's good. We'll see you, then?"

"Yeah, Mother." He had neither the strength nor the will to explain anything to his mother, nor was he in any mood to play referee between his sister and her boyfriends.

A dark sullen night was already frowning on him. He cast a downhearted glance at his living room and his gaze shifted to his wine bar. The bar was Daisy's brainchild and it stood out, like a shrine, in the far corner of his living room beckoning the worshipper for a moment of instant relief. There was a time when he could have sought refuge there. Tonight was, however, not such a night.

The woods...the woods, his mind groped, and without reflection he raced to the door.

It was a full moon and the psychedelic light of the far away planet bathed him in radiance, rendering him almost shadow-less – the silhouette of his stunted shadow a humbled dwarf in the encompassing brightness.

Enfolding him in a therapeutic embrace, a breath of cool current breathed peace all around him, pacifying his downcast heart, somewhat. A slight northerly breeze nudged the leaves to a subtle rustling match—a natural symphony for the chirrups and twittering nightlife. He sauntered about some more, a needy partaker in the tranquil setting.

Not a single one of these was his own master, he thought, conviction swelling his heart with every step, *nor was his shadow his own boss – see, how it submits to the natural laws of the Lord?*

Also, marveling at the infinite shimmer above, he wondered in awe: *You've accepted your lot, haven't you? Submitting your will to the Will of the Creator Designer without fuss or fanfare, right stars?*

Only man complicated life, he threw himself at a nearby tree. *He was such a man*, he quaked against the steady trunk of the firm tree. And then, he was felling tears – the steady stem a shoulder to lean on.

With the exception of those troubled times at the hospital with his wife, he never did cry as an adult. In the intimate solitude of the noble tree, he now let the tears pour. And at that very moment, he wished he were one with his shadow, the stars and the moon and the noble trunk.

A few days later, he called Daisy's office, only to be told that Daisy had been taken ill the previous day.

"A severe case of appendicitis," Daisy's colleague told Mike. "She's in hospital."

Putting down the receiver Mike immediately rushed to the said hospital. The troublesome appendix had already been removed. Daisy forced a weak smile and gestured for Mike to sit down. Shoving the bundle of flowers he brought for Daisy on a passing nurse, Mike lowered himself onto the hospital sea.

"I'm sorry, Daisy. Very sorry," he murmured awkwardly.

"Never mind," she said putting on a brave face. "It's all right. I'm quite okay. I may lose the baby, though," she grimaced, her insides a dull dying void.

"I'm really sorry," he mouthed, hardly comprehending the pain of a woman bidding farewell to a loved life.

"No, it's not your fault. It's our way of life that's at fault," swallowed Daisy.

"How long will you be here?" He broke into statistics; as if the number of days one stayed at a certain place was of any meaning to an ebbing life.

But daisy just didn't care. For her, the time it took to extinguish the life out of her womb could hardly be measured in days, nor in seconds, or minutes or hours, or even years.

"A few more days, I suppose," she sighed. "You're relieved about the baby, aren't you, Mike?" She darted a disillusioned glance at his direction.

"I...I...I really don't know what to say, Daisy," he mumbled, the passion she felt for the dying life he helped plant in her womb an emotion beyond his reach – yet hoping against hope that he cared for the welfare of the woman carrying this dying part of him.

"I really don't know. Maybe you should concentrate on getting well," he coughed, his bottom aching from perching on the sterile hospital seat. *It wasn't the first time he found himself perched on a sterile hospital seat, and perhaps it won't be the last*, he thought, then as he thought so, his gaze flattened on his leather shoes. He bought them on Daisy's insistence in a small town in southern Europe during their wild trip to the continent. They were very expensive shoes, not only handmade but also custom-made. The type of shoes, said the proud shoemaker, that would last a lifetime, "I still wear my father's shoes," bragged the proud shoemaker, "and if you're careful and live long enough you might see your own son walking in those shoes."

Mike swallowed at the shoemaker's remarks at the back of his mind, the word *son* a sparkling flame in his yearning heart. But Mike's heart wasn't at all with this unknown part of him. His being was fully immersed in his son in Rako Island, for he nursed him through babyhood. He was his mother when his mother snapped. The nurses taught him how to measure the milk for him, and he just about managed to feed him after a bawl or two, sometimes three but never exceeding that. The soiled baby napkins he'd just dump in the wastebasket, but that was before he learnt how to make the baby burp after feeding. And the smelly diapers, he never did get used to, but he changed them, anyway. He was the one who dreamt up his name. He cuddled him to sleep. He knew he was his father because he had known him; tickling him, yet again, for another beam of that toothless grin.

Daisy's son, if the fetus were a son, was never a known son to Mike. He had neither a face nor a name. And he had never heard him babble as babies do. This son of Daisy's, if he were a son at all, was known only to Daisy.

"You're all the same," Daisy wept, barricaded with self-pity; his remoteness a barren rift in her heart. "And please don't ever come near me. Just go and don't ever show your cruel face!"

As foretold by the doctor, a six-week pregnant Daisy miscarried shortly, thereby adding to the year's statistics of aborted unwanted unknown fetuses.

Chapter Nineteen

Young Hearts

Although the island became home away from home for the children and the love and care they received there should've sufficed them, yet, the family was hard pressed to admit the fact that all was not well with the little ones.

In spite of everything there still remained in the young ones' hearts a space they just couldn't fill, hard as they tried. The specter of the absentee father remained an issue they simply couldn't ignore.

More often than not it was Nasra who refused to let go and reinforced Mohammed's memory of his father. Thoughtless remarks by adults who hardly took the children's sensitivity into account had also helped focus the children's attention on the absent father.

A knock at the door, and Nasra would order Mohammed, "Go open! It's Daddy!" And the excited Mohammed would rush to the door.

One day, a breathless Nasra crashed into the door, as she'd run all the way from the *madrasah*, "Grandma, Daddy's here. He was just here. We saw him."

"No, Nasra, you're kidding me!" Grandmother said.

"Yes, Grandma, it was him! Mohammed, say it, tell Grandma!" Nasra yelled.

"Yes! Yes!" said the little boy excitedly. "We saw him, Nasra said we saw him. He wore glasses, and he didn't see us. So we ran..."

"Did he say anything?"

"No, but it was him, I swear, it was him, and I think he got lost," Nasra was in tears, fearing Grandma wouldn't believe her. They did see someone who resembled their father. He also wore glasses, like their father. He was in a car on the other side and drove past quickly. Nasra had a glimpse of him and was sure it was her father.

"If you saw him, then he'll come here, without any doubt," said the grandmother. "He knows the address. He won't get lost, again. Now cheer up. He'll come, *inshaAllah*."

A broken hearted Fatima drew the two into her bosom.

Open discussions pertaining to their parents' problems were also now a thing of the past. When a thoughtless aunt blurted out a word about the absent father in front of the children, Fatima would quickly change the topic.

The crux of the matter was the children missed their father. And with every passing month, the little hearts yearned for the absent father.

The suspense pained Anisa as well. But placed as she was in such a delicate situation, there wasn't much she could do about it.

"I don't know what to do," she told her uncle. "Why don't I just annul the marriage here and tell the kids everything's all over? In any case, I don't think I'm married to him, in the strict sense of the word, if you know what I mean." She was in a tight spot.

"If he doesn't deny he's Muslim," her uncle would say, "how can you be so sure you aren't married to him? And if you aren't married to him how can we neutralize a marriage that doesn't exist?"

"He used Islam...all he wanted was to get married, that's it," she lamented. "And you helped him. Why did?"

"Let's face it, Anisa, you forced my hand, and I did what I thought was proper. You were marrying the man, anyway, with or without our blessings, now, don't tell me that hasn't been the case?"

She nodded. "I'd no choice, under the circumstance, but he didn't have to dupe me."

"You forced it on him, if you didn't lead him on, he needn't use Islam." Her uncle said.

The scenario was very clear to everyone. By the time Anisa decided to introduce Islam into her life, the man's emotions were already entangled with her own. Her uncle was very much aware of this glaring fact, and said so to her face for the hundredth and one time.

"Uncle!"

"Nevertheless," said her uncle. "Ali did seem promising the few times he was here. He prayed with us at the *masjid*. Willing to learn. I myself taught him how to pray, and I still have that first letter he sent me and your mother."

"So you're still siding with him? After what he did to me?"

"I think I've sided with you long enough. It isn't justifiable any longer. I suggest you write to him and get a straight answer. We can't simply terminate a marriage you think doesn't even exist. There's something called fair play, I suggest that you involve him in your plans. It's better that you depart from each other on good terms."

"What am I supposed to do? Beg him to do something? Allah knows I tried."

"Well, he has children here. And you know how they feel about him. You can't take that away. And Allah knows with what feelings they'll grow up if their parents don't act as adults."

"*Ya Rabb*! What have I got myself into?"

"Done is done," said her uncle. "We can't turn the clock back. The situation would've been simple enough hadn't there been these children. But as things are, it's indeed a very sticky situation. And then there is the fact of his conversion to Islam. If we don't treat him well, he might even end up renouncing Islam altogether, I see that hasn't ever occurred to you."

"If I knew what I know today!"

"Be sensible Anisa. Write to the man. He's human. You'd been away for two whole years. You left him without telling him anything. To expect him to correct your mistakes for you isn't fair in the least. He met what he thought was an exotic girl without a single care in the world, in fact, you gave him all the wrong signals. How was he to know that he was falling into a world that he wasn't prepared in the least?"

"I know I made mistakes, my life has been nothing but a series of blunders, only Allah knows how I've suffered from my deeds," she groaned. "But why is it that everyone's getting pleasure from my pain?"

"So Anisa made mistakes? Should he be punished for Anisa's blunders?" Her uncle stated. "Anisa, everyone takes only what he sows. To you what you sow, and to Ali what he sows. Show a sense of responsibility, Anisa. Ali's a son of Adam too, and he deserves fair treatment."

"What about Islam?"

"No one can force Islam. The Messenger of Allah couldn't convince his own dear uncles. Learn from that fact."

"He's my children's father. What if his disbelief rubbed on them?"

"That's kind of late, don't you think?"

"Am so confused, I don't know what to do."

"Anisa, faith doesn't come cheap. You have to want it," said her uncle. "Even at the deathbed of his most beloved uncle, Abu Talib, the holy Prophet couldn't save the hardened soul of his uncle from the justice of God. Anisa, what the holy Prophet failed to do, you can't do. Anymore than you can triumph where the church failed."

"I'm just trying to help my children."

"Faith's an internal matter."

"As if I didn't know!"

"There's also something called compassion," her uncle went on, "no matter what you've done or not done in ignorance or rebellion, at this very moment your Creator recognizes and is appreciative of the least of efforts on your part, in the correction of those mistakes. And Allah is most forgiving, Anisa."

Ya Allah! she sighed again.

"Nothing passes by the Lord," her uncle said softly. "He saw you on the wrong track. And right now He's aware of your plight. Anisa, if your blunders didn't involve others, the situation wouldn't have been so tangled. You owe it to your children, yourself and this man whom you've forced into an area he didn't choose for himself."

Ya Rabb!

Right now, your health's as sound as could be. Cut the rope short. Write to the man and get a straight answer. He's your children's father. You've a voice and a brain. Use them."

"But how?"

"Trust in Allah, He has given you speech. Use that faculty. Allah is very much aware of your situation. Show that you trust Him to be the solver of your human problems. No one is above error. State your side of the story."

"What can I do now that I hadn't tried already?"

"Open the communication line. Start a dialogue."

"Just like that?"

"You've nothing to lose. He has children here, and he's very much aware of it."

"You haven't lived with the man"

"Then let's get to know him."

Chapter Twenty

The Call

Nor can a bearer of burdens bear another's burden.
If one heavily laden should call another to (bear) his load
Not the least portion of it can be carried (by the other),
Even though he be nearly related.
(Qur'an: 35:18)

Two years and thirty one days. Still no sign of her. He had a month's leave coming in two weeks. Should he go there, enlist the American Embassy's help and kidnap his own children? The woman had no sense and not an ounce of self-respect. She was past redemption. He had long toyed with the idea of writing to the erratic woman. However, no word of his could simply match the idiocy of her behavior. It was an idiocy that went beyond forgiveness. And there was no use wasting one's words on such a silly head.

But what if he, for a moment, tried to pretend to forget the enormity of her idiocy, went to the primitive place in good faith and tried to knock some sense into her silly head? Although she deserved dirt and mud, the woman was far-gone and to stoop to her level would be double murder. She'd already murdered him with her idiocy.

But, what if all sense and morality failed? Then he'd just have to stoop to her level and murder himself by paying her back in kind: The abduction of his own children loomed large in the horizon.

If so, how was he to go about it? How was he to locate his own children in that sandy enclave, without being spotted by one or other of those nosy aunts of hers? The whole community, it seemed, were either an uncle or an aunt. Everyone n the primitive place was either a grandmother or a grandfather to his own American children. He'd just have to enlist the American authorities there to pose as one of those myriads of grannies and seize the children at the candy store.

The least the US government could now do for him was to get his children back. Allowing an alien to carry away two American citizens through the customs and under the noses of the security officers and the FBI was a matter of national debate, and a security debacle at the international level. The least the people he voted for could now do was to restore the nation's lost credibility, for the land would never be the same if aliens were to be allowed to abduct nationals, under the noses of the security and the FBI.

What if the children failed to recognized their own dad. Would they rush to him? Or would they run away from him?

Exactly three days, prior to his departure to Rako Island, among the heap of junk mail, there appeared a bulky envelope.

Rushing back to the kitchen table he ripped the envelope open. The sight of two recent snapshots of his two children brought sweat to the brows of the father. Nasra's toothless grin and Mohammed's puzzled face drove a wedge in the heart of the father. They looked healthy enough. Sweat rushing down his spine; he now unfolded the letter. There were thirteen pages of his erratic wife's untidy handwriting.

Assalamu 'alaikum, Ali, began the kidnaper.

We're all doing well, and are in the best of health, alhamdulillah. I really don't know where to start or with what to begin. No matter, what conclusions you might've reached about me, Ali, I still care about you. A day doesn't pass that I don't pray for you.

But I'd be lying if I said I'm the same person you married some seven years ago. I can't even pretend to be so. A change over which I had no control has taken root at the deepest part of my heart. You were there and saw everything that had happened.

Ali, I came face to face with death, and if I told you it was a pleasant surprise, I'd only be pulling your leg. It was at this juncture of my life that I was forced, literally, forced by the grace of Allah to see and be a witness to the fragility of life, and how ill equipped I was should a final exist occur to the wretched soul that was mine. It was then that I was made to see how little I knew who I really was and what I stood for.

Born to honest believing parents, I was inculcated from a young age to be an honest person. Not that I remember ever disbelieving in my Creator, but I did not follow His light. I rebelled and rebelled against the light I knew personally was there, and chose to walk in darkness. I acted against my own nature and became my own oppressor.

I've to be honest with you, Ali, my downward slip did not start with you. The slippery descent began long before our lives crossed. I

317

*very much doubt our paths would've ever crossed had I heeded my
mother's last words to me before my departure form Rako Island.*

*Having betrayed my identity I became like those of whom Allah
says in the Qur'an: 'They see but see not, and hear but hear not'.
Such was the dismal outcome of my unnatural way of life that I almost
drowned myself. You were there; I'm not called 'the crazy woman' for
nothing.*

*This world belongs to one God. The God, Allah. There's no other
Reality. This one God is our common destination. No matter how we
choose to travel, our destination will be the same. Islam is the way to
this destination. You're not above the law. No one is. Ali, the sleek
skyscrapers which I took for real in my simpleton days will one day
become dust and rubble, and there will come a time in one's life when
between one and God there remains not a speck of self-deceit, nor a
shred of doubt as to where real sovereignty lies.*

*I'm not here trying to preach to you, Ali, what I'm trying to say is
that I just want to be myself. That's all I want in life, to be who I'm
and be what the Creator has intended for me—a willing servant—for*

318

it's only in that state that I'll ever be fulfilled. Now that I know what I'm doing, I find it hard, indeed, impossible, to take another turn.

We have two children together. Their care, livelihood and progress in life depend on both of us. Even if we end up flinging container-full of mud and dirt at one another, we'd still want a decent treatment for our flesh and blood. I'm grateful for your material support, Ali. But just as they'd die from lack of bodily sustenance, so too would our children perish from the malnutrition of the spirit; numerous civilizations had perished from that disastrous need.

Since the kind of history we had at school isn't up to mark on the subject of these woeful annihilations affecting planet earth, let me please draw your attention to the copy of the translation of the Qur'an I used to place on your side of the bed. Ali, the Holy Book of the outlandish Muslims happens to be the only untainted spiritual reference book available on the world market, today.

Please open it and take a hard look at the dismal endings of those who were caught in the act of playing God. Take a peek at the dismal fate of Pharaoh and the peoples of 'Ad and Thamud. Then return your gaze to the media and the-powers-that-be.

319

Don't get mad, take a deep breath, Ali, open the book and take a close look at the useful termination of the perverts who normalized their base inclinations and trashed the warning of the prophet Lut. Then return your gaze to the popular culture of your untamed civilization. Indeed, it pays, as the Creator would've us do, 'to travel the earth and see the end of those who rejected faith'.

Needless to say, the Creator intended only one way for these children of ours. If we, their parents do not show this one-way to them, who will?

Why didn't I think about that before is a dilemma as old as them. Tossing and turning the question in my foolish head has nowadays become a big yawn to me too.

Forget the liberal views of your society, Ali. They simply don't cut. Coming down to the nitty-gritty, when you find your tiny earthly feet on the other side of the fence, unprepared and totally naked – except for a sack-full of sins, you want to climb back fast and do everything right. Believe me, I'm speaking from experience. In the eyes of God the grateful and the ungrateful are not equal.

You know all about my regrets, Ali. I've nothing new to add to them. As it is, we are ourselves two living witnesses to the impracticability of lumping two opposing directions of life together. For the sake of harmony and peace of mind for all concerned, in any one given situation, a common front is inevitable, or chaos becomes the lot of all.

Granted, in my ignorance and simple mindedness, I did try to force down your throat an alien culture. Actually, I thought I was doing us, and more so, you, my ignorant husband, a great favor by trying to change you into something you weren't cut out for in the first place.

But as I was at one time forced to admit to the senselessness of my own digression from the path I knew was straight, so too am I forced to acknowledge today the futility of trying to modify one who isn't ready for real alteration.

Ali, if change doesn't come from within, no amount of outside coercion will do the job. In other words, your poor wife only labored in vain. That's why as of today and throughout the remainder of this letter, I'll be calling you with your real names, Mike Peterson, and not the despised label you incurred at the mosque. There's more to faith than a mere tag, Mike.

You never did pretend to like those funny names. The way you recoiled every time I shamed you in public and in front of your peers, by calling you by these funny names didn't at all escape the confused mind that was mine. None of it was ever your fault, as you could hardly be expected to understand the purport and the message of what these names convey.

Mike, if you failed to see the beauty of these names with your own civilized eyes and heart, how could I make you see that beauty through my own alien primitive eyes? Such an endeavor was indeed the highest tip of foolishness itself. Your poor wife only labored in vain. How you submissively came upon our son's name will have to remain a mystery, at least for now.

This laboring in vain on the part of your primitive wife was hardly the right medicine. Let there be no compulsion in religion, truth stands out clear from error. The destination is well known to all. The criteria to judge the right from the wrong, we've all got for free. It's up to each and every one of us to abuse or utilize that gift. 'No bearer of burdens can bear the burdens of another', says Allah. The last Messenger of Allah has left no stone unturned to bring this pure teachings home to mankind, and it's by following him that we'll find success.

If there's anything I hate in this world, it's to cause you further confusion, embarrassment or misery. For as my uncle says: I first noosed you, then led you on and on until retraction of steps became humanly impossible. And now that we're permanently entangled with one another, it's a no win situation.

I'm not here making excuses for leaving you the way I did. I was desperate, for there came a time in our troubled lives when the best medicine became tail-and-flight or I'd surely have crushed under the mighty weight.

I see I'm on the eleventh page of what I thought would be a short missive, breaking the boggy stalemate of the past two years. Even after I've poured out all my heart, I find I'm still at a loss as to how to resurface from this boggy mess and come to a decent place of rest.

The word 'sacrifice' comes to mind but I'm in no position to shout directives from this primitive soil as to what is to be sacrificed and who is to shoulder this great deed. I've no ready answers.

All I know is your children are a part of you. They need you, but they also need true guidance, and I can't see you providing that.

Mike, if you are unable to live up to the ideals of Islam, the least you can do for your children (and that's where personal sacrifice comes in) is to let them be.

Please see my humble letter for what it is: An incentive to break the deadly standoff and an opening to what I hope to be a long intelligent dialogue, before drastic ideas materialize into hasty actions.

Before I start on the fourteenth page, let me leave you in peace and pray to Allah to open your heart to the Truth. You owe it to yourself. Aameen.

Chapter Twenty-One

Shifting Sand

It was a Friday evening. Anisa and her family were all sitting out at the terrace – savoring the cool night under the open sky, when suddenly, from the farthest corner of the courtyard, Mohammed's shrill call fractured the peace.

"Bastard! Bastard! Come and catch me!"

Nasra was on the other side and was busy playing with her dolls, and had ears only for them.

All eyes turned on the little boy. None of the people sitting there had yet heard the word under this part of the sky. They exchanged glances of anxiety.

Anisa's uncle jumped in his seat, "What did you say just now, Mohammed?"

"Bastard! Bastard! Come and catch me!" repeated the little boy in a singsong.

"Who taught you this?"

"Nafisa," said Mohammed.

Nafisa was Nasra and Mohammed's playmate. Her family was just two houses away and happened to be the only Muslim family on their row. Nafisa was slightly older than Nasra.

No one could explain it, but Nafisa's mother, Leila, had always this thing against Anisa. However, Anisa's family downplayed the hostility and in spite of the naked dislike, the family was always there for the Muslim neighbor, helping her now and then.

Leila was about Anisa's age. And if the two women happened to walk on the same side of the street, Anisa would retrace her steps and take another route—such was her fear of the woman's tongue.

The last time she said salaam to the woman, Leila laughed and gushed a remark that had Anisa weep for days. "I saw him with my own eyes," said Leila with a smile, "and I haven't noticed any resemblance between him and his children!"

At first Anisa didn't catch what the woman was hinting at. But as she related the episode to her cousin, Nora, the purport hit her where it hurt the most.

"So the woman's insinuating that the children weren't even Mike's?" Anisa broke into hysterics and for days her hands became claws, just waiting and hoping for a chance to bounce on the hurtful woman. However, her mother's sanity prevailed and Anisa thought it best not to add injury to insult.

Avoiding her wasn't easy, either, since the woman treated herself as part of the family.

Immediately she heard the name Nafisa from the boy's mouth, Anisa slowly extricated herself from the crowd and went into the bedroom she shared with her kids. She perched on the edge of the bed and breathed her injury away.

Her mother then entered after her.

"So here's where you've been hiding?" she said as she treaded slowly towards the bed, bracing for a hysterical Anisa.

"Yes, Mother," said Anisa, catching her reflexive hands in mid-air. Her eyes were dry as a rock on an arid cliff—*no tears to wipe off!* *She must have run out of pain,* she thought glumly. Her hands returned to her like two old seared hides, useless; *no more tears, hands*, she sighed dryly, *no more stock*. This woman's pain had dried on the banks of Rako Island.

"I hope you're not taking the child's words to heart," her mother advanced. "It's probably something she picked from the others, you know, other kids."

"Like who, for instance?" Anisa asked. If Anisa's pain had dried on the banks of Rako Island, her mother's suffering was yet too deeply buried to enjoy even a whiff of air.

"Actually," said her mother, "there're some ill behaved boys down the lane; everyone knows."

"I know there's only one person in this lane who's capable of such behavior," said Anisa.

"Suspicion is a sin, Anisa, now don't start it. I'll speak to the kid tomorrow and tell her not to use such foul language."

"And who's going to teach the mother not to impart such wicked behavior to her young?"

Nora came in at this point.

"I know it's her," said Anisa's cousin. "I was going to shut her mouth for her, but knowing Aunt Fatima I had to swallow my words, but I'd no idea she'd do such a thing to her own child."

"This one-way pretense in the name of good neighborliness isn't helping anyone," said Anisa. "High time I added to the woman's vocabulary. I bet her dictionary's in dire need of good words!"

"No! There'll be no such thing," jumped Anisa's mother. "Out of the question. You're not going anywhere near the neighbor. She's not only our neighbor; she's also a Muslim woman. I'll talk to her gently. We don't want any hostility. Our neighbors deserve more than our hostility. And if the neighbor happens to be Muslim, we have double duty. Is that understood?"

"All right, all right. Understood," vaporized Nora. "I wouldn't mind some fruitful action, though. It's long overdue. This dilly-dallying with the Muslim villain won't get us anywhere. Mind you, the woman's unsound. If she's such a limping sister, why not show her *her* limp? After all, what're friends for?"

"She's our neighbor."

"Neighbor or no neighbor the woman needs some telling," said Nora. In fact, I wouldn't mind a little chat with the limping sister. It might make her stand upright a bit." Nora stopped.

"Nora! Leave this to me. And not a word to anyone." If there was anything Fatima hated it was the spoiling of people's names.

"This one's dynamite! She deserves more than the spoiling of name. She needs some nice medicine to apply to her limp, believe me!" said Nora who had the added burden of helping her as well, all in the name of good neighborliness and Islamic brotherhood! Only a saint could succeed in belonging to such a one-sided convention!

"And I always thought brotherhood was to be a two way traffic— did I miss something, Aunt?"

"This is a momentary lapse," Anisa pressed her lips, "and shouldn't be confused with the larger picture."

No sooner was Fatima out of the bedroom, than Nora broke into laughter. "I'll bet Aunt's going to dish out a nice plate of *halawa* before she pays her dues to the Muslim villain! By the way, I think we've run out of sugar!"

"Then, we might as well rush to the store and fetch some, so that our distinguished Muslim neighbor could get on with her life!"

The following morning, a plate of *halawa* balanced in her hand, Anisa's mother walked over to the Muslim neighbor's house.

Leila greeted her with an "*Assalamu alaikum*, Aunt Fatima, do come in and relieve yourself of this heavy weight in the hand," she gushed.

"*Wa'alaikuma salaam*, Leila, how have you been doing?" Fatima replied with caution.

"*Alhamduilillah...*,but the baby's been crying all night. I'm rushing him to the clinic, is Nora around, by any chance? I need someone here for Nafisa when she comes back from school."

"But of course." The ever-ready Fatima offered, forgetting her errand, "I'll send her here straight away."

The two women prattled on thus for a while. Fatima at last found the tongue to say what she came to say.

"Leila dear," she cleared her throat, "what's this new word the kids are using lately?"

"What new word?" Leila almost dropped the baby she was rocking on her knees.

"You mean you haven't heard the word?" Fatima asked.

"Your own grandchildren use the word. Why are you here blaming mine? *Ya Allah*! Aunt Fatima! You haven't been yourself since that daughter of yours came back to the island! *Ya Allah*! What's happening to the neighborhood and to old Aunt Fatima?"

"Leila dear," Fatima said firmly, "first of all let's seek refuge with Allah from the accursed *Shaitan*"

"*Auzubillah*!" spat the younger woman as though she were shooing away a fly.

"*Shaitan*," said Fatima, "is an enemy of good neighborhoods. *Shaitan* is indeed an enemy of mankind. We don't want to please him. Our enemy is pleased when we hearken to him, Leila. He sees us although we can't see him. Is it our aim to please this enemy of Allah, Leila?"

"*La Ilaha Ila Allah*!" Leila exclaimed. "I seek refuge with Allah from the accursed *Shaitan*. But what's come over you, Aunt Fatima? Why are you acting so strangely?"

"Nothing's the matter with me, Daughter. I came here to see if we could, together as Muslims and neighbors, seek refuge with Allah from the accursed *Shaitan*. And then try to expunge this unnecessary word from the neighborhood. We're one community, Leila. And it's only one word. One simple word. Is that too much to ask?"

"Yes, it's indeed one tiny word," the younger woman agreed. "But why are we making so much fuss about this one tiny word? I mean why should we bother at all if this tiny word doesn't apply to us?"

"This tiny word, Leila, brings to mind a saying related from our beloved prophet."

The younger woman cocked her ears. "And what does the Messenger of Allah say?"

"He has said," Fatima said, "he who truly believes in Allah and the Last Day should speak good or keep silent."

"'He who truly believes in Allah and the Last Day should speak good or keep silent.' It's beautiful, but what's the connection?"

"The connection is silence is preferable to even one tiny word if that one tiny word's unnecessary, which brings to mind another saying of our beloved prophet."

"And what's that?"

"Believers are like the parts of a building to one another – each part supporting the others."

"Yes, I know Aunt Fatima," Leila sighed. "You're absolutely right. Standing together is a need the believers can evade at their own risk."

"Exactly!"

"The question is how are we to eradicate this hurtful word from the neighborhood so we Muslims could stand together?" Leila wondered.

"Leila dear, I'll leave that to you, *inshaAllah*," said Fatima, overcome by Leila's quick change of heart. *So that was all it needed?* She praised Allah.

The two women rambled on some more about this and that, but this time in a totally different vein.

Miracle of miracles the said word was soon expunged from the neighborhood. For lack of toppings from Nafisa, Mohammed soon forgot all about it. Somehow, Nasra never caught it in the first place. And soon after, the neighborhood environment began to lighten up.

"Mother, I had no idea you were such a seasoned diplomat, *MashaAllah!* Your *halawa* has paid off, finally!" Anisa said after being greeted by a waving Leila from the end of the lane, three times in a single week!

"It wasn't the *halawa*, it was the wise words of our holy Prophet that did it, and praise be to Allah!"

While Anisa savored the new friendly air, Mike's explosive reply with which he hoped to blow up into pieces the silly kidnapper, was now shooting its nose into the amiable environment. The explosive had at last landed in the hands of the kidnapper.

There were only three tiny pages. The man had no imagination, none whatsoever. No date. No dear Anisa. Not even a hello and certainly no other pleasantries. The first line started right at the top of the page where the date would've been, had she been the writer.

I'll bet, he wrote, *the word heartless doesn't figure in the very long list of my dear wife's inherent traits. Why is it that the very people who cry change and mercy are always the least changeable and the least merciful? And why is it that when these very people choose to metamorphose, they, the criers of change and mercy, mutate into even worse dispositions? What an irony! What a joke!*

The busybody you are, making those new discoveries of the infinite flaws in the character (although these were always visible to everyone else other than the owner herself), I guess you can hardly be expected to have eyes or ears for other people's needs, including those of your own flesh and blood.

And here, let's not waste our breath on what the term sacrifice really entails. Suffice it to say that such a term means just one thing.

The busybody you are, I very much suspect you already know in that warped brain of yours who and what's to be sacrificed. I would actually pretend to be more game and it would perhaps make me feel less wary if you didn't mince words and told me in a straight language to dish out to you a beautifully wrapped gift of my own head, the only head I have got.

I know it isn't the done thing. No wife in her right mind (let's for a moment assume that this woman's in her right mind) would ask her own husband to sever his head off and dish it out to her. But under the circumstance of such a bizarre request, I would at least know where I stood in the reality of things.

Right now I'm at a loss as to what I'm asked to do. Such is the lack of intelligence on my part that I don't even know how to refer to myself anymore.

Identity crisis comes to mind: am I a divorced man or am I the cleverly noosed idiot who allowed himself to be burglarized in broad daylight?

On the question of my confused wayward western soul, me thinks, the answer to the question can be safely quoted straight out of the pages of my brilliant wife's long-winded sermon. Quote: No bearer of burdens can bear the burdens of another: unquote.

As it is, my brilliant wife's already loaded. Adding more weight to the already laden soul would be heartless. My wayward souls' help, me thinks, must come from less loaded quarters. It's only fair: No bearer of burdens can bear the burdens of another! I love it. For once, my wife seems to be getting the message, straight and pure. And as she admitted, hers was indeed a labor in vain!

Safi Abdi

Finally, the next time she puts into her brilliant head to steer aright the drifting western soul that I am, I suggest that she seeks help with her communication skills.

In the meantime, let her be forewarned, hers truly is at this very moment mapping out a strategy of abduction. So let her be prepared for the Rescue Mission! Amen!

Having packaged and posted the explosive, a somewhat calmer Mike cancelled his planned trip to Rako Island.

To his family and colleagues' mortification, he deferred his vacation to an unspecified date in the future. So secretive and off limits had he become of late that the only living being who knew of exactly where Mike was heading for his vacation was the travel agency who did his itinerary. All the others knew was that the morose Mike had a month's leave. And was deserving of some fun.

If fact, his mother would rather her boy spent time in a more congenial environment than the four walls of his cheerless home. The last time she sprang a visit on him she came upon Mike hacking away at the bar, which Daisy had so lovingly fitted, and his mother stayed long enough to see the whole place converted into a bookshelf!

His mother couldn't even remember when he last paid a proper visit to them and the visits, when they came, were no longer done with spontaneity.

Not that he minded paying his old parents a visit, but, now that his sister Charlotte had moved house nearby the parents, seeing the parents also meant suffering one or other of his sister's bed-friends.

The last favorite boyfriend and his two nephews' latest step-dad, was a mean spirited fellow. Mike's nephews hated the imposter, at first sight. He too hated him, at first sight. The imposter was two meters high and had a quarter of a meter's hair that dangled in a pony-tail between his rather broad shoulders; giving the man the look of a horse standing on its hind hoofs.

He was a favorite *son-in-law* of Mike's parents, the clown of their golf dinners, the roaster of their Sunday barbecues, and the cracker of archaic party jokes. Mike's sister Charlotte doted on him. And it seemed as though no one took note of the baby earrings that got stuck in the impostor's giant ears.

And as if all the negative qualities of his character weren't enough to nail him for life, the scamp was also a racist – a reckless, spineless racist – his favorite butts of ridicule were the Arabs, the Blacks, and the Colored, in that order. Why he chose that order was in itself a riddle to Mike.

And during the occasions Mike suffered the man's insults, he couldn't help but wonder if these slurs weren't specifically tailored for his consumption? After all, wasn't Mike the proud father of colored kids?

While these slurry party jokes upped everyone else's ego, an incensed Mike would hurl belligerent looks at the man, from a safe distance.

Mike was deeply sorry for his nephews. His sister had no taste, exposing her two children to this childish giant of a man, with the tiniest of baby earrings stuck to his giant ears.

While Mike worried himself sick over the bad influence this man had on his nephews, his family were equally troubled over the older son's melancholic demeanor.

"Since Daisy's miscarriage," the anxious mother confided in her best friend, Daisy's mother, "Mike's turned totally weird. It's as if he's in this dark world."

"There's nothing like an aborted pregnancy," returned Daisy's mother. "Only God knows if Daisy will ever conceive again. Mike has at least these other children…"

"You mustn't say that, Maggie," Mike's mother said. "Believe me, Daisy's child could've been more dear to me than some alien's progeny…I'm their grandmother…I should perhaps not say such things. But still, there's nothing like one's own kind; I mean, certain things just don't add up."

"I know what you mean."

"I simply don't have the words to describe the kind of ordeal we've all been through, all these ears. A total stranger in our midst; for a while we simply stopped breathing."

"Daisy' no longer Daisy." Daisy's mother whispered.

"Talk about gloom!"

"The only thing that's left is the fight for her sanity."

"Talk about sanity!"

"These late nights are taking their toll on her."

"He's become an affirmed monk! Squatting in that cheerless home! A few lively nights won't harm that boy!"

"These tranquilizers she's been popping, there's no breaking the vicious circle!"

"I sometimes wonder if he really misses the alien's children?"

Chapter Twenty-Two

Praying at the Beach

I am as My servant thinks I am. I am with him when he makes mention of Me. If he makes mention of Me to himself, I make mention of him to Myself; and if he makes mention of Me in an assembly, I make mention of him in an assembly better than it. And if he draws near to Me a hand's span, I draw near to him an arm's length; and if he draws near to Me an arm's length, I draw to him a fathom's length. And if he comes to Me walking, I go to him at speed.

(Hadith Qudsi)

Anisa did not know how many times she had read Mike's letter. Still clutching the ball of fire in her hand she returned to the balcony where the rest of the family still sat, eagerly waiting for news.

"He's on his way," she breathed, holding up the letter for evidence. "This is no less than a warning."

She surrendered the letter to her uncle then added, "The man's out of his mind. No self respecting person pens down such nonsense. This is the kind of scenario I'd been warning you of. Now check it out for yourself."

She was sizzling hot, caught in a scorching whirlwind, conjuring up the kind of design the man was mapping out at that moment. A 'rescue mission' he wrote. Mike never did have a good word for the FBI. So they were the last people he would entrust with his precious mission. She was lost in thought, trying to figure out how best he could carry out his precious rescue mission. *Come to think of it, the Mossad would do this for free*, she thought glumly. Perhaps the Zionist army was backing him? *Attacking Muslim children wasn't exactly an annoying sport for this army,* she reminded herself.

"Let her be forewarned," Omar read out the last sentence, "hers truly is at this very moment mapping out a strategy of abduction! Let her be prepared for the rescue mission!"

Averting his gaze from Anisa, he said, "You want my opinion, Anisa?"

"It's about time," she sighed.

"We're in business, Anisa, let's keep up the dialogue." He passed the letter over to Nora. "I need a second opinion, though."

After a minute or two, Nora had also arranged her face in a mirthless posture.

"He is right," she shook her head, "I mean, about the communication skills. We all need some help there, don't we? Yeah, yeah, Ali is right."

Sensing the whimsical looks on their faces, Anisa looked from one to the other. She snatched the papers from Nora, "I knew it! I knew it!" she boiled. "As the saying goes, give the fool a rope to hang himself! If I kept my peace, none of this rubbish would've been heaped on my head! Indeed, a strategy of abduction!"

A convoy of Zionist tanks rumbled through Anisa's mind and she could see it happen in broad daylight: *the baby snatch!*

"I still believe this to be a dialogue, say, some sort of a dialogue, the beginning of something," Omar said.

"I did ask for an intelligent dialogue. This is, however an insult and a warning of a forthcoming event!"

"*Allahu Akbar!*" her mother said. "Seek refuge with Allah from the accursed *Shaitan*! We need some semblance of sense here."

"A strategy of abduction, indeed!" she sighed.

"If the man was serious about the abduction," her mother said sensibly, "he wouldn't be advertising it. He's not a child, you know."

"He's an American, and an American would do just that!" she seethed. "This is their way of catching the enemy off guard!"

"This doesn't make sense," her mother replied, "Ali may not be an enlightened Muslim but I very much doubt he's that childish."

"Whoever said he was a Muslim, let alone an enlightened one! And as for being a child, well, well, this man's the biggest child of all. His body may have expanded, but I very much doubt his brain has passed the toddler stage! Huh! That inflated child's no Muslim!"

"Well, you said it, and we took your word for it!" Fatima fired at her daughter.

"High time my children and I left this neighborhood," she said, bolting out the door. "It just isn't the right place for us!"

Still muttering the phrase 'rescue mission' under her breath, she stormed into the *madrasah* and bolted out in the same speed, with the startled children in tow.

She didn't know where she was taking the children at this time of day. Hand in hand, mother and children loafed around the city. Seeing their mother's condition, neither Mohammed nor Nasra opened their mouths. It was late afternoon. The sun was still baking hot and as the three walked and walked, the sweat trickling down their backs, not a word was uttered.

However, as they reached the beach and the cool breeze from the ocean took some of the heat off the clammy bodies, Mohammed could no longer hold his tongue.

Taking in the scene of roasting human flesh at the strand, he said, "Mommy, what're they doing here?"

Before the mother could respond, Nasra said, "They're not doing anything, silly, they are on holiday."

"But what're they lying there for? And where do they always leave their clothes?"

"They want to bake until brown, boy!" said Nasra. "But they'll never ever look like Mommy even if they grilled to the bone and laid there all their lives."

"Nasra!" The mother gasped.

"I swear," the little girl said, "that's what Aunt Leila said. It wasn't me who said it."

"Aunt Leila?" Anisa's brows shot up and lay suspended in mid forehead.

"Because they're naked," Mohammed said after some reflection, "that's why they can not look like Mommy. I look different when I'm naked too! When I have clothes on I look respectable. That's normal."

Lost between the children's conversation, and for want of support Anisa threw her body onto the soft sand of the beach. Copying his mother, Mohammed tossed his tiny body alongside hers.

"If Daddy was here," he said, putting his hands behind the back of his head, "would he be lying there too in one of those tiny *tiny* under pants? I wish he were here though, with or without clothes, I don't mind, really."

"My daddy's not here, either," the mother said. "And you haven't seen me complaining."

"All the children I know," Nasra said clasping her hands behind her head and squinting at the still bright sky, "all the children I know," she repeated, "have fathers, except for Nasra and Mohammed."

"What about Adam?" asked Mohammed. "You saw how they took away his father in a box, not even telling the boy where they were taking him. All the grown ups did was cry like babies and take Adam's father away."

"A silly boy like you who knows only how to talk! How many times do I have to tell you that the old man happened to be dead when they took him away? And that Adam is an orphan, just like our mother. We are not orphans, Mohammed!"

"But Adam saw his father go away, I haven't, and I'm still waiting! And now I'm suddenly so very thirsty. Mommy, can I have some ice cream, please?"

Anisa blinked away a long torturous tear.

"Children, I'm very sorry. I don't have any money on me. I left my purse at home." She wiped the lone tear with the back of her hand.

"Hey, children," she added after a short pause, "I've good news for you, your father is alive."

"Then why isn't he coming? Why can't he come, let's say, tomorrow?" Nasra suggested.

349

"But my dears, your father is so far away. He just can't make it to tomorrow, that much we must understand…"

"He doesn't have to walk, he can ride that huge white plane in the sky…Mommy, let's go home now."

"We'll go, but first, can you promise me something?"

"Yes?"

"Don't ever talk to anyone about your father, not even to Aunt Leila, okay?"

"Then let him come! If he comes, we stop talking, and start playing like we used to do…" Nasra said.

"Grandfather said Mom and Dad need to talk, you know, real talk, your father and your mother, they never thought things through, they just got married."

"What's that? And why this talk all over sudden? You just said everyone should stop talking, can't he just come, must you talk as well?"

"Of course, he can come. I can't prevent that, now can I?" The mother said, looking her daughter in the eye. "But it's best that Dad and Mom write to each other first. This is supposed to give them chance to know each other better."

"But we know him." Nasra said sharply, giving her mother a strange look, "and I think you know him too. And now why everyone's pretending so suddenly…Mom doesn't know Daddy and Daddy doesn't know Mommy, what's going on?"

"I think I know what's going on," the little girl replied to her own question.

"And what is it that you know that I don't?" The mother asked in a hushed voice.

"You were kidding when you said to Daddy: 'I love you, I love you', and I know that's what some people say when they want to get married," Nasra said, digging her hands in the sand, "but then, you left him, just kidding, weren't you?"

"Nasra! That's not a nice thing to say!"

"But Daddy is not a bad person, so why did we leave him?"

"My dear girl, all I'm saying is your dad is in need of something and he doesn't know it. I never said he was bad. It's just that there is this thing missing from his life and that's why we can't be with him when *he isn't so hundred percent*...do you know what I'm saying?"

"If you know what's missing why don't you help him find it?" asked Nasra though she didn't quite understand what it was that was missing. "He lost his glasses and isn't able to see us anymore?" The little girl wondered. "Isn't that why he isn't so hundred percent anymore?"

"Tsk...Tsk...Tsk..." the mother said. "Oh, how I wish it were so! No dear, you guys got me wrong. There's more things missing in this man than meets the eye, and the only one who can help this man find himself is the Almighty Allah. So if you'd help me we will ask Allah to come to our help. Now say this prayer after me."

"Okay!" The children chorused.

"Repeat after me: Please Allah, make Daddy listen," the mother prayed.

"Repeat after me: Please Allah, make Daddy listen," the children prayed.

"Don't say 'repeat after me'!" their mother screamed. "Just say, please Allah, make Daddy listen."

"Please Allah make Daddy listen."

"Say: Please Allah accept Daddy," the mother prayed.

"Say: Please Allah accept Daddy," repeated the children.

"You kids are spoiling the prayer!" she screamed at them.

"It's Mohammed. Mohammed can not pray!"

"No, it's not Mohammed. Mohammed wants cold drink!" The little boy began to wail.

Ashamed of herself and cursing Aunt Leila in her heart, Anisa buried her feet in the soft sand.

"I'm sorry, please accept my humble apology. This is not exactly a place of prayer. Maybe we should go now and get that ice-cream, eh?"

"Are we done with the prayer?" Nasra asked.

"Yes, that's enough for today," she said in a lighter note, and then they all got up to shake the sand off their clothes.

After a few minutes of walking and reflection, Nasra said, "Mommy?"

"Yes, dear?"

"If I pray to Allah alone every day, will Daddy listen to Allah?"

"*InshaAllah*, Allah is able to do all things," Anisa replied, her mind in a trauma over the mental drafting of a response to Mike's letter.

Mike's questions before their marriage at the mosque now came back to her.

"If Islam's peace, why isn't there peace in the Muslim world?" he asked.

"But only those who truly live their lives in accordance with Islam will get that peace. You have to live within the peaceful way of Islam to get that peace, Mike," she would say. But did she know what she was talking about? She now wondered. And the answer she got now was: *No.* Anisa might have carried a Muslim name but the way she chose for herself was anything but the way of peace. *Yet she talked peace!*

Mohammed's small voice broke into her dilemma.

"Mommy, I really want to pray to Allah. I promise not to spoil the prayer again."

"Me too," the mother whispered.

"Then, we all pray, after we've all cooled down with cold water and ice-cream," Nasra said brightening up.

"*InshaAllah*," the mother sighed.

All the time the children and their mother were having this talk, Omar and Fatima were in a tug-of-war of their own.

"Poor child!" Fatima sighed. "We've all turned our backs on her. Now she has no one to turn to. Anisa is all alone."

"As long as you call this mother of two child, mark my words, Fatima, Anisa will forever be the child. My niece's got no sense of humor. And certainly doesn't see things from the lighter side! It's *she* that she should blame! Not him!"

"*Allahu Akhar*! Omar, what's so humorous about the specter of child abduction?"

"If I know Anisa she probably jotted down whatever came to her head. What's the man supposed to do? Smile back after two years of anger, human anger, and then a naked bomb? Isn't it only natural that he too be allowed to breathe a little bit?"

"But what could be in her letter that could've spurred such a dangerous threat?"

"It wasn't a dangerous episode when our daughter kidnapped his children. Now that he mentions such an eventuality—which I'm sure will never come to pass if we acted a little more humane—then the word danger comes to everyone's mind."

"What was actually in this dangerous letter of his?" Fatima asked fighting hard to sound impartial.

"Your daughter may have read sinister things into that letter. But as far as I can see, the man's just given his anger a vent. That's all. There's no finality to his words. And he does seem ready for a real dialogue, not a narrow-minded outburst. And certainly no more silence. Anisa will just have to keep up the dialogue she started. She has everything to gain by it, and certainly nothing to lose, under the circumstances. I'm not a mind reader, but I do suspect that Ali has had time to think things over, and this gives me hope that perhaps all is not lost."

"I hope you're right, Omar. I hate to see her suffer so. The children are suffering too," Fatima said.

"Let's not forget he is human too and has feelings like everyone else."

Two weeks later, Mike became the recipient of another letter. He did expect a response, but not this quick.

Tearing the envelope open, his heart missed a beat as he caught a glimpse of his children's enchanting smiles. In one shot, Nasra was in school uniform! In the other, the runaway wife was holding both his children on her lap. Except for the face and the hands, her body was all covered up, her dark features blending with the dark garments. She'd never looked more packed in. His children were however plain to see.

Wondering what she was up to this time, he hurriedly began to read the letter:

Assalamu 'alaikum, Mike, she wrote.

Thanks a bunch for the lovely message. It's not everyday that a wife gets the privilege of being showered with such high-powered praises from a most dear husband. I tell you, it takes more than a lorry-full of pepper and salt to down such a deluge of praises. I'm a survivor, though. Many thanks!

Yesterday, after receiving this most heart-wrenching message, your children and I had a heart to heart talk, followed by a short prayer at the beach. They're too young to understand the situation. But, one thing's for sure, they love their father and there is nothing they'd love more than to see him drop from heaven.

After our short prayer at the beach, I promised myself to do everything in my power to restore my children's rights, but I can't work miracles. Our children don't know that. They see their father riding in a big white plane and they can't understand why it can't happen today, or at the very latest, tomorrow.

I had to tell them this that you and I had to get to know each other before their father could come home gliding on the wings of that huge airplane. A long sensible talk is what we need, and that's what I said to the children.

Right now, my mind's too muddled up to think out a proper way of conducting this sensible dialogue for which the kids and I prayed for only yesterday, without causing undue damage to the ego of their father.

Mike, it takes two to kindle a fire, it also takes two to put out that fire.

If it were up to my emotions alone, I wouldn't be here sweltering in this heat, leading toddlers' prayers at the beach, or writing stupid letters. I also know how much you care about me. But what's the point of it all if we can't live together in peace and harmony? What's the meaning of love if it can't give tranquility and peace?

Isn't it written that when a man and a woman are left on their own then Shaitan becomes the third? Perhaps what we thought as love was nothing more than shaitanic whisperings and false promises of the heart? Therefore, one wonders, how true is this love of man when his heart contains nothing but pride and ingratitude? And how can a mere mortal sing of love when his heart, the very heart given to him by God, cringes at the mere mention of the Giver of hearts? In the eventuality of such a love affair, of hearts united by Shaitan and human desires, how peaceful and tranquil would such a union be?

I don't expect Mike to answer these, these are my own thoughts, and I'm simply thinking out loud.

Safi Abdi

Mike, there is no coercion of faith in Islam. If a slave fails to see the need of his own heart, no other slave can loan out his heart to him and if a slave refuses to use his ears and eyes no other slave can see or hear for him.

You've every right to believe that I've let you down, Mike. Seen from your secular point of view, I've let you down.

But I'm not sorry that I did what I did and I've every right to change and make choices for myself. And see to it that the children I've nurtured inside of me for nine whole months are spared the turmoil that was our life before I turned tail. I may appear to you foolish but to them I'm their mother, and this mother has every right to change, for it's her birthright to find her Path, and it's her birthright to be herself.

Truth is, we simply can't go back to the kind of trauma that split us in the first place. It's a matter of life and death. Sanity is at stake here: yours and mine. And specially mine.

All I want for us is peace and sanity and a life that makes sense to both of us. You already know what it takes to achieve that peace.

The woman in the picture is also ample proof to you, that the Anisa you thought you married is irrevocably gone. She's been done with. She'll never come back. She's dead to this world. The woman-in-the-picture had met her in direct combat and she is now mortally dead. The best you can do for the Anisa you married is to kiss her goodbye. Let me repeat my condolences to you: Mike: The woman you married is deceased.

Mind you, this battle was no bed of roses for this woman in the picture. But the Anisa you married had to depart and I wouldn't resurrect her for the world.

This might sound like an ultimatum, but you do have a choice in the matter: Either accept this woman-in-the-picture for what she is and live with her in peace and harmony or else separate from her in good faith.

It may sound cruel to you, but if we're to have a future together; if we are to give our children the kind of healthy environment that's due to them, you, Mike Peterson will have to make all the changes. This woman-in-the-picture has already made her changes. It's now up to the father to make these changes as well; real changes that come from the heart, and not mere lip-service.

Mike, we haven't created these children. For all we'd know, they might have been someone else's children hadn't Allah not given us the opportunity to be their parents. Allah had created Adam and he had neither father nor a mother. Allah had caused Jesus to be, and Allah had no need for a father to complete this creation of his, so this father-mother issue is a thing ordained by Allah, and true credit should be to Him alone. For these children came from his presence, their very life depends on Him, and He is their destination. Our earthly connection maybe useful to them, but this need is only of a temporary nature.

Bearing this in mind, what right do we have to deprive these children from reaching their rightful goal in life?

Sssh, don't say I should've thought of that before! I know we should never have gotten involved in the first place. I'm also aware that I'm right now clutching at straws. I can't turn the clock back, so I've nothing to lose by clutching at the straws, for I did promise my children that I'd do anything in my power to do my bit, but there are limits as to what this woman-in-the-picture can do. She can clutch at straws but she can't spin their father into a God-fearing husband. Neither can she open this man's eyes, nor can she be his ears or heart. Not that she hasn't tried, but as this man very well knows, this woman only labors in vain.

This man she married is perhaps too good to own up the truth. This woman-in-the-picture is, however, a simple plain person and she can't be expected to assume airs and pretend nonchalance. The simple primitive soul that she is, how could she ever again pretend when every cell in her being has already said no—no more pretence.

Knowing all these and more, how could she in her right mind (let's just pretend she's in her right mind) chase fancies, now that she knows where these fancies would be leading her? Seeing all these, how could she with both eyes open lead her own sweet soul to a fire whose fuel is 'people and stones'?

She wouldn't do that for anyone, not even for her own flesh and blood, and certainly not for the Mike Petersons of this world.

My children did not create me. Allah created me for a purpose. When, on the Day of Judgment, the trumpet is sounded, and dead people from their sepulchers rise, on that day, they, my own children, would be too busy with their own affairs to think about their old mother. So, too, from your sepulcher will you be.

Mike, I can't force you to love and show gratitude to your Lord, but now that I know what I'm doing, I'd be lying if I said I'd settle for less than that.

Sooner or later, you'll come to know that everything I said was nothing but the truth.

I did have a Muslim name, but I was at one time lost myself. But like many erring Muslims, I knew I had a Lord, and in the privacy of the heart He gave me, I spoke to Him. With the lips He gave me, I begged Him to get me out of the rut I put myself. In the privacy of the tall gentle trees, I cried my desperation to Him. When each and everyone of you saw me as an alien, to my Lord I became a worthy being. And in the privacy of the heart He gave me I acknowledged His kindness to me.

Mike, my father knew how to talk to his Lord. He spoke to Him with all his heart, body and mind, and he did try to impart to me something of what he had. The shallow being I was I never did learn this simple mechanism, this direct communication with the Being who had my life in His Hand, I never did learn. I knew how to bow and could kneel but never did I learn how to reach to this Being who held my heart in His Hand. And as I slipped further and further away from the rope that held me to the Source of my life, the kneeling and the bowing that I did without heart, these also became a thing of the past.

And I became a toy for another power – the toy you married and called love. But this toy of a woman was not to remain a toy forever for this toy had a heart and she had a most gracious Lord. A Lord so great, a Lord so near. A Lord who has taught her how to rise up. A Lord who has taught her how to speak to this Being who gave her speech and the criteria to judge the right from the wrong.

When I became more alien than ever in that hospital bed, this Lord was all this alien had. The only ear that heard and gave weight to her call, coming with speed in the hour of need. And I was grateful. And with the heart He gave me I acknowledged my need of Him.

Although the toy you married is buried and gone, this woman is still the defective person she used to be. Struggling yes, but way behind the person she'd love to be. Take heart, the phrase the ideal

Muslim will never take place in the personality of your alien wife. In my day-to-day affairs, when the enormity of my own feeble mindedness hits me anew in the face, there are times when I can't understand why Allah puts up with me at all.

You've to feel it inside of you, this magnanimity of His, this boundless grace, this unlimited generosity. He knows we sin by day and night, yet He has told us to ask of Him forgiveness with the heart and the lips He gave us. Every limb and every tiny cell of our body is aware of its need of Him, for He is the sustainer. He's given us everything we have, all the things we call ours are actually His.

Being the creatures He has created 'bare and alone', there isn't a thing we can contest. Neither does He need our praises; for He is above any word we can say about Him.

He has made you compassionate, loving and reasonable, now that you know where to find Him, you can talk to Him in the privacy of your own heart. Mike, you'll never know how swiftly the Creator comes to the humble seeker until you've done your part. Speak to Him, and He will answer. You've one single life. Start today, in His

Name for He's indeed Most Gracious Most Merciful. Think hard, Mike, and start the journey today, inshaAllah.

May Allah be with you; I'll now leave you in peace, and please don't try anything funny. Your children long for you, but they couldn't have been in better hands. Aameen.

Putting the pages face down on the kitchen table, Mike did not know whether to laugh or cry. *That preacher-born-again-wife*! She had done it again! Had always the knack for *rubbing people up the wrong way*! So his alien wife was now dead? And *he* was now a widower in mourning?

Now doubt, this new *woman in the picture* was of a tougher mettle, hiding darkly behind dark clothing. And despite all the ramblings, she'd sounded her orders bell clear: *Depart on a spiritual journey, dear widower, but while you're at it, hands off your flesh and blood!* What a brilliant idea coming from a most brilliant wife!

This widower had a different opinion though. If he was to embark on this spiritual journey on his own, he'd have to do it in very close proximity of his own flesh and blood, and with the full knowledge of knowing the little ones were being nicely tucked in their own warm western beds, on every night of this spiritual journey!

It was only fair. And it was no thanks to his erratic wife's sloppy, one-sided speech, that, he Mike Peterson, was also just as capable of putting two and two together about the reality of things…once he put his mind to it. That too in the privacy of his own *Western* heart!

If his wife was now bent on going full time as a preacher, she might as well pay for her own stationery, with her own money, and not with the children's monthly allowance.

That his God was a very fair God, that he also knew and no thanks to the born-again-wife for that knowledge either. His spiritual journey was his business alone and *he* and no one else's. He was already at it, but it was too personal a matter to share with anyone.

One thing was worth celebrating, though. Something was making the brilliant kidnapper into a desperado. From what he'd just read, Rako Island wasn't exactly a bed of roses, no more. Mike could hardly contain his own pleasure at these deductions. Whatever it was that was making her so desperate for reconciliation, albeit on her own terms, was a favorable wind and he welcomed it with all his heart. A sense of well being inflating the widower's heart, a bitter sweet taste of revenge on his smiling lips, Mike got up from the kitchen table to make a nice cup of steaming American coffee for himself. An eye for an eye and a tooth for a tooth.

If he was going to be crucified, anyway, he might as well choose the place and time. Thanks to his wife's timely tip, the rescue operation was now within reach of take-off. Now that he knew the children played at the beach, the rescue plan smacked of instant success! Why hadn't he thought of that before?

He already knew, the boys, his brothers-in-law, Hassan and Hussein, were very fond of the beach. He'd just have to spend a few weekends at the beach, incognito, and without apprehension by an inquisitive aunt. The beach was a neutral territory and was off-limits to all relations and friends, the kind who would surely have made his skin creep, if he were to operate at the vicinity of the candy store. At the beach, he could easily roam around and mingle with the people without fear of some old aunt or other making eyes at him.

Meanwhile, his contact will have to secure the boys' friendship. A game of ball perhaps? The boys were very fond of playing football at the beach. A nice game of ball while the children built castles in the sand would've to become a nicely developed routine.

The rescue operation itself was to be a very swift, very tidy job. They did long for their widowed father, so said the heartless mother. He was now sure, at least Nasra would recognize him at sight. But he wasn't leaving anything to chance.

The steaming cup in hand, Mike settled himself comfortably in his easy chair. After a few minutes of relaxed concentration, and a second reading of his wife's long-winded sermon, his steady hand reached for the phone.

Chapter Twenty-Three

The Baby-Snatch

Sporting a rather crispy mustache, a neat beard, and wearing a pair of white slacks, a colorful shirt and a gray hat, with a Japanese camera casually slung over his shoulder, the American tourist queued at the tiny airport's passport control.

It was already past midnight, and as Mike's passport was stamped for entry, the airport official's gaze met the American tourist's eyes. The airport official gave a nod of recognition. Mike returned the nod with a wave of his left hand. But, except for these two and for the two men who patiently waited outside in the old black Sedan, this nod meant nothing more than a casual hello.

The minute he came out, Mike spotted the car. The driver watched through the rear mirror as the American tourist quickly wheeled his suitcase towards the vehicle where the two men sat and waited for him to put the suitcase in the luggage compartment.

Opening the car door, Mike slid into the back seat. The occupants, both locals, immediately turned their bodies to shake hands with him. He already knew their trade names: Stalk and Chili. The airport official whom he had met on arrival, and whose job was to begin at the police check at the departure hall, after the completion of the rescue operation, was also another invaluable member of the team.

The contact who put all these together was, however, not to be contacted at all in Rako Island, not until the American tourist homed safely with his goods. The contact was too important to be seen with the two conmen who sat together with Mike in the car.

Stalk put the car into gear and the three men sped towards a five star hotel, just a five minutes' walking distance from the strand, where the American was to stay for a month or so, until the goods were safely in hand.

On their way to the hotel, Mike was given a rapid re-run of the plan, which now contained another alternative. If the past weeks' findings were anything to go by, Stalk now impressed on him, his departure from Rako Island might even happen earlier than stipulated.

And the venue of the operation, added Stalk, need not be confined to the beach.

The *madrasah* was just as good a place as any, Mike was told. In fact, this location seemed to the men sitting in front of him far less complex than the beach. And since the children's attendance there was on a regular basis, the chances were much more greater.

Although the *madrasah* was only a stone's throw from the family's home, it was situated in such a way that the view from the family's home was impossible because of the cluster of buildings all around it. Since there was also virtually no traffic in the vicinity between the housing complex and the *madrasah*, the area was also safe enough for the kids to walk or play on their own.

During the four weeks' surveillance the men carried out the children were seen to walk the short distance in the company of another child, a girl of Nasra's age, and on several occasions, without even adult supervision, Mike was told.

Pulling the car into a stop at the hotel entrance, Stalk walked Mike to the reception and once again impressed on the reluctant Mike the feasibility of the *madrasah* option.

The following day, having slept off some of the jetlag, a refreshed Mike met his helpers at the hotel bar. It was past midday. They were already there, sitting at a table overlooking the sea, conversing in low tones over two empty coffee cups and an untidy ashtray, as they patiently waited for Mike to make his appearance.

Wearing a replica of what he wore on arrival, Mike casually walked over to the men's table. Waving to a passing waiter, he ordered coffee for all three and the three immediately set to work on the plan.

The men were a peculiar pair. Stalk did most of the talking. Chili drowsed on every word, a seal on his mouth unless spoken to directly. They did complement each other in a rather weird way and seemed more hurried than Mike to get it all over with.

Perhaps, the hefty money, some of which was already paid to his contact's account number had pressed the right buttons. But still some show of reservation on the part of these two could have done wonders for Mike's own fragile resolve.

Since it was mid week and the kids weren't expected at the beach, at least, not until the weekend, anyway, Mike reluctantly agreed to the men's suggestions, or rather unconcealed coercion, that he accompany them to the said *madrasah*, that very afternoon.

"But, shouldn't we take things easy, at least today?" voiced Mike wavering, weakening, enervated by the confining hotness of his whereabouts. He didn't know why, but it seemed, he was playing for time; even catching himself a few times, half wishing on a nosy aunt or an old grandmother to come to the rescue before the rescue mission came to pass. But the place he sat with the two knaves wasn't exactly the right spot for an old grandmother or a nosy aunt to pop in.

"The sooner it's all done the better," Stalk said, gesticulating with a tobacco debilitated hand, conspicuously hurried. "Why wait and waste time, man?"

"Indeed, why wait and waste time. I didn't travel thousands of miles to wait and waste time," returned Mike with all the resolution he could muster.

"Good." Stalk's sooty fingers gestured.

"What if someone saw me?" Mike asked, worried.

"No one will know you, with your goggles, hat and new beard. And in any case, we'll park the car at a safe distance. We've already marked out a nice spot. And you won't even have to get out of the car until the *goods* are for grabs. Just don't wear that rainbow shirt too often. We don't want too much attention."

Goods! The slime was calling his children *goods*! His hands tuned into fists behind the coffee mug.

"What about this other child?" he asked with a gulp of his coffee.

"I agree, this could pose a slight problem," said Stalk, as yet another cigarette snaked out of his ancient shirt pocket. "But," he said, belching out a smog of invisible dust and dangling the poor cigarette between two jagged fingers, "it's no bigger hurdle than what we'd have at the beach…"

"What's to be done about the girl, hey Chili?" He waved the fleecy stick under his friend's nose.

"Been thinking," drowsed Chili. "Once we know the time's ripe for the actual nabbing, we break up the kids. No one will suspect anything. I engage the girl in talk. She's only a child. I give her sweets and pretend I know her. It can be done as easily as I'm sitting here. In the meantime, Stalk makes good with the *goods*."

"Brilliant, Chili boy!" Stalk dispatched yet another putrid cloud right into the face of the goods' father.

"Well, well, what can I say?" said Mike, feeling cheated, cheating and depressed. His association with the knaves he hired through the third party making him sickly and stinking.

This was, however, no time for finesse, nor did the goods' father have any time for vacillation. He'd already wasted two years on hesitation. He was a father on a mission. The success of the mission depended on these two heels for whom his children were nothing more than transferable matter – express goods that changed hands at the press of a button.

Although the overt eagerness was arduous on his nerves, and he was wary of the *madrasah* option, he reckoned, these two broken men had a job to do and they were earning a living. The only difference between his mode of survival and theirs was that his was done without the constant finger pointing of an accusing self. He was sure they too had a conscience that could point fingers, given one tenth of the chance he had.

They probably had children of their own. And these children were flesh and bones that needed feeding, non-stoppable nourishment. The whole set up reeked of necessity, *pure human necessity*—he was starved for his children and they were starved for dough—and *his* money was there for grabs, so he might as well show who was the boss.

Clearing his throat, he now said in what he hoped was a no nonsense tone, "Perhaps, we shouldn't be seen together so much," he said, the light-weigh eyes an azure slit, radiating superior airs, sparking formidable powers. "What say you we meet downtown, say later on in the afternoon? I don't know about you guys, but I'm starving."

"But of course." Stalk's hand flailed in mid air as though combating an invisible opponent. A good look at the *new* man, and his insides were suddenly a bag of ice. Darting a cowering glance at his ancient Citizen watch, he said, "You been here before, American? You know your way around?

"Am not exactly a new kid in town," said the commander in chief. "You say where and when."

378

That same afternoon, Stalk pulled the car into a stop in a parking lot behind the *madrasah*. Twenty or so minutes later, Mike got a glimpse of his two babies. And as they walked passed him, hand in hand, on their way home from the *madrasah*, the strength and the resolution he'd been praying for all afternoon, now came over him. Two whole years of separation! He almost popped out of the window, and would've shot out of the car to scoop up his precious goods hadn't Stalk's fluttery hands not pinned him down to the seat.

Chapter Twenty-Four

Life in America

It was a Monday afternoon, exactly eleven days from the date of the American tourist's arrival in Rako Island. As the hands on the departure hall's wall clock struck 3:30 PM, the American tourist, now accompanied by his two children, was swiftly helped into a waiting Tokyo-bound Boeing aircraft. A smiling hostess came forward to help place the children in their seats, on each side of the father.

As the last person came on board and the *Fasten Seat Belt* signs lit up, a breathless Nasra repeated the question, "Where's Mommy, Dad? When can I see her?"

"Don't worry, dear," mouthed the father, "she should be in any minute. Here I've a nice surprise for you guys," said the father in a hushed voice, drawing the children's attention to the travelers' bag he held on his lap. He unzipped the bag to reveal a most exquisite assortment of candy, bubble gum, Barbie-dolls, tiny high-tech warplanes, police cars, finger-size-doll-costumes, ambulances...

"Wow!" breathed Nasra and the kids dived for the displayed goods.

Once up in the air, Mike's breathing came back to normal. Reclining comfortably back in his seat, the triumphant Mike released a deep breath. It was perhaps the first normal breath that left his throat since that first afternoon he laid eyes on his children.

Thank God, it was all over. Ten days of siege, ten days of tension and ten sleepless nights that left him in a frantic daze! He knew he was such a heel...lower than even the level of his heels.

His associates did a brilliant job, though – reveling in the eight-day siege at the *madrasah* and the two-day day siege at the beach, as if that were a normal sport; their tainted hearts thumping for the reward that would be theirs once the game was over.

On the third night of the grisly waiting, the American tourist, Stalk and Chili were no longer unknown trade labels. They were becoming bosom buddies, time-knitted triplets. No longer was Stalk a flighty leaf, caught in the negative currents of Rako Island. Nor was Chili the hot non-feeling stuff he thought he was.

Stalk was the only son of an old bedridden mother. He never did get married; nursing his ailing mother since the day he was ten and his father disappeared into the vast ocean, while fishing from a hazardous slippery spot. Stalk was there, a lone helpless witness to his father's frantic hand, still clutching the fishing rod before the huge furious wave lapped him up, rod and hand. Stalk never did return to school. However, he and his mother returned to the shore two days later to reclaim the half-eaten corpse of his father from the blowing sand. Strangely enough, his father's clothes, though tattered out of recognition, still clung to the half-eaten body. Stalk never did get to know the consumer of his father's body.

Chili had ten children and a wife to feed. Sixteen years ago, a creaky tired boat had dropped him off the shores of Rako Island. His own island became the scene of a bloody, silly unrest and he and his wife were the only survivors of his whole clan. He had heard stories of the peaceful thriving island on the other side of the vast ocean and was full of sustained hope for the future.

The tourist business was just budding then and Chili joined the gaiety as a third rate entertainer in one shoddy joint, where he worked at night, singing hoarsely, live, to the tourists' tipsy moods, and then slept off the nightly shift during the day, quietly with his wife. And to make up for his lost clan, Chili and his wife brought to the world one clansman after another, within fourteen years of their arrival in Rako Island.

As Chili, night after night, cracked his way through the benumbed crowds, he knew that none of the people who tuned in to his unhappy bawls had any inkling of either his sad past nor did they give a damn about his unfortunate present. That he was a solitary clansman, fighting for an increase of a whole population, the frivolous passing throngs never could guess. And before he knew it, he was the father of ten demanding children and a temper-ridden wife to boot. To escape these nightly rasping shifts and to release himself from his wife's daily nags, Chili found a job as an independent courier for an underground gang whose business he dared not find out. It was a very irregular job, that allowed him to sleep at night in peace and shake off

383

his wife during the day and that suited him just fine. The job that was at hand now was one such easy job.

For both Stalk and Chili this was the first time either of them had ever come so close to their jobs. In fact, Mike's children were the only flesh and blood goods they had ever handled. And as Mike listened to the men's woes over dinner, as he needed the company and they needed the break; before long he was appreciating in earnest the men's eagerness for their seedy job.

And all the luck was on his side. Stalk and Chili proved their mettle. Their calculations were superb. The *madrasah* was a Godsend.

Chili's plan was faultless. At the appointed time of 2.00 PM, while the three children made their way to the *madrasah* on their own, a smiling Chili took the older girl aside, while an amiable Stalk struck a good rapport with the goods.

Tagging the goods by their names and pointing his fingers at the car park, he sang, "Look! Your father's home! Over there!" And as the children and their new friend neared the parking lot, the appearance of the now clean-shaven father couldn't have been more timely.

Everything seemed to be happening at rocket speed. By the time the children got over the shock of seeing their father, the driver was already speeding towards the main road. As Mike stole a backward glance at Chili and the little girl who were too deeply engrossed in conversation to notice the passing car on the other side of the compound, his heart's pounding could be heard in the seventh heaven.

They had just an hour to boarding time. And approximately half an hour's drive to the airport. They had two or so hours before the children were missed at home, that being the time of their return home from the *madrasah*, unless Chili failed to persuade the girl to follow him to a nearby amusement park.

No sooner did they arrive at the airport, than Stalk took leave of the American and his children, and the airport official took over and within seconds the American tourist and his children were ushered through the passport control and into the waiting aircraft.

He'd already paid in advance to the boss for their services. But Mike had no idea how much of what he paid to the contact's bank account would reach the men's pockets. However, since the job was done tidier than his wildest imagination, Mike was able to bring genuine smiles to the men's faces; this gesture somehow elevating the shame he felt using their condition. The men were no longer anonymous underlings, though, Mike never did find out the men's real names.

Meanwhile, back in his wife's neighborhood, a six-some, Anisa, her mother, and uncle, Nafisa, the children's *madrasah* mate, and her mother Leila, and a neighbor who said he saw what happened through his window, were all present at the local police station, to file their report of the missing children.

It was approximately a few minutes past 5.00 PM.

The police officer on duty was an old acquaintance of Anisa's uncle. And after the exchange of pleasantries, once Omar briefed him on their errand, the sergeant got to work.

Writing down the necessary details, and having questioned the little girl, he then turned his attention to the witness.

"Mr. George Poona?"

The man nodded, then proceeded to tell what he saw from his window.

"It must have been slightly over 2.00 PM, I'd just come back from work and having already seen the car in the parking lot, I rushed to my room to get a change of clothes, so I could once again take my position at the window."

"But why didn't you report if you knew what was going on?"

"I didn't say I knew anything, I was perhaps just curious. And the men did nothing to arouse any suspicion, just mild curiosity."

"For how long has this been going on? And how many people did you see?" The officer prompted.

"The very least, a week, if I'm not mistaken, but they always seemed to be waiting for something and so increased my curiosity. You can't blame me for that, nothing exciting ever happens around here."

"You didn't answer my second question…again how many people did you see?"

"In the beginning, just two, but, one day I noticed something move in the car, it was then that I realized that there was a third party, perhaps someone who didn't want to be seen?"

"Describe what you saw today."

387

"By the time I went to the window, this young lady here was already chatting with one of the men, there were few other children around, some noise, I couldn't really hear what they were saying. The second man was also in conversation with two other children, and it didn't strike me as odd, you see my attention was on the object of my curiosity, the person inside the car. And then surprise, the object of my concern suddenly sprang out of the car and before I knew it some of the children in the playground and the man were hugging, and that's when I heard my wife call…"

Then?

"Then, I quickly changed and ignoring my wife's calls rushed down the steps to catch sight of the man. But by the time I came down, the car was gone…"

"Then what did you do next?"

"I came back to tell the strange episode to my wife."

"When did you decide to report?"

"Only after we saw all the commotion in the neighborhood," he admitted.

"You knew a little bit about the children's history, didn't you?"

"A small place like this," the man admitted, "things do go round, especially with the women yapping all day long."

"Then you must be well informed," the policeman threw at him.

"I'm not complaining."

"Then I'm sure you've had a glimpse of the third party, the object of your curiosity. And who knows he might even have looked foreign?"

"Maybe, but how was I to know he was after the children?"

At this point, the officer turned to Omar, "You are positive the father is involved?"

"Positive. He's already warned us, but we haven't taken him seriously."

"Then we'll get to work immediately, and will inform you as we proceed." The officer shook Omar's hand, nodded his head at Anisa, and they all trooped out of the office.

Twenty-four hours later, when she knew he'd be home, for that was about the time it took to fly from Rako Island, Anisa placed the first long distance call she made since she came to Rako Island.

Mike confirmed Anisa' worst nightmare. However, he snorted into her ear, the children couldn't have been in better hands. The happy father had just put his children to bed, and when day light broke, he said, he was headed to his lawyer, just a *small* precaution, said he, so that should the mother try anything *funny* the *widower* would have nothing to be ashamed of. The children were at long last on Western soil, warming their own beds, but, added the father, the children's mother was more than welcome to join her flesh and blood. The ball was now firmly placed in her hands, and the *widower* wished *his* deceased wife well.

"You fool! Bring my children back!" was all the bereaved mother could utter before she slammed the phone on the cruel tyrant.

But, much to the gratifying surprise of everyone, and to the great relief of her family, Anisa' rage and delirium fell short of everyone's estimations. Once the children's safety was confirmed, and she realized her own powerlessness in the matter, a calmness of mind and sanity she didn't know she possessed took a firm hold on her. She wasn't going to give up her children. But if she were going to get them back, she'd need to do so with a calm, clear head. For, if she now went off after him in a huff, or filed for divorce, she might even risk losing the children forever. He was on secular soil. And he was in a fighting mood.

And what jury would put themselves in her shoes and for a second, pretend to be her, a Muslim woman, and then try to understand what made her act the way she did? What secular mind would be liberal enough to stretch beyond the confines of its secular mindset?"

That when she ran she did so only to protect her children from their irreligious father and that by running away, she thought she was doing everyone a favor, including her husband, for whom her alien way of life posed an antithesis, and that when she ran away, she was a desperate woman, a desperate mother, and not a cold blooded kidnapper.

Wouldn't admitting to that in public and in a court of law make her into a big joke in the eyes of the emancipated world?

On the other hand, if they parted enemies, and he secured custody of the children amid cheers and plaudits, wouldn't he try to turn the children against her? Or worse still against all sense of justice? And wouldn't an associate of low life and a bosom friend of Rako Island's underworld be just as capable to coalesce with the devil himself?

She was convinced that she'd said enough, done enough, and though she hadn't been the best of speakers, she knew beyond all doubt that she'd been sincere to him.

She never wished him harm. He was the father of her children, and her only fault was that she tried too hard to be a window for him and hoped that he'd share her concerns. His own trials were on a different plane, but because of her, he also suffered and went through enough to make him understand what she so desired to communicate.

That those tribulations of hers weren't for nothing, that too he knew. He was there. He saw with his own eyes the reflexive changes they brought on her. That itself should've been a sufficient sign for him.

If he didn't revel so in his own mundane heart, and didn't sadistically delight in her plight, she was convinced, he, too, would've tasted at least something of what she felt.

As it was, whatever she tried to say fell on dead ears. She wasn't going to waste any more breath, and now she vowed to keep her peace, and let Mike find his own way. Her children were a gift from God, not acquired chattels.

Once again, her faith was put to the test, but this latest crisis had within it a power that had made her stronger than she had ever been. And as she was once sustained in the hour of need by prayer so too in this way passed Anisa's days and weeks.

And for five months and seven days Anisa and her family lived on the fringes of hope.

For Mike and for his children, things went smoothly for a while. The social worker he was assigned to instantly helped him find a place in the country's educational ladder.

On his way to work, the father would drop the children at their respective institutions. And unless pressing business matters demanded his urgent attention, he'd then pick them up on his way from work. And for a while, everyone seemed to make allowances for him. The poor father! The poor children! Poor Mike!

His family became a pillar of support for him—his mother's grandmother instinct coming back to life. After all, they were her flesh and blood, and minus the alien *mother*, weren't they simply adorable!

The boy, 'Med', for that was the name Mohammed's grandmother now coined for her grandson, was a tanned replica of his own father. That boyish grin brought back memories of Mike's own boyish grin. And the family returned to the family albums for confirmation. Seeing Nasra now was like seeing Charlotte at seven. The resemblance was startling…when one went past the tan and the curls, "Look at that chin!" the grandmother would say. "Here…see that scraped knee! Bloody as hell! It must run in the family!" And the said aunt couldn't have been more flattered for at seven Nasra had already the promises of a natural beauty.

During those heady days of complete contentment with life, Mike even entertained ideas of the runaway wife knocking on his door and begging for forgiveness—not that anyone else cared—for to his family, the alien got what she deserved, more so because of her bizarre religious leanings.

"They're all terrorists," Charlotte said. "Islam terrorizes people and the only answer to terrorism is counteraction. That's the only language they understand."

Since the children's return home, Charlotte had taken on the role of the ideal aunt, baby-sitting her niece and nephew. Mike was held up at work that day and Charlotte had picked up her niece and nephew from school. On seeing Mike's car pull into Charlotte's driveway, Mike's mother also came over for a chat. Charlotte's boyfriend, Ted, was at work at the wine bar mixing drinks for himself and for Charlotte. The children were on the lawn, learning the ropes of skating at the hands of their cousins, Charlotte's sons.

As on many such occasions, the conversation, inadvertently, turned to Mike's alien wife. It seemed as though the mere mention of Islam always brought people's minds to Mike's runaway wife. While Mike was in no mood to defend Anisa and was hard pressed to agree to some of the allegations hurled at her by his sister and mother, he had his reservations about equating the religion of Islam with Terrorism.

"I can't agree with you, there, Charlotte," he said amused at his sister's blank ignorance. "I maybe knew to the faith, but if there's anything I've learned to be careful of it is the equation of Islam with Terrorism."

"And I always thought you were Muslim *only* on paper!" Charlotte's partner threw at Mike. Now that Mike's mood had lightened up with the children's return, his attitude towards Ted had undergone a tremendous change. And Ted had taken this as a sign of a blooming camaraderie.

"Well, Ted, I'm now as authentic as they come," Mike laughed, but he wasn't in the least comical, though his family took it so.

"I somehow can't see you as a full-fledged terrorist," put in Ted, suppressing a smile. "But if you ever get the urge to throw a few bombs I'm all yours, Mike!"

And before Mike got wind of Ted's remark, his mother's declaration stole the show.

"Their so-called holy book," she said in a sweeping remark, "is a copy of the holy Bible, verbatim."

"I had no idea my mother was into scriptures!" Mike said.

"Everyone knows," Charlotte said. "It's so obvious, isn't it?"

"But how can you be so sure of something you haven't even seen, let alone read?" Mike asked, still sporting a whimsical look on his face. "And which Bible, if I may ask, was plagiarized?"

"The holy Bible, of course!" His mother threw at him. "Have you any doubt that the author of the Qur'an has plagiarized the holy Bible?"

"But we've so many versions, Mother, which version do you mean?"

"Well, he must've plagiarized the original version."

"We don't even have the original version. We've so many other versions. Now which one was plagiarized?" Mike was enjoying himself.

"Well, he must've plagiarized the original," she said thoughtfully, "and if we had the original today, we would've amble proof, but as I see it we really don't have any proof!"

"What if the Muslims have the proof and they are hiding it?" Charlotte said. As the manager and owner of her own company,

Charlotte had very bright ideas when it came to business, but otherwise she was a complete flop, her high IQ, notwithstanding.

"Okay, let's for a moment go along with this allegation of yours, I say allegations, okay, not true, but I'm willing to go along with it, just for the sake of argument," Mike paused, then added, "now if the author of the Qur'an plagiarized the Bible, then he did a brilliant job by expunging all the doubtful ingredients that make up the Bible as we know it today, take the concept of the trinity, for example, and the list could go on...forgive me for saying it, but wouldn't you say that was a brilliant job? More food for thought!"

"Yeah!" Ted said enthusiastically. "I must give Mohammed credit for that! That trinity stuff, it's just way beyond my head, forgive me for saying this Charlotte, but this concept of God having a child just doesn't stand up to reason! I don't think I've it in my Bible either! Someone very smart must have copied the Qur'an and taken it out!"

"You do have a point there, Ted." Mike looked at Ted with sudden interest. *Wasn't this the man that Mike despised so much*? Ted just didn't have the looks of a man given to thinking. Mike's gaze returned to the man who was now feeling the yellow ribbon holding

398

his ponytail with his free hand. Perhaps the tiny ribbon was too tight on the man's horsy neck? Mike wondered, without voicing his alarm. To be honest, Mike never did see the man, his gaze always being stolen by the pretty ribbon on the man's horsy neck.

"Now that you say it, Ted," said Mike averting his gaze from the pretty ribbon, "I just can't help wondering who is plagiarizing who?"

Mike never did have a good word for the Bible, and between the two of them, Mike now reflected, it was Anisa who showed more leniency towards practicing Christians. He never did understand that part of her until he began to read the Qur'an in earnest.

And excepting that time she flipped after the birth of their son, she never really said anything damaging about Christianity as a religion.

If anything, she was always deriding him and his family for being so much in love with the world, and kept chiding her quickly aging mother-in-law for being too caught up with the humdrum of temporary life—at a point in time, she'd say non-diplomatically, when back in Rako Island, people of her mother-in-law's age had already invested in their *burial garments…*

But as compared to his family's scathing remarks about Islam, he now reflected, hers was more like the admonitions of a mother to a particularly stubborn child.

"Hallelujah!" Mike's mother cried. "These Muslims, they're all going to hell; men, women and children. Son, if I were you I'd put on the breaks…"

"No, Mother, I am too deeply in it now, the teachings of Islam are just perfect for me. And after all, this is America, and freedom of speech and thought, and freedom of religion is enshrined in our constitution, your son's simply following the book…" Mike grinned.

"Then if Islam's so mighty superior, why did God choose Arabs of all people? And now that you're being taken in with this mighty argument, I think I can safely ask you this, and I'm entitled to an answer—but why was America kept in the dark? Why weren't we involved in the kingdom of God?"

Mike burst out laughing. If she weren't so full of herself his mother could have gone places, but as it was, her pride had always stranded her in the middle of nowhere—and he knew he had in him something of her. Thank God, she wasn't as severe in outlook as his sister Charlotte.

"Mother, I think I've overstayed my welcome, Charlotte's making some noises, but before I go let me put this to you that God chooses whom He pleases. We're nothing but mere mortals and it isn't our place to dictate to God. And if He chooses Arabs to convey His message, I say, let that be more food for thought."

"But I'd feel much better if you put on the breaks You've no excuse, now, you've your children and you've nothing missing in your life. Find someone and be happy."

And his mother meant well. And now that her grand children were safe, she hoped for an absolute snapping of all ties with the woman and her faith. But he had to admit, the children cared. He had to admit it too, that he also cared, albeit in a different way...if only for the satisfaction of seeing her beaten?

Much to Mike's private disappointment, however, the erratic wife didn't recant, nor did she try to retaliate. Complete silence. Total inertia. Weeks stretched into months. Not even a whimper of grief. Whatever happened to the frays for which he prepared himself?

Wasn't this the impulsive, emotion-ridden Anisa he knew and counted on?

Once the exhilaration he felt at his own chivalry wore itself out, and the spark began to leave the body of the heroic feat, to Mike, the reality of life, the reality of being a single male parent was now becoming something of a burden, all the familial concern, notwithstanding.

And as if the feeling of desolation that now threatened his day to day affairs, and the drudgery of the routine itself weren't enough, his own children, the children for whom he longed for all this time, and for whose sake he'd become a criminal of a sort, also turned into his own worst critics.

It didn't even take them a fortnight to get homesick, and mommy-sick, and grandma-sick, and what-not-else-sick. Even at the height of his high-flying period, the two rascals not only ignored to take part in the general revelry, but they also chose to keep their little feet firmly on the edge of hope.

And despite all the clever diversions, a day didn't pass without mention of the erratic wife's name in his home. Stories of how she used to do things abounded, and memories of how she spellbound them with her stories flitted the air. A better cook than *she* also never existed, for *her* cake was the best of all cakes—even when she herself didn't do the baking! And when the annoyed father pointed out that if *she* didn't doing the baking how could *her* cake be the best, Nasra would just laugh and say, her mother was the best of all those who went shopping! And that when *she* bought things it was like she made those things herself! And when Mike pointed out that all the money their mother used for her shopping was in fact his, Nasra would just slam at him that Dad was now being green in the eyes! Because Mommy could never say such a thing about their dad! And that she would never be green in the eyes when they said good things about their dad because she just happened to be a *good* Muslim who prayed *five times* a day! And she wasn't so irregular as Dad, and then Mohammed would butt in and complain that he himself had been missing out his Friday prayers, and it was all thanks to Dad!

"Doesn't it ever get Friday here? he asked the bewildered father. "When do people do their Friday prayers here, Dad?"

"But you're under-aged young man!" Mike retorted. "For God's sake, no one expects you at the mosque!"

"But we used to go to the mosque with Mommy and it used to be so much fun!" Then it was back to Mommy and how so much better everything was with her!

The saintly amiable daughter of two years ago was now no long there. What he was now fated to deal with was a contentious, tantrum-ridden child, who refused to eat at will, and refused to play at will, and with a tongue as long as his arm.

Even after downing all the candies and the ice-creams, and the showers of pity and familial coos, the little girl told her grandmother, "I think my other grandmother in Rako Island is that little, tiny, tiny bit better than my grandmother in America."

"Oh yes?" The disheartened grandmother's head popped out of the kitchen sink.

"So. So."

"And what makes her so perfect, I wonder?" the grandmother asked coyly.

"You can't even guess, can you?" the little girl licked at her ice cream.

"Let's just say I like to be told things."

"She's Muslim, now you see?"

"Aha!"

"She prayers to Allah everyday."

"Then she must be a Super Granny!"

"I guess so," Nasra murmured, licking the ice cream from her lips. "Grandma, can I go watch cartoons, now?"

"Of course, dear, you run along, and don't forget to take your popcorn with you."

Later in the evening, a distraught grandmother lamented to her husband, "Poor young things," she said, "imagine the ordeal of being exposed to a society that did nothing but prayers! For two whole years, these poor things had seen nothing but prayers! Two whole years of prayers! Poor Mike!"

"Ah...don't let that get you down now," chuckled the grandfather. "They'll soon get this out of their system. Poor souls, guess what Med said the other day when I took him fishing?" said the grandfather as a way of cheering up his wife, before pausing to light his pipe. "The poor fellow yelled: 'Allah!', related the grandfather with a shake of his pipe, "Son," said the grandfather, "where's Allah?" Then said he: 'Grandpa, watch out what you say about Allah! Beware, you're a grandpa! God! What kind of a grandpa is this?'"

At this the grandparents roared with laughter: Poor things! Poor children! Poor Mike!

Children were children and the grandparents were obliged to forgive the little one's attitude for as long as it took them to de-acclimatize their little minds.

However, to Mike, it seemed the little ones were not only an ungrateful pair, they were also thick-skinned faultfinders, who found fault with everything their father did for them, from the way he dressed them to the toys he showered them with.

"Your toys are too noisy!" The little fellow declared the other day, after his father reprimanded him for unceremoniously taking apart the high-tech war planes and the police cars.

"Then you buy your own toys, young man!"

"Give money, I buy." The little boy's pointed nose went up in the air.

"You buy with your own money!"

"Mommy can buy with your money!"

"No! No! Not with my sweat! With her money!"

One day as the father was trying to help his daughter out with her home assignment, Nasra suddenly looked up from her books: "Why is it that some people are bad these days, Dad?"

"They don't have to, Nasra," said the father looking up from his Herald Tribune. "In act, we can all try to be good. But some can't help being bad. So welcome to the real world, Nasra."

"Aha! So, that's why Dad and Mommy are taking turns to be bad?" frowned the little girl.

"Now, now, Nasra, it's not like that at all, now step on it. I haven't got all day. And you need your beauty sleep."

After a short interval she looked up again thoughtfully chewing the pencil, "Why don't you ever tell us to pray? Are you like the others, Dad?"

"Well, my name's Mike Peterson. And I don't have to remind you of anything. You guys are grown up enough to know what your doing, anyway!"

"Well, then, remind yourself more often, you're not doing things well, yourself. You're never on time when it comes to prayers, is it because there's no mosque around here?"

"Now, now, aren't we digressing? You were supposed to be doing your assignment, weren't you?"

"But what if you suddenly died, what then, Dad? And they took you away in a box, like Adam's father? And you're an old man…"

"Ah!"

"Daddy's a baby!"

And as the months dangerously stretched before his eyes, without the runaway wife making so much as a tiny whimper, the texture of Mike's repose began to change shade, first slowly and then with a speed he didn't reckon possible.

Chapter Twenty-Five

Unsettled Needs

On a lovely Spring day, as Mike began to load the children into the car for a weekend trip to his parent's place, Nasra declined to go at the last minute.

"Come on in, dear. It'll be fun."

"Nasra's not going anywhere."

"What's the matter now…come?" He opened the door for her.

"I'm staying, Dad. You go and have fun. I can't have fun."

"But Mac and Joe will be there too. And so is Ted." The father tried a smile as he tried to coax the little girl into the car.

"But I don't like that man!"

"Which man?"

"The one with the big ears," she sobbed.

"You mean Ted," asked the father somewhat taken aback. "And I always thought the two of you were buddies."

409

"Well, I just don't like his pony-tail. He looks, well, I don't know what!" she sobbed. "He…he doesn't look like anything! He lost his studs and now he has these terrible holes in his ears…and how they hurt. Ouch!"

"Don't you worry about this man. If he doesn't know any better, then let him hurt. He's not hurting your ears, now is he?"

"But he said he'll dig another hole in his nose. Dad, I don't like him. This man hurts himself."

"If he wants to dig holes in his nose, that's his business. Let him dig!"

"But he's going to hurt his nose. Ouch!"

"Now, Nasra, let's be reasonable. We're going to Grandma, we aren't visiting this man."

"But he's got this big scorpion on his shoulder too! Daddy, this man, he'll kill himself."

"But it's his shoulders, and the bloody scorpion's on his shoulders, why should we care? Now, come on and get in the car…"

"But I love Mommy. I hate scorpions."

"I know you love Mommy and hate scorpions, now, if you'll be a good girl…"

"I love Mommy too!" Mohammed butted in with a wail.

"Okay! Okay! So you guys aren't going nowhere, hah? Then stay put!" Mike slammed the car door shut and the three stomped back into the house.

Once inside, the kids were soon running up and down the steps, collecting toys here and there and then before he'd gotten over the shock of having been beaten, yet again, the rascals were racing each other to the playground.

With so much time on his hands, Mike moved around the house aimlessly tidying up this and that—God, how he was beginning to loathe these long weekends! With so much on his mind and nothing of interest to do. And for the first time in five months that he actually found himself wandering in mind: *Floor*! That was it! He could call Floor! Or perhaps just drive there. It was a good two hour drive. Then before he knew what he was doing he reached for the phone: "Hello!" A man's voice came on the line and he didn't sound like Floor's husband. *What if Floor just wasn't there anymore? What if she just*

411

died? Mike thought. His daughter had brainwashed him, and now he was thinking like her. *What if you suddenly died, Dad, and you are an old man? What if the earth suddenly quaked and gave up all it's ghosts, and everyone fell under, and nothing remained on the face of the earth? What then?"*

"Floor?" Mike asked quickly before his thoughts sent him to another delirium.

"A second, please," the man replied.

"Good day!" Floor cracked.

"Floor!"

"Mike! Where the hell have you been? And where are you?"

"What are you doing today?"

"Well, there's only one way to find out!"

Two or so hours later, Floor met Mike and his children at the door. On her trail were her daughter Peggy and one giant of a man.

"You son of a gun!" she said lightly as she scooped up the children, one after the other. "You son of a gun!"

"Remember me?" she pinched Nasra's nose.

"I know you, you are Floor. And that's your Peggy."

Then Floor was ushering everyone in, "Well, this is Jack," she introduced the giant.

After a few minutes, Jack was on his feet again.

"We'll see you later, Jack," Floor said and Jack was dismissed.

"That was my favorite giant," she said to Mike. "Poor fellow, no woman had ever so much as darted a lid at him. And now that he thinks he met the woman of his life, he's dying to tie the knot! He's got a heart as big as him, but I'm too old, and my arthritis are killing me, what say you, Mike? Should an old girl like me put her health at risk?"

"He would do," Mike replied, warming to Floor's gaiety. "And you could do worse!" His mood was already lighting up. The children were out playing in the playground with Peggy, and having made some more coffee the two went out to sit and lounge by the poolside.

"Boy, am I glad the mouse's out of your hair!" Floor said shortly. "When I don't like people, I make sure they know it!"

He didn't comment.

"Now tell me, shameless Westerner, what've you done with my friend? And why isn't she with her kids, anyway? Tell the old girl, now what's the matter?"

After beating around the bush, Mike had at last found the tongue to lay it all on Floor. After hearing him out, Floor broke into laughter, "Talk about the devil," she said. "I wouldn't put it past you…somehow, I knew it the minute I saw you! You son of a gun! So now the ball's firmly in my friend's court? I can't see Anisa giving up on her children, though – the woman must be up to her neck with mighty plans, and there goes the circle! But frankly, why don't you give her a call?"

"What you mean, give her a call?"

"Am no psychologist, Mike, and I'm not given to spiritual contemplation, for as your crazy wife used to say, 'this woman's name's Floor, something's terribly wrong with her spirit, it's just not there, it's dead and buried under the floor!'"

"Yeah, those were the days," Mike shook his head.

"But if what your saying's right," Floor said seriously, "and I know, and the whole damn medical profession knows that whatever

414

problems you guys had was religious based, then why can't you just tell her what you just said to me?"

"But how could I ever give in to her when she never even once accepted me? And to crown it all, the woman not only stuck off, she abducted my children as well! How am I to forget that?"

"Well, you did pay her back, didn't you?" Floor grinned.

"Then why doesn't she get in touch with her children, am not standing in the way, am I?"

"I can't answer that anymore than I can understand your confession, but if what you're saying's correct, that you feel in that strange heart of yours that you're now one of them Muslims...then why are we wasting our time?"

"Yes, I do know I'm Muslim. I don't know how it all started or when it really began, but once I knew I was one of them Muslims, I just couldn't get rid of it, hard as I tried, this feeling of knowing who I've become."

"You were never normal, Mike," said Floor, all the while looking at him, as if deriding herself for not seeing him, until that moment, for what he was. "You were always one of them, weren't you?"

"Was I that strange?"

"Yes, but do go on, lay it on the old girl," she sat back in her chair, to get a better view of him.

"No doubt, I was angry with Islam. Islam turned my life upside down. I've been on an emotional roller coaster since I met Islam."

"You're telling me!"

"The key word is upside down!"

"And inside out!"

"But once I knew that the God of the eccentric Muslims was the one and the same God of America, and that Allah wasn't simply another eastern deity, it was then that I knew that I couldn't simply walk away from that knowledge. The proof was within me..." Mike wavered.

"Go on."

"You won't believe it, but my whole world's turned into a pulp— you name it, my buddies, my love life, my wine bar – Islam has kissed them all goodbye, and I haven't even lifted a finger to protest."

Floor rolled her eyes, "So now, what have we got here?"

"My religious declaration's none of her business."

"I'd still give her a call."

"After what she's done to me, no way!"

"This is crazy. Mike, you're not making sense. What're you afraid of, anyway. It's not like you at all...what's Islam doing to you? Now tell me what's this thing that so cramped Mike's style?"

"I'm still grappling with the basics, Floor," he said, "but the Islam I've come to know the last year or so, isn't really your run-of-the-mill stuff, nor is it the off-the-cuff media spun theories we know so well. A lot of the things we know of Islam are simply not there in reality...I mean there's more to Islam than meets the eye. Once you put your mind to it, let me warn you, you're hooked...there's no escape...and to say no is like denying the sky is blue...it's that apparent."

"Then we might as well not think about it!" Floor laughed.

"There's nothing arbitrary about Islam. We humans, we are all the same. We have the same needs. I've always felt this need for direction—though I didn't realize it—and it's not because of her..."

"Man, did I miss something!" Floor laughed. "Congratulations!"

"Once a Muslim always a Muslim, that's how I feel."

"I really miss the big mouth, you know," Floor said soberly. "We were like family. After she left, I realized how selfish I must have been during her illness. I was so full of my troubles that I didn't realize how much she needed me."

"You couldn't have been more supportive, Floor," Mike said.

"Still, I can't help wishing I did more." Floor switched on Mike two huge sad eyes. "Now what are you going to do?"

"Nothing," he said firmly. "She might have been your friend, but she'd never been mine."

"So you want out?"

"I'm not ruling out that option."

"Then welcome to the world of the divorcees!" she said. "I wish I could help though. By the way, you're staying for the night, aren't you? The guestroom's all yours. We could do with the company. What do you say to a Kosher pizza, stranger?"

"Thanks Floor, you been such an angel, but I think, I'm in a coping mood right now."

"On the other hand, you could leave the two little monsters with us? That should give you plenty of time to straighten things up in that warped head of yours. We bring them back on Sunday. You see, Jack's crazy about this new car he bought…"

"You win," Mike said, as they got up and strolled over to the playground. "But first let's find out what the little ones have to say about this new arrangement."

Chapter Twenty-Six

The Phone Call

A month later, and just a few weeks away from the children's summer holidays, an excited Fatima called her daughter to the phone.

It was a Saturday morning. The family had already done their morning prayers, but except for Fatima everyone had again gone back to bed to catch up with more sleep.

"Anisa! Anisa! Telephone! It's Ali!" Fatima shouted shrilly.

A bleary eyed Anisa grabbed the receiver. Having been awakened by the ringing of the phone and Fatima's shrieks, the whole family now rushed to the sitting room.

"Hello Mike! Hello!" Anisa screamed looking around her with the countenance of someone totally dazed. Everyone was staring at her, waiting for her to speak and say something. Her mother pushed her onto the telephone stool, "Sit! Sit down!" she commanded.

"Hang on a minute, I've a young lady here who's dying to have a word with you." Anisa heard squeals in the background.

A breathless Nasra came on line.

"Mommy, we're coming to visit, very soon. Dad made all the arrange...arrra...Daddy what did the woman say?"

"Arrangement...arrangement..." whispered the father.

"Arrangents? Never mind, Mommy, it's Nasra again Daddy made all the whatever...we're not supposed to tell, but we've lots of presents for you."

"My baby! What did you say? Hello? Nasra? Are you there?"

"Med is her. He wants to say something."

"Who?"

"Mommy! Mommy!" Mohammed's shrill voice cut into the mother's eardrum, but before he could say his piece, Nasra was back with more news.

"Mommy, can you guess how many teeth I've lost? Say it quickly."

"Let me see...10? 300?" They'd been gone for an epoch.

"Mommy can't even guess, the number is 4. Now speak to Med. He's crying."

"Med?"

"Mommy, I lost a tooth, and I kept bleeding, buckets and buckets. The doctor said: 'brave man, brave young man...,'" Mohammed's voiced trailed off as Mike came back on line.

"Hello there!"

A lump came to her throat.

"Yes, Mike, I'm here. But why did you let the doctor mess with Mohammed's mouth? And why is he bleeding buckets all of a sudden? Could you please explain what this is all about?"

"He fell down from the stairs, no big deal, really, the boy's blessed with some imagination...runs in the blood, doesn't it?"

"But where were you? And why was he left to bleed to the last? What were you doing? Weren't you looking after him?"

"I look after him all the time. But I can't walk for him. He's got plenty enough legs of his own! But don't you worry, the gentleman's still in one piece."

"And what have you done to his name?"

"His name's intact, too, and you'll be seeing him in a few weeks."

Then she was crying, "Talk!" her mother nudged her, "don't stop, you're on line, talk!"

"Tell me, Mike, and be honest with me, what plans have you got for Rako Island this time? Are you handing the children over the counter...the customs, or what?"

"Customs?" he screamed. "Now why are you involving the customs, if I may ask?"

"Never mind, just bring them, I know they need me, we won't involve anyone, not the customs, not the police. Let's please solve this in a civilized manner, okay? Now what am I supposed to do? Just wait and count the seconds?"

"I'll call you about the flight details. It's our bedtime, now. Give my regards to everyone, will you? And not a word about the customs or the police. Hello? Are you there?"

"Yes, Mike?"

"And say hello to Omar, will you?"

A dazed Anisa turned to the equally stunned family.

"You heard what we said? They're coming! They're coming!" She flew from the stool and darted straight into her mother's arms, then they were all jumping up and down, hugging each other, as if they'd just met; a scene so funny that an observer would've mistaken the house for a mental institution.

"When?" everyone was a-buzz with questions.

"Coming here?"

"To Rako Island?"

"You can't be serious?"

"Whatever happened to Mohammed's tooth?" asked the concerned grandmother.

"I knew it! I knew it!" Omar threw himself onto the sofa for support. "I knew it! *Ina Allahu 'Ala Kuli Shayin Qadiir!*"

Later, at breakfast, Anisa once again went over the telephone conversation with the others.

"Nasra said she lost four more teeth. That makes the total number of missing teeth six," she said lost in thought and munching away at the pancakes.

"How could all six be missing when the two she lost here were already grown before she left?" asked the grandmother.

"What else did they say? Give us the meat," Nora said.

"Mohammed fell over the stairs and knocked one of his front teeth loose. The doctor had to remove the brave young man's bleeding tooth, the tooth bled buckets, they said."

"Anisa, please, we've all had some biology, please," Hassan laughed. "We know teeth don't bleed as a rule."

"These teething problems aside, what did your husband say?" Nora's patience was wearing thin. "And why would he want to hand the kids over the counter? And why would he involve the police? One wonders what sort of family is it that would resort to the authorities for every little thing? We can't even solve our own problems, we need to bring in the authorities, as well, it's now become a routine...hello husband...in comes the police. Tell us now, Cousin, what did your husband say?"

"My husband? You mean Mike? Or perhaps you meant Ali?"

"I had no idea we were dealing with two different characters! See what I mean?"

"Mike said nothing. Nor did Ali say anything!"

"So whoever it was he called to say nothing?"

"You saw me on that phone, now don't tell me I didn't learn anything? He even said to say hello to Omar, well?"

All eyes turned on her.

"He did say something about the customs," she added. "We did mention the police...yes...didn't we go there after the abduction?"

"What did Mr. Mike Peterson say? Didn't he say they were coming?" Nora asked, totally out of touch with Anisa.

"You'll be seeing them in a few weeks, wasn't that what he said?" The still dazed Anisa look around her again. She wasn't dreaming. She could now see and feel the sun's heat, but she kept up the munching, anyway, just to prove to herself that this wasn't' just another dream...She'd never eaten in her sleep before.

"*Alhamdulillah!*" Omar said at last, "at least now we know he is coming and that he is bringing the children with him. I'm also sure Ali has reached a positive decision. I knew Ali would come to his senses, I'd always known he would."

"*Alhamdulillah*! Fatima replied. "You were proven right, Omar, but after what nightmare!"

Chapter Twenty-Seven

Candid Wrangling

...And nearest among them in love to the believers are those who say "we are
Christians." Because amongst these are men devoted to learning. And men who
have renounced the world, and they are not arrogant.
And when they listen to the revelation received by the Messenger, thou wilt see
their eyes overflowing with tears, for they recognize the truth:
(Qur'an: 5: 82-85)

The night they had been waiting for had finally come. Anisa and
her family did not sleep that night. By midnight everyone was ready
to go. As Nora and Anisa came out of the bedroom to meet the others
outside, Fatima's shock at seeing her daughter's appearance came
through.

"Can't you do better than that?" She gasped at the dowdy look of
her daughter, draped unceremoniously in materials that had seen
better days.

"Doesn't she look terrible?" echoed a grim Nora. "I wonder where she's dug them up from? I've never seen them before. What's she trying to prove, anyway?"

"You're not going to meet your family in this fashion, now there's no time for arguments. If you don't know any better, ask Nora to help you. We're waiting in the car." Fatima and Omar got into the car.

"I hope she doesn't scare him off," Fatima told Omar. "Whoever said one had to be in tatters to look Islamic! Allah is indeed beautiful. Can't help wondering what kind of message she's trying to convey to the poor man!"

"You worry too much, Fatima. Anisa's all right. *InshaAllah*, they'll iron this thing out. I hope to convince him to stay on in the island."

"Ya Allah!" said Fatima raising her hands in prayer. "You're indeed able to do all things."

A few minutes later Anisa and Nora joined Fatima and Omar in the station wagon. And at exactly 1.45 AM. the jumbo jet's passengers had begun to trickle into the arrival hall where they made lines at the passport control. At long last, Anisa was able to behold her children and husband among the throngs of people. Fortunately for Mike, the airport official who helped him kidnap the children was no where in sight.

As Mike and the children approached the door, Anisa went berserk, "*Ya Allah*! There! There! It's true! See how they run to me! I assure you this is real!"

"*Ya Rahman*! Just look at them!" The grandmother's eyes brimmed with tears.

Having cried over her children, Anisa had at last awakened to Mike's presence, who by now had shaken hands with everyone else. She extended a lame hand, and he took it lamely.

Once out at the parking lot, Omar deposited the luggage in the boot and they all piled into the station wagon. It was parked just a few steps away from where the black Sedan that helped him kidnap his children was parked. Mike's eyes were a hazy blue as his emotions entangled themselves with Stalk and Chili. But none of the people who crowded in Omar's car could sense any trace of remorse in his light weight eyes.

"So you at last got the heart to part with the old pick up, Omar?" he asked, fleeing his own empathy with the absent men who helped him abduct his own children. *Would they be mad at him? Shredding their happy endeavors so?*

"Ali, I couldn't afford to keep it going any longer," Omar said. "I just can't get used to this automatic gear, though. I feel like I'm in the passenger's seat. I miss the hard labor of changing gears. Driving this thing, I don't feel I'm in control at all. This car doesn't need me. It can very well take care of itself. Makes me feel redundant!" Omar complained as he turned the key and put the car easily into drive, and just sat there with his hands rested on the wheels as though he weren't doing anything at all.

"At least, it's large enough for the family," Mike said.

"Ali, that's some consolation!" Omar laughed.

"Mommy is crying again!" said little Mohammed pulling at his mother's scarf as he made himself comfortable between his Mom and Dad.

"I'm not crying, dear. I'm just happy. Now open your mouth and let me see that tooth you lost to the doctor."

"It's not there anymore," Nasra shouted from the back seat where she sat with Nora. "The doctor put it in his pocket!"

Ten minutes later, Omar reluctantly brought the car into the driveway of the hotel where Mike was already booked, on his own request, "Sure you won't change your mind? You know we've plenty of room at home…you don't have to do this. No matter what happens between you and your wife we like to believe that we are still your family."

"Thanks, Omar. But I think I'll be just fine here. I'll see you tomorrow." Mike patted Omar's shoulder.

As he turned to kiss Mohammed goodbye, Nasra's eyes widened in apprehension, "Where's he going now?"

"We don't have enough room at home, tonight, Nasra," Anisa put in quickly. "Daddy is coming back tomorrow."

"*Alahamdulillah!*" the little girl said, "I thought he was leaving again!"

The following day Mike met Omar at the door, he'd just returned from Asar prayers. The two shook hands.

"*Assalamu 'alaikum*! We expected you for lunch," Omar said. "Have you had anything to eat?"

"I'd a late lunch at the hotel, then took some time to pray Asar and Dhuhur." Mike said, and the two made their entrance into the living room.

An hour or so later of chatter and prattle and tea, Mike and Anisa suddenly found themselves all alone in the house.

Omar was the first to excuse himself on the pretext of an urgent errand at the shop. Then Fatima remembered an old widowed woman she was going to visit at the hospital. The brothers were already gone after lunch. That left Nora and the children. And before they knew it, they too were out of sight and out of earshot.

"I wonder where everyone's gone," Anisa murmured, then made a dash for the front door. This was *it*! She was on her own—with Mike! But wasn't this the moment she'd waited for—and dreaded? Returning to the sitting room, she said glumly, "We're on our own, Mike. Would you care for some more tea?"

"Too sweet, I wouldn't mind some coffee, though."

"How thoughtless of me!" She dashed out of the room. "I'll get you some in a jiffy." She returned in the same speed with hot water, a mug of Nescafe and a large table spoon.

"One spoon?" she asked holding up the large spoon.

"Make it two or three, it doesn't matter."

"Three of this?"

"Never mind about the coffee, let's go get some fresh air." He got up to go.

"Let's wait a bit so we don't lock them out."

"You can give me that coffee now," he said, sliding back into the chair.

Why did she have to wear black of all colors? His mind screamed, reminded of the black Sedan Stalk rented for the rescue mission.

"By the way, that's a nice scarf you've got on your head…black isn't it? Lovely color…a bit too dark, but…" he said airily.

"Thanks! Didn't know you liked dark colors…yes…black's a bit too dark…but nice…but guess what they call me at work?"

"I could never guess things with you, but go ahead, lay it on me."

"The black woman!" she laughed.

She was sure he was now ready for whatever it was he came for...*good!* About time they kissed *goodbye!* Two and half years of hanging in the air wasn't exactly a balm for the nerves. She wasn't dreaming at all, *Mike was back in Rako*, and he didn't come empty handed...

"But that's lovely," he said politely, "so you're working now—I remember Nasra mention that—and you're wearing these nice black scarves to work?" He put his hand to his mouth to stifle a yawn.

"Yeah, isn't that nice!" she said, taking another sip of the tea and adjusting the scarf.

"But you wouldn't wear them inside your home unless you had male strangers in the house, isn't that right?"

"You sure learning the rules, Mike," she replied, wondering whether he was hinting at something or showing off some new knowledge he'd stumbled on in her absence? Now that he wasn't involved with her, she thought, he could look at things with an open mind. *Good for him...the country boy's come a long way!*

"Have you seen your poor old parents lately?" she asked, injecting into her voice more concern than she really felt—not that she had anything against the oldies. In fact, since the children's abduction, she had come to sympathize with Mike's motherly concern.

"My poor old parents? I didn't pass on their warm greetings, did I?"

"Your poor nephews, they must be big boys now…let me guess, eleven and thirteen? Whatever became of their poor father?" The last person she would waste breath on was his sister Charlotte, the kids were altogether a different matter, *poor unlucky things*! she thought. But now that they were parting ways, she might as well show some sign of concern for the sister as well. Pouring another cup of tea for herself and trying to muster up as much pity as she could, she said with a flutter of her lashes, "Poor Charlotte! How much she must've suffered bringing up those kids on her own!"

"Well, she had it coming. She can't blame it on anyone else."

"You should feel some sympathy for her. After all, she's your sister." She fixed her gaze on the white wall above his head.

"Well, my sister can take care of herself. She's a grown woman, you know."

"I've as yet to see her act grown up! Unless she's got her act together the last couple years!" she blurted out against her better judgment. "Anyway, she's family. And family's forever. More coffee, dear?"

"Yes, dear, but just one spoon, but not that spoon," he said eyeing the large spoon. "Teaspoon, please, if you have any around."

"How stupid of me, I nearly killed you!" She blew into the kitchen to get a teaspoon. *Ya Allah*! He was up to something and he wasn't saying it. Wasn't it time she broached the subject? No, she pinched herself, let it be *him* who splits the beans…

"By the way," he said, as she handed him the cup, "I've a letter for you from Floor."

"You're not kidding! Floor! Writing to me! After what I said to her! The fundamentalist that I'm why would Floor waste her precious letters on me, sister of terrorists! And how's the poor daughter? And that strange man of hers? We were the best of friends, sharing everything but faith! Poor old Floor, she must be mad at me! But how is she? Can't help missing her. Is the coffee better now, dear?"

"Tastes like one, thanks dear."

437

"How about my other friends, met anyone of them?"

"Your friends?"

"How silly of me! Busy as you were doing your own thing," she said, then for want of saying something, added. "Well, you must excuse me, I almost forgot to wish you Merry Christmas and Happy New Year! You must've invested in a lovely tree now that your old wife's not in the vicinity?"

"Well, well, well…and to think we were in the middle of summer…wrong as usual, aren't I?"

"You must've celebrated last Christmas, though?"

"Oh! Last Christmas! Why didn't you say so! Last Christmas was simply fantastic! You know, for the first time in my adult life that I'd gone bananas—I was Santa Claus and the neighborhood kids loved it."

"A pity you didn't have the children with you then?"

"But we'd a lovely Easter with eggs and what not—that made up for the lost Christmases!"

She knew she wouldn't rest until she found out exactly what it was that brought him to Rako Island. There was something terribly unnatural about the way he was conducting himself...

"I think we should go out now," she said, wary. "What do you say we go to the beach?"

Outside on the main street, they hailed a cab. It was that time between afternoon and sunset. But it was typically warm and the two strolled slowly among the throngs of people at the beach getting ready to go home. At last they found a deserted place at the farthest edge of the beach.

"Mind if we sit here?" he asked politely.

"Sure," she said as she removed her sandals to sit on them, then seeing the wet sand, he changed his mind.

"Never mind, we'll walk back. It's soon getting dark anyway. I'm starving, what say you to a meal? But, hey, haven't you forgotten *Maghrib*?"

"Ah? No, no—not today. You see, I'm on holiday. The woman's period."

"You're on holiday because of the period? I got it!"

439

"I thought we were going to talk."

"Haven't we been talking enough?"

"And saying nothing?" If all he wanted was a divorce why was he procrastinating this way?

"I didn't thank you for that nice letter, did I?" he asked shortly.

"That nice letter? Which one?"

"Cute letters, both of them, but that last piece, that was the cluster bomb. A remarkable letter, by any standard. And the picture, Oh, what a killer!"

"The children's picture?"

"The other one, too, you know, the lady in the picture, wasn't that my wife?"

"With Mohammed and Nasra on her lap? That one?"

"You're a born letter writer, Anisa. What a waste of talent! Ah, there comes a cab! Taxi! Taxi!"

The driver screeched to a stop, "Where to, sir?"

"You just drive," Mike said, hopping into the front seat. "I'll think of something."

"You've no place to go, sir?" The driver eyed him.

Anisa shouted from the back, "The Meridian. The fish is good there."

The driver winked at the foreigner, "The fish is good in Rako Island. And where do you come from, sir?"

"America."

"America! Unites States of America! Good place. Yes, sir?"

"The best."

"Good movies, yes, sir?"

"Only the best."

"What else is best there, sir?"

"Huge place, best place."

'That's best, sir, very powerful, too." The driver rapped his knuckles against the wheel to demonstrate just how powerful. "I saw the war on TV, sir. The planes, they were simply the best. Up, up, down, down, giant metal birds. Shoot, shoot, drone, drone, just like dragons. Just like in films. With planes like that who needs bravery, sir?"

"Take it easy, man, but let me get this straight," Mike threw a glance at the driver, "what war are we talking about?"

441

"The Gulf War! Which other war can we talk about? Very interesting war, sir. And where were you, sir? Weren't you serving in the army?"

"Bad timing," Mike admitted.

"Busy kidnapping your own children, weren't you?" Anisa's hands became fists under her handbag. She promised herself not to ever mention that chapter of her life even to herself. It was a chapter that was best buried.

"You missed a very interesting war, sir. Just like in movies. You know the dead people did not matter at all. We were watching a movie, sir."

"A movie?" Mike hurled at the driver. "Was that what this war was all about? A movie?"

"Simply the best," the driver replied. "None of us taxi drivers really cared for the dead or the crying women. The planes, they were the hot topic. Bu these other things, the ruins these planes left behind, they just didn't matter. It was that kind of war that's either lost or won. Sir, let me be frank with you, America won that war."

"America shouldn't try to take exclusive credit for that war," Anisa hurled from the back. "America did not win that war. Whole Muslim armies were involved in that war. And if it wasn't for these stupid Muslims, we wouldn't be talking about this war at all."

"In any case, sir, it was a very interesting war." The driver screeched to a stop in front of the hotel. "Sir, how is Mr. George Bush these days?"

"Mr. George Bush?"

"Who else? Yes, Mr. Bush your president, the man who put all the planes together, how does he feel, sir? Any signs of remorse about what he has done, sir?"

"You mean, the George Bush?" asked Mike as he took out his wallet to pay the driver. "How the hell would I know of his feelings? And like I said I'm a busy man. So pre-occupied have I been of late that had someone shelled the hell out of my own house I wouldn't have noticed. Thank you."

"Enjoy your fish, sir," said the driver as he pocketed the fat tip.

"What an interesting fellow!" Anisa hissed as they got seated at a table in the restaurant. "You were of course very busy doing your own thing, but let *me* tell you something, America couldn't have won that war. The stupid Arab world won it for America. It was them who invaded each other."

"That's not what the man said."

"But what did he know of this war? All the poor man saw was a movie! He was right about the dead people, though. Indeed, a very interesting war. If there ever was a stimulating war, this one was peerless! And like the driver said, it was a war won by machines! So much for bravery!"

"A movie? Was that what it was all about? A movie? And why would a world leader have any regrets about this movie, if you don't mind *me* asking?"

"Well, I don't know about that, but the movie this world leader orchestrated was surely perfect – the perfect recipe for regrets—you had dead Arabs on both sides!. On both sides of the fence, innocent Muslims! – what a perfect occasion for celebrations!"

"And if the occasion calls for such a celebration, why the regrets? As it is, the world's over-populated. And if the latest population chart's anything to go by, it's this part of the world that's truly congested, so why the regrets?"

"Who gives a hoot?" she cried. "Who gives a cent? Whoever spared a tear for a grieving women? The world's male population, leaders and laymen, they're just the same, they just don't give a damn about women. No one cares, not even Rako Island's taxi drivers. Dead women don't give fat tips. Most of them can't even afford thin ones, when alive. This man's of course blameless, busy as he was nabbing innocent poor children!"

"Like I said," he said, averting his gaze from the scarf, "that was one hell of a letter and busy as I was I still got the time to read all seventeen pages of this highly spirited letter. Well, what do you say to that?"

A notebook and a pen in hand, a smiling waiter ambled over to the table.

"The best fish on the menu, please. My wife came all this way just to partake of this great fish," Mike said casually.

"Something from the chef's specials is good, sir? And may I recommend the same for the husband as well, sir?" The waiter asked politely.

Done with the amiable waiter, Mike now turned to Anisa.

"Like I was saying, this spirited letter was simply the best, if there is anything that can claim superiority over American bombs, today, it's this letter. I made sure it traveled with me, and it's right here in Rako Island, gracing my secular briefcase. Mike Peterson's carrying a Muslim letter in his mundane briefcase and my wife here is talking about watching a silly war on TV. She's mad because this mundane person didn't make time to watch dead people on TV. I didn't kill those people, dear, I didn't even know of their death, this man you see before you was already dead when these planes took to the skies. So, how was he supposed to know of the dead?"

"If this man was really deceased," she took a deep breath. "I assure you he wouldn't be here paying fat tips. Nor could his departed soul lurk in posh hotels, lying in wait for a chance to pounce on Muslim children!"

446

"Which brings me to the question of my passport," he said. "I was never ever given the chance to ask, but why in God's name did my wife steal my passport? To wreck the enemy boat, and give the crazy woman time to make her escape good?"

"You did get your paper back, however, the truth is, even if my poor uncle didn't speed things up, this man's chances of pouncing on Muslim kids was just as great. The underdeveloped being that I'm, I did miscalculate the extent a developed mind could go to—dear husband, you don't need a silly paper to do business—congratulations, your powers extend the heavens!"

"This letter was an eye opener," he said. "This fool actually thought he knew something about the sender, but no, said the letter bomb, no, no, you don't know nothing about this woman…"

"The letter bomb…say you?" she asked, cautious. *The man wanted out*, she was positive now, her suspicions being confirmed by the second. *Out*, that's what he wanted. And what better hands to dump the kids? No fool this man. The signs were there for all to see. *A woman*! That was it! And this woman, she now realized, was most probably a flop with kids. What else was making him so goosey? He

447

was in love, and he didn't know how to confess this huge feeling to his old wife. It wasn't exactly the kind of thing a man in love would do. Confess to the ex-wife! It wasn't the done thing in polite circles. And Mike was a gentleman. All this dust he was raising now was simply a cover up. A lesser man would've just posted the children; a one way ticket to Rako Island would have sufficed. But not Mike—he'd travel thousands of miles, just to make sure that he'd done things right—what a miracle, though! Wasn't that what she prayed for day and night? Mike wanted *out*.

"That beautiful letter, dear," she said, managing a very thin smile, "what was in that beautiful letter that ruffled the hair?"

"Come to think of it, it does have the makings of someone's life story."

"Mind if I go to the ladies to wash my face?" she asked, she needed time to reconstruct her thoughts and prepare herself for the bomb: *Anisa, I want out.*

Once in the ladies, she put her face under the tap, splashing cold water on it.

She was alone in the mirrored room, and she could give herself a critical look. Her looks weren't exactly her first priority these days, yet she could now see, reflected from all sides in those endless mirrors, that she was still *together*, and if Mike was opting for out, the mirror reinforced her confidence, it wasn't because she was *falling apart*. Their problems were deeper than skin and bone, and she wished him well.

Apparently, she thought, briefly dwelling on the looks of this new competition, or more appropriately, this *filler* (for she wouldn't call her competition, as it was *she*, *Anisa*, who did the ditching, and this new being who filled *the* vacuum had only filled a vacuum) was none other than a she-copy of him and, therefore, a perfect recipe for peace and harmony—the harmony that Mike so desired but never found with Anisa. Then just as she was returning to the filler's looks, and wondering how natural this woman would really look put beside Mike, that she heard voices at the door. Anisa hastily opened her bag and taking out a wrinkled Kleenex from underneath her wallet she quickly wiped the water from her face and strode back to the restaurant. The food was already on the table when she arrived.

"How's Omar, by the way?" he asked without raising up his head from his plate. "I understand his wife's passed away?"

"He's okay, my uncle's a man of faith. And he knows that life and death are in the Hands of God. So he's been very patient. And all Praise is to Allah."

"Can't really help liking the man," he said as he chewed on a mouthful of fluffy white rice dipped in steamed fish. "A good man. Had there been more people like him around, I assure you, the world's troubles would've seen a marked reduction. A very sincere man, you knew where you stood with him...not like some people we know." He looked up from the plate, and waved his fork at her. "Two people so closely related yet so different – yeah, yeah, Omar and *his niece* are as far apart as East is from the West."

"Aha?"

"Omar's tops."

"Wish I could say the same about your dear sister, though. But never mind, there's no point in crying over spilt milk. One minute you think you are family with her, the next minute she turns you into a complete E.T, sometimes even more alien."

"An alien's an alien," he said as a matter of fact.

"It's in her make up, this snaking business."

"You've something on your face, hang on," he reached out to pick up something from her forehead.

"Eeee!," he inspected the slimy wet tissue between his fingers. "What's this?"

"Just wiped my face with a Kleenex, bad quality, I suppose. Made in Rako Island, not the real thing."

This *other woman* must be really neat, she thought, definitely not the type that would spoil her precious face with old Kleenexes that stick on the face.

"So, where do you work and what kind of work is it that sends you to the malls everyday?" he asked "You didn't mention it in that letter-bomb you dispatched to the old widower."

"It must've slipped my mind."

"Then, it can't be that serious."

"How's that very important work of yours that always stood between you and your prayers? And how's your buddy Bill? Isn't he

451

married yet? And how's that delightful mother of his? I'm sure she's given up all hope of ever becoming a decent mother."

"Why would anyone want to get married? Bill maybe crazy, but, I guarantee you, he ain't that crazy," laughed Mike.

She nodded.

This other woman he was crazy about, she thought, she was all for marriage and so was he and now he wanted to pretend like he was crazy, so he could marry her…or *live with her*, or whatever.

"Absolutely. Only crazy people got married, for crazy reasons." She put another spoonful into her mouth. "But who cares about people and what they think where matters of the heart are concerned? As long as one gets married to the *right* person, guess, that's all that matters," she said, preparing for the bomb.

"The right person, you say? It isn't everyday that a right person comes along, Anisa," he replied philosophically, taking another sip of the mineral water.

"All the more reason why one should grab the chance when the said right person comes along—especially after all these years of whiling away one's time with the wrong sort, you know, the alien sort," she poked her free hand at her chest.

"You could've fooled me," he raised his eyebrows wondering what the hell she was talking about now.

And idea suddenly struck her mind, "You know that first night you called, wasn't there another person spending the night with you guys?" she ventured.

"Another person?"

"Never mind, you don't owe me nothing, but frankly speaking, you may say to me anything, I'm a changed woman, and it's your life. I've no right to interfere with your life, like you dare not include yours in mine, right? After all, we come from different worlds, being different earth-wares, and all that. And our ways will never meet."

"Anisa, our ways have already met."

"Mike, how you of all people could utter such nonsense?" she cried. "Ours was a *mighty* collision. What happened to us can't be called a meeting. In real life, our ways will never meet. Collisions do occur, but meetings? No way. A happy meeting isn't for us. Only collisions. And sad stories."

"I've no need for sad stories, Anisa. I'm paying for the meal, and I intend to enjoy it," he said, but as he raised his spoon again his glance fell on the black table cloth beneath his elbows and he started with panic. His eyes shifted to Anisa's headgear, same color! Why black of all colors? His mind screamed. She could've worn blue, and this would match perfectly with her dress, why did she have to make the head black? And why did the Sedan had to be black? He knew he was done in, and his good brain just wasn't functioning well, but right now any other color could've done him service.

Oblivious of his discomfort, she persisted, "Let's face it, Mike, these sad stories do abound. You name it. Unhappy memories. Unhappy spouses. Confused kids. Sick wives. Confused husbands. Confused doctors. Angry husbands. Confused in-laws. Tiresome global jaunts. Baby abductions. We must beware, these *collisions* make neat families."

"You could say that again!"

"See, we don't even look the same, and appearance does count in this world of colors. I knew that long ago, remember how different we looked in the water, even then?"

"Right as usual!"

"People just can't help staring when they meet us," she continued in a frown, "look at that waiter over there? He's done nothing but stare and is probably waiting to be salaried for his endeavors. See the old couple in the corner? They haven't blinked once since we came in. Let's face it, we make an odd couple, Mike."

"Odd is the word I been searching for all night long, you just took it out of my mouth, a marvel how your tongue's always beating me to things…now let me say after you: Odd, isn't it?" he stated, thinking of the hey days of *her* reform, when she first donned the scarf. She did look odd then. But there was something about the way she now carried herself that told him things were different for her now. *Seemed like she'd passed the painful stage, and made peace with her God.* He thought. He could see that she'd crossed some hurdles too…*and perhaps weakened her Satan, somewhat*? But he wasn't about cheering her. The last thing on his mind was to bring smiles to her lips and make her say: *I told you so. I am home, Mike. See, how settled I'm now in my faith? See how happy I'm to be me? The other*

455

was simply a put on. She'd to go, the Anisa you married. But look at you? Look at this new you that can see things?

"Very odd," she broke in to his thoughts. "Whether we're in your hometown or in my home turf, people are people and they can't help staring when they see an *odd couple*. And now that I've this thing on my head, you just can't blame people, can you? Mike, we're intruding into each other's privacy."

"You could say that again!"

"Like I was saying we don't even look alike, even our shadows would tell us."

"They would." Another glance at the table, and the table cloth was moving before his eyes. Was he getting dizzy?"

"You people think you came from the apes. Right?"

"I went to school, Anisa," he said refocusing his gaze. "And I've always been an A student. And I understand you went to school, too, and they taught you the Darwin theory, unless of course you were in the habit of flunking subjects?"

"I never did take my text book seriously on that subject. I did take in a lot of other stuff, but somehow I never took in that theory, and it was just as well, one problem less."

"Good!"

"And by the way, what's so special about Darwin? Why are you so hung up on him? The man's dead and went to his grave without ever getting his jumbled ideas together. Don't you think it's time you looked for facts instead of whiling away your energies on a weightless impression whose contriver is already dead?"

"But his theory is with us, and it does keep things in perspective."

"Like you guys are at the top of things, right?"

"Always Mrs. Right!"

"Now honestly, tell me about this other person," she said, eager. "It's a free world. I mean, you know my type, I'm not the interfering sort. You don't graze in my turf, either, see how you don't even interfere with my headgear anymore?"

"I wouldn't mind a different color, though, but that's altogether beside the story, isn't it?

"But your willing to give it a try and be liberal about the whole thing," she said, quite impressed with his progress but still dying to get to the bottom of his errand.

"After all," she persisted, "we happen to share the same earth. You just can't throw us out, that doesn't mean you didn't try, but it just doesn't work that way. So why bother? Why worry about my headgear? What would you care if I wrapped my head with a piece of cloth? It isn't your head that's wrapped, it's not even your wife's any longer if your really serious about this other person. Honestly, now that you're on my native soil, I can be very hospitable, and very understanding, you know us, you been here before," she took a breath, then continued.

"Yes, you've met my family, and you know that in our own underdeveloped ways, we can be really very accommodating. You just admitted yourself that my uncle was a great guy. I even heard you say to him: *Salaamu'alikum* this very afternoon. And not long ago you even reminded me of my evening prayers. Now, that's what I call a miracle, exactly what your children and I prayed for right on that beach!"

"How could I forget? You mentioned it rightly in that nice piece your wrote to the widower."

"Now you can tell me everything, the whole happy story, any day. Right now, I'm all ears."

She'd just cleaned up her plate. The fish was simply ethnic perfect. She was on her soil. She could take anything, anything her children's father wished, would be done.

"You heard what my uncle said," she said. 'No matter what happens between you and your wife, we'd like to believe that we're your family', those are my uncle's words." What her uncle said was exactly how everyone else in her family viewed him. Family.

"That's, however, altogether beside the point, and you didn't travel thousands of miles to compare our families. I'm sure there's a weightier issue at hand. And now that our children are no longer two hapless bones of contention, I'm willing to tackle this weighty issue with the father of my children."

The friendly waiter was strolling towards them. There were very few people in the restaurant now and he was able to give the couple his undivided attention.

459

"Anything else, sir, anything for Madam?" He poised his pen on his notepad and darted glances from the one to the other.

"What would you like to have for desert, Madam?" Mike asked.

"Sorry, dear, Madam's not spoiling the stomach with more stuff."

"Thanks, man, the wife's not spoiling the fish with more stuff."

"Just coffee for the husband, sir?" The waiter grinned. "Thank you, sir."

"Thank you, too, sir."

"Now about helping you out with this weighty issue," she broke into a hurried monologue, "I want you to know that what you're doing is great. I mean the two of you are made for each other. The most terrific couple in your native country. Same shade of skin. Same unwrapped heads. You're both insured for life. You laugh at the same jokes. You won't have to propose with all the awkwardness in the world. Actually, you won't even have to propose at all." She paused to take a sip at her orange juice.

"And she won't be bored easily at the golf courses. She won't embarrass you by asking silly questions about the mouse holes and the tiny balls. With this other person, Mike Peterson will remain Mike

460

Peterson, forever," she paused, then went on. "Names like Ali Ahmed, bring back memories of the mind boggling images of the sword swiveling dervishes. Who in their right mind would want to suffer such outlandish nametags, anyway? Mike, your mother's right."

"My mother's always right, so what's new?"

"Patience, Mike, I promised the kids this very dialogue, so hear me out, will you?"

"Then make it short, will you?"

"Now where was I? Yes, like I said, with you and this person, it's like—welcome freedom—my sweet sister-in-law-fashion."

"Ah! So that's where we were heading again? My sister?"

She wasn't about to be side-tracked. "I assure you," she carried on, Your journey together with this person will be a very pleasant one. You guys can have the finest and the brightest Christmas tree in the neighborhood. What a cheer to your old mother! With this person, there won't be no more mountains to climb. Nor more reading of brain-jolting stuff. You won't have to get wiser at all by reading heavy stuff. The two of you can read all the books in the world and yet remain the same simple souls forever."

He darted a glance at his watch; it was on a totally different time zone…he was feeling dizzy again, "You just go ahead and tell when you're done," he said as he reclined back in the chair and tried to rest his head.

With this other person, prayer mats shall be a thing of the past, she said. And the fridge could back to life with all things forbidden.

"That was some shot, I hope you're done now?" he yawned.

"Well? What say you to all these? It's your life, Mike. You either live it full, the only way that makes you feel cushy or you go on denying yourself, which hopefully won't be the case, if you let the old wife take over the burden of the hampering pair. Mike?"

"Tell me when you're done," he said, his right hand kneading his head which was now in the throes of a blinding headache.

"Between you and me, Rako Island's just as good a place for the kids. You guys can come here for your vacations, come summer, come winter. You guys are welcome to this one season we've got here—throughout the year just one season. The strand's beautiful. The island's service-oriented. She'll love the milky, mushy sand."

She paused for an interlude, but finding no interruption, she went on, "I mean with a bikini, you can perch anywhere and everywhere."

"Bikinis don't get in the way. Bikinis are made that way," he sounded, quoting someone else, for by now his brain was at it's lowest ebb, and he just couldn't be bothered to come up with a remark of his own.

"If you've a bikini on your body nobody will look."

"What's there to look for? Everything's out in the open. I hope we are done now?"

"Cover up that body and you're inviting trouble!" she said. "Isn't that why we're given the look, and from mouth to mouth our simple covering has become the talk? Look how they look from behind the veil! They say. They must be carrying bombs under those silly wraps! Yeah, we're heading the 21st century, what the hell are they hiding anyway. Isn't that what you were thinking when your wife decided to take out the wrap?"

"Get it on with it, get it off your chest."

"But that's all history," she said paving the way for friendship and understanding. "Now's the time for friendship, you and I and this bikini friend of yours, we're not going to be suspicious of each other. We've children together. And unless you guys are too old to start a family, we'll have even more together…Is something wrong, Mike?"

"It's just this headache," he sighed. "You may proceed now, while I nurse this stupid head of mine. Waiter!"

"Your coffee's on it's way, Sir."

"I think he's suffering from jet-lag," she diagnosed, the seasoned traveler she was. "I hope the management has reserved some painkillers," she smiled at the waiter. "As you can see, this man is a guest. And foreigners do expect decent service. That's why they come to Rako Island."

"I think your wife's right, Sir. My wife's always right, too. At least, about sicknesses and foreigners. I'll get you some Panadol with the coffee, Sir."

The polite waiter staggered away from the problem couple. *My God, what a weird couple,* he thought, *wait until my wife hears this.*

"You know Anisa, this diagnosis is about the greatest thing that's happened to us since the fish. My lady, you're right again. You know am just powerless without my beauty sleep, so how about calling it a day, after I've had my Panadol?"

Anisa glanced at her watch. It was 8.55 PM. Still not a single word about his errand. And now he was getting a splitting headache. *It must be tough on him*, she reminded herself. If he hadn't kidnapped the children, he wouldn't have been in this spot now—*popping Panadol in a restaurant*! For a moment, she was tempted to ask whether the kids cried during the seizure, but decided against it. The last thing on her mind was to plant more sinister ideas into his head – as it was he'd plenty going for him.

"Your Panadol, Sir." the waiter placed the coffee, two tablets and a bottle of water in front of Mike, and the latter immediately paid up. Never had Mike come across a more concerned waiter, more like a good friend on standby. The man deserved a bonus.

"Time we pulled up the old legs," he said, coining his own phrases now that he had the Panadol in his hand. "You do have work in the morning, if I'm not mistaken?"

"I'm on leave."

"Hello there! I'm on vacation, too! The children are on vacation…why don't we all do something together? Say tomorrow? So where shall we meet?"

"You know, if we have the children around, we won't be able to talk about things, honestly, let's not involve them until we've had something concrete. Your daughter Nasra has squirrel ears."

"Between you and me, she's also blessed with a tongue as long as my arm! You could say it runs in the family!"

"So this person and she, they aren't thick at all, are they?" laughed Anisa.

"Wife, to be honest with you, I really do not have the faintest idea of where this is all leading. Maybe a good night's sleep will jump start my brain, but as it is, I'm clueless. So why not call it a day, and go on vacation from all talk until I'm myself again? And let's not forget who is the guest here…"

Soon the waiter was racing them to the port and waving for a Taxi.

Luckily, this cab driver was a churlish type. And it was just as well. For Anisa was now drained of all energy, and Mike just couldn't wait for the door to shut before he was snoring in the front seat.

No sooner did Anisa raise her hand to tap on the door than Nora swung the door open.

"Sssh. Let's go to the kitchen, they've all gone to bed," she said, leading the way to the kitchen.

"Now the good news first. And please no bad news tonight. Just give the good news and I'll put my head to rest," Nora said making herself snug in her favorite corner.

"What good news?" sighed Anisa as she slumped on a chair.

"You tell me," Nora's heart missed a beat. "Isn't that why I passed up my beauty sleep? Just to hear the good news? We're entitled to good news, my friend, you can't deny it anymore. Now, come on and open up."

"Well, I hate to disillusion you, sister, but there isn't much to tell, not that I'd heard all evening any voice other than my own, so, there, except that he's now trying to act more gentlemanly, if you know what I mean."

"Guess, it's long overdue."

"Now that my children are back, I guess, I should cool it down and not complain anymore."

"What's the matter, Anisa? He said something and you're not telling?"

"There's nothing to tell. The man's living with another woman. And he isn't telling it like it is. It's written all over him. He thinks he can fool me. But I know him. He doesn't think I know him, that's the problem. Can you believe it, I even invited her to Rako, come summer come winter…"

"So generous," Nora rolled her eyes.

"We're family, after all. He invited me and the children to this family get together tomorrow. Said he was entitled to his holiday and I'm obliged to make his holiday a success because he happens to be on my native soil!"

"Said you were obliged to make his holiday a success? What could he mean by that?" whispered Nora.

"Not in so many words," Anisa said. "Nora, you haven't lived together with these people as closely as I have."

"You've done it all for us, Anisa, that's more than we can handle, and for your info, I wouldn't repeat your experience if I lived several lives. Now tell me about you and Mike. Tell me all you know."

"So you think you know more than you know, don't you? But what would you know other than what is chosen for you to know? So you read their weekly magazines and lap up the daily papers? And read books, written, and censored by them? So you watch TV? What do you ever get to see therein other than what you are shown, Nora? Take my word for it, these people they don't talk straight. And they're racists. Can you believe it, we haven't even said salaam before he started poking fun at my scarf, just because it happens to be black!"

"So Mike's a racist? That's nice to know, Anisa," Nora yawned.

"You wouldn't notice those things, would you? No, you wouldn't, not in years."

"Nora, you don't know Mike. You are a Muslim. Muslims never get to know people. Muslims take people at face value. That's the big problem facing the Muslim world, they never get to meet the person behind the face…"

And then she was telling Nora a story she'd never shared with anyone.

"Let me tell you something, Nora."

"Get on with it, Anisa," groaned Nora. "And please don't drag me into your troubles. I like to keep my innocence."

"In the hey days of our relationship," she related, "we used to attend parties and such. In his home town everyone knew everyone. Everyone had a smile and a kiss on the cheek for everyone. How naïve I must've been taking their smiles for other than what it was."

"Anisa, please."

"And then in one of these happy nights," Anisa waved away Nora's remark, "this woman comes up to me, all smiles, with arms stretched as an ironing board, 'Look what we've got here?' she cooed. 'So this is the cute little darling I been hearing about?' She arched her bare back a little to one side so she could wink at someone else. 'Anisa Ali', said I, hugging her copiously. 'Aaali! Aaali!' she whispered into my ear. 'Aaali honey darling, you know you're the handsomest darling I ever saw, you know, in a very, very dark, dark way, ha! ha! ha! Aaali! Aaali!'

'Handsome in a very, very dark, dark way?' said I, still clinging to her bare back as though that were the only straw on the cliff, then whispered I, like one overwhelmed, 'Now that you mention it, I also think you're the naughtiest darling in town, you know, in a very, very white, white way! What's your name white-hide?'"

"Phew!" Nora heaved a sigh. "I feel like I've just been driven up a barren hill, I'm parched, do you mind passing some cold water from that fridge?"

"Nora, bad company is bad for you. Can you imagine me criticizing a creation of God, and blaming someone for being white? I could've had my tongue torched for uttering such blaspheme! See what happens when one consorts with the wrong sort. When they smile, you smile back, when they say green you learn to say yellow, black, white, they snub, you snub back. You could say I was unlucky, but the only unsmiling person I met there was Floor. Floor never did smile at you."

"How terrible!"

"In all the years I'd known her, Floor never did fake a smile. When she smiled, it was real, nor did she call you honey. No honey. No smile. No colors. That's Floor."

"How about his parents, your children's grandparents?" Nora managed.

"My in-laws?" Anisa grinned. "Nora, I may disagree with my mother-in-law, but that girl has my respects. Even if she were to throw me from a cliff, I'd still salute her before I hit the ground. She's no Floor, but she's just as constant. No surprises."

"Huh?"

"She doesn't hate me anymore than I hate her. It's just that she's overly protective, you know how mothers are. The old lady's family, that much I can guarantee you, and it so happened that I'd be the first to know of her bad back, but that was of course when we weren't rowing."

"So you guys don't hate each other no more? But that's good news. Why didn't you share it before, so I could console myself with this piece of good news…"

"But this sister of his, she's no family, the way she smiled at me. And then, boom! Nora, my sister-in-law lasted only for a few months. After that just barren looks, then complete silence, it was horrible, I felt bereft. Nora, that woman's a closed cupboard, and she's the only one holding the key."

"Let's just hope that Mike's not a closed cupboard, too," breathed Nora.

"You just give me one good reason why he would be any different?" replied Anisa. "And no matter what happens, he'll never say what he means. You've to be a darn good guesser to keep your neck above water."

"Well, he doesn't have to confess to anything. Why should he?"

"You think he's brimming with good news?"

"At least he's come to his sense. Cousin, that's more than I can say about you."

"You don't get it, do you? The man is under threat to dump the kids, or else."

"Is he settling for divorce, then?"

"You think he cares for divorce? What'd he gain from it that he hadn't got already? I mean even if he didn't divorce the old wife, what'd he lose?"

"I think I'm going to bed, Anisa, this is depressing," lamented Nora. "Honestly, I expected some good news. The normal good news normal people normally hear once in a while. We are also normal people. We also like to hear some normal news, but I guess good news is meant only for others." Nora yawned. *What a family!* Marriage No.1. Marriage No.2. Fray. Counter fray. Abduction. Counter Abduction. Put this union's problem on the desk of the Security Council, and no matter how many hands went up in the air, the UN would never solve this one…

"There's no end to anything," Nora said. "There wasn't even a beginning. Not for up here, anyway. None of us were even there when it all started. *MasahAllah!* No beginnings and no ends. And we're to grovel in the mud with this headless, tailless union! I've school tomorrow. Salaam!"

"And by the way," Nora threw from the kitchen door, "don't say anything to your old mother until you guys have had this family united nations conference, or whatever."

With a huge yawn, Nora slid through the half closed kitchen door. She was really beat. What an anti-climax! All day long, she'd been feeling on top of the world, euphoric, happy for everyone, for her old aunt, for her cousin, for the poor man, for their children, hoping for a positive outcome. Kept telling herself all day long that here was at last a union that worked. *A united nations union that really worked.* A union that was now at the brink of settling things, one way or the other.

She even told, or rather, boasted to their Muslim neighbor, Leila, about the imminent official reunion of her cousin and her Muslim husband.

"You know Leila, he can't live without her." She went purposely over for a little brag that very afternoon. "Ali has at last come to his senses, and I think these two are just perfect for each other."

"*InshaAllah!*" Leila said. She'd been rather chummy with Anisa since the children's abduction and felt really sorry for her. "I'd still exercise caution, though," said Leila, before adding wisely with real remorse in her heart (which no one seemed to feel or welcome). "You know Anisa's not the first woman marrying outside the faith. And she won't be the last. Every now and then I hear stories about women who made the same mistakes."

Only the other day, Leila heard this unbeliever mouth..."You already know what the horrible *kafir* said...forget it," Leila stopped with a wave of her hand, refusing to repeat after the *kafir*. It was too monstrous of him to say what he said about Islam. But Nora already knew from the man's Muslim wife.

"But that's not true of everyone," put in Nora. "Leila, Ali Ahmed's not like that. A bit slow, yes, but not that shallow, and he's a true believer, it's written all over him, why else do you think he is in Rako?"

"I hope to believe you, Nora," Leila swallowed. "But I do have my reservations about these men."

"But this other woman's story is totally different, Leila. She can't even practice her own faith, and if she so much as breathes a word about Islam to the kids he promised he'll head straight for the Church, just to teach her a lesson! And you know what? The last time this man went to Church he was in his mother's arms, half a century ago!" Nora said.

"They're all the same," said Leila. "And if these women don't stop and take a breather before they take a leap with total strangers, then they'll just have to reap the fruits of their own folly. And the fire of hell is eternal, Nora."

"But, Leila, you can't compare my cousin to these other women..."

"Well, Anisa's lost her sanity, too, hasn't she? I remember how she looked when she came here. All the more reason why she should be more careful now."

Leila's stomach was of late a spider's conundrum, webs of guilt and remorse. And the hardest knot of all was Anisa. Worse still was the fact no one seemed to feel the pain she felt. Her neighbors were still helpful and friendly, but she didn't have to be a genius to know that they felt ten times bitten, many shy.

"I wish Anisa well," she said to Nora. "And I don't want to see her hurt again."

"Let's not forget that Ali Ahmed's traveled thousands of miles just to be with his family," concluded Nora before she left Leila. And now, this! What a let down! What an unlucky family! And what unlucky children! They did nothing but jabber about Mom and Dad all day long. And now how was she ever going to face Leila and the neighbors?

Following day, Anisa was already up at dawn. He did not say when he was coming to pick them up, but she got ready, any way. To her mother's queries she answered, "Poor man, he was beat. Cutting miles in a second in that infinite sky. You know, Mother, how exhausted I was when the kids and I came? The waiter gave him Panadol with his coffee. The service is getting better everyday. They even keep painkillers just in case. I'll bet they'll soon be on orders to keep tranquilizers as well!" she joked away her limbo, but her mother wasn't fooled in the least.

"So, we're still floating in suspense? And you didn't settle anything?" she shook her head. "I think they're awake now," she added, referring to the kids. "You had better get them ready, before their father comes along." After all the things that happened, Anisa's mother was grateful for every little good thing that came her way.

By 8.00 AM, Mike was at the door. Saying salaam to his mother-in-law, he ushered his excited children into the waiting cab. A few minutes later, his wife joined them at the back.

Thirty minutes later the driver pulled to a stop at the harbor. And before they knew it they'd piled into one of these cruise boats that take people for trips to nearby resort islands. Mike was as yet undecided as to what to do next. They'd gone on such cruises before Mohammed was born and all the troubles began. If Anisa was surprised by the boat she didn't say it. She was feeling rather tired and spent, after all the things she said the night before she was in no form to say or do anything. All she could do now was to keep sitting where she sat in the cool shade of the boat, sip her coke in peace, and play referee between Mohammed and Nasra, and if there was any more energy left in her, then she could reserve it for later. He was right about the vacation. Nobody knew what this family of four were thinking, but as the boat's engine rumbled and cut it's way through the white of the massive waves, they looked as normal as anyone else, and the children babbled with excitement, "Look! Med's putting the straw into his ear!"

"Med?" Anisa echoed, wondering where she'd heard the name before.

"And who's Med, dear?"

"I'm Med!"

"Mohammed, you're kidding your old mother! You and I, we'll have to talk! And nor more straws into the ears." She tugged at his ears.

"Ali, who's this Med person, dear?" she asked him purposely calling him 'Ali'. "Is she a new addition to the family?"

"Just a nickname, dear. Nothing special. I'll tell you all about it, it's a long story. Now about that vacation…?"

It took an hour and forty minutes to reach the island. There were few hotels there, but they didn't check into any. Hand in hand, the family moved from place to place, shopping here and there, haggling over the prices. The prices skyrocketing at the sight of Mike and plummeting at the lips of Anisa. When the seller said, seven dollars, Anisa would just grin away and say, 'give him four, honey'.

By lunch time their hands were full with all kinds of ethnic stuff. Ethnic shirts for the husband, ethnic skirts for the wife, ethnic dresses for the daughter, ethnic shirts for the boy, hats and ethnic belts for the kids. It was time to move on, for the kids were getting restless and showed signs of lost interest.

They found an outdoor restaurant with bright sun umbrellas at the beach. A few tourists lay spread-eagled on the sands. A little further down, tiny rock splinters and slippery marble stones glistened, scattered; strewn about the shore as if drizzled from above. Multi-colored pebbles vied for attention under the glimmering baking sun. There were sea shells of every size and shape; some rounded, some already withered by time and tide.

At that moment, her mood reflected the ambience of the benign ocean. The coastline stretched as far as the eye could see, and beyond. Untroubled waters extended to the east and caressed the blue gentle sky at the horizon.

"If it wasn't for these spoil-sports," she stated, tossing her hand at the sleeping human penguins, "wouldn't the strand be a nice place to be, Mr. Ali?"

"You know you never fail to amaze me," he said ignoring her remark. "After all that ethnic stuff, I still have money left in my pocket. And just for the record, why Mr. Ali? Have you forgotten my name? And why is it that you have problem keeping your promises? Isn't that highly un-Islamic?"

"We're on vacation, aren't we, Mr. Ali?"

"No, Anisa, there's no holiday for us. I'm down here to do some home work. Now, how about coming down to the nitty-gritty?"

The children were now out of ear shot.

"Fire away! I'm all ears." She blew hot air into space.

"Give it your best shot, why do you thing Mr. Ali's here? To keep his wife away from the malls, perhaps?"

"I give up." She admitted. "You do the talking, I've had it. My batteries are flat." She sighed away her foolishness, and wondered why she kept up the yapping about nothing all night long. And now she was sick and tired of her own voice. "As long as I don't have to listen to *me,* I'm okay, Ali. So fire away. And keep it going for as long as the sun shines, just make sure I'm supplied with enough Soda."

"I didn't even get the message until you started that mighty haggling over the silly ethnic shirt! So, cheer up, my friend, you guys aren't the only low-IQ-ed species on the planet. Ah! So my wife's finally awaken up to the reality of life? But that's nice to know. I tell you there's nothing more flattering to a man's ego than to be accosted by a jealous woman! How sorry I'm now to have missed last night's show! If I knew last night what I know today, I wouldn't be popping Panadol, I'd be holding a party at the restaurant! But the thick head that I'm I didn't get it, so my wife's jealous of the other woman? And the bikini-thing's making her nervous? He! He!"

"You see those two tiny things over there, the one in the pinky dress, and the gentleman who almost bled to death under my keep," he went on, "they're what hastened my hand. Can't see what they see in this woman, but one thing's for sure, they made my life a living hell, and I'm not sorry to share them with Rako Island's biggest fool."

"Thanks," she said in a small voice. "I really don't know how to thank you, the last months had been hell for me, too. And if I seem crazy to you, your suspicion's right. I still can't believe I'm awake.

Come pinch me, Ali, and tell me this is happening to me. And that this isn't yet another wandering of the mind."

"For crying out load, don't get me wrong, I didn't come here because of you, see those two things over there, see how they play to abandon, does Anisa understand what I am saying, or perhaps she needs an interpreter?"

"Good idea!"

"Anisa, I'm declaring to you, although I don't have to, that, I, Ali Ahmed, alias, Mike Peterson, am just as good a Muslim as Anisa Ali. And the rest is between him and his Lord."

"*Alhamdulillah*, Ali, we've come a long way," she said. "But now that we know this much, I think we should stop there and not add more things. Let's think coolly over what you've just said."

"Hear me out," he said. "I'm not done yet. First, about this name Med. It's one of my old mother's brilliant ideas. Let's face it, Anisa, people are people."

"I should've guessed." A lament escaped her. "Six months out of my sight and you know what? Mohammed's name is cut into three parts and the poor boy is made to walk away with only a third, so as to make his grandmother happy! What a shame!"

"I trusted you, Anisa. That's why I married you. I'm not in the habit of marrying people I don't trust. But I didn't know Islam. I was ignorant about Allah. I knew even less about Jesus. I mean what did I know about Jesus?"

"Absolutely nothing," she groaned. "Because if you did know about Jesus then we wouldn't have a problem, would we?"

"Indeed, the Western world's felling the forest, and all in the name of a man about whom they know absolutely nothing! Yes, we eat turkey at Thanksgiving but did I ever bother myself about who I was thanking? And by the way, why turkey? Why not lamb? Would it be any different if we'd chicken and not turnkey? And who invented this turkey business, anyway?"

"Mike?"

"We're talking about turkey and eggs and trees, and you're lambasting me for a minor headgear!"

"I knew you were ignorant, Mike but really not that oblivious," she shook her head, frowning at her own heedlessness. "But who has done this to you?"

"Yeah, all these years of thanksgiving, thanking not who I should be thanking."

"*Allahu Akbar!*"

"So you think I don't know that, do you?"

"Fire away!"

"Allah is greater, that's what *Allahu Akbar* means, dear wife. Muslims are saying it every minute and every second, but do they know what they're saying? You already knew how to say *Allahu Akbar* when you married this turkey eating guy, didn't you? You knew all these and even more yet you wedded me."

"*Subhanallah!*" she glared at him.

"You didn't trust me," he continued, "yet you chose to wed me, not once but twice! You didn't tell your folks about this turkey eating guy you wedded, did you? But there was no hiding from Allah, was there? Apparently, your family came first, and to think that Allah was first with you! Hiding from the family, while God watched—small wonder then that my twice married wife lost her mind—knowledge kills people, doesn't it?"

"Mr. Peterson!" she squirmed, humiliated. *For how long has he been rehearsing for this?*

"You were not mad when you wedded this turkey eating guy," he said, a sadistic smirk smeared on his face. "Remember how many beer bottles crowded my table on that fateful night when our eyes first met across the lights? Don't tell me you don't remember, loud mouth you even commented it."

"But the irony is, Anisa, you didn't mind sitting at that table," he blasted. "You also knew," he leaned back in his chair, savoring every word that left his mouth, "pork is a stable diet in my home turf, it just can't be replaced. Like you guys have fish out here, it's an island you live on. You're destined to eat fish."

"For how long have you been rehearsing for this?" she asked.

"Where I come from, pork is big business, we can't turn the clock back."

"Please, Mike, let's call it a day."

"You also knew that bacon and eggs are simply inseparable, yet you wedded me."

"Phew!"

"You know that witty miss piggy in the Muppet show?" he said, "she was my idol when you wedded me."

"Mike, are you all right?"

"Anisa, the Western world's in love with piggy so much so that no decent establishment's without a piggy idol. Go nor further, check out the banks!"

"Much as I'd love to see you pulverized, I wouldn't want to see the West enjoying your demise, so take care, Mike."

"You knew all these, you laughed about them in private, and in public, yet you married a fan of witty piggy! So what was the use of saying *Allahu Akbar*?"

"I'm going to the restroom, Mike, cheerio." She slung her hand bag over the shoulder. "Children!" she yelled.

It was 3.00 PM when Anisa and the children returned. The boat was not leaving until 6.00 PM. He had plenty of time to say his piece. He was rather parched, though, his throat suddenly hit by a wave of drought, cracking and brittle dry. Slowly he removed his shoes and socks, then beckoned to a passing waiter. Within no time the waiter had bounced back with the order and everyone had coke and ice cream.

"Like I said," he began once the children were out of earshot. "You knew about all these things and yet you married me. Ridiculous, wasn't it? Wasn't that why you recoiled every time one or other of your Muslim brothers and sisters made eyes at us? You were ashamed of me, weren't you, Anisa?"

"Come on take a gun and shoot like a man. Step into your cowboy shoes and shoot me!" But he wasn't listening to her at all.

"I guarantee you," he went on digging his bare feet in to the earth and relishing the cushy softness of the sand. "It wasn't my skin that made you recoil. Associating with a fan of witty piggy, wasn't that what got under your skin?"

"I think I've had about enough," she wheezed. Tearing herself away from the duress of their bond, she gazed at the neutral sky. A white solitary cloud channeled through the blue blanket of the firmament, and hung afloat, suspended in mid air. A lone bird circuited the dangling cloud, perhaps seeking cover from the intense brightness? She wished she were that bird.

His words pierced into her plight. "All these phobias, all this hysteria about washing and scrubbing Ali Ahmed, alias Mike Peterson proper, all these orders with the 'Ali, did you brush your teeth?' or 'Go take another bath!' – weren't all these because of my piggy past?"

"Be a man, just shoot me, will you?"

"Even though," he seethed, "I quit the bloody flesh before we even grazed under the same roof, you wouldn't trust me. You hated yourself, consorting with a man whose very heart once ticked on pig meat!"

A dull scream escaped her. "Mohammed! Stop there! Please go help him before he drowns himself!"

"Mohammed's not drowning. He's still building his castles. He hasn't moved an inch," he said, carrying on with his monologue.

"A prisoner of her own desires. Pregnancies. Children. And when she ultimately decided to make good her way of life, she put into that silly head of hers that she could perform miracles and make something out of this piggy fan, at will and without much ado!"

Did he travel this far just to chafe salt and pepper on her sores?

"You're hurting me," she groaned.

"You thought you could perform miracles!" he persisted.

But then before he knew what was happening, the alien wife was gone. The half-alien children were gone. One day he'd an alien family, the next day, nothing. If he shouted from one corner of his house his own voice came back to him, but he wasn't about confiding his personal woes to her.

"The rest is history, Anisa."

"Let's get on with life then, and put this sad history behind us, shall we?" she sobbed, but this fell only on deaf ears.

"I thought I knew the woman I was marrying, but I didn't. That was one hell of a surprise."

"I didn't even know myself," she sniffed.

"Of course, I said yes to everything my wife said was important in life." He fired in authentic rage. "When she said, 'down with the pig'

I said, why the hell not! When she said, 'out with the beer' I said out with the beer!"

Mike paused a little and went over some of the things that bothered him in his head. Every time his wife said: out with the beer, his insides would scream. *Come on, Mike, you're not making sense. You can't throw everything all at the same time; we can accept the throwing of the pig, but the wine? Have you lost your sanity? A glass of wine is exactly the right medicine for you now. Are your ears plugged? Haven't you heard the professionals?*

You get lost, he'd retort at his insides, *and keep that glass for the professionals. I don't need a glass of wine to lose myself, I've a wife who drives me crazy. And it's she who knows what's best for my tummy!*

And his insides would just laugh at him: *Hypocrite!*

"You turned me into a double dealer," he now leveled at her. "When my fridge said, no, no, I turned to the streets and to my mother's fridge."

Another painful lump threatened to drop out of her mouth. An invisible concussion quaking in her insides, she pondered the profound blunders of her life.

"Mohammed! Stop smudging that sand on your face!" he paused to yell. The worst part was, he reflected, as he watched his son wipe his smudgy face with an equally soggy hand, he didn't even understand why he was throwing the beer at a time when he needed it the most.

"You were pushing into me a faith without reasoning. Faith without conviction is a faith on a gold platter. Easy-come-easy-go-kind-of-thing."

"Oh really?" she coughed, kicking her sandals off and burying her feet in the hot clammy sand.

He waved her whimpers aside. "I remember vividly what you said to me during those crazy days at the hospital. *You* Anisa, had received your faith on a gold platter, and took everything for granted, as though you had entered into a *special* treaty with God, while all the while you did nothing but break the law, with every step you took and with every breath you inhaled. Of course, you were a *born Muslim* so you could get away with murder, just by virtue of your being born to Muslim parents! But believe you me, your *jihad* didn't start the day you were born, your little exertions started in that sickbed, and I hate to disillusion you, Anisa, but that's when you first became Muslim, and not before! And God sees and is aware of everything! So if anyone is a Muslim convert, it is *you*!"

"Go on, shred the already torn being and let's hope that lightens the burdens of your own omissions!" she shrieked.

"For the first time in her life, Anisa became candid. Told me a lot of things I didn't know about my wife. Pain opens doors, and the door of honesty is opened by pain." He paused, then continued, "Then Anisa saw with her own eyes that she were in effect no better than Mike. And that he, the drifting Western soul, Mike Peterson, and she, Anisa Ali Haaji were in effect one and the same. Wasn't that why my good wife lost her sanity? Because she just couldn't stand her bad side. It was too much, for the good side knew so many things about the bad side and there was no way the good side could separate from the bad one. So crack went the nut!"

What a bafflement to the *good one* to know that she and the *all-bad-boy* were one and the same! The man with the no-faith badge on his forehead and the woman whose very life-pattern was supposed to have been built on piety were in fact only two sides of the same coin!

"What a puzzle for the medical profession! None of those kindly souls really got wind of what ailed my alien wife. Even after the stomach healed they had problems healing the sick woman!"

"I never did thank them, did I?" she asked, suffering to the marrow.

"You don't have to cry, Anisa. I'm just getting acquainted with my wife…"

"That's exactly what the kids and I prayed for, but I didn't think it'd hurt so much," she choked.

"Incidentally, I didn't thank you for all the books you brought into our home. But you didn't even give me a chance to read them, now did you?"

"You didn't do too badly yourself," she bounced back to life. Time she put up some resistance…

"Wives don't make good prophets," he said calmly, and without any sign of agitation. "I really don't know if this is pure coincidence, but, in history, there had never been a woman prophetess. I've nothing against wives, but they just don't make good prophets. When one is in the business of being God's agent on earth one thing one can't do without is patience. Anisa, you were never fit for the role! You just don't have what it takes to be a mouthpiece for God!"

Why didn't he just hand the kids over the counter? she sighed.

"I searched every page of those books and I couldn't come up with a single prophetess. See, it's God who chooses prophets, and when He does choose, He chooses with care. He doesn't choose every Tom, Dick, or Harry. Nor does he choose the Anisas of this world. He chooses patient people, people of integrity, people whose words and deeds are the same, not half-baked hypocrites!"

"Shoot me! Come on!"

"My dear wife, prophets don't appoint themselves! They're chosen!"

"I'm not staying her," she moaned, cemented to the plastic seat.

"Of course, there're so called prophets cropping up every now and then, but they're not chosen. These prophets are self-elected and they all share a common malady: falsehood."

"I'm getting out of here."

"But don't you lose heart, I'm not so dimwitted as to equate my dear wife with these false prophets."

"Ha!"

"You thought you were doing me a favor by telling me to throw the pig," he flurried on. "You thought you were leading me to the right path. But you were actually leading me to another wrong path. Wife, congratulations, you christened me!"

"I christened you?" He must be mad, she thought. She did try to Christianize him, but that was only in desperation, not that she ever succeeded.

"Now, now, now…"

"Truth is, you're the one who christened me and not my folks. You wanted me to believe without conviction. That's Christianity, not Islam!"

497

"That's what you think, but it's a free world, Mike. Say what you will but the truth will always remains the same. Constant. The only one who's changing sides is you. So Mr. Mike Peterson's changing position? And is now sporting some conviction to boot? The first conviction of his life?"

There was a time when she'd embrace anything, any whiff, any drop, and the slightest hint of a conviction would put her heart at ease. But no, not today, the timing just wasn't right, "So you're Muslim now...so what!"

"People who've read the Qur'an understood my position," he went on in the same heartless fashion. "No compulsion in religion— but my wife, she just couldn't wait to lead me astray."

She'd had just about enough, and now he was blaming her for his own faithlessness, "How dare you accuse me of leading you astray?"

"You knew all about the silly things about my life," he said, non-perturbed, "the eggs, the tree, the piggy idol, the doggy business, the bottles in the wall, and more, but, did Anisa truly understand all the silly things in her life, Anisa's life, until our son Mohammed came on the scene? By then, it was too late."

"Please Mike, I've had it."

"I never refused anything...all I ever wanted was some understanding from the woman, who, on her own free will, snake-charmed my feelings, my base Western self. Now don't tell me you didn't have a hand in it? You had a hundred hands in it! No fire without smoke, Anisa!"

"So, I was in it, too? But that's all in the past, let's please not talk about old accidents."

"But you and I, we're not alone in this old accident." He pointed at the two little figures by the seashore. "You see those tiny things over there, they're also involved in this old crash of ours. There's no escape for Anisa, but to face the truth. She's loaded with a mighty cargo, my children."

He paused a little and she was grateful for the respite. For the first time since he arrived that she was able to take a good look at him. *So the man was growing a mustache?* she wondered. No wonder he looked foreign, and acted like one, too! She cupped her hand on her mouth, yes, there was something funny about his head, too. *Ah! he was losing hair!*

"Mike, I hope you're not getting bald?" she asked, standing over him, and trying to figure out if her suspicion was right. "You never told me it was in the family?"

He was not to be side-tracked.

"Our son's name's no longer a mystery to me," he said. "And it had to come from my lips. That was a sign, but it didn't come from you. That sign was from Allah, my Creator, the only one for whom I count."

Ya Allah! He'll never stop!

"In reality, no one really likes me," he said softly as if speaking only to himself, a feeling of dejection permeating him. "When I needed them most, my own kids turned their little backs on me. As for you, you never did pretend to like me."

"Liked your mother, though, somehow, she had problem seeing it," she said hoping for some digression from the man's disturbing monologue. "There were times when I wished the old lady dead, but hey, the lady's thousands of miles away." And once things got sorted out, one way or the other, she thought, she might even give the old lady a call? Write a nice letter? Or better still invite her to Rako

Island? Generosity never did kill anyone, she thought. And who knows the trip might even enlighten the old girl on the ways of the world?

"By the way, is she still on that funny ointment? The one she got from the friendly immigrant? And how's the therapy going? I did tell her to go easy on those golf clubs. She's not getting any younger, people her age are already on a mad rush to secure grave sites—here in Rako."

"I'd no idea my mother was on a funny ointment," he lamented on. "See, no one really tells me anything funny. Darn! If my colleagues ever found out about my change of heart, I assure you, I'd be the first electrified clown in the US!"

No one ever liked him. Not even the Jeffersons, he had to admit, "Since you guys left, I get nothing but brush-offs. Their dog and I were never the best of friends, but now the black beast can't even stand my car!"

"Racist!" she slammed at him.

"It's him and you that can't stand me!" he fired back.

"So what are we going to do about it?" she said.

"Allah knows best!"

"Who taught you this?" she gasped anew.

"Anisa," he said, "thanks for the books, but you ain't no prophet."

"So you now understand the *shahada?*" she changed the subject, "But that's great."

Once the mind and the heart grasped that unequivocal affirmation of the Oneness of God, he told her, there was no way any thinking being would want to walk away from that knowledge. Once he understood that his God wasn't imperfect after all, he knew he was home. He didn't understand a lot of other things then, but he knew he had a head start. He could now proceed with the knowledge of knowing that the Greatness of God was total and unlimited. His highness unreachable. His mightiness unmatched. His power supreme. His holiness above all perfection. His justice all-encompassing. The king of all had absolutely no need for partners.

"Can you imagine how proud I felt about myself?" he said. "My God wasn't at any one time a mortal, neither was He ever a slaughtered lamb. He was above anything I could think of. And yet I had a direct access to Him. No priests in the middle, and no-wife-intercession!"

He didn't want to cause any more heartaches to his wife, "But your miracles, Anisa, never saw the light of day with me and you're not the cause of my faith. My God did it. He's the One who turned me to those books. Not you. Your success stopped at Christianity!" Uninterrupted he blazed on. "Now, that's something, a Muslim woman telling her husband to believe without conviction. That's what you been telling me, thanks, but no thanks, that's what I been telling you."

"Not even a word of thanks? After all I had done for you?" The ingratitude of man! *Small wonder he was losing hair and mounting whiskers to make up for the loss!*

"You know that's exactly why Christianity failed in the West," he went on, "People just can't be bothered with being noosed and blindfolded. That's why the missionaries are investing so much in you guys. They don't love you anymore than they love their real clansmen up North."

She had to stop him. "Mike, dear," she gushed, "now that we know this much, let's say *alhamdulillah* and leave well alone, please, dear?"

There was no stopping him, though. "You see," he went on. "to find out exactly what it was that made my alien wife tick I'd to dig into history books."

"What have I to do with history?"

"Because you just happened to be part of the Church, that's why," he said, sharp-edged. "Isn't that why the Church invested in old Anisa and brought her to America to pursue her studies? But mark you my words, the Church's a complete failure. It bungled with my ancestors, it blundered with Anisa, and it's bound to screw up with these grateful refugees they're now feeding in the third world. *Belief sans conviction*, that's their motto. That was also the motto you tried on me, doing the Church's work on me!"

"I think I've had more than I can take," she said. "You never did have a good word about the Church, Mike so please save your words. The Church lost you long ago. In fact, the Church had never found you. So, even if you're now thinking of signing your name off the

Church records, take my word for it, you won't be missed, simply because you never belonged."

"The Church's a complete flop." He blazed on. "I sometimes wonder, if that wasn't the reason why they sent you to me in the first place! Maybe I should have a few words with that old school nun of yours and tell her a few things about the kind of nuns they're dishing out to the West! They are themselves going south, and they're sending us Southerners to do the job for them! Foreigners like my wife here!"

"Cool it, dear husband, no one's going to miss you. There are more than one billion Christians today, a tiny figure off that huge body won't rock the boat. The world's safe, but thanks for sharing your change of heart with your poor wife."

"We Westerners," he said, "we're fed up with the Church. Whether it comes from the East or the West. They can't fool us no more. We don't need the Church. On the contrary, we feed the Church and the Church also expects us to feed their sad, grateful refugees."

"Please lower your voice," she whispered, "and keep your spiritual awakening to yourself. No one else's interested, you know."

"The West's no longer enthralled with the big eared priests who like to listen to their little secrets. So disillusioned are we up there that we've reached a stage where we can't even be bothered into admitting our little foibles to the willing ears."

"Wow!"

"To get a fair idea of what it was all about, this poor man had to tail a few Church-going folks."

"You were attending weddings, didn't you?"

"Only fools attend Church weddings," he cried, "I've passed that stage. But I raise my hat to Muslims like my dear wife here. They were right about that, too, yes, we Westerners we go to Church just for fun and for play and for company and for instant stardom. And the Church knows better than to mess with us."

"Good!" she hissed. "Seems like, Mr. Peterson's getting the message, finally, and why, if this poor woman may ask, would the Church waste its time with someone like you?"

"Thanks to the Church," his voice rocketed, "I wasn't even a Christian until you came along to do what the Church failed to do: christen me! Woman, you make Sister Anne proud."

"Never mind about your little brain, Mike, said my dear wife," he sizzled. "As long as I keep mine ticking don't you worry, dear. Drop that piggy love, and not a drop of that beer, you hear! said my dear wife."

He took a deep breath of tangent air, then added. "To understand what made my little wife's head tick, this man had to travel back in time, back to Europe, and up and up and all the way to Scandinavia."

"You see, dear wife," he continued, "my ancestors were coerced into Christianity, never was it a matter of choice, so chop went many a head—*Christ or Chop*? asked their crusading king. *Enough chopping please*, they said, *haven't we lost enough heads already*? Stop the crusade, ordered the king: *Christ is in. Thor is out.* But was Thor ever really finished?"

"Man, do I know you!"

It was late afternoon, their shadows were getting longer by the minute, corrugating in the white fluffy sand. His shadow didn't look like anything, but the sky was blue and the white waves surfed smoothly over the dark blue waters, fanned by the courteous breeze.

"Unlike the Church," he thundered, "your intentions weren't brutish at all. You didn't christen me just to rule over me. You thought you were doing your old man a favor – this creature you were imprisoned with for life, your children's father, that was the only difference between Anisa and the Church!"

"*Ya Rabb!*"

"Makes you feel better, doesn't it? I also know that you'd like to take some credit for my conversion, but between you and me, Allah is the One who showed me the way. But thanks for the christening, it felt like being hurled into the Church pond, right after being baptized."

Complaining, complaining, complaining, when will it ever stop?

"The Almighty turns even the bad into good, and this neglect had turned my attention to the books my wife left behind in the huff."

"Thanks for pointing out that little favor."

He had to admit, she had done something the Church never could have done, first she converted him, then when she left him, she left him with real books that afterwards straightened his little brain and helped him understand why he did everything his wife ordered him to do.

"Thanks for not leaving me with the wrong titles..."

"Thanks for pointing that out, too."

"It was tough," he proceeded, "listening to every page of those books pointing the finger at my face and telling me simply: *Man you're wrong about things. Your wife was right, her many flaws, notwithstanding.* A mighty blow to the ego, don't you think?"

"Now what?"

"I've decided, and this is a choice I've to make, and not because I've been pushed by any other consideration than to say 'no' to my ego. And I hereby state that I've chosen my life over my ego, and that's no thanks to Anisa. But as regards my prayers and my sacrifice and my life, let me say this to you, my dear wife, my prayers and my sacrifice are for Him alone who has showed me the way. There's something called *shirk* in Islam, the act of setting up partners with God, and it'd worry me if I did things because someone else said so. And not because I, Mike Peterson, was doing it for only one purpose, the purpose of pleasing God alone."

Mike was drawn to this as he realized where his wife would be leading him, if he listened to her.

He now turned his whole body to her and as he began to shake the sand off his feet to put on the socks and the custom-made shoes, he said, "This man knows his needs. He doesn't need his wife's mothering and her Church representation techniques. And now I guess it's about time I thanked my wife for her ears! What say you to a stretch of the legs before that boat ride back?"

And as he began to stretch his legs, something caught his eyes and his gaze fell on his expensive shoes. God! He let out a breath. The shoes that were supposed to last two lifetimes were nearing their death and the wearer would be lucky if they made it to the boat.

But why did it take him this long to tell her this? She was lost in thought. *So she laughed about the trees and the eggs?* She now turned to the poor husband who was in full contemplation over his lousy shoes.

The poor man, she though, *might never have seen the light of day hadn't his ancestors the presence of mind to give in to the pressures of their crusading king.* And she was filled with compassion she hadn't felt for him in years.

"I swear no one ever told me about the beheading or the subsequent rebellion, for that matter," she said in earnest. She'd always known there was something basic missing in Mike's spiritual makeup, but she had no idea that this was rooted in a centuries old rebellion against the Church.

"You can't blame me for laughing at the eggs, Mike," she said softly. "You guys were the ones who created this farce, this tragic comedy."

Having wowed her with their mightiness and their technical prowess, how could she help wondering if they were breaking simple earthly eggs with their mighty alien friends in outer space?

"Believe me, no one said anything about the sad story behind all the celebrations," she said in a small voice, deriding herself for having misconstrued the faithlessness of a man whose very ancestor's body was held together by a string of non-committal surrender to a crusading king...

"How could you blame me for laughing and shaking my non-existent head when all I knew about you was what I saw with my own displaced eyes?" She could no longer hold the tears.

"Mike Peterson," she held out her hand, "have you by any chance any tissue paper? Not some poor quality ones that stick on people's faces, but good first class ones?"

Chapter Twenty-Eight

The Ending

And He it is Who accepts repentance
from His slaves, and forgives sins,
and He knows what you do.
(Qur'an: 42:25)

Afterward, as they walked silently towards the boat, each lost in thought, he broke into her thoughts, "You know I can't go back, not right away, anyway."

"You mean?"

"We're setting up home in Rako Island," he said, then added, "*inshaAllah*."

"You must be crazy? You know what you're saying. Oh, Ali, are you sure you're you? *Ya Allah*! There comes the boat. Nasra! Mohammed!"

By 9.00 PM, Anisa and her family were back home. Nasra was the first to break the news, "Grandma, Grandpa, Dad and Mom are getting married again, just in case they didn't do it well the last time, have you ever heard anything like that, Nora?"

"Marry? Again? And why would Daddy want to marry Mommy? Would someone please explain? What's going on, folks?" Nora jumped in her seat. After her conversation with Leila and then Anisa the night before, she had given up all hope of ever solving her cousin's marital problems.

"Nora, please, I see this family, this united nations team is going to be just fine. This is breaking news and the neighborhood needs to beware of it." Omar said, then unable to contain his own enthusiasm, he turned to Mike.

"*Assalamu 'alaikum*, Ali, come and be seated," he said motioning Mike to sit near him. "We were just about to leave for the police station! You know after *Isha*, we just didn't have much else to do, so we let our imaginations run, you know how it is in Rako…You see, we were hundred percent sure you reverted to your old ways, well almost…"

514

"And you feared I dumped your daughter somewhere and abducted the kids, right?"

"Don't tell me you're telepathic, too?"

"To be frank with you, the idea did cross my mind, more than several times, but then once I remembered the God of the East and the God of the West, I felt a little bit better about my future wife," he burst out laughing.

"Dad, Mom isn't your future wife," gasped Nasra. "She's your wife, everyone knows. *Ya Allah*! I don't understand what's happening to these people, these old people will never grow up!"

"And how did he remember the God of the East and the God of the West, I wonder?" The grandmother's rolled her eyes.

"Two and half year's a long time, ladies," Omar grinned.

And then the telephone was ringing. Anisa dashed into the living room to pick it up.

It was her mother-in-law! And she was dying to be in on anything her blind son was cooking in Rako Island.

"Poor boy, she yelled into Anisa's ear, "he didn't even have the nerve to tell me that he was kidnapping my grandchildren. I'd to needle it all out of Floor."

"Nor did he breathe a word to me."

"By the way," she continued, "I've Nasra's teddy-bear right here with me, remember the one I bought her when you were in that sick bed? And how's Med?"

"Med is good," Anisa grinned, for once humoring her mother-in-law. "But how's that bad back of yours? I hope you're taking it easy…?"

"Grandpa and I are going on a tournament," said the grandmother, "I thought you should know."

"I'd go easy on those golf clubs," said the concerned daughter-in-law. "Remember what the friendly immigrant said about creaky fragile bones?"

"Toothpicks for the worms!" The grandmother laughed. "By the way," she added, "I hear the poor man's been deported…"

"Where could they possibly take him?" Anisa wondered. The last she heard his hometown was no longer on the map.

"I've no idea...but take care...I'll catch you later."

The End

Safi Abdi

Glossary

Alhamdulillah!	Praise be to Allah!
Allahu Akbar!	Allah is Great!
Assalaamu 'alaikum	Peace be on you
Auzubillah!	Seek refuge with Allah
Rabb	Lord and Sustainer
Ya Rabb!	O Lord and Sustainer!
Ya Allah!	O Allah!
SubhanaAllah!	Glory to Allah!
Ya Rahman!	O Merciful God!
Salaam	Peace
Ma 'salaama	Peace be with you
Ina lilahi wa in ilaahi raajiun!	From Him we come and to Him we return
Masha'Allah!	It is the will of Allah!
BarakaAllah!	Allah Bless!
InshaAllah!	Allah-willing
Kafir	Non-believer

Kufr	Covering up of truth
Muslim	One who submits to the will of Allah
Fajr	Morning prayer
Dhuhur	Noon prayer
Asr	Middle prayer
Maghrib	Evening prayer
Isha	Night prayer
Juma'	Friday prayer
Shahada	The first Pillar of Islam
Sura	Chapter of Qur'an (There are 114 Suras in Qur'an)
Aya (ayaat pl)	Verse of Qur'an (Aya means sign)
Salat	Five daily prayers
wudu	Ablution before prayer
Haram	Forbidden by Law
Masjid	Mosque
Madrassah	Qur'anic school
Alaihi salaam	Peace be upon them (referring to prophets of Allah and the angels)

Lut	Lot
People of Lut	People of Lot (Those who indulged in Perversity—wiped from the face of the earth)
Hadith Qudsi	Sacred Hadith (the sayings of the Prophet Muhammad as revealed to him by the Almighty)
Jahiliya	The period of ignorance before the coming of the last Prophet.